WHAT'S SO FUNNY?

This Large Print Book carries the
Seal of Approval of N.A.V.H.

WHAT'S SO FUNNY?

DONALD E. WESTLAKE

THORNDIKE PRESS

An imprint of Thomson Gale, a part of The Thomson Corporation

THOMSON
━━━━━✦━━━━━ ™
GALE

Detroit • New York • San Francisco • New Haven, Conn. • Waterville, Maine • London

Thorndike Press® Large Print Mystery.
The text of this Large Print edition is unabridged.
Other aspects of the book may vary from the original edition.
Set in 16 pt. Plantin.

LIBRARY OF CONGRESS CATALOGING-IN-PUBLICATION DATA

Westlake, Donald E.
    What's so funny? / by Donald E. Westlake.
        p. cm. — (Thorndike Press large print mystery)
    "A Dortmunder novel"-T.p. verso.
    ISBN-13: 978-0-7862-9839-6 (alk. paper)
    ISBN-10: 0-7862-9839-1 (alk. paper)
    1. Dortmunder (Fictitious character) — Fiction. 2. Bars (Drinking establishments) — Fiction. 3. Organized crime — Fiction. 4. New York (N.Y.) — Fiction. 5. Criminals — Fiction. 6. Robbery — Fiction. 7. Large type books. I. Title.
PS3573.E9W47 2007b
813'.54—dc22   2007024289

Published in 2007 by arrangement with Grand Central Publishing, a subsidiary of Hachette Book Group, USA.

Printed in the United States of America on permanent paper
10 9 8 7 6 5 4 3 2 1

For Larry Kirshbaum — welcome aboard

■ ■ ■ ■

PART ONE:
KNIGHT'S ERRAND

■ ■ ■ ■

1

When John Dortmunder, relieved, walked out of Pointers and back to the main sales floor of the O.J. Bar & Grill on Amsterdam Avenue a little after ten that Wednesday evening in November, the silence was unbelievable, particularly in contrast with the racket that had been going on when he'd left. But now, no. Not a word, not a peep, not a word. The regulars all hunched at the bar were clutching tight to their glasses as they practiced their thousand-yard stare, while the lady irregulars mostly seemed to be thinking about their canning. Even Andy Kelp, who had been sharing a bourbon with Dortmunder down at the far end of the bar while they waited for the rest of their group to arrive, now seemed to have settled deeply into a search for a rhyme for "silver." All in all, it looked as though a whole lot of interior monologue was going on.

It took Dortmunder about one and six-seventeenth seconds to figure out what had changed while he was away. One of the seldom used side booths, the one nearest the street door, was now occupied by a person drinking something out of a tall clear glass, revealing both ice and bubbles within, which meant club soda, which probably meant nonalcoholic. This person, male, about forty-five, who apparently still permitted his grandmother to cut his thick black hair, wore on his lumpy countenance the kind of bland inattention that did not suggest interior monologue but, rather, intense listening.

A cop, therefore, and not only that but a cop dressed in what he no doubt thought of as civilian attire, being a shapeless shiny old black suit jacket, an emerald green polo shirt and shapeless tan khakis. He also seemed to subscribe to the usual cop belief that the male body was supposed to have bulges around the middle, like a sack of potatoes, the better to hang the equipment belt on, so that your average law enforcement officer does present himself to the public as a person with a lot of Idaho inside.

As Dortmunder moved around the corner from the end of the bar and started past the clenched backs of the interior monologists, two things happened which he found disturbing. First, the lumpy features of the cop over there suddenly became even more bland, his eyes even less focused, the movement of his arm bringing club soda to his mouth even more relaxed and even.

It's *me!* Dortmunder screamed inside, without letting anything — he certainly hoped — appear on the surface, it's me he's after, it's me he wants, it's me he's got the tag sale duds on for.

And the second thing that happened, Andy Kelp, with such studied nonchalance he looked like a pickpocket on his day off, stood from his barstool, picked up his glass — and the bottle! their shared bottle! — and turned, meeting no one's eye, to sit in the nearest of the side booths, as though to be more comfortable there. Not only that, but, once seated, he contrived to lift his feet under the table and put them on the bench seat on the other side, so that not only was he more comfortable here, he was *alone.*

They all know it's me, Dortmunder acknowledged to himself. Even Rollo, the meaty bartender, his back to the room as he taped a home-lettered-on-shirt-cardboard-in-red-Crayola WE DON'T ACCEPT FOOD STAMPS sign to the backbar mirror, even Rollo, by the unusually cementish appearance of those stocky shoulders, made it clear

11

that he too knew why Cap'n Club Soda was here, which happened to be himself, the individual who had just entered the arena.

Dortmunder's first thought was: escape. But then his second thought was: can't. The only exit was just beyond the cop's black wool left elbow; unachievable, in other words. Maybe he should turn around and go back to Pointers, take a seat there, wait the guy out. No; the cop could just follow him in and start talking.

Then what about hiding out in Setters? No, that wouldn't work either; an irregular would be sure to come in and start yelling and carrying on.

Whatever this is, Dortmunder thought, I gotta go through with it. But not without my drink.

So, with barely any break in stride at all for his own interior monologue, he headed down the bar toward that distant but worth the detour drink. And as he went, the cop signaled to him. Not with any blunt stare or finger-point or *hey you,* none of that. All he did was pick up his glass, smile in an appreciative way at the club soda inside it, then put the glass back down on the table and look nowhere in particular. That's all he did, but more plainly than an invitation edged in black it said, comon over, siddown, let's get acquainted.

First things first. Dortmunder reached his glass, saw there wasn't enough liquid left in the bottom of it to put out a firefly, drained it and turned hopelessly toward the booths, carrying the empty glass. Along the way, not looking at Kelp, who likewise did not look at him, he paused beside that first table to replenish his glass from their bottle — *their* bottle! — then trudged on down the row of booths to stop next to Mr. Doom and mutter, "This seat taken?"

"Rest yourself," the cop said. He had a soft deep voice, a burr with some gravel in it, as though he might sing the Lord's lines in some church choir somewhere.

So Dortmunder slid in across from the cop, keeping his knees away from those alien knees, and put his head back to sluice down a little bourbon. When he lowered glass and head, the cop was sliding a small card across the table toward him, saying, "Let me introduce myself." He didn't exactly smile or grin or anything like that, but you could tell he was pleased with himself.

Dortmunder leaned forward to look down at the card without touching it. A business card, an ivory off-white, with fancy lettering in light blue, it read in the middle:

and in the lower right corner an address and phone number:

> 598 E. 3rd St.
> New York, NY 10009
> 917-555-3585

East Third Street? Over by the river? Who ever had anything to do way over there? That was a part of Manhattan so remote you practically needed a visa to go there, and if you needed a reason to go there, there weren't any.

Also, the phone number was for a cell phone, that was the Manhattan cell phone area code. So this Johnny Eppick could *say* he was at 598 East Third Street, but if you called that number and he answered, he could be in Omaha, who's to know?

But more important than the address and the phone number was that line under the name: *For Hire.* Dortmunder frowned at that information some little time and then, head still facing downward, he swiveled his eyes up to look toward Johnny Eppick, if that's who he was, and say, "You're not a cop?"

"Not for seventeen months," Eppick told

him, and now he did grin. "Did my twenty, turned in my papers, decided to freelance."

"Huh," Dortmunder said. So apparently, you could take the cop out of the NYPD, but you couldn't take the NYPD out of the cop.

And now this no-longer-cop did a very cop thing: out of an inside pocket of that black suitcoat he took a photo, color, about twice the size of the business card, and slid it forward beside the card to say, "Whadaya thinka that?"

The picture was what looked like an alley somewhere, grungy and neglected like all alleys everywhere, with what looked like the rear entrances to a row of stores in an irregular line of brick buildings. A guy was moving near one of those doors, carrying a computer in both arms. The guy was all dressed in black and was hunched over the computer as though it were pretty heavy.

Dortmunder didn't really look at the picture, just gave it a skim before he shook his head and said, with regret, "Sorry, I never saw him before."

"You see him every morning when you shave," Eppick said.

Dortmunder frowned. What was this, a trick? Was that *himself* in the picture? Trying to recognize himself in that burdened figure there, that crumpled-over dark comma against the bricks, he said, "What's goin on here?"

"That's the back of an H & R Block," Eppick told him. "It's Sunday afternoon, it isn't tax season, they're closed. You took four computers out of there, don't you re-member?"

Vaguely, Dortmunder did. Of course, when you're at your job, after a while the work all blends together. Carefully, he said, "I'm pretty sure that isn't me."

"Listen, John," Eppick said, then paused to pretend he was polite, saying, "You don't mind if I call you John, do you?"

"Kinda, yeah."

"That's good. John, the point is, if I wanted to turn some evidence on you over to some former co-workers of mine, you'd already be in a place where everything goes clang-clang, you know what I mean?"

"No," Dortmunder said.

"It seems to me pretty clear," Eppick said. "One hand washes the other."

Dortmunder nodded. Pointing his jaw at the picture, he said, "Which hand is that?"

"What you want, John —"

"Well, the negative, I guess."

Sadly Eppick shook his head. "Sorry, John," he said. "Digital. It's in the computer

16

forever. One you won't be carrying anywhere, not even to that fence friend of
yours, that Arnie Albright."

Dortmunder raised a brow in surprise.
"You know too much," he said.

Eppick frowned at him. "Was that a threat,
John?"

"No!" Startled, almost embarrassed,
Dortmunder stuttered, "I only meant, you
know *so* much, I don't know how you'd
know all that much, I mean, whadaya wanna
know all that much about *me* for, that's all.
Not you know *too* much. *So* much. You
know *so* much, uh, Mr. Eppick."

"That's okay, then," Eppick said.

At this point there was a slight interrup-
tion as the street door beside their booth
opened and two guys walked in, bringing
with them a touch of the outer nippiness of
the air. Dortmunder sat facing that door,
while Eppick faced the bar, but if Dortmunder recognized either of these new customers he made no sign. Nor did Eppick seem
to notice that fresh blood was walking past
his elbow.

The first of the fresh blood was a carrot-
headed guy who walked in a dogged unre-
lenting manner, as though looking for a chip
to put on his shoulder, while the other was
a younger guy who managed to look both

17

eager and cautious at the same time, as though looking forward to dinner but unsure what that sound was he'd just heard from the kitchen.

These two didn't become aware of Eppick until they'd already entered the place, the bar door closing behind them, and then they both faltered for just a frame or two before moving smoothly on, unhurried but covering ground, passing Andy Kelp with no recognition on either side and making their way without unseemly haste around the end of the bar and out of sight in the direction of Pointers and Setters and the phone booth and the back room.

Hoping Eppick had made nothing of this exit and entrance, and trying to ignore the army of butterflies now investigating the nooks and crannies of his stomach, Dortmunder tried to keep the conversation on track and his voice unbutterflied by saying, "I mean, that's a real question. Knowing all this stuff about me and having this picture and all this. What's the point in here?"

"The point, John, is this," Eppick said. "I have a client, and he's hired me to make a certain retrieval on his behalf."

"A retrieval."

"That's exactly right. And I looked around, and I looked at old arrest records,

18

you know, MOs of this guy and that guy, I still got my access to whatever I want over there, and it seemed to me you're the guy I want to help me in this issue of this retrieval."

"I'm reformed," Dortmunder said.

"Have a relapse," Eppick suggested. "Recidify." Picking up the picture, he returned it to his coat pocket, then pushed the business card closer to Dortmunder, saying, "You come to my office tomorrow morning, ten a.m., you'll meet my employer, he'll explain the whole situation. You don't show up, expect to hear knocking on your door."

"Urm," Dortmunder said.

Rising up out of the booth, Eppick nodded away, grinned in an amiable fashion, and said, "Give my hello to your friend Andy Kelp. But it's just you I want to see in the morning."

And he turned and walked out of the bar to the outer sidewalk, leaving behind a sopping dishrag where there once had been a man.

2

When Dortmunder's breathing had returned to normal, he twisted around on the seat to look for Kelp, who had already departed for the back room. He knew he was supposed to follow the others back there now, where, instead of the original agenda, they would expect him to answer a whole lot of questions. He didn't think he'd enjoy that.

Facing the other way — toward the street, in fact — trying to decide what to do, he was in time to see another arrival push through the door, this one distinctive in every way. If people come in sizes, this guy was jumbo. Maybe even colossal. What he looked mostly like was the part of the rocket that gets jettisoned over the Indian Ocean, plus a black homburg. In addition to the homburg, he wore many yards of black wool topcoat over a black turtleneck sweater that made it seem as though his massive head were rising out of a hillside.

This fellow stopped just inside the closing door to lower a very large beetled brow in Dortmunder's direction. "You were talking," he said, "to a cop."

"Hello, Tiny," Dortmunder said, for that was, improbably, the monster's name. "He isn't a cop any more, not for seventeen months. Did his twenty, turned in his papers, decided to go freelance."

"Cops don't go freelance, Dortmunder," Tiny told him. "Cops are part of the system. The system doesn't do freelance. *We* are freelance."

"Here's his card," Dortmunder said, and handed it over.

Tiny rested the card in his giant palm and read aloud: " 'For Hire.' Huh. There's rent-a-cops, but this isn't like that, is it?"

"I don't think so, no."

Tiny with great gentleness handed the card back, saying, "Well, Dortmunder, you're an interesting fellow, I've always said so."

"I didn't go to *him,* Tiny," Dortmunder pointed out. "He came to me."

"But that's it, isn't it," Tiny said. "He came to *you.* Not Andy, not me, just you."

"My lucky day," Dortmunder said, failing to hide his bitterness.

"A cop that isn't a cop," Tiny mused, "that you could rent him like a car. And with you he wanted a nice conversation."

"It wasn't that nice, Tiny," Dortmunder said.

"I been in the limo outside," Tiny said, that being his preferred method of transportation, given his immensity, "I spotted you in there, I figured, maybe Dortmunder and this cop want to be alone, then I see Stan and the kid go in, no introductions, no high fives, and now the cop comes out, and turns out, what he wanted with you, he wanted to give you his new card, he's opened shop, cop for lease."

"Not a cop, Tiny," Dortmunder said. "Not for seventeen months."

"I think that transition takes a little longer," Tiny suggested. "Maybe three generations."

"You could be right."

"Again," Tiny agreed. "You wanna talk about it, Dortmunder?"

"Not until I think about it a while," Dortmunder told him. "And I don't really want to think about it, not yet."

"So some other time," Tiny said.

"Oh, I know," Dortmunder said, and sighed. "I know, there will be some other time."

Tiny looked around the bar. "Looks like everybody else is around back."

"Yeah, they went back there."

"Maybe we oughta do likewise," Tiny said. "See what Stan has in mind. It isn't that often a driver has an idea." He gazed down at Dortmunder. "You coming?"

With a second sigh — that made two in one day — Dortmunder shook his head. "I don't think I can, Tiny. That guy kinda knocked the spirit out of me, you know what I mean?"

"Not yet."

"What I think," Dortmunder said, "I think I should go home. Just, you know, go home."

"We'll miss you," Tiny said.

3

"So, John," May said, over the breakfast table, "what are you going to do?"

After a troubled night, Dortmunder had described his meeting with Johnny Eppick For Hire to his faithful companion, May, over his usual breakfast of equal parts corn flakes, milk, and sugar, while she listened wide-eyed, ignoring her half-grapefruit and coffee black. And now she wanted to know what he was going to do.

"Well, May," he said, "I think I got no choice."

"You say he isn't a cop any more."

"He's still plugged in to the cops," Dortmunder explained. "He can still point a finger and lightning comes out."

"So you have to go there."

"I don't even know *how*," Dortmunder complained. "All the way east on Third Street? How do I get there, take a ferry around the island?"

"There's probably buses," May said. "Across Fourteenth Street. I could loan you my MetroCard."

"That's still a hell of a walk," Dortmunder complained. "Fourteenth, all the way down to Third."

"Well, John," she said, "it doesn't seem worth stealing a car for."

"No, I guess not."

"Especially," she said, "if you're gonna visit a cop."

"Not for seventeen months."

"Uh huh," she said.

The bus wasn't so bad, once he and the driver figured out how he should slide May's mass transit card through that little slot. It was an articulated bus, so he found a seat next to a window in the rear part, beyond the accordion. He sat there and the bus groaned away from the curb, and he looked out the window at this new world.

He'd never been so far east on Fourteenth Street. New York doesn't exactly have neighborhoods, the way most cities do. What it has is closer to distinct and separate villages, some of them existing on different continents, some of them existing in different centuries, and many of them at war with one another. English is not the primary language in many of these villages, but the Roman alphabet does still have a slight edge.

Looking out his window, Dortmunder tried to get a handle on this particular village. He'd never been to Bulgaria — well, he'd never been asked — but it seemed to him this area was probably like a smaller city in that land, on one side or the other of the mountains. If they had mountains.

After a while, he noticed the scenery wasn't bumping past the window any more but was just sitting out there, and when he looked around to see what had gone wrong the other seats were all empty and the driver, way up there in front, was twisted around, yelling at him. Dortmunder focused and got the words:

"End of the line!"

"Oh, yeah. Right."

He waved at the guy, and got off the bus. The walk down to Third Street was just as long as he'd been afraid it would be, but then that wasn't even the end of it. Not knowing how long it would take to get to such an out-of-the-way location, he'd given it an hour, which turned out to be fifteen minutes too long, so he had to walk around the block a couple times so he wouldn't be ridiculously early.

But at least that did give him the opportunity to case the place. It was a narrow dark brick corner building, a little grungy, six stories high. The ground floor was a check-cashing place, with neon signs saying so in many languages in windows backed by the kind of iron bars they use for the gorilla cages in the zoo.

Around the side on Third Street was a green metal door with a vertical row of buttons next to names on cards in narrow slots. Some of the names seemed to be people, some businesses. There were two apartments or offices per floor, labeled "L" and "R." EPPICK — that's all it said — was 3R.

Stepping back, Dortmunder looked up at the windows that should be 3R, and they were covered by venetian blinds slanted up to see the sky, not the street. Okay; fifteen minutes. He went for a stroll.

It was still five minutes before the hour when he'd completed the circuit twice, wondering what the proper word was for a Mongolian bodega, but enough was enough, so he pressed the button next to EPPICK and almost immediately the door made that buzz they do. He pushed it open and entered a tiny vestibule with a steep flight of stairs straight ahead and a very narrow elevator on the right. So he took the elevator up, and when he got off at three there were the stairs again, flanked by two doors, these of dark wood and marked with brass figures 3L and 3R.

Another button. He pressed it, and another door gave him the raspberry. This door you had to pull, he soon figured out, but the buzz was in no hurry, it kept buzzing at him until he got the idea.

Inside, the place was larger than Dortmunder had expected, having taken it for granted a building like this would consist of a bunch of little rooms that people would call a "warren of offices." But, no. Many of the warren's interior walls had been removed, a rich burgundy carpet had been laid to connect it all, and on the carpet were separate areas defined not by walls but by furniture.

Just inside the door that Dortmunder was closing was a small well-polished wooden desk facing sideways, to see both the door and the room. Next to the desk stood Eppick, wearing his winner's smile plus, this morning, a polo shirt the same color as the carpet, gray slacks with expandable waist instead of belt, and two-tone golf shoes, though without cleats.

"Right on time, John," Eppick said, and stuck out a gnarly hand. "I'm gonna shake your hand because we're gonna be part-ners."

Dortmunder shrugged and stuck his own hand out. "Okay," he said, limiting the part-nership.

"Lemme introduce you," Eppick said, turning away, keeping Dortmunder's hand in his own, an unpleasant experience, "to our principal."

Dortmunder was going to say he didn't know they had any principles, but then decided not to, because here was the rest of the room. To the right, along the wall under the windows with their upward-slanted venetian blinds showing strips of pale blue late-autumn sky, was a blond oak confer-ence table with rounded ends, flanked by eight matching blue-upholstered chairs. On the left side, where there were no windows because of the next building in the row, was a conversation area, two dark blue sofas at right angles around a square glass coffee table, and a couple of matching chairs just behind them, ready for overflow. To the rear behind the conversation area was a galley kitchen, with a simple table and six chairs in front of it, and in the final quarter, behind the conference table, stood a Stair-Master and other gym equipment. Not what Dortmunder would have guessed from an ex-cop. Not from an ex-cop called Eppick, anyway.

"Around here, John," Eppick said, and led Dortmunder around in an orbit of the front desk, aiming for the front left corner of the space, where a high-tech wheelchair that looked as though it were ready for space-walks squatted facing the glass coffee table, opposite one of the blue sofas, with the other sofa against the wall to its left.

Someone or something hunkered in the wheelchair, inside black brogans, black pants, a Navajo-Indian-design throw rug draped over the shoulders, and a scarlet beret on top. It seemed large and soft, just barely squeezing into the available space, and it brooded straight ahead, paying no attention to Eppick as he led Dortmunder forward by the hand.

"Mr. Hemlow," Eppick said, and all at once he sounded deferential, not the self-assured cop at all any more, "Mr. Hemlow, the specialist is here."

"Tell him to sit down. There."

The voice sounded as though it were coming from a bicycle tire with a slow leak, and at first Dortmunder thought Mr. Hemlow had pointed at the sofa to his left with a chicken foot, but no, that was his hand.

Speaking of hands, Eppick finally released

Dortmunder's and gestured for him to get to that sofa by walking around behind Mr. Hemlow in his wheelchair, which Dortmunder did, while Eppick went away to take up a lot of the other sofa, crossing one leg over the other as though he wanted to show how relaxed he was, but not succeeding.

Dortmunder sat to Mr. Hemlow's left, leaned forward, rested his forearms on his thighs, looked eye-to-eye with Mr. Hemlow, and said, "Harya doin?"

"I've been better," grated the bicycle tire.

Dortmunder was sure of that. Seen up close, Mr. Hemlow was seven or eight different kinds of mess. He had a little clear plastic hose draped over his ears and inserted into his nostrils to give him oxygen. His face and neck and apparently everything but those chicken-foot hands were bloated and stuffed looking, as though he'd been filled up by a bicycle pump trying to solve the tire leak. His eyes were small and mean-looking, their pupils a very wet blue, so that, under the red beret, he looked like a more than usually homicidal hawk. What could be seen of his skin was a raw-looking red, as though he were originally a very pale person who'd been left out in the sun too long. His posture sucked; he sat on his shoulder blades with his wattles on his torso, which seemed to be shaped more or less like a medicine ball. His right knee twitched constantly, as though remembering an earlier life as a dance band drummer.

While Dortmunder sat absorbing these unlovely details, Mr. Hemlow's watery eyes studied him in return, until all at once Mr. Hemlow said, "What do you know about the First World War?"

Dortmunder thought. "We won," he guessed.

"Who lost?"

"The other people. I don't know, I wasn't there."

"Nor was I," Mr. Hemlow said, and gargled out something that was either a laugh or a death rattle, though probably a laugh, because he went on living, saying, "But my father was. He was there. He told me all about it."

"That musta been nice."

"Illuminating. My father was still fighting in that war two years after it was over, what do you think of that?"

"Well, I guess he must of been a real gung ho type."

"No, he was under orders. And you know *who* he was fighting?"

"With the war over?" Dortmunder shook his head. "I don't think you're supposed to do that," he said.

"In 1917," Mr. Hemlow said, "the United States entered the war. It had been going on in Europe for three years already. That was the same year as the Russian Revolution. The czar was thrown out, the Communists came in."

"Busy year," Dortmunder suggested.

"The British," Mr. Hemlow said, and apparently spat, though nothing seemed to come out. "The British," he repeated, "kept a great pile of munitions at Murmansk, a deep-water port on the Russian coast of the Barents Sea, north of the Arctic Circle."

"Cold up there," Dortmunder suggested.

"Didn't matter," Mr. Hemlow told him. "All that mattered, after the Revolution, they had to keep those munitions away from the Red Army. So that's why — there's no war declared here, nothing legal about this at all — my father and several hundred other US Army and US Navy personnel went up there to fight alongside the British and keep the goddam Red Army from getting those arms. Stayed there for two years, after the war was supposed to be over. Lost three hundred men. Finally, late in 1920, the Americans came home. Only time American troops ever fought Russian troops on Russian soil."

"I never even heard about it," Dortmunder said.

"Most haven't."

Eppick said, "It was news to me, too, and I thought I knew some history."

"American soldiers," Mr. Hemlow said, with what sounded like satisfaction, possibly even pride, "are a light-fingered group, always have been. Over many a mantel in America hangs stolen goods."

"Spoils of war," Eppick explained.

"That's what they call it," Mr. Hemlow said. "Now, near the end of the invasion, a platoon of American soldiers, nine lads including my father, and their sergeant, Alfred X. Northwood, came across a surprising item in a port warehouse in Murmansk. It was a chess set, a gift for the czar, from I don't know whom, which had been shipped in by sea just in time to meet the Bolshevik Revolution, and it was the most valuable thing those boys had ever seen in their lives."

Dortmunder said, "A chess set."

"The pieces were gold, inlaid with jewels. It was too heavy for one man to lift."

"Oh," Dortmunder said. "That kind of chess set."

"Exactly. It was worth millions. In the chaos of war and revolution, nobody even knew it existed, packed away in a wooden crate."

"Pretty good," Dortmunder said.

"Most of the boys in that expeditionary force," Mr. Hemlow said, "were from Ohio and Missouri, so they made an agreement. They would take that chess set back to the States and use it to finance a dream they'd been sharing, to open a chain of radio stations across the Midwest. If they'd done it, they would've died rich men."

"Uh huh," Dortmunder said, noticing that "if."

"Sgt. Northwood," Mr. Hemlow went on, "took the ivory-and-ebony chessboard. One of the lads took the teak box that held the pieces. The other eight, including my father, took four chessmen each, knowing each of them could smuggle that much home."

"Sounds good," Dortmunder agreed.

"Back in the States," Mr. Hemlow said, "out of the army at last, they met with ex-Sgt. Northwood in Chicago, and all gave him their part of the loot, for him to convert into the loans they needed."

"Uh huh," Dortmunder said.

"They never saw Northwood or the chess set again."

"You know," Dortmunder said, "I kinda saw that coming."

"They searched for him, for a long while," Mr. Hemlow said. "Fewer and fewer of them over the years. Finally just my father and three of his friends. Their sons all were told the story, and when we seven boys were grown we took what time we could from our regular lives to look for Northwood and the chess set. But we never found either one." Mr. Hemlow shrugged, which was more like a generalized tremor. "The generation after us didn't care," he said. "It was all ancient history. Two of the boys from my generation are still alive, but none of us is in any condition to go on with the search."

Delicately, Dortmunder said, "This Sgt. Northwood, he probably isn't around any more either."

"The chess set is," Mr. Hemlow said. "The boys were going to call their company Chess King Broadcasting. One of them drew up a very nice logo for it."

"Uh huh," Dortmunder said, hoping Mr. Hemlow wasn't about to show him the logo.

He wasn't. Instead, he lowered his head, those watery eyes now turning to ice, and he said, "I am a wealthy man. I am not in this for the money. Those boys were robbed of their dreams."

"Yeah, I get that," Dortmunder agreed.

"Now, unexpectedly," Mr. Hemlow said,

"I seem to have an opportunity, if I live long enough for it, to right that wrong."

"You know where the chess set is," Dortmunder suggested.

"Possibly," Mr. Hemlow said, and sat back in his wheelchair to fold his chicken feet over his paunch. "But for a moment," he said, "let us talk about you. What did you say your name was?"

4

"Diddums," Dortmunder said, and winced, because that was an alias he loathed that nevertheless bounced out of him at the most unfortunate moments, like his own private Tourette's.

Mr. Hemlow gazed on him. "Diddums?"

"It's Welsh."

"Oh."

Smoothly, Eppick said, "John uses a number of different names, it goes with his specialty."

Could a gourd on a medicine ball look grumpy? Yes. "I see," Mr. Hemlow said. "So what we know so far is that this gentleman's name is *not* Diddums."

"It's probably not even Welsh," Eppick said.

"It's definitely John," Dortmunder said.

Eppick smiled and nodded. "That's true. Something like me. You never been a Johnny, have you?"

"No," Dortmunder said.

"That's where the pizzazz is," Eppick assured him. "You saw it on my card. 'John Eppick' wouldn't have done anywhere near as much."

"I can see that," Dortmunder agreed.

"Of course you can. Johnny Eppick. It's something to aspire to. Johnny Guitar."

"Uh huh."

"Johnny Cool. Johnny Holiday. Johnny Trouble."

"Johnny Belinda," put in Mr. Hemlow, surprisingly.

Eppick didn't want to disagree with his employer, but he didn't want Johnny Belinda either. "That's a special case, sir," he said, and hurriedly turned back to Dortmunder, saying, "Johnny Rocco. Johnny Tremain. Johnny Reno."

"Johnny Mnemonic," suggested Mr. Hemlow, a man who probably didn't so much go to look at movies as have movies come to look at him.

"Sir, I don't think that one's up there with the others," Eppick suggested.

Dortmunder, who didn't go to the movies unless his faithful companion May insisted, nevertheless did have something of a grab-bag mind, which he now realized contained a movie title belonging to this crowd:

"Johnny Got His Gun."

Neither of the others liked that one. Eppick said, "John, we are talking in the order of Johnny Yuma, Johnny Midnight, Johnny Jupiter, Johnny Ringo."

"Johnny Appleseed," Mr. Hemlow added.

"Wel-ll," Eppick said, "that's a little far afield, Mr. Hemlow."

Dortmunder said, "Johnny Cash?"

"Johnnie Walker," announced Mr. Hemlow.

Dortmunder turned to him. "Red or Black?"

"Oh, Black," Mr. Hemlow said. "Definitely Black. But that isn't the point." Shifting his mass in the general direction of Eppick, he said, "The point is, you do vouch for this man."

"Oh, absolutely," Eppick said. "I have used the entire resources of the NYPD to research the kind of specialist we need and, of those not currently counting the days on the inside, John here is just about the best you can get. He's a thief when he wakes up in the morning, and he's a thief when he goes to sleep at night. An honest thought has never crossed his brain. If he were any more crooked, you could open wine bottles with him. In his early days he did some time, but he's learned how to avoid that

40

now. I guarantee him to be the least trustworthy, most criminal scalawag you'll ever meet."

"Well," Dortmunder said, "that's maybe a *little* overboard."

Still talking to Mr. Hemlow, Eppick said, "You trust me, and I trust John, but it's even more than that. You know where to find me, and I know where to find John. He'd double-cross us in a minute if he —"

"Aw, hey."

"— thought he could get away with it, but he knows he can't, so we can all have perfect trust in one another."

"Excellent," said Mr. Hemlow, and nodded his head at Dortmunder a while, not in rhythm with his twitching knee, which was a distraction. "So far," he said, "I like what I see. It would seem that Johnny has chosen well. You keep your own counsel. You don't bluster, but you do stand up for yourself."

Dortmunder could not remember ever having been the center of attention to this excruciating a degree, not even in a court of law, and he was beginning to chafe under it. Itch. Not like it so much. He said, to try to shorten the interview if at all possible, "So you want me and somebody else to go get this chess set for you, so all you —"

Mr. Hemlow said, "Somebody else?"

41

"You said it was too heavy for one man to lift."

"Oh, yes." Mr. Hemlow did that nodding thing some more. "That's what my father told me, that impressed me at the time. I hadn't thought of the implications, but you're right. Or, could you do it in multiple trips?"

"When you're burglaring," Dortmunder told him, showing off a little expertise, "you don't do more than one trip."

"Yes, of course, I do see that." Turning to Eppick, he said, "How long will it take you to find a second person?"

"Oh, I think John could come up with somebody," Eppick said, and grinned at Dortmunder. "Your friend Andy, maybe."

"Well," Dortmunder said, "he'd probably have to look in his appointment book, but I could check, yeah." To Mr. Hemlow he said, "So it looks to me like there's only two questions left."

"Yes?" Mr. Hemlow cocked that puffy head. "Which questions are those?"

"Well, the first is, where is it."

"Yes, of course," said Mr. Hemlow, a little impatiently. "And the second?"

"Well, you might not think it to look at me," Dortmunder told him, "but I got a family crest."

42

"Have you?"

"Yeah. And it's got a motto on it."

"I am anxious to hear this motto."

"Quid lucrum istic mihi est."

Mr. Hemlow squinted; the red-headed hawk in flight. "I'm afraid my Latin is insufficient for that."

"What's in it for me," Dortmunder translated.

5

Mr. Hemlow roared with laughter, or at least tried to, with various noises emanating from his head area that might, with redubbing, have added up to a roar. Then he said, "Well, what would be in it for you might be millions, I suppose, if you were to manage to elude Johnny here. A rather more modest sum if you do your part like a good boy."

"Plus continued life in the free world," Eppick added.

So they were cheapskates, these two, it had all the earmarks. Dortmunder had seen it before, guys with big ideas who just needed a little bit of his help, his knowledge, his experience, but didn't want to pay for it. Or didn't want to pay enough.

On the other hand, if he announced he wasn't going along with these birds, that alley photo could very well come back to bite him on the hind parts. So, at least for now, he would follow Mr. Hemlow's advice and do his part like a good boy. Therefore, he said, "Without knowing where this thing is, or how it's guarded, or anything about it, I don't know how much trouble I'm gonna have to get my hands on it, or what expenses I'm gonna run up, or if it's maybe more than two people needed for the thing, or whatever. So right now, I'm with you, but I gotta tell you, Johnny Eppick here says I'm the specialist you want, and if I decide, being the specialist, that it can't be done, or it can't be done without too much danger to *me,* then I'm gonna have to tell you now, I'm gonna expect you to go along with how I see it."

Eppick frowned, clearly not liking the broadness of this escape clause, but Mr. Hemlow said, "That sounds fair to me. I think you will find the task worthy of your skills, but not to include a level of peril that might incline you to forgo what would certainly otherwise be a very profitable endeavor."

"That's good, then," Dortmunder said. "So where is it?"

"I'm afraid I'm not the one who's going to tell you that," Mr. Hemlow said.

Dortmunder didn't like that at all. "You mean, there's more of you in on this? I thought everybody else died or got old or didn't care."

"Except," Mr. Hemlow said, "my grand-daughter."

"Now a granddaughter," Dortmunder said.

"It is true," Mr. Hemlow said, "that the generation after mine took no interest in the stolen chess set, nor the ruined dreams of their grandparents. It was all just history to them. However, Fiona, the daughter of my third son, Floyd, takes a *deep* interest in the story of the chess set, precisely because to her it *is* history, and history is her passion."

Dortmunder, whose grasp on history was usually dislodged by the needs of the passing moment, had nothing to say to that, so he merely did his best to look alert.

Which was apparently enough, because Mr. Hemlow almost immediately went on, "Fiona, my granddaughter, is an attorney, mostly in estate planning for a midtown firm. She's the one who took an interest in the story of the chess set, came to me for what details my father might have given me, did the research and found, or at least believes she's found, the chess set."

"Believes," Dortmunder said.

"Well, she hasn't seen it personally, of course," Mr. Hemlow said. "None of us will, until you retrieve it."

Eppick said, "The granddaughter was just happy to figure she solved the mystery, there it is, case closed. It was Mr. Hemlow explained to her the lost dreams and alla that."

"She agreed, at last," Mr. Hemlow said, "to a retrieval of the chess set, for the future good of the family, to make up for the ills of the past."

"Got it," Dortmunder said.

"But she has conditions," Mr. Hemlow warned.

What have I gotten into here, Dortmunder asked himself, and was afraid he was going to find out the answer. "Conditions," he said.

"No violence," Mr. Hemlow said.

"I'm in favor of that," Dortmunder assured him. "No violence, that's how I like it every day."

"One of the reasons I picked you, John," Eppick told him, "is how you don't go in much for strong-arming against persons."

"Or property," Mr. Hemlow said.

Dortmunder said, "Property? Come on, you know, sometimes you gotta break a window, that's not *violence*."

Conceding the point, Mr. Hemlow said, "I'm sure Fiona would accept that level of mayhem. You can discuss it with her if you wish."

"Or not bother her about it," Eppick advised.

"So I'm gonna see this Fiona," Dortmunder said, and looked around. "How come I'm not seeing her now?"

Eppick said, "Mr. Hemlow wanted to vet you, wanted to reassure himself that I'd made the right choice, before sending you on to the granddaughter."

"Oh, yeah?" To Mr. Hemlow Dortmunder said, "So how am I? How do I vet?"

"That I have mentioned my granddaughter's name," Mr. Hemlow said, "means I have agreed with Johnny's judgment."

"Well, that's nice."

Mr. Hemlow said, "Johnny, would you phone her?"

"Sure." Eppick stood, then paused to say to Dortmunder, "You free this afternoon, if she can make it?"

"Sure. I'm between engagements."

"Maybe not any more," Eppick said, and grinned, and said, "You wanna write down the address?"

"I do," Dortmunder told him, "but I don't have anything to write with or on."

"Oh. Never mind, I'll do it."

Eppick went over to the desk by the front

door, sat at it, played with a Rolodex a minute, then dialed a number. While he waited, he started to write on the back of another of his cards, then paused to punch out four more numbers, then finished writing, then said, "Fiona Hemlow, please. Johnny Eppick." Then another pause, and then he said, "Hi, Fiona, it's Johnny Eppick. Just fine. I'm here with your granddad and we got the guy we think is gonna help us with that family matter. I know you wanna talk to him. Well, this afternoon, if you got some free time." Cupping the phone, he said to Dortmunder, "She's checking her calendar."

"For this afternoon?"

Eppick held up a finger, and listened to the phone, then said, "Yeah, that should be long enough. Hold on, lemme see if he's clear." Cupping the phone again, he said to Dortmunder, "This afternoon, four-fifteen to four-forty-five, she can fit you in."

"Then that's good," Dortmunder said. "I happen to have that slot open." In truth, he himself did not live that precise a life, but he understood there were people who did.

Into the phone, Eppick said, "That's fine. He's — Hold on." Another cupping, and he looked at Dortmunder to say, "Do you really still wanna go on being Diddums?"

"No, do the name," Dortmunder said. "The only one I didn't wanna know it was you, so that's too late, so go ahead."

"Fine. Fiona, his name is John Dortmunder, and he will see you at four-fifteen. Give me a call after you talk to him, okay? Thanks, Fiona."

He hung up, stood up, and brought to Dortmunder the card he'd written on the back of, where it now read:

Fiona Hemlow
C&I International Bank Building
613 5th Ave
Feinberg, Kleinberg, Rhineberg, Steinberg, Weinberg & Klatsch
27

Dortmunder said, "Twenty-seven?"

"They got the whole floor," Eppick explained. "Hundreds of lawyers there."

"We're all very proud of Fiona," Mr. Hemlow said. "Landing at such a prestigious law firm."

Dortmunder had had dealings with lawyers once or twice in his life, but they mostly hadn't come with the word "prestigious" attached. "I'm looking forward," he said.

6

In conversation over breakfast with his Mom, before she went off for a day of driving her taxi for the benefit of an ungrateful public, Stan Murch gradually came to the conclusion that he wasn't just irritated by what had happened last night, or what in fact had not happened, but he was really very pissed off about it and getting more so by the minute, and who he blamed for the whole thing was John Dortmunder.

At first his Mom didn't get it: "He wasn't even there."

"That's the point."

He had to explain it all about seven times before she saw what he was aiming at, but at last she did see it, and it was really very simple and, straightforward. At the O.J. last night, they had been a little group of people who would come together like that from time to time for what they hoped would turn out to be profitable expeditions and

51

employments, and there was always at least that one preliminary conversation to kick it off, to see if this new project sounded like it might work, to see if everybody wanted to come on board. Each of them in the group had his own specialty — Tiny Bulcher, for instance, specialized in lifting large and heavy objects, while he himself, Stan Murch, was the driver — and John Dortmunder's specialty was in laying out the plan.

Now, it wasn't often that Stan brought the original idea to the group, but this time he had one, and it was a good one, and if Dortmunder had been there he would definitely have understood the concept and started working out how to make it a reality, and all of that, and by now they'd be on their way. Instead of which, Dortmunder isn't even at the meeting, he's out in the bar with some cop.

But everybody else wants to know what the idea is. So Stan tells them, and they hate it. Because Dortmunder isn't there to tell everybody how it could work, the idea gets shot down like a duck. So it's all Dortmunder's fault.

After his Mom took off in her cab, Stan continued to brood a while longer, and then he decided the thing to do was call John and see if he's ready to take a meeting *now,* just the two of them, and after that they could get everybody else to come around. So he called John, but got May, who said, "Oh, you just missed him, and I'm halfway out the door myself, I got to get to work."

"Do you know where John went?"

"He had a meeting at ten this morning —"

"With the cop?"

"Oh, did he tell you?"

"Not yet. Where's the meeting, do you know?"

"Lower East Side, some funny address. John had never been anywhere around there before, he was going to take a bus."

"You got the address?"

"He wrote it down a couple places, so he wouldn't forget. I'll look, Stan, but I don't have much time. I don't wanna be late. They're short on cashiers at the Safeway as it is. Hold on."

So he held on, and about three minutes later she came back and said, "It's 598 East Third, and the cop is named Eppick. He says he's retired."

"Then why does he want to talk to John?"

"You'll have to ask him."

"I intend to."

■ ■ ■ ■

If you only need a car for a few hours, there's nothing better, after taking the subway up out of Canarsie, than to go to the parking garage under one of the big Manhattan office buildings, where they have sections set aside for employees of the various businesses upstairs, so the car you choose will not be missed before five p.m., by which time you've returned it. Also, being in white-collar employment, they tend to drive pretty nice cars. All you need is to find somebody who leaves his parking-space ID in the car, which many people do.

It was in a recent Audi 9000, forest green, 17K on the odometer, that Stan cruised the area of 598 East Third Street, a neighborhood not used to seeing cars of that quality abroad on its streets. Being New York, though, everybody in the district was cool about it.

May had said the meeting was scheduled for ten, and Stan got there at quarter past, so it should still be going on. In the check-cashing place? Unlikely; more probably somewhere upstairs. Motor running and flashers on, to assure the world he was not abandoning this nice car, Stan left it beside a handy fire hydrant long enough to run over and look at the names for the upstairs tenants, and found it right away: EPPICK. He hadn't known it was spelled that way.

It was a long meeting John was having with this cop, as Stan waited in the car next to the fire hydrant, now with flashers on but engine off. Ten fifty-two read the very nice dashboard clock when at last John came out and started to walk away. Stan honked, but John just kept walking, so Stan had to start the engine, open his window, chase John around the corner, and yell, "Hey!"

Nothing. John just kept plodding forward, head down, arms and legs moving as though the machinery were a little rusty, and apparently now operating without functioning ears.

"Hey!" Stan yelled again, and honked, all of which had the same effect as before. Nil. *"John! Goddam it!"*

Now John stopped. He looked alert. He stared up at the sky. He stared at the building he was going past. He stared back the way he'd come.

What is this? You hear a horn, you don't look at the street? Stan pressed the heel of his palm against the horn and left it there, until at last John turned to gape, then pointed at Stan as though telling somebody,

"I know that guy!"

Having captured his subject's attention, Stan released the horn and called, "Come on over. Get in."

So John came around and took the passenger seat and said, "What are you doing around here? This one of your routes?"

"I wanted to talk to you," Stan said, driving forward. "Where you headed?"

"You wanted to — You mean — How did you —"

"I called and talked to May. Where you headed?"

"Oh. Well, I got a meeting up in midtown this afternoon, that's all."

"All of a sudden, you take a lot of meetings."

"Not my idea," John said.

Stan figured he'd find out sooner or later what was going on. Meanwhile, there was his own little scheme to consider. He said, "Whadaya say, I drive you up there, put this car back, we grab a bite."

"Sure. Why not?"

There was nowhere to eat on Park Avenue. There was nowhere to eat on Fifth Avenue. On Sixth Avenue and Seventh Avenue the streets were filled with tourists standing on line to eat in places exactly like the places they'd eat in back home in Akron or Stuttgart or Osaka, except back there they didn't have to stand on line.

Stan and John eventually found a dark bar with food on a side street between Eighth and Ninth Avenues, where the plump but not soft waitress said, "How you fellas today?"

"Hungry," Stan said. "We just walked across Manhattan."

"I hear they got buses now," she said, and distributed menus. "You want a drink while you read?"

They both wanted beer. She went away and they studied the menus, and John said, "Can you tell the difference between ostrich burger and bison burger?"

"Bison's got four legs."

"Burger."

"Oh. No. Turkey burger I can tell. All those others I think they come outa the same vat, back there in the kitchen."

"I can remember," John said, "when 'burger' only meant one thing, and the only word you ever had to stick in front of it was 'cheese.' "

"You're showing your age, John."

"Yeah? That's good. Usually I show twice my age."

The waitress having returned, Stan ordered the bison burger and John the ostrich burger, and then John said, "You wanted to talk to me."

"Well, with all these meetings you got, you didn't get to *our* little meeting last night."

"No, that cop come along."

"And he's still along, I guess."

"It looks like it's gonna be a long story, I'm not sure. I know you wanna know what it's all about."

"Naw, John, I don't poke and pry in somebody else's business."

"Nevertheless," John said, "to make up for it, my not getting to the meeting last night, I'll tell you the story so far. The ex-cop is working for this rich guy that wants to what he calls 'retrieve' something that got stolen from his father eighty years ago."

"Wow. That's a long time."

"It is. So this afternoon," John said, "I'm supposed to meet the rich guy's grand-daughter, because she's the one knows where it is. So I'm not even sure if it's possible, or if it's real, but you don't just say no to a cop. Or an ex-cop either."

"No, I get that," Stan said.

"So now," John said, "tell me yours."

"What I wanna do," Stan said, and the waitress appeared, with two platters, and said, "Who had the ostrich burger?" and they couldn't remember. So she just put the platters down, accepted an order for another couple beers, and went away, which meant they didn't know exactly what they were eating, but that was okay.

Around a mouthful of either ostrich or bison, John said, "You were gonna tell me what you wanna do."

"I wanna hand to you," Stan said, and paused for a beer delivery, and said, "the idea I was presenting to everybody — except you — last night."

"Sure. I wanna hear it."

"It's out in Brooklyn."

John looked pained. "I dunno, Stan," he said. "That place I went to today was Brooklyn enough for me."

"That's the trouble with all you guys," Stan told him. "You're all Manhattancentric."

John looked at him. "What kinda word is that?"

"A word from the newspaper," Stan said. "And therefore authentic."

"Okay."

"It isn't all Manhattan, you know. There's four other boroughs."

"Maybe three," John said.

"What? Who you throwin out?"

"Staten Island. It's over in New Jersey

someplace. You can't even get there on the subway. Any place you have to go to by *boat* is not part of New York City."

"Governors Island."

"So? That's an island."

"So's Staten."

Looking exasperated, John said, "You moving to Staten Island? Is that the news you wanted to bring me?"

"No, I'm very happy in Canarsie."

"Just a little defensive. So tell me the idea. Did everybody else love it?"

"Let me tell it to you, okay?"

"Go."

"Because I'm in Canarsie," Stan said, "I drive a lot, which people in Manhattan don't do. So I see things that people in Manhattan don't see. So out along the Belt Parkway, they're building this mosque, you can see it from the road."

"Mosque."

"Yeah, you know, a religious place that —"

"I know what it is, Stan."

"Okay. So they're building it, I read about it in the paper —"

"The Manhattancentric paper."

"Maybe the same one, I dunno. It said, they're getting a lot of Arab oil money for this mosque, they're building one that's gonna be like the big one in London with the golden dome, only, this being New York City, they ran into some problems."

"Naturally."

"Cost overruns, extra permits they didn't know about, unions they never heard of, the whole thing grinds to a halt."

"Of course it does," John said. "Didn't they know that?"

"Well, they're religious people," Stan said, "and they're immigrants, and nobody ever *tells* anybody how New York works, everybody just does it."

"I almost feel sorry for these people," John said.

"Well, don't feel *too* sorry. They shut down now, but they're gonna start up again next spring, with some more oil money, and now they know a little more about the system, so this is just a delay is all."

"I'm happy for them," John said. "But up till now I don't see your idea in here."

"The dome," Stan said.

John just looked at him, ostrich or bison visible in his open mouth. So Stan said, "The dome got delivered before they shut down, and it's gold. Not solid gold, you know, but not gold paint either. Real gold. Gold plate or something. It's sitting out there on this empty construction site, it was delivered when the walls were supposed to be up, but of course the walls *weren't* up, so it's sitting there, with this crane next to it."

"I think I'm getting this," John said. "It's your idea, we use the crane, we pick up this dome — How big is this dome?"

"Fifteen feet across, twelve feet high."

"Fifteen feet across, twelve feet high. You wanna pick this up and take it away."

"With the crane, like you said."

"And where you gonna stash this thing?"

"That's part of what we gotta work out," Stan said.

"Maybe you can take it to Alaska," John said, "and paint it white, and make everybody think it's an igloo."

"I don't think we could get it that far," Stan told him. "All the bridges. And forget tunnels."

John said, "And who's your customer, the American Dental Association?"

"John, it's *gold*. It's gotta be worth I don't know how much."

"You don't have a place to hide it," John said. "You take it down the street with this crane, you don't have any way to disguise it, camouflage it. You don't have a customer for it. So who at the O.J. last night liked the idea?"

"There were some naysayers," Stan admitted.

"How many?"

"Well, all of them. But I figured, *you* could see the possibilities."

"I can," John agreed. "Just this morning, that cop — who, by the way, isn't a cop any more, not for seventeen months — just this morning he was telling the rich guy about me, how I took a couple falls in the early days but learned how to have that not happen any more, and *this* is part of the learning. I don't go down the street with a fifteen-foot-wide, twelve-foot-tall hot golden dome out in front of me." He shook his head. "I'm sorry, Stan. I can see how it was for you, you looked at this great big gold thing out there beside the Belt, you read about it in the paper, all you could think about was the gold. It's *my* job to think about the problems, and what this dome is is one hundred percent problem."

"Maybe I'll go do it on my own," Stan said. He was really feeling dumped on.

"One thing," John said. "If you do it on your own, don't get your Mom involved."

His Mom was the only other gang he could think of. Stan said, "Why not?"

"Because she'd rather drive her own cab than do the state's laundry. I gotta go."

Standing, John said, "If you're gonna want me to talk with you about an idea like that, you pay for lunch. See you later."

7

It turned out, the C&I International Bank Building, up there on Fifth near Saks, was operating under an alias, or at least a later modification of its original name, which you could read inside in the lobby. On a marble side wall was a big black board in a gold frame with all the tenants listed in white block letters in alphabetical order, and across the top of this board it said Capitalists & Immigrants Trust. So, somewhere along the line, somebody stopped liking that name and decided C&I International would go down smoother, though mean less. Maybe the capitalists and immigrants had stopped trusting.

Feinberg, Kleinberg, Rhineberg, Steinberg, Weinberg & Klatsch was indeed, according to this board, on the twenty-seventh floor, so Dortmunder took a 16–31 elevator with a couple messengers and looked at the reception area while they transacted their businesses with the receptionist.

It was a large though low-ceilinged place with gray carpet and gray furniture in the two seating areas and black desk space in front of the receptionist and along the wall behind her. The walls, a soothing dusty green, were mostly covered with big swirling pieces of abstract art in non-startling colors, so you could feel you were hip without having to do anything about it.

The receptionist, once the messengers cleared the area and Dortmunder could step forward in their place, was just exactly too beautiful to be real, though she seemed unable or unwilling to move any part of her face. She looked at Dortmunder's hands for the package, didn't see one, and finally made eye contact, so Dortmunder could say, "Fiona Hemlow."

She reached for a pen: "And you are?"

"John Dortmunder."

She wrote that on a pad, applied herself to her phone bank, murmured briefly, then said, "She'll be out in a moment. Do have a seat."

"Thanks."

The seating area had gray glass coffee tables among the gray sofas, but nothing to read, so Dortmunder sat on a sofa and looked at the paintings and tried to decide

66

what they looked like. He'd just about come to the conclusion that what they mostly resembled was the bowl after you've finished the ice cream when a very short young woman in black skirt, black jacket, high-necked plain white blouse and low-heeled black shoes marched in from a side aisle, looked around, gave Dortmunder a real estate agent's smile and strode over, hand out: "Mr. Dortmunder?"

Rising, he said, "That's me."

Her handshake was firm but bony. Her black hair was short, curled around her neat small ears, and her face was narrow; good-looking in an efficient sort of way. She looked to be in her mid- to late twenties, and there was no point even looking for a familial resemblance between her and the medicine ball in the wheelchair.

She said, "I'm Fiona. You met my grand-father."

"This morning, yeah. He gave me the background. Well, some of it."

"And, I," she said, being perky in some-how a subdued fashion, which was maybe how girl lawyers effervesced, "will give you the rest. Come along, I'll escort you back."

He followed her down a hall with doors on one side, all open and showing small cluttered offices, each with a neat middle-aged man or woman at a desk, intently concentrating on the phone or the computer or a bunch of pages. Then she went through an open doorway at the end of this hall into a much larger space all broken up into small pieces, like an egg carton, with chest-high walls every which way so you could see what everybody was doing. The people at the machines in these little cells were generally younger than the ones in the private offices, and Dortmunder had already come to suspect that Fiona Hemlow's work environment was in this mob scene somewhere when she said, "I arranged a small conference room for us. Much more private. No distractions."

"Good."

To get to this small conference room, she had to lead him a zigzag route through the people-boxes, and he was surprised the black composition floor wasn't covered with lines of breadcrumbs left by previous people afraid they wouldn't be able to find their way back.

A perimeter of the boxes was reached, and Fiona led the way along a wall to the left with alternating closed doors and plate-glass windows, through which he could see the conference rooms within, some occupied by two or more people in intense head-thrust-forward conversation, some empty.

Into an empty one she led the way, shut the door, and said, with a smile, "Sit anywhere. A beverage? Coke? Seltzer?"

Dortmunder understood that in the business environment it was considered a gesture of civilization to offer the guest something to drink without booze in it, and probably a hostile act to refuse it, so he said, "Seltzer, yeah, sounds good."

She went away to a tall construction on the end wall that contained everything necessary to life: refrigerator, a shelf of glasses, TV, DVD, notepads, pens, and paper napkins. She poured him a seltzer over ice and herself a Diet Pepsi over ice, brought him his drink and a paper napkin, and at last they could sit down and have their chat.

"So you found this thing," Dortmunder began. "This chess set."

She laughed. "Oh, Mr. Dortmunder, this is too good a story to just jump in and tell the end."

Dortmunder hated stories that were that good, but okay, once again no choice in the matter, so he said, "Sure. Go ahead."

"When I was growing up," she said, "there was every once in a while some family talk about a chess set that seemed to make everybody unhappy, but I couldn't figure out why. It was gone, or lost, or something, but I didn't know why it was such a big deal."

She drank Diet Pepsi and give him a warning finger-shake. "I don't mean the family was full of nothing but talk about this mysterious chess set, it wasn't. It was just a thing that came up every once in a while."

"Okay."

"So last summer it came up again," she said, "when I was visiting my father at the Cape, and I asked him, please tell me what it's all about, and he said he didn't really know. If he ever knew, he'd forgotten. He said I should ask my grandfather, so when I got back to the city I did. He didn't want to talk about it, turned out he was very bitter on that subject, but I finally convinced him I really wanted to know what this chess set meant in the family, and he told me."

"And that made you find it," Dortmunder said, "when nobody else could."

"That's right," she said. "I've always been fascinated by history, and this was history with my own family in it, the First World War and invading Russia and all the rest of it. So I took down the names of everybody in that platoon that brought the chess set to

America, and the other names, like the radio company they wanted to start, Chess King Broadcasting, and everything else I thought might be useful, and I Googled it all."

Dortmunder had heard of this; some other nosey parker way to mind everybody else's business. He preferred a world in which people stuck to their own knitting, but that world was long gone. He said, "You found some of these people on Google."

"And I looked for brand names with chess words," she said, "because why wouldn't Alfred Northwood use that kind of name, too? A lot of the stuff I found was all dead ends, but I'm used to research, so I kept going, and then I found Gold Castle Realty, founded right here in New York in 1921, and then it turned out they were the builders of the Castlewood Building in 1948. So I looked into Gold Castle's owners and board of directors, and there's Northwoods all over it."

"The sons," Dortmunder said.

"And daughters. But mostly now grandsons and granddaughters. It had to be the same Northwood, came here from Chicago when he stole the chess set, used it to raise the money to start in real estate, and became hugely successful. They are *very big* in New York property, Mr. Dortmunder. Not as famous as some others, because they don't want to be, but very big."

"That's nice," Dortmunder said. "So they've got this chess set, I guess."

"Well, here's where it gets even better," she said, and she so liked this part she couldn't stop grinning. "The original Alfred X. Northwood," she said, "married into a wealthy New York family —"

"Things kinda went his way."

"His entire life. He died rich and respectable, loved and admired by the world. You should see the obit in the *Times*. Anyway, he died in 1955, aged seventy, and left six children, and they grew up and made more children, and now there are seventeen claimants to Gold Castle Realty."

"Claimants," Dortmunder said.

"The heirs are all suing each other," she said. "It's very vicious, they all hate each other, but every court they go into they get gag orders, so there's nothing public about this information at all."

"But you got it," Dortmunder said, wishing she'd quit having fun and just tell him where the damn chess set was.

"In my researches," she said, "I came across inklings of some of the lawsuits, and then it turned out *this* firm represents Livia Northwood Wheeler, Alfred's youngest daughter, who's suing *everybody* in the family, no partners on her side at all." Leaning closer to him over the conference table, she said, "Isn't that delicious? I'm looking for the Northwoods, and everything you could possibly want to know about their business for the last eighty years is in files in these offices. Oh, I've done a lot of after-hours work, Mr. Dortmunder, I can assure you."

"I'm sure you have," Dortmunder said. "Now, about this chess set."

"It used to be," she said, "on display in a bulletproof glass case in the corporate offices of Gold Castle Realty in their thirty-eighth floor lobby of the Castlewood Building. But it is an extremely valuable family asset, and it is being violently fought over, so three years ago it was removed to be held by several of the law firms representing family members. Four of these firms are in this building, For the last three years, the chess set has been held in the vaults in the sub-basement right here, in the C&I International bank corporation vault. Isn't that wonderful? What do you think, Mr. Dortmunder?"

"I think I'm going back to jail," Dortmunder said.

8

She blinked. "I'm sorry?"

"Don't you be sorry," he said. "I'll be sorry for both of us."

"I don't understand," she admitted. "What's wrong?"

"I know about banks," he told her. "When it comes to money, they are very serious. They got no sense of humor at all. You ever been down to this vault?"

"Oh, no," she said. "I'm not authorized."

"There it is right there," he said. "Do you know anybody *is* authorized?"

"The partners, I suppose."

"Feinberg and them."

"Well, Mr. Feinberg isn't alive any more, but the other partners, yes."

"So if — Wait a minute. Feinberg's name is there, head of the crowd, and he's *dead?*"

"Oh, that's very common," she said. "There are firms, and not just law firms either, where not one person in the firm name is still alive."

"Saves on new letterhead, I guess."

"I think it's reputation," she said. "If a firm suddenly had different names, then it wouldn't be the same firm any more, and it wouldn't have the reputation any more."

Dortmunder was about to ask another question — how a name could sport a reputation without a body behind it — when he realized he was straying widely away from the subject here, so he took a deep breath and said, "This vault."

"Yes," she said, as alert as a dog who's just seen you pick up a ball.

He said, "Do you know what it looks like? Do you know how you get there? Does it have its own elevator?"

"I don't know," she said. "I suppose it could."

"So do I. These partners that can get down there, can you talk to them about this? Ask 'em what it's like?"

"Oh, no," she said. "I've hardly ever even *seen* one of the partners."

"The living ones, you mean."

"Wait," she said. "Let me show you something." And she stood, went over to the construction that contained everything, and came back with a sheet of paper. She slid it across the table to him and it was the company's letterhead stationery. Pointing, she said, "These names across the top, that's the name of the firm."

"Yeah, I got that. All the way to Klatsch."

"Exactly. Now these names down the left side, those are the actual current partners and associates."

"The ones that are alive."

"Yes, of course."

He looked, and the names were not in alphabetical order, so they must be in order of how important you were. "You're not here," he said.

"Oh, no, I'm not — Those are the partners and associates, I'm —" She laughed, in a flustered way, and said, "I'm just a wee beastie."

Dortmunder waved a finger at the descending left-hand column. "So these guys —"

"And women."

"Right. They're the ones can go down to the vault, if they got business there."

"Well, the top ones, yes."

"So not even all of them." Dortmunder was trying not to be exasperated with this well-meaning young person, but with all the troubles he now found staring him in the face it was hard. "So tell me," he said, "this chess set being down there in that vault, how is this good news?"

"Well, we know where it is," she said. "For all those years, nobody knew where it was, nobody knew what happened to it. Now we know."

"And you love history."

Sounding confused, she said, "Yes, I do."

"So just knowing where the thing is, that's good enough for you."

"I . . . I suppose so."

"Your grandfather would like to get his hands on it."

"Oh, we'd all like *that*," she said. "Naturally we would."

"Your grandfather hired himself an ex-cop to help him get it," Dortmunder told her, "and the ex-cop fixed me up with a burglary charge if I don't bring it back with me."

"If you *don't* bring it back?" Her bewilderment was getting worse. "Where's the burglary if you *don't* bring it back?"

"A different burglary," he explained. "A in-the-past burglary."

"Oh!" She looked horribly embarrassed, as though she'd stumbled upon something she wasn't supposed to see.

"So the idea was," he told her, "I come here and you tell me where the chess set is, and I go there and get it and give it to your grandfather, and his ex-cop lets me off the hook."

"I see."

"This vault under this — What is this building, sixty stories?"

"I think so, something like that."

"So this vault way down under this sixty-story building, probably with its own elevator, with a special guest list that your name has to be on it or you don't even get to board the elevator, in a building owned by a bank that used to be called Capitalists and Immigrants, two groups of people with *really* no sense of humor, is not a place I'm likely to walk out of with a chess set I'm told is too heavy for one guy to carry."

"I'm sorry," she said, and she sounded as though she really was.

"I don't suppose you could get a copy of the building's plans. The architect plans with the vault and all."

"I have no idea," she said.

"It would be research."

"Yes, but —" She looked extremely doubtful. "I could look into it, I suppose. The problem is, I couldn't let anybody know what I was looking for."

"That's right."

"And I don't actually see how it could help," she said. "I mean, I don't think you could, say, dig a tunnel to the vault. So far as I know, there is no actual dirt under midtown, it's all sub-basements and water tunnels and steam pipes and sewer lines and subway tunnels."

"I believe," Dortmunder said, "there's some power lines down in there, too."

"Exactly."

"It doesn't look good," Dortmunder suggested.

"No, I have to admit."

They brooded in silence together a minute, and then she said, "If I'd known, I'd never have told Granddad."

"It isn't him, it's the ex-cop he hired."

"I'm still sorry I told him."

Which meant there was nothing more to say. With a deep breath that some might have been called a sigh, he moved his arms preparatory to standing, saying, "Well —"

"Wait a minute," she said, and produced both notepad and pen. "Give me a number where I can reach you. Give me your cell."

"I don't have a cell," he said. But I'm going to, he thought.

"Your landline, then. You do have a landline, don't you?"

"You mean a phone? I got a phone."

He gave her the number. Briskly she wrote it down, then said, "And you should have mine," and handed him a small neat white business card, which he obediently tucked into a shirt pocket. She looked at the landline number he'd given her, as though it somehow certified his existence, then nodded at him and said, "I don't promise anything, Mr. Dortmunder, but I will do my best to find something that might help."

"Good. That's good."

"I'll call you if I have anything at all."

"Yeah, good idea."

Now he did stand, and she said, "I'll show you out."

So he tried a joke, just for the hell of it: "That's okay, I left a trail of breadcrumbs on my way in."

She was still looking blank when she shook his hand good-bye at the elevators; so much for jokes.

Riding down, alone this trip, he thought his best move now was go straight over to Grand Central, take the first train out for Chicago. That's supposed to be an okay place, not that different from a city. It could even work out. Meet up with some guys there, get plugged in a little, learn all those new neighborhoods. Get settled, then send word to May, she could bring out his winter clothes. Chicago was alleged to be very cold.

Leaving the C&I International building,

he figured it'd be just as quick to walk over to the station when here on the sidewalk is Eppick with a big grin, saying, "So. You got it all worked out, I bet."

9

"Not entirely," Dortmunder said.

"But you're working on it."

"Oh, sure."

"And naturally you'll have to consult with your pals, whoever it is you bring in on the job. Who do you figure you'll work with this time?"

Dortmunder looked at him. "You told that grandfather," he said, "how I learned a few things over the years."

"You're right, you're right." Eppick shrugged and grinned, not at all put out, dropping the whole subject. "So let's take a cab," he said, and crossed the sidewalk to the curb.

Helpless, Dortmunder followed. "Where we taking it?"

Eppick's arm was up now, but he didn't bother to watch oncoming traffic, instead continuing his cheerful grin at Dortmunder as he said, "Mr. Hemlow wants to see you."

"He already saw me."

"Well, now he's gonna see you again," Eppick said, as a cab pulled to a stop in their general neighborhood. Eppick opened its door, saying, "Hop in, I'll tell you about it."

So Dortmunder hopped in and slid across the seat so Eppick could follow. Eppick slammed the door and told the turbaned driver, "Two-eleven Riverside Drive."

Dortmunder said, "Not your office."

"Mr. Hemlow's place," Eppick said, as the cab headed west. "Mr. Hemlow's a distinguished man, you know."

"I don't know anything about him."

"He's retired now," Eppick said, "mostly because of this illness he's got. He used to be a chemist, invented a couple things, started a couple businesses, got very rich, sold the stuff off, gives millions away to charity."

"Pretty good," Dortmunder said.

"The point is," Eppick told him, "Mr. Hemlow isn't used to being around roughnecks. He didn't know how he was gonna take to you, so that's why the first meeting was at my place. We knew we'd have to check in with you again after you saw the granddaughter, but Mr. Hemlow decided you were okay, or okay enough, and it isn't easy for him to get around town, so this time we're going to his place."

"I guess I'm honored," Dortmunder said.

"You'll be honored," Eppick told him, "when Mr. Hemlow's got the chess set."

It was a narrow stone building, ten stories high, midblock, taller wider buildings on both sides. The windows were all very elaborate, which made sense, because they faced a tree-dotted park sloping down toward the Hudson, with the West Side Highway and its traffic a sketched-in border between grass and water and New Jersey across the way looking good at this distance.

Eppick paid and they got out of the cab and went up the two broad stone steps to where a dark green–uniformed doorman held the big brass-fitted door open for them and said, "Yes, gentlemen?"

"Mr. Hemlow. I'm Mr. Eppick."

"Yes, sir."

The lobby was small and dark and looked like a carpet salesroom in a mausoleum. Dortmunder and Eppick waited while the doorman made his call, then said, "You may go up."

"Thanks."

The elevator had an operator, in a uniform from the same army as the doorman, although Dortmunder noticed there weren't any operator type controls, just the same buttons that in other elevators the customer has to figure out how to push all by himself. But here the operator did it, and by looming over the panel in a very stiff manner he made sure nobody else got close to the buttons.

"Floor, sir?"

"Mr. Hemlow, penthouse."

"Sir."

The operator pushed *P* and up they went, and at the top the operator held *Door Open* while they exited, so he was either being very conscientious or he was hoping nobody'd notice he wasn't actually required.

Apparently Mr. Hemlow had the entire top floor, because the elevator opened onto his living room, a broad muted space with a wall of large old-fashioned windows overlooking the river but too high up to show the park or the highway. Mr. Hemlow himself waited for them in his wheelchair, and said, "Well, Johnny, from the smile on your face, things are going well."

"Oh, they are, Mr. Hemlow," Eppick assured him. "But mostly I'm smiling because I just love this room. Every time I see it."

"My late wife thanks you," Mr. Hemlow said, a little grimly. "It's all her taste. Come along and sit down." And his motorized wheelchair spun around in place and took off at a pretty good clip, which was probably why he didn't have any rugs on the nice hardwood floor.

Dortmunder and Eppick followed him over closer to the view, where Mr. Hemlow did his spin-around thing again and gestured to them to take a pair of easy chairs with an ornate antique table between them and a good view of the view. However, he then rolled himself into the middle of the view and said, "So tell me where we stand."

On the wing of the airplane, Dortmunder wanted to tell him, but instead said, "Could I ask you, did your granddaughter tell you where they're keeping this chess set?"

"She said a group of law firms was holding it while some lawsuit was being worked out. Apparently, it used to be in an extremely well-guarded place."

"So that's good," Eppick said, and grinned at Dortmunder. "Some law firm won't be so tough to break into, will it?"

"It's not in a law firm," Dortmunder said. "Not in their office."

Mr. Hemlow said, "But my granddaughter said it was."

"They got," Dortmunder told him, "whatchacallit. Custody. The outfit your granddaughter works for, this Feinberg and all of them, except Feinberg isn't with us any more, but that's okay, it's the reputation that counts. Feinberg and them, and some other law companies, they're all in these lawsuits together, so they all got custody of the chess set together. So Feinberg and three of the other companies are all in this C&I International Bank building, so where the chess set is is in the bank building vault, like three sub-basements down or something, under the building, guarded like an underground vault in a bank building."

"Sounds difficult," Mr. Hemlow commented.

Dortmunder was prepared to agree with him wholeheartedly, with details, but Eppick came in first, saying, "That won't stop John and his pals. They've come up against worse problems than that, eh, John?"

"Well . . ." Dortmunder said.

But Eppick wasn't listening. "It seems to me, Mr. Hemlow," he said, "the hard work's all been done here. At the start, you didn't even know where it was. Could've been anywhere in the world. Could've been broken up in different places."

"True," Mr. Hemlow said.

"Now we know where it is," Eppick went on, "and we know it's right here in New

York City, in a bank vault. And we have a person with us, John here, has been inside bank vaults before. Haven't you, John?"

"Once or twice," Dortmunder admitted.

"So the only thing left to discuss," Mr. Hemlow said, "is where you'll deliver the chess set once you've laid your hands on it. You'll probably have it in a van or something like that, won't you?"

"Probably," Dortmunder said. If everybody wanted to spin out a fantasy here, he was content to go along. However; Chicago.

"I think the best place for it, at least at first," Mr. Hemlow said, "would be our compound in the Berkshires. It's been closed for a few years since Elaine died, but I can arrange to have it open and staffed by the time of your arrival."

Eppick said, "Mr. Hemlow? Some kind of country place? You sure that's secure enough?"

"It's enclosed and gated," Mr. Hemlow told him. "Not visible from the road. Elaine and I used to go to Tanglewood for the concerts in the summertime, so we built the compound up there, our rustic retreat. After Elaine passed and I became less . . . mobile, I stopped going. The rest of my family seems to prefer the ocean, for some reason, though why anyone would wish to be immersed in salt water all summer is beyond me. At any rate, the place is there, it has never been broken into or bothered, and it's the safest location I can think of."

"If you don't mind, Mr. Hemlow," Eppick said, "me and John here, maybe we oughta go look at it. Just to see if there's any little tweaks to be done, help out a little. Better safe than sorry."

Mr. Hemlow considered that. "When would you go?"

"First thing in the morning," Eppick told him. "I'm sure John isn't doing anything much, in the daytime."

Except fleeing to Chicago. "Naw, I'm okay," Dortmunder said.

"With your permission," Eppick said, "I'll rent a car and bill you for it later."

"Take my car," Mr. Hemlow said. "I hadn't planned to use it tomorrow. Pembroke knows how to get to the compound, and he'll have the keys."

Doubtful, Eppick said, "You're sure."

"Absolutely." From the left arm of the wheelchair, moving that medicine ball body with little grunts, Mr. Hewlow produced a phone, which he slowly buttoned, saying, "I'll leave Pembroke a message to — Oh, you're there. Very good. I'll want the car around front at" — as much as possible, the head on the medicine ball cocked to one side in a questioning way — "nine?"

"Fine," Eppick said.

"Good. Yes. It won't be me, you'll be driving Mr. Eppick and another gentleman up to the compound. You still have the keys? Excellent." He broke the connection and said, "You should be back late afternoon. Come up and tell me what you think."

"Will do."

"Thank you for coming," Mr. Hemlow said, so Eppick stood, so Dortmunder stood. Good-byes were said, they walked to the elevator while Mr. Hemlow watched from back by the view, and neither spoke until they were out on Riverside Drive, when Eppick said, "So you'll be here at nine in the morning."

"Sure," Dortmunder said.

Eppick did a more successful cocking of the head. "I get little whiffs from you, John," he said, "that you're not as keen as you might be on this job."

"That's not easy, that vault."

"But there it is," Eppick pointed out. "If you're thinking, maybe you'll just get out of town for a while until this all blows over, let me tell you, it isn't *going* to blow over. Mr. Hemlow's into this for sentimental reasons, but I'm in it for profit, and you'd better be, too."

"Oh, sure."

"Police departments around America," Eppick said, "are getting better and better at cooperation, what with the Internet and all. Everybody helps everybody, and nobody can disappear." Lacing his fingers together to show what he meant, in a gesture very like a stranglehold, he said, "We're all intertwined these days. See you at nine."

10

When May got home from her job at the Safeway with the daily sack of groceries she felt was a perk her employers would have given her if they'd thought of it, the apartment was dark. It was not yet quite six o'clock, but in this apartment, whose windows showed mostly brick walls four to six feet away, midnight in November came around three p.m.

May switched on the hall light, went down to the kitchen, stowed the day's take, went back up the hall, turned right into the living room to see if the local news had anything she could bear to listen to, switched on the light there, and John was seated in his regular chair, in the dark, gazing moodily at the television set. Well, no; gazing moodily *toward* the television set.

May jumped a foot. She let out a little cry, clutched her bosom, and cried, "John!"

"Hello, May."

She stared at him. "John? What's the matter?"

"Well," he said, "I'm doomed."

For the first time in years, May wished she still smoked. Taking the other chair, she flicked ashes from that ancient cigarette onto the side table where the ashtray used to be, and said, "Was it that cop?"

"It sure was."

"And did Stan find you?"

With a hollow sardonic laugh, John said, "Oh, yeah. He found me."

"He can't help?"

"Stan doesn't help," John said. "Stan *needs* help, him and his golden dome. If my only problem was Stan Murch and his golden dome, I'd be sitting pretty, May. Sitting pretty."

"Well, what *is* the problem?"

"The thing the cop wants me to get," John said. "It's a golden chess set — more gold — and it's supposed to be too heavy for one guy to lift."

"Get somebody to help."

"It's also," he said, "in a sub-basement vault under a midtown bank building."

"Oh," she said.

"And this guy, this seventeen-months-not-a-cop," John said, "he let me know, I try to leave town, he's got these millions and mil-

93

lions of cop buddies on the Internet and they'll track me down. And he would, too, he's a mean son of a bitch, you can see it in his forehead."

"So what are you going to do?"

"Well," he said, "I figure I'll just sit here until they come to get me."

"You don't mean that, John," she said, though she was afraid he actually did mean it.

"I've done jail before, May," he reminded her. "It wasn't that bad. I got through it."

"You were less set in your ways, then," she said.

"You can pick up the old routines," he said. "Probly a few guys still there I knew in the old days."

"Or there again."

"Yeah, could be. Old home week."

May knew John had a very bad tendency, when things got unusually difficult, to sink with an almost sensuous pleasure into a warm bath of despair. Once you've handed the reins over to despair, to mix a metaphor just a teeny bit, your job is done. You don't have to sweat it any more, you've taken yourself out of the game. Despair is the bench, and you are warming it.

May knew it was her job, at moments like this, to pull John out of the clutches of despair and goose him into forward motion once more. After all, it isn't whether you win or lose, it's just you have to be in the goddam game.

"John," she said, being suddenly very stern, "don't be so selfish."

He blinked at her, emerging slowly up from a dream of prison as a kind of fraternal organization. "What?"

"What about *me?*" she demanded. "Don't you ever think about *me?* I can't go to jail *with* you, you know."

"Yeah, but —"

"What am I going to do with myself, John," she wanted to know, "if you're going to spend ten to fifteen upstate? I've made a certain commitment here, you know that, I hope."

"May, it's not me, it's that cop."

"It's you that's sitting there," she told him, "like you're waiting for a bus. And you *are* waiting for a bus. To jail! What's the matter with you, John?"

He tried, though feebly, to fight back. "May? You *want* me to *try* to get down into that vault? Never mind the vault, you want me to try to get into the elevator that leads down to the vault? The bank's *money* is down there, too, May, they will be very alert about that vault. And, even if I was crazy enough to try it, who am I gonna get to help carry? Who else would try a stunt like that?"

"Call Andy," she advised.

11

The dome didn't look like gold at night. There were work lights around the construction site, even though no work was being done at the moment, to deter pilferage, which would usually mean boards or Sheetrock panels, not golden domes fifteen feet high, and in those work lights, as far as Andy Kelp was concerned, the dome looked mostly like a giant apricot. Not a peach, not that warmer fuzzy tone, but an apricot, except without that crease that makes apricots look as though they're wearing thong bathing suits.

Andy Kelp, a bony sharp-nosed guy in nonreflecting black, tended to blend in with the shadows at night when he moved from this place to that place. The place he was moving around in at the moment was just beyond the chain-link perimeter fence enclosing the mosque construction site, now temporarily on hold while the recently transplanted community got up to speed on the New York City culture and ethos.

And the reason Andy Kelp was moving around here at night was that, while he still thought the idea of heisting something this size and weight, particularly from people who have been known to be slightly hot-headed in the past, was a terrible notion, the one thing he didn't have was John Dortmunder's opinion. He was pretty sure John would see the scheme the same way everybody else did, but unfortunately John hadn't been at the meeting in the back room of the O.J. to put his stamp of disapproval personally on the idea, having been waylaid by some cop.

So, because of that gap in the chain of evidence, and because he wasn't doing much of anything else at the moment, he'd borrowed a car from East Thirtieth Street in Manhattan and driven out here to Brooklyn to give the golden dome the double-o. He was now coming to the conclusion that his first conclusion had been right all along, as expected, when the phone vibrated against his leg — silence can be more golden than any dome — so he pulled it out and said, "Yar."

"You busy?" The very John Dortmunder whose absence last night had brought him out here.

"Not really," Kelp said. "You?"

"We could maybe talk."

Surprised, Kelp said, "About the job?"

Sounding surprised, John said, "Yeah."

Kelp took a step back to study the dome from a slightly different angle, and it still seemed to him too big and too unwieldy and just downright too unlikely, so he said, "You mean, you want to do it?"

"Well, I got no choice."

So John felt compelled to go after all this gold; think of that. Kelp said, "To tell you the truth, I was thinking, you cut a piece off it, could be," though he hadn't thought of that till this very minute. But if John believed there might be something in this gold mountain, that could get Kelp's creative juices flowing, too. "Is that your idea," he asked, "or what?"

"Cut a piece off *what?*"

"The dome," Kelp said. "You'll never get the whole dome, John, I'm looking at it and —"

"The dome? You mean, Stan's Islamic dome?"

"Isn't that what you're talking about?"

"And you're *out* there with it? You're whacking *pieces* off it?"

"No, I'm just giving it the good lookover,

99

the whadawe see when we see this idea."

"Stan there?"

"No, I just come out by myself, spur of the moment kinda thing. I don't wanna encourage Stan, get his hopes up. John, *aren't* you talking about the dome?"

"You think I'm a moron?"

"No, John, but you said —"

"You wanna meet? You wanna talk? Or you wanna stay out there and cut filets outa the dome?"

"I'm on my way, John. Where and when?"

"O.J., ten. It's just the two of us, so we won't need the back room."

"So it isn't a solid job yet."

"Oh, it's solid," John told him. "And I'm under it."

12

When Dortmunder walked into the O.J. at ten that night Andy Kelp had not yet arrived, and the regulars, freed from last night's Eppick-inspired verbal paralysis, were discussing James Bond movies. "That was the one," the first regular said, "where the bad guy went after his basket with a laser."

"You're wrong about that," the second regular told him. "You happen to be confusing that one with that guy George Laserby, he was the Bond only that one time — What was it called?"

Dortmunder angled toward the other end of the bar, where Rollo the bartender repetitively rag-wiped one spot on the bar's surface as though he believed that's where the genie lived, while a third regular said, *"In His Majesty's Secret Police."*

The second regular frowned, as Dortmunder almost reached the bar: "Wasn't that

Timothy Danton?"

The third regular frowned right back: "Timothy who?"

"Danton. The polite one."

"No, no," the first regular said. "This is much earlier, and, it's a laser, not a laserby, a light that slices you in half."

The third regular remained bewildered: "This is a *light?*"

"It's green."

"You're thinking," the second regular told him, "of *Star Wars.*"

"Rollo," Dortmunder said.

"Forget *Star Wars,*" the first regular said. "It was a laser, and it was green. Wasn't the bad guy Doctor No?"

"Doctor Maybe Not," said the joker. There's a joker in every crowd.

"Rollo," Dortmunder explained, and Rollo came slowly up from REM sleep, stopped his rag-wiping, focused on Dortmunder, and said, "Two nights in a row. You could become a regular."

"Maybe not," Dortmunder said, echoing the joker, though not on purpose. "But tonight, yeah. Just me and the other bourbon." Because Rollo knew his customers by their drink, which he felt was the way to inspire consumer loyalty.

"Happy to see you both," Rollo said.

"It's just the two of us, so we don't need the back room."

"Woody *Allen,*" demanded the ever-perplexed third regular, "played James *Bond?*"

"I think that was him," said the second regular, showing a rare moment of regular doubt.

"Fine," said Rollo, and went away to prepare a tray containing two glasses with ice cubes and a full bottle bearing a label that read *Amsterdam Liquor Store Bourbon* — "Our Own Brand." "Drink it in good health," he said, and pushed the tray across the genie.

"Thanks."

Dortmunder turned around, carrying the tray, looked to choose just the right booth, and Kelp appeared in the bar doorway. He entered, saw Dortmunder, gazed around the room, and pointed at the booth next to him, the one where last night — just last night! — Dortmunder had met his personal ex-cop doom.

The same booth? Well, the farther from the Bondsmen the better. Dortmunder shrugged: Okay.

Once they were seated facing one another and their glasses were no longer empty, Kelp said, "This is about that cop."

"You know it. Johnny Eppick For Hire."

"How much of that is his name?"

"The front half."

"So he used to be a cop," Kelp suggested, "and now he's a private eye."

"Or whatever. He's working for a rich guy that wants this valuable heavy golden chess set that just happens to be in a sub-basement bank vault in midtown."

"Forget it," Kelp advised.

"I'd like to," Dortmunder said. "Only he's got pictures of me in a compromising position."

"Oh, yeah?" Kelp seemed very interested. "What, is he gonna show them to May?"

"Not that kind," Dortmunder said. "The kind he could show to the cops that didn't retire yet."

"Oh." Kelp nodded. "Miami could be nice, this time of year."

"I was thinking Chicago. Only, Eppick thought of it, too. He says, him and the Internet and his cop buddies would find me anywhere I went, and I believe him."

"How much time you got?"

"Before my arrest, arraignment, plea bargain, and bus ride north?" Dortmunder shrugged. "I can stall a little, I guess. But Eppick is leaning, and the guy he works for is old and sick and wouldn't be interested in any long-term plans."

"Sheesh." Kelp shook his head. "I hate to say this, but better you than me."

"Don't hate to say it," Dortmunder advised him, "because you're already kinda involved."

Kelp didn't like that. "You two've been talking about *me?*"

"He already knows you," Dortmunder said. "He researched me or something. Last night, when he left here, he looked down toward you and said, 'Give my hello to Andy Kelp.' He knows about Arnie Albright. He knows us all."

"I don't like this," Kelp said. "I don't like your friend Eppick even *thinking* about me."

"Oh, is that how it is?" Dortmunder wanted to know. "Now he's my friend?"

"You know what I mean."

"I'm not sure I do."

Kelp looked around the room, as though to fix the location more securely in his mind. "You asked me to meet you here tonight," he said. "Now I get it, you asked me here because you want me to help. So when are you gonna ask me to help?"

"There is no help," Dortmunder said.

Kelp slowly sipped some of his bourbon, while gazing at Dortmunder over the glass. Then he put the glass down and continued to gaze at Dortmunder.

"Okay," Dortmunder said. "Help."

"Sure," Kelp said. "Where is this bank vault?"

"C&I International, up on Fifth Avenue."

"That's a big bank," Kelp said. He sounded faintly alarmed.

"It's a big building," Dortmunder said. "Underneath it is a sub-basement, and in the sub-basement is the chess set that's out to ruin my life."

"I could go up tomorrow," Kelp offered, "and take a look."

"Well," Dortmunder said, "I'd like you to do something else tomorrow."

Looking hopeful, Kelp said, "You already got a plan?"

"No, I already got a disaster." Dortmunder drank some of his own bourbon, more copiously than Kelp had, and said, "Let me say first, this Eppick already figures you're in. He said to me today, 'I suppose you'll work with your pal Andy Kelp.' "

"Conversations about me," Kelp said, and shivered.

"I know. I feel the same way. But here's the thing. It's just as important you get to see this Eppick as it is you get to see some bank building."

"Oh, yeah?"

106

"Tomorrow morning," Dortmunder said, "in the rich guy's limo, we're going upstate somewhere, Eppick and me, to see if what the rich guy called his compound is secure enough for us to stash the chess set after we ha-ha lift it."

"You want me to ride upstate tomorrow," Kelp said, "in a limo with you and Eppick."

"And a chauffeur."

Kelp contemplated that, while back at the bar, "Shaken but not slurred!" piped the joker.

Kelp observed his glass, but did not drink. "And why," he wanted to know, "am I doing this?"

"Maybe we'll learn something."

"Nothing we want to know, I bet." Kelp did knock back a little more bourbon. "What time are we doing this foolish thing?"

13

Being a wee beastie in a huge corporate law firm in midtown Manhattan meant that one did not have very many of one's waking hours to oneself. Again tonight it was after ten before Fiona could call her home-buddy Brian and say, "I'm on my way."

"It'll be ready when you get here."

"Should I stop and get anything?" By which she meant wine.

"No, I got everything we need." By which he meant he'd bought wine on his way home from the studio.

"See you, hon."

"See you, hon."

The interior of Feinberg et al maintained the same lighting twenty-four hours a day, since only the partners and associates had offices around the perimeter of the building, and thus windows. In the rest of the space you might as well have been in a spaceship far off in the emptiness of the universe. The only differences at ten p.m., when Fiona moved through the cubicles to the elevator bank, were that the receptionist's desk was empty, the latest Botox Beauty having left at five, and that Fiona needed her employee ID card to summon and operate the elevator. It wasn't, in fact, until she'd left the elevator and the lobby and the building itself that she found herself back on Earth, where it was nighttime, with much traffic thundering by on Fifth Avenue.

Her route home was as certain as a bowling alley gutter. Walk across Fifth Avenue and down the long block to Sixth and the long block to Seventh and the short block to Broadway. Then up two blocks to the subway, where she would descend, swipe the MetroCard until it recognized itself, and then descend some more and wait for the uptown local, riding it to Eighty-sixth Street. Another walk, one block up and half a block over, and she entered her apartment building, where she chose a different card from her bulging wallet — this was three cards for one trip — in order to gain admittance, then took the elevator to the fourth floor and walked down the long hall to 4-D. That same third card also let her into the apartment, where the smell of Oriental food — was that Thai? the smell of peanuts? —

was the most welcoming thing in her day.

"Honey, I'm home!" she called, which they both thought of as their joke, and he came grinning out of the galley kitchen with a dishtowel tucked in around his waist and a glass of red wine in each hand. As tall as she was short, and as blond as she was raven-haired, Brian had wide bony shoulders but was otherwise as skinny as a stray cat, with a craggy handsome face that always maintained some caution down behind the good cheer.

"Home is the hunter," he greeted her, which was another part of the joke, and handed over a glass.

They kissed, they clinked glasses, they sipped the wine, which they didn't know any better than to believe was pretty good, and then he went back to the kitchen to plate their dinners while she stood leaning in the doorway to say, "How was your day?"

"Same old same old," he said, which was what he usually said, though sometimes there were tidbits of interest he would share with her, just as she would with him.

Since he worked for a cable television company, Brian actually had more frequent tidbits to offer than she did. He was an illustrator there, assembling collages and occasionally doing original artwork, all to be background for different things the cable station would air. He belonged to some sort of show business writers union, though she didn't quite see how what he did counted as writing, but it meant that, though his income was a fraction of hers, his hours were much more predictable — and shorter — than hers. She thought wistfully from time to time that it might be nice to be in a union and get home at six at night instead of ten-thirty, but she knew it was a class thing: Lawyers would never stoop to protect themselves.

Brian brought their dinners out to the table in what they called the big room, though it wasn't that big. Even so, they'd crowded into it a sofa, two easy chairs, a small dining table with two armless designer chairs, a featureless gray construct containing all the elements of their "entertainment space," two small bookcases crammed with her history books and his art books, and a small black coffee table on which they played Scrabble and cribbage.

They'd been a couple for three years now, he moving into what had been her place after he broke up with his previous girlfriend. They had no intention of marrying, no desire for children, no yen to put down roots somewhere in the suburbs. They liked each other, liked living together, didn't get on each other's nerves very much, and didn't see too much of one another because of the nature of her job. So it was all very nice and easy.

And he was a good cook! He'd had an after-school restaurant slavey job in his teens, and had taken to the concept of cookery as being somehow related to his work as an artist. He enjoyed burrowing his way into exotic cuisines, and she almost always relished the result. Not so bad.

Tonight, as her nose had told her, dinner came from the cuisine of Thailand, and was delicious, and over it she said, "My day wasn't exactly same old same old."

Interested, he looked at her over his fork. (You don't use chopsticks with Thai food.) "Oh, yeah?"

"A man I talked to," she said. "The most hangdog man I ever met in my life. You can't imagine what he looked like when he said, 'I'm going back to jail.' " And she laughed at the memory, as he frowned at her, curious.

"Back to jail? You're not defending crooks now, are you? That isn't what you people do."

"No, no, this isn't anything to do with the

firm. This is something about my grand-father."

"Daddy Bigbucks," Brian said.

She smiled at him, indulging him. "Yes, I know, you're only with me because of my prospects. Money is really all you care about, I know that."

He grinned back at her, but with a slight edge to it as he said, "Try going without it for a while."

"I know, I know, you come from the wrong side of the tracks."

"We were too poor to have tracks. What I've done, I've shacked-up up. Tell me about this hangdog guy."

So she told him the chess set saga, about which he had previously known nothing. He asked a few questions, brought himself up to speed, then said, "Is this guy really going to rob a bank vault?"

"Oh, of course not," she said. "It's just silly. They'll all see it's impossible, and that'll be the end of it."

"But what if he tries?"

"Oh, the poor man," she said, but she grinned as she said it. "In that case, I think he probably will go back to jail."

14

In Dortmunder's dream, it wasn't his old cell at all, it was much older, and smaller, and very rusty, and flooded with water knee-deep. His cellmate — a hulking guy he'd never met before, but who looked a lot like Hannibal Lecter — leered at him and said, "We like it this way."

Dortmunder opened his mouth to say he didn't at all like it this way, but out from between his lips came the sudden jangle of an alarm clock, startling him awake.

John Dortmunder was not an alarm clock kind of guy. He preferred to get out of bed when the fancy struck him, which was generally about the crack of noon. But with the necessity this morning of being way over on the Upper West Side at nine o'clock, he knew he had to make an exception. Two days in a row with morning appointments! What kind of evil cloud was he under here, all of a sudden?

Last night, May had helped him set the alarm for eight in the morning, and now at eight in the morning May's foot helped him bounce out of bed, slap the alarm clock silly until it shut up, then slope off to the bathroom.

Twenty minutes later, full of a hastily-ingested mélange of corn flakes and milk and sugar, he went out into the morning cold — it was *much* colder out here in the morning — and after some time found a cab to take him up to Riverside Drive, where a black limo sat in front of Mr. Hemlow's building, white exhaust putt-putting out of its tailpipe. The skinny sour guy at the wheel, with the white hair sticking out from under his chauffeur's cap, would be Pembroke, and the satisfied guy in the rear-facing backseat, encased like a sausage in his black topcoat, would be Johnny Eppick in person, who pushed open the extra-wide door, grinned into the cold air, and said, "Right on time. We're all here, climb in."

"One to go," Dortmunder told him.

Eppick didn't think he liked that. "You're bringing somebody along?"

"You already know him," Dortmunder said. "So I thought he oughta know you."

"And he would be —"

"Andy Kelp."

Now Eppick's smile returned, bigger than ever. "Good thinking. You're starting to put your mind to it, John, that's good." Slight frown. "But where is he?"

"Coming up the street," Dortmunder said, nodding down to where Kelp walked toward them up Riverside Drive.

Kelp had a jaunty walk when he was going into a situation he wasn't sure of, and it was at its jauntiest as he approached the limo, looked at that smiling head leaning out of the limo's open door, and said, "You're gonna be Johnny Eppick, I bet."

"Got it in one," Eppick said. "And you'll be Andrew Octavian Kelp."

"Oh, I only use the Octavian on holidays."

"Well, get in, get in, we might as well get going."

The interior of the limo had been adjusted for Mr. Hemlow's wheelchair, so that a bench seat behind the chauffeur's compartment faced backward, and the rest of the floor was covered with curly black carpet, with lines in it that showed where the platform would extend out through the doorway when it was time to load Mr. Hemlow aboard. The bench seat would really be comfortable only for two and Eppick was already on it, but when Dortmunder bent to enter the limo somehow Kelp was already

in there, seated to Eppick's right and looking as innocent as a poisoner.

So that left the floor for Dortmunder, unless he wanted to sit up in front of the partition with the chauffeur and not be part of
the conversation. He went in on all fours
and then turned himself around into a
seated position as Eppick closed the door.
The rear wall, beneath the window, was also
covered with the black carpet, and wasn't
really uncomfortable at all, anyway not at
first. So Dortmunder might be on the floor,
but at least he was facing front.

"All right, Pembroke," Eppick said, and
off they went.

Kelp, with his amiable smile, said, "John
tells me you know all about us."

"Oh, I doubt that," Eppick said. "I only
know that little part of your activities that's
made it into the filing system. The tip of the
iceberg, you might say."

"And yet," Kelp said, "I don't seem to
have any files on you at all. John says you're
retired from the NYPD."

"Seventeen months ago."

"Congratulations."

"Thank you."

"Where was it in the NYPD," Kelp won-
dered, "did they make use of your talents?"

"The last seven years," Eppick told him,

not seeming to mind the interrogation at all, "I was in the Bunco Squad."

"They still call it that? 'Say, did you drop this wallet?' That kinda thing?"

Eppick laughed. "Oh, there's still some street hustle," he said, "but not so much any more. You watch television half an hour, you know every scam there is."

"Not every."

"No, not every," Eppick conceded. "But these days, it's mostly phone and Internet."

"The Nigerians."

"All that money they're trying to get out of Lagos and into your bank account," Eppick agreed. "Amazing how often we find the sender in Brooklyn."

"Amazing you find the sender," Kelp told him.

"Oh, now," Eppick said. "We do have our little successes."

"That's nice," Kelp said. "But now you're out on your own. John tells me you got a card and everything."

"Oh, I'm sorry," Eppick said. "I should of given you one." And, sliding two fingers under the lapel of his topcoat, he brought out another of his cards and gave it to Kelp.

Who studied it with interest. " 'For Hire,' " he read. "Doesn't narrow it much."

"I didn't want the clients to feel constricted."

"You had many of those?"

"Mr. Hemlow is my first," Eppick said, "and naturally the most important."

"Naturally."

"I don't want to let him down."

"No, of course not," Kelp agreed. "Here at the beginning of your second career."

"Exactly."

"Yet John tells me," Kelp said, "this little thing you put him on the send for, he tells me it isn't gonna be easy."

"If it was gonna be easy," Eppick said, "I woulda sent a boy."

"That's true."

"I got every confidence in your friend John," Eppick said. Looking at Dortmunder, who was at that moment shifting position this way and that because after a while and a few stops at red lights the limo floor and back weren't quite as comfortable as he'd thought at first, he said, "I believe also that John has every confidence in me."

"Sure," Dortmunder said. When he crumpled himself into the corner, it was a little better.

15

Judson Blint typed names and addresses into the computer. Here it was, nearly ten in the morning, and he still hadn't finished with Super Star Music, while stacked up beside his left elbow were the letters, the applications, and the checks — lovely checks — for Allied Commissioners' Courses and Intertherapeutic Research Service. What a long way to go.

For some reason, the mail was always heaviest on Fridays. Maybe the post office just wanted to clear everything out before the weekend. For whatever reason, Friday was always the day that made this job seem most like a job, instead of what it actually was, which was three extremely profitable felonies.

Take Super Star Music, on which he was still working at ten in the morning. Advertising in magazines likely to draw in the young and the gullible, Super Star Music promised to make you rich and famous by setting *your* song lyrics to music. Alternately, if it's music you got, they'll give you lyrics. Now, most amateurs do simple marching-beat doggerel, so there's lots of music out there to match; just shift the rhythms around a bit. As for lyrics, *Bartlett's Familiar Quotations* has some pretty good ones, or there's always what's in the next envelope right here.

Allied Commissioners' Courses, on the other hand, would teach you everything you needed to know to make a fine living as a detective; sure. And if Intertherapeutic Research Service's dirty book doesn't improve your sex life, check your pulse; maybe you died.

Judson Blint's task in this triple threat ongoing skimming of the pittances of the reality impaired was simple. Each day, he opened the envelopes, typed the return addresses into the computer and attached the labels to the right packages. Then he carried the outgoing mail on a large dolly down to the post office in the lobby of this building, brought up the next batch of suckers, and carried the checks to the inner office of J.C. Taylor, who'd originally thought up all this stuff and would give him twenty percent of the intake simply for doing the clerical work — usually between seven and eleven hundred a week.

He'd been at this scam since July, when he'd first come to Manhattan out of Long Island, fresh out of high school and convinced he was the best con artist of all time, until J.C. saw through him in a New York minute but gave him this job anyway, for which he would be forever grateful. Also, it had already led a bit to even better things.

He was thinking about those better things, feeling sorry again that Stan Murch's idea at the O.J. the other night had been such a loser, because it was time to pick up a little extra coinage here and there before winter set in, when the hall door opened and, before Judson could do his spiel — "J.C. Taylor isn't in at the moment, have you an appointment, I'm terribly sorry" — Stan Murch himself walked in. He shut the door behind himself, nodded at Judson, and said, "Harya."

"Hi."

"I was in the neighborhood."

Of the seventh floor of the Avalon State Bank Tower on Fifth Avenue near St. Patrick's Cathedral? Sure. "Glad you could drop by," Judson said.

There were chairs in this small crowded room, other than the one at the desk where Judson sat, but they were all piled high with books, either detective or sex. Stan looked around, accepted reality, and leaned back against a narrow clear spot of wall beside the door. Folding his arms, he said, "That was really too bad about the other night."

"Yeah, it was."

"I just had the feeling, you know, the guys didn't quite get the concept."

"I had that feeling, too."

"You in particular," Stan said. "A bright young guy, not stuck with old-fashioned thinking."

"Well, it just seemed to me," Judson said, wanting to get out of this without acknowledging there was anything to get out of, "the other guys had a lot more expertise than me, so I oughta go along with the way they saw things."

"I got a certain expertise, too, you know," Stan said, and looked as though he were thinking about getting irritated.

"*Driving* expertise, Stan," Judson said. "You got the most driving expertise I ever saw in my life."

"Well, yeah," Stan said, but would not be deflected. "On the other hand," he said, and the inner door opened.

They both turned to look as J.C. herself walked in from her office, saying, "I heard voices. Hello, Stan. Keeping my staff from their work?" A striking if tough-looking brunette of around thirty, who moved in a style somewhere between a runway model's strut and a cheetah's lope, J.C., when she came into a room, particularly dressed as now in pink peasant blouse and a short black leather skirt and heeled sandals with black leather straps twining halfway up to the knee, it was impossible to look away.

Stan didn't even try. "Just exchanging a word or two, J.C.," he said. "Exercising our chins."

"Talking about the golden dome?" J.C. asked him.

Stan didn't like that. "Oh, Tiny told you," he guessed, Tiny Bulcher being J.C.'s room-mate somewhere around town, a pairing that seemed to those who knew them to have been made, if not in Heaven, possibly in Marvel Comics.

"Tiny told me," she agreed. "He said it was the dumbest idea he'd heard since Lucky Finnegan decided to walk from the Bronx to Brooklyn stepping only on the third rail." To Judson she explained, "Lucky was very proud of his sense of balance."

"If no other sense," Stan said.

Judson said, "Somehow, I have the feeling he didn't make it."

"They're trying to find another nickname

for him," J.C. said. "Something about bar-beque."

"The golden dome," Stan said, his eye being on it, "is not as dumb an idea as some people think it is."

J.C. gave him a frank look. "Which people, Stan, don't think it's a dumb idea?"

"Me for one," he said. "My Mom, for two."

J.C. pointed a scarlet-tipped finger at him. "Do not get your Mom involved."

"I'm just saying."

Judson said, "It's too bad John couldn't be there to hear the idea."

The silence that followed that remark was so extreme that both Judson and J.C. bent deeply suspicious frowns on Stan, to find him red-faced and struggling to find a deflecting comment. J.C. said, "You told him."

"We had a preliminary conversation on the subject, yes."

J.C. said, "And he hated it."

"It's true he doesn't yet see the potential," Stan said. "So all I was gonna suggest to Judson here, let's drive out, drive along the Belt, take a look at it, gleaming there beside the highway, it's like the dome of gold at the end of the rainbow."

Judson said, "I think that was a pot."

"A dome is a pot," Stan said. "Upside down."

"It is true," J.C. said, "that Judson here is a beardless youth —"

"What? I shave!"

"— but that doesn't mean he's green between the ears."

"Thank you, J.C."

J.C. considered what she was going to say next, as she hitched a hip onto the corner of the desk. "You know how it is sometimes," she said, "you see a very beautiful, very desirable woman, and man, how you'd like to get your hands on that?"

They both nodded.

"And then you find out," J.C. said, "she's unobtainable. That's all, just unobtainable. You know what I mean?"

They both nodded.

"So you feel sad a little while," she said, and they both nodded, "but then you move on, something else grabs your eye, all you've got left is a little nostalgic feeling for the never-happened," and they both nodded, and she said, "Stan, that's what that dome is. You saw it, you lusted after it, you tried to figure out how to get your hands on it, but it's just not obtainable. Try to think about something else."

The silence this time was more contemplative, and Judson deliberately gazed the other way while Stan worked his way through the seven stages of loss, or however many of those stages there are.

"Well," Stan said, at last, and Judson dared to look at him, and Stan had a recovered look on his face. "I guess for a while," he said, "I'll be taking some alternate route."

16

It turned out Mr. Hemlow's compound wasn't upstate after all, but upstate plus, which meant, having driven straight north out of the city up through New York State for more than two hours, they suddenly veered off to the right oblique, like a basketball forward going in for a layup, and here they were in Massachusetts. And still not there.

Long before Massachusetts, Dortmunder had come to the realization that the only way he was going to survive this trip was by not sitting on the floor, which was bonier than it had seemed at first and also did a certain amount of jolting and juking, less noticeable to people up there on the comfortable upholstery. His alternative, after several failed experiments, was to lie on his back on the floor and stretch his legs out, so that his ankles were more or less between the ankles of Eppick and Kelp. In that position, left arm under his head for a pillow, he could feel foolish but also believe he would somehow live through all this.

Being on the floor like that, he didn't get to see a lot of the scenery go by, nor to participate much in the conversation proceeding above him, though he could certainly hear everything those two had to say to one another. After an early period of parry-and-feint, in which Eppick tried to interrogate Kelp while pretending he wasn't doing any such thing, and Kelp pretended to answer all those questions without ever actually conveying any solid information — much like a politician at a press conference — they settled into their anecdotage, each telling little incidents from other people's lives, never their own. "A guy I know once —" and so on. Eppick's little tales tended to finish with the miscreant in handcuffs, while Kelp's had the rascal scampering over the rooftops to safety, but they obviously both enjoyed the exercise and each other.

From time to time, in order to give his cramping left arm a rest, Dortmunder would roll over onto his right side, use his bent right arm beneath his head as a pillow, and let the twinging left arm lie straight down his side. At those times, he was in even less contact with the rest of the world, so much so that, at one point, he actually fell asleep, though he would have said that was impossible. That is, before —

"Snr— ? Wha?"

"We're here, John," Eppick said, and stopped poking Dortmunder's shins with his toe.

Dortmunder sat up, incautiously, became painfully aware of many of his body parts, and braced himself against the floor, which was not vibrating.

The limo had stopped. Blinking gummy eyes, Dortmunder looked past the looming forms of Eppick and Kelp, and saw the steering wheel. Where was the chauffeur? Whatsit, Pembroke.

Oh. Out there in the woods.

They were on a dirt road now, surrounded by huge Christmas trees, and when Dortmunder twisted around — ouch — he saw out the back window that they were very close to some sort of paved road, on which, as he watched, a truck piled high with monster logs went rolling by.

Meanwhile, this dirt road had come to a metal gate in a simple three-strand wire fence extending away to left and right into the sweeping lower branches of the Christmas trees. What Pembroke was doing now was working at two padlocks holding the halves of the gate shut.

Watching Pembroke at it, Dortmunder thought, that doesn't look very high-tech to me.

Kelp said, "That doesn't look very high-tech to me."

"It doesn't have to," Eppick said, and pointed. "See those square white metal plates at every post? Those'll be the notices. This is an electrified fence."

"Oh," Kelp said.

"It won't kill you," Eppick said, "but it will make you change your mind pretty quick."

Now Pembroke was walking the two sides of the gate open, first to the right, then to the left. Beyond the opening, the dirt road angled rightward and almost immediately disappeared among those big dark tree branches.

Pembroke slid back behind the wheel, drove forward past the gate, got out, shut the parts of the gate behind him but didn't refasten the padlocks, got back into the limo and started them slowly forward onto this private land.

As they drove, Eppick twisted around frontward to say, "Pembroke, a question."

"Sir," Pembroke said, but kept his eye on the road curving back and forth ahead of them, nothing visible now but long curving green branches of pine needles and this well-maintained dirt road.

Eppick said, "Yesterday, Mr. Hemlow called this the compound. How big is it?"

"In land, sir?"

"Well, yeah, in land."

"I believe, sir," Pembroke said, while steering massively left and massively right, using his whole upper body as though this were a toboggan on fresh snow, "the compound consists of just under thirteen hundred acres."

"And the whole thing is circled with electric fence?"

"And alarmed, sir, yes."

"Alarmed?" Eppick sounded impressed. "Where's the alarm go off?"

"Boston, sir."

Less impressed, Eppick said, "Boston? That's the other end of the state."

"It is the capital of Massachusetts, sir. Orders received from Boston, by e-mail or fax, are acted upon much more rapidly than orders received from Great Barrington."

"Oh, I get it," Eppick said. "And is that back there the only entrance?"

"Oh, no, sir. The staff entrance is around to the other side of the hill."

"Staff entrance," Eppick echoed. "Staff

entrance into this . . . forest."

"Yes, sir."

"Thank you, Pembroke."

"Sir."

Eppick faced the others. "Pretty good," he said.

Dortmunder had decided not to lie down any more, no matter what happened. Seated on the floor, semi-braced against the right door, with his left hand stiff-armed to the floor, he felt the limo sway to and fro as they continued their slow and steady serpentine progress through the forest, the road now tending more or less steadily uphill.

All these pine trees, and all so gigantic. It was like driving through a magic forest in a fairy tale. Dortmunder had just thought of that fanciful idea when the limo rounded yet another spreading tree, and in front of them appeared what at first looked to be several truckloads of dark brown shingles dumped in a pile in a clearing in the forest, but which, on further study, proved to be a sprawling three-story wood-shingle house with dark green window frames and a dark green shingle roof, as though it were more plant than structure and had grown in this place. A broad veranda girdled the house, both inviting and secretive.

To the right of this building was a pocket

version of itself, being a garage with three green wooden doors, and this was where the dirt road became blacktop, opened to embrace all three doors, and stopped. To right and left, in among the trees, two more structures could be seen, also pretending to be abandoned piles of shingles, both of them smaller than the main house but larger than the garage.

As Pembroke angled the limo toward the garage door nearest the main house, Eppick said, "Those other buildings guesthouses?"

"On the left, sir. On the right is staff quarters."

"Who lives here now?"

"Oh, no one, sir." Pembroke stopped the limo and switched off the engine. "There has been no one on the property, sir," he said, "since the last time Mr. and Mrs. Hemlow attended a concert at Tanglewood more than three years ago. That would have been in August, sir."

17

Brady tried to find his place in the Kama Sutra even while Nessa kept on galloping beneath him at cheetah speed, putting him in a position similar to the person who has to rub his belly and pat his forehead at the same time. Got it; *that* page! Brady bent to his lesson, and Nessa abruptly stopped.

Brady reared back. "Already? No!"

An urgent hand reached around behind her to grasp his hip. "A car!" she cried, her words only half muffled by the pillow.

Now he too heard it, the throaty purr of some expensive automobile rolling up toward the house. Flinging the Kama Sutra away, he leaped off the bed and ran across the large master bedroom toward the front windows, as behind him Nessa scrambled into her clothes.

A long sleek black limousine rolled to a stop at the garage door behind which Brady's battered Honda Civic sat, as Brady peeked around the curtain. The car doors opened down there and four men climbed out, one at first on hands and knees until two of the others helped him up. The one from the front seat in the chauffeur's hat would be a chauffeur, and he's the one who led the others toward the house, taking a key ring from his pocket.

The door wasn't locked! Racing back across the room, grabbing his jeans from the floor but nothing else, Brady shrilly whispered, "Hide everything!" and tore out to the hall as behind him Nessa, already hiding the Kama Sutra under a pillow, wailed, "Oh, Brady!"

No time. Out Brady went, and down the broad staircase to the living room three steps at a time, naked as he usually was when around Nessa, his jeans flapping in the air behind him. Across the living room he dashed, jeans hand behind him, free hand reaching out ahead, and got to the door and snapped the lock just as he heard the first footsteps echo across the veranda.

Pausing one millisecond, his back against the door, to pull on his jeans and study the living room, at first he saw nothing out of place, but then, there it was, a beer bottle he'd left behind on the coffee table after dinner last night.

Running again, he arced past the coffee table and grabbed the bottle on the fly, as he heard the key in the front door lock and heard the doorknob turn. The door started to open, and *through* the doorway he went, and hurtled down the broad corridor to the kitchen, the only other room on the ground floor that would contain evidence of their intrusion.

A voice behind him, back in the living roam: "Well, this is some rustic."

Who *were* those people? They come here, they have a chauffeur, they have keys, but they've never seen that incredible living room before?

It was, that living room, as Brady would agree, some rustic, and so was the rest of the house. The living room, thirty feet wide and twenty feet deep, with a huge stone fireplace on one end wall, was two stories high, with a cathedral ceiling, the whole thing done in rough wood, the beams with the bark still on, the walls rough-surfaced boards, the plank floor dotted with old Navajo rugs, the furniture large, deep, comfortable, what God would buy for His own weekend place. Suspended above it all was a huge chandelier that pretended to be a whole lot of kerosene lamps with glass chimneys but was actually electrified and on a dimmer.

Brady had run to the kitchen to try to clean it up before they came back here, but now his curiosity was aroused. He stood an instant, not knowing whether to sneak back and listen or proceed with his kitchen police, when the kitchen's side door opened and Nessa appeared, dressed, having come down the back stairs.

Good. "Clean it!" he whispered, waving at the not-clean kitchen — they tended to go to bed immediately after meals, though they knew they shouldn't — and tiptoed back down the corridor, now hearing a second voice say, with a kind of weary seen-everything sound, "I guess this is what you call your compound."

A third voice, brisk, in charge, said, "Upstairs should be the best place to stash something."

What? Brady kept even closer, just out of their sight. Meanwhile, the second voice said, "No, it isn't."

There was a little pause then, that might have been uncomfortable, and the third voice said, "Pembroke, why don't you wait in the car?"

"Sir."

Nobody spoke then until the front door opened and closed, and then the take-charge third voice said, "Upstairs. Farther from the doors and windows. More hiding places."

"Too heavy," said the weary second voice, "for one guy to lift."

"Oh."

"Don't worry, Johnny," the first voice chimed in, much the most chipper of them, "we'll find a good spot somewhere down here."

"Then I suggest," the third voice said, as though trying to recapture command here, "we might just as well sit over there by the fireplace a few minutes and think about it."

"Fine idea."

"Sure."

Oh, good, Brady thought, and, scampered back to the kitchen, where Nessa was hurriedly shoving used plates, pots, silver, cups, glasses and cereal bowls into cupboards, drawers and the broom closet. "Stop!" he whispered. "Not there."

In just as harsh a whisper, Nessa said, "Brady, we've got to *hide* all this."

"Upstairs."

"What?"

"They're not going upstairs. They're looking for a place down here to hide something, so they'll open *everything,* and they're sure to see all that stuff. Carry it all up, just out of sight up the stairs, and I'll keep an eye on them, warn you when they're coming."

"How come *I* get the dirty job?" she demanded, but he'd already fleet-footed away again, this time peeking around the doorway to see the trio at their ease on the armchairs at the far end of the living room, looking very much like a genre painting of the day the mob broke into the Winter Palace.

Brady, a mob of one, sat on the floor by the doorway and listened while they had a little conversation out there, saying absolutely nothing else of interest, like what it was they wanted to hide and why they wanted to hide it. But that was okay. Brady had all the time in the world.

Brady Hogan and Vanessa Arkdorp were both seventeen, both born and raised in the town of Nukumbuts, NE (known to the local high school wags as Numbnuts), each aware of the other living a mere three blocks away but not making much of it until this past June when, at the town swimming beach on the Gillespie River (from a forgotten and generally unpronouncable Plains Indian name), they truly noticed one another for the very first time and immediately knew what their future was going to be: each other.

It was all very easy during summer vacation. Brady had a part-time job at the Wal-Mart, which took up little of his attention, but which he had to have because the family had fallen on hard times since Brady's father had been laid off from the grain processor four years ago. Nobody else blamed Brady's father for what was, after all, merely the fickle finger of economic fate, the roulette wheel of capitalism rolling on past your number, but Brady's *father* so thoroughly and obviously blamed himself that after some time everybody else began to agree with him, which meant he was never considered for any of the few jobs that did open up, and life was less than tranquil at the Hogan house these years.

Also, neither Brady nor Nessa was the scholarly type; once you knew your numbers and your alphabet, school was, face it, a drag. They were only going back for their senior year at Central Middle Combined High (twenty-seven minutes by bus, twice a day) because all of the parents they knew had an unreasoning horror of the word "dropout," as though it meant something similar to "vampire."

The principal physical result of Brady's Wal-Mart job was this very used Honda Civic, which he operated over the summer both to go to and from work and to boff Nessa on just about every bit of empty ground in the northeast part of the state. So, when the idea first occurred to them — both simultaneously, it seemed — that they might go somewhere else in the world in September other than back to dear old Central Middle Combined, the first asset they had was Brady's little red car, and the second asset was all the cash they could find in their parents' homes, which wasn't much. And other assets?

Well, principally, Brady's deftness. He'd never been in trouble, not in real trouble, though there'd been a few close calls. But back when he was ten years old he first realized he could get through just about any lock there was in Numbnuts, and did, for years, partly for fun and partly for profit (CDs, candy, beer, condoms). With his dexterity, and the Honda, and Nessa at his side, was he a world-beater or what? Guess.

Right now, nobody in their families had any idea where they were. In fact, nobody in the whole world had any idea where they were. Starting in early September, they'd just roamed at first, south and east, and then north and east, and eventually just liked the look of the Massachusetts pine forests. Still, they might have moved on had they not stumbled upon this electric fence in the woods.

Naturally, as you would, as I would, they asked each other why anybody would put up an electric fence in the woods. They followed the fence to a gate — which was, in fact, the staff entrance — and from there found the big house with the little houses around it. The outbuildings were all shut down, but the big house had water and electricity and even useful food in a freezer, as though the owner hadn't realized he wouldn't be coming back, and maybe still didn't know it. They had made good use of the freezer food, and supplemented it by little late-night visits to towns fifteen and twenty miles away. They'd been here three weeks now, in a place that, from the dust all over everything when they arrived, had not been occupied for years and showed no signs of potential future occupancy as well. It was all theirs. Heaven, they called it, and they were probably right.

But now their heaven had been invaded by some very dubious people lounging around in the big living room by the big fireplace, talking about where to hide whatever it was. Which, he noticed, whatever it was, they didn't have it here with them. From what they said to one another, this trip was to find the hiding place, then another trip would be to bring the thing itself. Kind of roundabout, Brady thought, but that was their business.

Which they weren't in much hurry to get done and over with, so Brady and Nessa could go back to bed. They just talked along, and then the one that thought he was in charge, that the others called Johnny, finally said, "What I've been thinking, you want to hide something, why not the kitchen? Lots of places there."

The weary one said, "We don't know how big this is yet, so how do we know what size place we gotta put it?"

"Just big enough," Johnny said. "I mean, how big could it be?"

"The purloined letter," the chipper one said.

Both of the others seemed stymied by that. Johnny finally said, "Was that supposed to be something?"

"Short story by Edgar Allan Poe," the chipper one said. "Whatsamatta, Johnny, you never went to high school?"

"Yeah, that's all right," Johnny said. "What's this letter? We're not talking about a letter."

So what, Brady asked, *are* you talking about?

"We're talking about something where you hide it," the chipper one told him, "that nobody's gonna find it. In the story, it's a letter. And where the guy hid it, turns out, was right there on the dresser, where nobody's gonna see it because what they're looking for is something *hidden*."

"Crap," Johnny announced.

The weary one said, "You know, Johnny, maybe not. You got something, you can't find it, turns out, it's right in front of you. Happens all the time."

"Nobody's gonna look at that set," Johnny insisted, "and not notice it."

Set? What the hell *is* it? Brady was about to go out and ask, unable to stand it any more.

But then the chipper one said, "How about this? We get it. On the way up here, we get cans of spray paint, black enamel and red enamel. We paint 'em all over, this team red, this team black, nobody sees any gold, nobody sees any jewels, it just looks like any chess set. We can leave it right out, like on that big table over there with all that other stuff."

Gold. Jewels. Any chess set.

Tiptoeing as fast as the first night he ever sneaked into Nessa's house back in Numbnuts, Brady made his way to the second floor, where Nessa, tired and sweaty, was just finished bringing all their dirty used stuff up from the kitchen. "Baby!" he whispered, exulting. "We're in!"

"They still here?"

"Just for a little while. Then we can go back to bed and I'll tell you everything."

"*Oh,* no."

This being the first time Nessa had ever said no to the idea of going back to bed, Brady stumbled to a halt on his way to the front window to watch and wait for the interlopers' departure, turned back, and said, "What?"

She gestured. Dirty kitchen detritus was all over the upstairs hall floor. "The *first* thing we're gonna do," she said, "is clean up this stuff. We can't go on living like this, Brady, we gotta have it neater around us."

There were warning signs in that sentence, but Brady was too distracted by two different kinds of lust to notice them. "You're right, baby," he said, and proceeded to the window, and grinned back at her. "Comere and I'll tell you all about it. We're gonna clean that stuff up because we're gonna stay here for a while. And we're gonna stay here because our ship is comin *in.*"

"What ship?" She came over to the window with deeply furrowed brow.

"Look, there they go," he said, and they watched out the window as the three men headed out for their limo, all talking at the same time.

Nessa said, "Will they be back?"

"Oh, yeah," Brady said, with a big wide grin. "They'll be back. Honey, we're *waitin* for them to come back."

18

So far as she knew, Fiona had only seen
Livia Northwood Wheeler once in her life,
more than a year ago, shortly after she'd
been taken on here at Feinberg. She'd had
no idea at the time, of course, that Mrs.
Wheeler's father had stolen an incredibly
valuable property from her own great-
grandfather and his friends, but she'd
noticed the woman anyway, because Mrs.
Wheeler was God knows noticeable, and
she'd said at the time to her cubicle buddy
Imogen, "Who's *that?*"

"Livia Northwood Wheeler," Imogen told
her. "She's richer than God. In fact, she
pretty well thinks of God as a parvenu."

Fiona watched the woman out of sight,
Livia headed toward the area of the associates' offices, following one of the secretaries
who, like most of the secretaries here, was
dressed much more elegantly than the
young female lawyers. This Mrs. Livia

Northwood Wheeler left in her wake an image of someone who might not actually be richer than God, but who certainly looked older than any deity you might care to mention. A very tall, unbelievably thin, ramrod-straight, hawk-nosed, gaunt-cheeked, laser-eyed creature with a helmet of snow-white hair that gleamed like radiation, she was garbed totally in black and walked with a stiff but determined gait, as though here to foreclose on your property and glad of the opportunity to do so.

That time, Fiona had watched her go with a slight shudder and the thought, "I'm glad she isn't here to see *me*," an opinion which seemed to be confirmed half an hour later when Mrs. Wheeler, led by the same secretary, marched through once more in the opposite direction, looking as though her session with her lawyer had neither mollified her nor increased her rage; so it must be a steady thing, like a sanctuary candle.

Now it was Friday morning, the day after her meeting with Mr. Dortmunder and the retelling of the story of the stolen chess set, and Fiona was graced with her second viewing of Mrs. Wheeler, this one identical to the first. Into view the lady marched, following a different secretary this time (secretarial turnover was much faster than lawyer turnover), and looking as though that sanctuary candle of discontent burned just as brightly in her breast as ever.

Fiona watched her go, this time armed with her knowledge of their secret and surprising link, and after the woman was out of sight it became impossible to focus her mind back on her work. There *was* this link, and Fiona found it fascinating. It was as though a character from a history book, a George Washington or a Henry Ford, were to suddenly walk by; wouldn't she want to share a word with the person, just to touch, however tangentially, that history? She would.

Fiona did very little to earn Feinberg's salary the next fifty minutes, but kept an eye on that route among the cubicles, knowing Mrs. Wheeler must eventually pass by once more, on her way out of the building. When at last, an eternity later, it did happen, Mrs. Wheeler again preceded by today's secretary, Fiona immediately leaped to her feet and went after them.

There was always a wait of a minute or two in the reception area before the elevator arrived; that would be her opportunity. She knew that what she was doing was wrong, to speak directly to a client with whom she had no legitimate intercourse, she knew she could even theoretically be fired for what she was about to do, but she simply couldn't help herself. She had to meet Mrs. Wheeler's eye, she had to hear Mrs. Wheeler's voice, she had to have Mrs. Wheeler herself acknowledge Fiona Hemlow's existence.

There they were, standing in front of the elevator doors. The secretary, Fiona noticed, wasn't even trying to make conversation with this gargoyle, nor did the gargoyle seem to expect much in the way of what, in other circumstances, might be called human contact. Well, she was about to get some.

Striding forward, covering her nervousness and insecurity with a bright smile and a brisk manner, Fiona gazed steadily at Mrs. Wheeler as she crossed the reception area, and just at the instant when the woman became aware of her approach, Fiona exclaimed, with happy surprise, "Mrs. Wheeler?"

The distrust came off the lady like flies off a garbage truck. "Ye-*ess?*" The voice was a baritone cigarette croak, but with power in it; a carnivore's croak.

"Mrs. Wheeler," Fiona hurried on, "I'm Fiona Hemlow, just a very minor lawyer here, but I did have the opportunity to work on just one tiny corner of your case, and I so hoped some day I would get the chance to tell you how much I admire you."

Even the secretary looked startled at that one, and Mrs. Wheeler, flies rising in clouds, said, "You do?"

"The stand you have taken is so firm," Fiona assured her. "So many people would just give up, would just let themselves be trampled on, but not you."

"Not me," agreed Mrs. Wheeler, grim satisfaction almost melodious in that croak of a voice. Fewer flies were in evidence.

"If I may," Fiona said, "I would just like to shake your hand."

"My hand."

"I don't want anything else," Fiona assured her, and tried for a girlish-chum sort of chuckle. "I could even get in trouble just by talking to you. But of all the people I've learned about since I came to work here, you're the one I absolutely the most admire. That's why — if it isn't too much — if it isn't an imposition — may I?" And she extended her small right hand, keeping that perky hopeful smile on her face and worshipful gleam in her eye.

Mrs. Wheeler did not take the hand. She didn't even look at it. She said, "If, Miss —"

"Fiona Hemlow."

"If, Miss Hemlow, Tumbril sent you after

me to butter me up, please assure him it did no good."

"Oh, no, Mrs. —"

But the elevator had arrived. Without another glance at Fiona or the secretary, Mrs. Wheeler marched into the elevator as though it were the captain's bridge and she were usurping command. Silently, the door slid shut.

The secretary said, "I don't think you ought to tell Jay that."

"I don't think anybody needs to tell — Jay — anything about any of this," Fiona said, and went her way, finding herself for the first time brooding on the whole issue of family feuds that go on generation after generation, and doubting very much that her own family, in such a situation against the Northwood family, would ever be on the winning side.

19

By surreptitiously running the last few feet to the limo — not an easy thing to do — Dortmunder managed to get absolute uncontested first shot at the seating. Settling with a sense of beleaguered triumph into that soft and comfortable backward-facing seat, he looked around to see Kelp sliding in next to him and was just as glad he wouldn't have to make conversation with Johnny Eppick the next two hundred miles.

Eppick himself, arriving at the limo one pace too late, smiled benignly in at the two on the bench seat, said, "Enjoy the trip," paused to shut the rear door, then got into the front seat next to Pembroke and said, "We'll go back to New York now."

"I thought we would," Pembroke said, and started the engine.

As the car rolled down the long drive, Kelp, facing that empty rear compartment of the limo, said in a conversational voice,

"We'll have to stop somewhere to eat, won't we, Johnny?"

No answer. The glass partition behind Pembroke was half open, but apparently that wasn't enough. Kelp winked at Dortmunder and raised his voice slightly: "Isn't that so, Johnny?"

Still nothing, so Kelp twisted around and spoke directly into the open section of the partition: "Isn't that right, Johnny?"

Eppick's head slued around. "Isn't what right?"

"We'll have to stop for lunch somewhere."

"Sure. Pembroke probably knows a place."

"Let me think," Pembroke said.

Kelp faced front — that is, rear — and said, "So they can't hear us unless we want them to."

Up front, Pembroke and Eppick were in conversation, presumably about lunch, but the words couldn't be made out from back here. Dortmunder said, "You're right, they can't. Is there something we want to say?"

"About that idea of mine with the chess set."

"The purloined chess set thing," Dortmunder said, and nodded. "That was pretty cute, I gotta say."

"It's more than cute for us," Kelp said.

"It is? How?"

"Once they're all painted red and black enamel," Kelp said, "who's to say that's the real piece or maybe some imitation we slid in, help keep all that gold from going to waste?"

Dortmunder frowned at Kelp's profile, but then, for security reasons of not being overheard, he faced the rear of the limo again as he said, "You're acting as though we're gonna *get* that thing."

"Never say die," Kelp advised.

"Die," Dortmunder said. "We're not gonna get into that vault."

"We'll burn that bridge when we come to it," Kelp told him. "In the meantime, you gotta talk to that granddaughter again."

"I already asked her for building plans," Dortmunder said. "She doesn't think she can get them."

"They'd be nice, too," Kelp said, "but what I'm thinking about is pictures of the chess set."

"Pictures?"

"It's been on display. It's part of a court case. There are gonna be pictures. If we wanna bring in a couple ringers on the day, we got to know what they look like."

"They look like chess pieces in a vault under a bank," Dortmunder guessed.

"Well, you'll talk to the granddaughter,"

Kelp said. "Can't do any harm."

The food in New England was part hard black and part soft white. Fortunately, they carried national brands of beer in the dark-brown-laminated, green-glass-globed, black-flounce-skirted-waitress imitation Klondike/Yukon something or other where they broke their journey, so starvation was held at bay.

"I like that seat, I think I'll keep it the rest of the trip," Dortmunder announced grimly when they left the scene of their designer lunch, and nobody even argued, so he got to sit up in the balcony with Kelp the whole rest of the way.

As they neared Riverside Drive, Eppick twisted around to the space in the partition and said, "You two don't have to see Mr. Hemlow. I'll report."

Grinning, Kelp said, "Gonna tell him the enamel chess set was your idea?"

Eppick grinned right back. "What do you think?"

"I think," Kelp said, "Pembroke can drop us off downtown."

Eppick frowned a little, not sure that was part of the deal, but Pembroke, professional eyes remaining on the road, said, "Of course, sir," so that was all right.

Soon they were easing to a stop at the

curb in front of Mr. Hemlow's building, and if the uniformed doorman who came trotting out and down the steps to open first the rear — "Not us, him," Kelp said — and then the front door had any attitude toward what was coming out of this particular limousine, it didn't show on his face.

Eppick, before departure, looked meaningfully back at Dortmunder and said, "You'll keep in touch. Progress, and all that."

"Oh, sure."

Pembroke's mild gaze was on them in the rearview mirror: "Sirs?"

"I'm the first stop," Kelp told him. "The West Thirties."

"Sir."

They set off, and Kelp said, "Not so bad, go home by limo."

"They'll probably raise my rent," Dortmunder said.

Kelp nodded at the floor. "Is that as comfortable down there as it looks?"

"Try it," Dortmunder suggested.

20

When her cubicle phone rang at seven-thirty, Fiona assumed it was a wrong number, or some other kind of mistake. Who would call her at the office, particularly after working hours? Certainly not Brian, who would always wait for *her* to phone *him* so he could put on tonight's gourmet dinner. Nor would it be any of her friends or relatives, who would never phone her at work, not even during the business day.

Ring, it went again, while she tried to think it through. A wrong number would be a distraction, but if she ignored it and let it go on into voice mail, then it would merely be a distraction postponed. In fact, having rung once — twice now — it was already a distraction, taking her away from the implications of mortmain as applied to this particular real estate bequest in this thinned-out old upstate Patroon family.

Ring. That was three; after four, it would

go to voice mail.

And what if Brian had been hit by a taxi or something and it was the hospital calling, needing to know his blood type or whatever? Not that she knew his blood type, and not that the hospital wouldn't be able to work it out for themselves, but nevertheless, just before the fourth ring that would have sent the call irrevocably down that black vertical chute into the echoless dungeon of voice mail, Fiona snapped up the receiver with her left hand, hit the button with her right, and was reaching for a pen as she said, "Fiona Hemlow."

"Hey, you're still there." The voice was vaguely familiar, a little rough, not the sort of person she would know.

Pen down, finger hovering over the button that would end this call, she said, "Who's that?"

"John. You know, yesterday we talked. Hold on." Away from the phone he said, "Gimme a minute here, do you mind? I got my party." Speaking to Fiona again, he said, "You know, in your office yesterday."

"Oh, John, yes, of course," she said, that dogged pessimistic face clear in her mind now, matching up perfectly with that weary voice. "You wanted to talk to me?"

"Well, not on the phone, you know, not

exactly. I been waiting outside here —"

"What? Outside this building?"

"Yeah. That's where you are, right? I thought, you come out, we could have a talk while we walk. Hold on." Off, he said, "*I'm being polite. You be polite.*" Back, he said, "I was beginning to think, maybe you went home early —"

"Never."

"So you go home late."

"Always."

"How late? I mean, instead of hang around, I could come back — Hold on." Off, he said, "You got a watch?" There was some sort of muffled complaint and then he said, "I don't *want* your watch, I wanna know what time it is."

"It's seven-thirty," Fiona said.

"See?" he said, off. "She knows what time it is, it's seven-thirty."

Fiona said, "How long have you been waiting?"

"Since five. You'd be surprised, you know, how many people come out of these buildings at five. So finally, I figured, I better check this here, so I borrowed this cell phone —" Off. "I *borrowed* it, you're getting it back."

"I'll come down now," Fiona said.

■ ■ ■ ■

The inadvertent supplier of the cell phone was long gone when Fiona reached the street, where John Dortmunder leaned against the front of the building like a small gray rebuttal to all the work ethic within. Approaching, she said, "Mr. Dortmunder, I —"

"John, okay?" he said. "Mr. Dortmunder makes me nervous. The only time I'm Mr. Dortmunder is when I'm being arraigned."

"All right, then," she said. "You're John, and I'm Fiona."

"It's a deal," he said. "Which way you walk?"

"Over to Broadway and up to the subway."

"Okay, we'll do it."

They got to the corner and had to wait for the light, during which he said, "Mainly what I want is pictures."

She couldn't think of what. "Pictures?"

"Of the thing. The thing in the vault."

"Oh," she said. "The chess set."

For some reason, he didn't like to hear those words spoken out in public. "Yeah, yeah, that's it," he said, and patted the air downward in front of himself as though wanting to tell her to pipe down without being rude about it. All at once, she was aware that other people, all around them, were standing here waiting for the light to change, and she piped down.

WALK. They walked.

"Well, of course we have pictures of *it*," she said, more quietly, as they crossed Fifth Avenue. "The entire — Well, the entire you-know was photographed and measured when the law firms accepted custody."

"Measured; that's good, too."

"I could e-mail it all to you," she said.

"No, you couldn't."

They had reached the other curb, where Fiona stopped, waited for the nearby walkers to move on, and said, "I could print it out for you."

"Oh, yeah?"

"That's better anyway. Absolutely no record."

"No record, that's good."

"We'll go back to the office," she decided, and they turned around.

DON'T WALK.

She said, "So you're really going to go ahead and do this, even though you hate everything about the vault?"

"Your grandfather and the other guy like to see forward motion," he told her. "I'm doing what I can to keep everybody happy."

WALK.

Shouldn't he be angry about this situation? Fiona felt he should certainly be angry at *her,* if not her grandfather, for making this whole thing happen. And yet, he just seemed fatalistic and tired, trying not to go into that vault but sliding there inexorably, after just that one push from her. "I'm sorry, John," she said.

"It isn't you," he said. "What I'm coming to a realization about," he said, as she withdrew from her wallet the card that would let her back into the C&I International building, "is, this is all the mistakes of my past life, coming back to haunt me. In order to pay for all those little misdemeanors and all those little lapses from all the time before I reformed, I gotta do an illegal entry into a bank vault that's impossible to get into and even if you could get into it, which you can't, doubly impossible to get out of, carrying a weight. Half a weight."

During this speech, Fiona had carded them into the building and now led the way toward the elevators, but "Hold on," he said.

Surprised, she turned to see him standing still in the gleaming high-ceilinged gray marble lobby. "Did you want something? The snack shop's closed."

"I wanted to look at it," he said.

"Oh."

So they both looked at the lobby, Fiona trying to see it now through John Dortmunder's eyes, seeing it for the first time, not her own eyes which hadn't really seen the lobby as anything but another blank part of her daily commute for over a year.

The place was very different through his eyes. On their left was the chest-high security station with the wall-mounted TV monitors behind it and the two gray-uniformed security men on duty, whom she'd barely noticed all this time because they knew and recognized her so that she never since the first week or so had had to show her Feinberg ID. But there they were nevertheless, looking in Fiona and John's direction with casual interest because they weren't at this moment in transit across the lobby but simply standing in one place, not a normal lobby occurrence.

What else? The three shops on their right with pane glass windows facing the lobby, selling (1) snacks and reading matter, (2) luggage, and (3) stationery and computer software, were all closed now, though well-lit within.

Across the rear wall of the lobby were the brushed-steel doors of the elevators. To their left was the marked door to the staircase, for emergencies, and to the right of the elevator doors was another brushed-steel door that Fiona had never noticed before. Twice a day she'd passed it, and never noticed.

With a silent glance at her, John walked toward the rear of the lobby. Fiona followed, knowing where he was headed. "I'll get the elevator."

"Good."

They both angled closer to that door on the right, him more so than her, but neither went directly to it, because after all two security men behind them had nothing better to do than watch people moving. However, she was close enough to see — so he must see it, too — that discreet gold letters on the door said NO ADMITTANCE and that it had a card slot like all the other entry card slots in her life, but no doorknob.

"Uh huh," he said, and she carded for the elevator.

Putting the card away in her wallet, she said, "You say you reformed?"

"Right."

"When was that?"

"When I met your grandfather."

"That's what I thought," she said, and the elevator door slid open.

Fiona's access to the Feinberg computer system was not total — there were distant tunnels of data, mostly involving money or foreign linkages, that required passwords beyond her station in life — but much of Feinberg's knowledge was available to her. Being a wee beastie in these offices meant being a utility infielder, on tap to assist any of the more important associates who might need a little delving and precedent hunting done, so her access had to be broad and deep, so quite naturally included the files on the chess set known in the court papers as Chicago Chess Set, its official provenance not going farther back than Alfred X. Northwood's long-ago train journey from that city to New York, chess set in tow.

"Chicago Chess Set," she read from the screen. "Yes, here it is. How much of it do you want?"

"All of it," he said, looking at the cover sheet on the screen, which showed the chess set brightly lit on a black velvet background, set up and waiting, gleaming, looking exactly like something created by royal gold-lust.

"All of it?" She reared back to look at him.

"You can't want *all* of it. The court hearings? There are hundreds of pages on this item of the suits, all by themselves, maybe thousands. You couldn't *read* all that."

"No, I don't wanna read all that," he said. "I want all the pictures and all the measurements."

"All right, let's see —" She checked the table of contents. "There's individual photos of the pieces —"

"Sounds good."

"Pages of dimensions of each piece."

"Not bad."

"Shots from different angles in different lighting."

"Lay it on me."

"In all," she said, "sixty-four pages."

"I'll borrow an envelope," he said.

Later that evening, over burritos with shrimp and rice — very nice — at their table in their candlelit big room, she told Brian about her latest encounter with John Dortmunder, and he laughed and said, "Is he really gonna try to go down in there and *get* that thing?"

"Well, he doesn't want to," she said, "but it looks like my grandfather and that other man are pressing him very hard. I just keep hoping they'll all realize it's just impossible and give it up."

"Hard to give up all that gold," Brian said. "*I'd* know how to get down in that vault."

"You would? How?"

"Say I'm shooting a documentary," he said. "Movie people can get in anywhere. 'Hi, we're doing a Discovery Channel special on bank vaults. How did you spell your name again?' You're right in."

Laughing around her burrito, she said, "Oh, Brian, I don't think Mr. Dortmunder could convince anybody he was making a movie for the Discovery Channel."

"No, probably not," Brian said. His eyes glittered just slightly in the candlelight. "Too bad."

21

Saturday morning, after May left for the Safeway, Dortmunder sat at the kitchen table and spread out the photos and spec sheets he'd been given by Fiona Hemlow last night. The chess set turned out to be a little smaller than he'd imagined, but also heavier: 680 pounds. Yeah, that would take more than one guy.

According to what it said on the description sheets, the chess pieces weren't actually gold all the way through, which would make them even heavier, but gold poured into forms around wood dowels, with three to five jewels set into each piece to make the two teams: pearls for the white gang, rubies for the red. The kings and queens were just under four inches tall, the others shorter. The gold had been shaped with extreme delicacy and care, as you would do if you were working for an absolute monarch.

Dortmunder had been looking at the pictures and reading the specs about half an hour when the phone rang, over there on the wall next to the refrigerator. It was going to be Andy Kelp, of course, and when Dortmunder got to his feet and walked to the phone and said into it, "Harya," it was.

"What's happening?"

"Well, I got the pictures," he said, reluctantly, looking over at the papers spread out on the table. He knew it was dumb to want to save that little trove of information for himself, but there it was.

"The pictures? Already?"

"And the specs, sizes, all that."

"I'll be right there," Kelp said, and was, walking into the kitchen, saying, "I didn't want to disturb you with the bell."

"I appreciate that," Dortmunder said. "How are my door locks holding up?"

"Oh, they're fine," Kelp assured him. "Let's see what we got here."

"One little puzzle," Dortmunder said.

Kelp had picked up a photo of the complete chess set, but now he looked at Dortmunder. "You mean, aside from how do we get our hands on it?"

"One of the rooks," Dortmunder told him, "is light."

"Light? How do you mean, light?"

Using the photo Kelp was holding, Dortmunder pointed to white king's rook and said, "That one's about three pounds lighter than this one," pointing to white queen's rook, "but that one's the same as the two on the other side."

While Dortmunder riffled through more photos, Kelp stared at the picture of the entire set. "You mean all of these others weigh the same?"

"Almost. There's little tiny differences because there's different jewels in each one. Here, here's the separate pictures of those two. The one on the right there is the light one."

"King's rook," Kelp read the caption at the bottom of the picture and looked at the squat golden castle decorated with four sparkly pearls. "I thought rook meant to cheat somebody."

"Outa three pounds, I know. But one of these pages here uses the word 'rook' and then that thing, that para thing . . ." He finger-drew in the air the icon of a lying-down smile face.

"I know what you mean," Kelp said.

"Good. (or castle) it says. So that's a word for it."

Kelp bent over the individual pictures of the two white rooks, then leaned back and shook his head. "Maybe," he said, "we'll be able to tell more when we've got 'em in our hands. Heft them."

Dortmunder frowned at him. "Got 'em in our *hands?* Don't you remember, they're still in that vault. This is just so Eppick and Hemlow think something's happening, but Andy, nothing is happening."

"I don't know why you're so negative," Kelp told him. "Look at these pictures. Every day, we get closer."

"Yeah, and I know to what," Dortmunder said, and the phone rang. "That's probably Eppick now," he said, getting to his feet. "Wanting to know is it time to send the arresting officers."

"Give the man credit for a *little* patience," Kelp suggested.

Dortmunder barked into the phone and Stan Murch's voice said, "The kid and I just finished breakfast, in a place over by his place."

"That's nice," Dortmunder said, and told Kelp, "Stan and Judson just had breakfast together."

"Why's he telling *you* that?"

"We didn't get there yet," Dortmunder said, and into the phone he said, "Why are you telling *me* that? This isn't something else about that dome, is it?"

173

"No, no," Stan said. "I gave that up."

"Good."

"Kind of like a lost love."

"Oh, yeah?"

"I'm traveling strictly Flatbush Avenue these days."

"Well, it's still Brooklyn."

"But no dome. Listen, the kid and me," Stan said, "were wondering, since the dome thing's no good, did you maybe have something going on with that cop."

"Mostly," Dortmunder said, "he's got something going on with me."

"If we could help —"

"I'm beyond help."

Kelp said, "Tell them come over. The more brains the merrier."

"Andy says you should come over to my place, bring your brains."

"We'll be right there," Stan said, and they were, but they used the traditional entry method of ringing the street doorbell, and it so happened they did so just as the phone rang again.

"You get the phone," Kelp suggested, standing, "and I'll get the door."

"Good." Dortmunder crossed to the phone and said, "Harya," into it as Kelp pressed the release button on the wall and walked away down the hall to wait for the arrivals to climb the two flights.

A voice that could only belong to Tiny Bulcher said, "Dortmunder, I worry about you."

"Good," Dortmunder said. "I wouldn't want to worry about me all alone."

"You having trouble with that cop?"

"Yes. Listen, Andy's here and now Stan and Judson are just showing up."

"You're having a meeting without me?"

"It didn't start out to be a meeting. People just keep showing up, like a wake. You wanna come over?"

"I'll be right there," Tiny said, and was.

There were four chairs around the kitchen table, and Judson could sit on the radiator, so once Tiny had been added to the mix they were all more or less comfortable. Since Dortmunder had just finished describing the current situation to Stan and Judson, Kelp did the honors with Tiny, including a description of Eppick's apparently broad and entirely unnecessary background data bank on everybody in the room.

"There are people," Tiny commented, "who, when they retire, they oughta retire."

"Tiny," Dortmunder said, "the way it looks, I'm the only one he's really putting the pressure on. When I don't get that chess set, I'm the one he's gonna blame, nobody else."

"San Francisco isn't a bad place to hang out sometimes," Tiny observed.

"I was thinking Chicago," Dortmunder told him, "and Andy suggested Miami, but Eppick knows all about that. He tells me, with all the millions of cops all connected now, he'll find me wherever I go."

Tiny nodded, thinking it over. "It's true," he said. "It's harder to disappear than it used to be in the old days. In the old days, you just burn your fingerprints off with acid and there you are."

"Ow," Judson said. "Wouldn't that hurt?"

"Not for twenty-five years," Tiny told him. "Anyway, you can't burn DNA off. Not and live through it."

Kelp said, "You know, we got another little conundrum here. I know it isn't as important as the main problem —"

"The vault," Dortmunder said.

"That's the problem I was thinking of," Kelp agreed. "Anyway," he told the others, "you see these pictures of these two rooks."

"Those are castles," Stan said.

"Yes, but," Kelp said, "rook is a name for them in chess. Anyway, everything weighs the way it's supposed to, except this one rook here is three pounds lighter than the other rooks."

They all leaned over the pictures, including Judson, who got up from the radiator and came over to stand beside the table, gazing down. Stan said, "They look alike."

"But you see the weight," Kelp said. "They wrote it down right there."

Stan nodded. "Maybe it's a typo."

"This stuff is all pretty careful," Kelp said.

Dortmunder said, "I don't find this as gripping as the main problem."

"No, of course not," Kelp said. "It's just a mystery, that's all."

"No, it isn't," Judson said. "That part's easy."

They all watched him go back to sit on the radiator again. Kelp said, "You know why this one's different."

"Sure." Judson shrugged. "You just got to put yourself in that sergeant's place, Northwood. There he is in Chicago with this thing, very valuable but it weighs almost seven hundred pounds. He's as broke as the other guys, but he's gotta get out of there fast before the platoon gets back. So he has a guy, maybe a jeweler, somebody, make up a fake, looks just like the real thing. That way, he can sell the pearls, sell the gold, get on that train, show up in New York in style and start his wheeling and dealing."

Everybody thought that was brilliant. Tiny said, "Kid, you're an asset."

"Thank you, Tiny."

Judson beamed all over. Since he also looked as though any second he might start to blush, everybody else went back to looking at the pictures and talking to one another, Kelp saying, "So when we do our own little switcheroo, we want to make sure we don't do this guy."

Dortmunder said, "What do you mean, our own switcheroo? We got a *vault* between us and them, remember?"

Stan said, "I gotta say, from my perspective, it does seem worth the effort."

"Effort isn't the question," Dortmunder said. "The vault is the question."

"So let's ask the kid," Tiny said. "Kid, you solved the mystery of the rook; very good. Here's question number two: How do we get into the vault?"

Judson looked surprised. "We can't," he said.

22

Dortmunder just sat there and let the conversation wash over him, like a hurricane over a levee. To have his own conviction of the impregnability of the C&I International vault confirmed by Judson Blint — out of the mouths of babes, as it were — merely put the rat poison on the cake. It was all over, in the immortal words of Charles Willeford, except the paperwork.

The others around the table didn't want to believe it. "There's always a way to do anything," Stan insisted.

"And if there isn't," Kelp said, "you make one up."

"Exactly."

"So make one up," Tiny suggested.

The silence that ensued was brief but telling, before Stan said, "Well, you can't do a bomb scare."

"Nobody," Tiny pointed out, "said you could."

"The idea with a bomb scare," Stan went on, "is they evacuate the building, then you can do what you gotta do, but it doesn't work that way. You try a bomb scare around this town, the building doesn't evacuate, it fills up to the brim, with cops, firemen, insurance adjusters, short con artists, farmers' markets, and documentary filmmakers. So forget the bomb scare."

"I'll do that," Tiny said.

"And you can't overpower the lobby guards," Kelp said, "you know, with handguns and masks and sets of cuffs and all that, on account of the camera surveillance."

"That's too bad," Tiny said. "It sounds like it might've been fun."

"Well, it won't work that way," Kelp advised him.

"So here's a question," Tiny said, and everybody except Dortmunder looked alert. "Let's say," Tiny said, "somebody went in there in disguise, to look like one of the people got the okay to go down to this vault. Not me, one of you guys. In a suit, shine up your shoes, like that."

Kelp said, "I think you gotta show ID."

"ID is not a complete impossible," Tiny said. "For instance, you follow one of the bank execs home one night, out to Connecticut, you come back with the ID, family finds him next morning, healthy but tied up and gagged in a car in a commuter railroad parking lot."

They thought about that, then turned to Dortmunder. Kelp said, "John?"

It was his own house, so he couldn't even go home. He roused himself to say, "Special elevator down from the lobby, special card stick into the elevator door, don't know what extra stuff they got downstairs, but the lobby guards know all the execs or they get fired."

"Also," Judson said, just to sink that boat one more time, "it weighs almost seven hundred pounds. You're gonna look funny carrying that in your suit."

Into the next silence, Stan inserted, "What if — ?"

They all, except Dortmunder, looked at him. Kelp said, "And?"

"I was just thinking," Stan said. "About safe-deposit boxes, you know. One of us gets a safe-deposit box, then we got a legitimate reason, go down to the vault."

"I think," Kelp said carefully, "it's a different vault, or a different part of the vault. Am I right, John?"

"Yes," Dortmunder said.

Tiny said, "Dortmunder, I didn't see this

place, I don't have it in my mind. We've got a lobby, we've got a bank, what've we got here? Walk me through it."

"It's a big building," Dortmunder told him. "Sixty stories high, half a block wide. The bank branch is on the corner, with its own way in and out. Lobby's in the middle, no door, anyway no public door, between them. On the side of the lobby away from the bank wall you got shops, inside shops, no street doors. At the back of the lobby you got your elevators and the special elevator."

"These lobby guards?"

"On the left, by the wall separates you from the bank."

Tiny nodded. "All very open," he said. "You're not gonna wheel that thing on a dolly across that lobby."

"As," Dortmunder said, "I said."

"Air ducts," Stan said.

Tiny looked at him. "You wanna push a seven-hundred-pound chess set through a building's air ducts? What about when they go vertical?"

Kelp said, "Street repair crew. Set up outside, dig down, run your tunnel under the sidewalk to the —"

"On Fifth Avenue," Judson said.

Kelp paused, frowned deeply, and shook

his head. "Never mind."

Stan said, "I know where I can get hold of a helicopter."

Tiny said, "I don't know what you're gonna do with it."

Kelp said, "What if we *did* set fire to the lobby? We come in dressed like firemen —"

Dortmunder said, "Marble doesn't burn."

The silence this time was uncomfortable from the very beginning, because everybody knew at once it was the final silence, but nobody wanted to be the one to declare the session over, the cure not found. Finally, Judson cleared his throat and said, "You got a nice warm radiator here, but maybe I oughta, I don't know, probably time to . . ."

"Me, too," Stan said, stretching as though he'd been asleep a long time.

So then everybody moved and stood up and walked around, except Dortmunder, to whom they all said good-bye as though he were somehow both the bereaved and the dearly departed. Dortmunder nodded, but did not stand.

Tiny, on his way out, rested a giant paw on Dortmunder's shoulder, adding to the weight of his burdens, and said, "If you don't like San Francisco, I got another suggestion. Biloxi."

Dortmunder shook his head. "Eppick —"

"I said Biloxi," Tiny reminded him. "Biloxi, Mississippi. Trust me, Dortmunder, they still won't talk to a Northern cop down there."

23

The lobby of the C&I International building did not look as Judson had expected from John's description. The openness, largeness, and airiness had somehow been left out. The space must have been three stories tall, sheathed in creamy mottled marble, with a sweeping wall of glass to face the street. The place mostly reminded Judson of a cathedral, particularly on a cloudless Sunday morning like this, with the thousand rays of thin November sun reverberating every which way through the lobby, reflected from all the other glass-and-steel buildings along the avenue.

It was like standing inside a halo. How could anybody ever bring himself to steal anything in a place like this? Never mind all the light, it was the saintliness that deterred.

And yet it was a bank. Over there were the two guards, behind their chest-high counter, the monitor screens set into the wall up behind them.

Would one of those screens show the vault, or at least the entrance to the vault? Why not?

Judson moved in the direction of the monitor screens, looking at black-and-white pictures of hallways and empty elevators, until he became aware that the guards were, in their turn, looking at him. Not because they suspected him of anything, but because he was the only thing they could see that was in motion. The shops on the other side of the lobby were closed on Sundays, and so were many of the offices on the floors above.

Belatedly deciding it would be a mistake to draw a lot of attention to himself, Judson veered from his monitor-bound route toward the register instead, deeper along that wall. They would think he was merely looking for one of the tenants here, wouldn't they?

Judson had no real business in the C&I building, not on Sunday nor on any other day. He had just been feeling so bad about John ever since he'd casually demolished everybody's hopes yesterday by saying flat out that they'd never get into that bank vault, and had seen the sag of John's face like a wedge of cheese in a microwave.

But why should they believe *him?* He was the kid, what did he know? Of course, it was just that all the others were pretending there was hope, to buoy John's spirits, and the kid had been too dumb to go along, so once he'd burst the bubble, there was nothing left for anybody else to say.

But was he right? Was it true that the vault was impregnable? Rising from bed in his Spanish Chelsea apartment this morning, he'd known the only thing he could do was look at the place for himself, just in case — just in case, you know — there might somehow, in some little tiny way nobody else had noticed, be a way to squiggle into that vault after all.

And back out. That was one of the most important life lessons he'd learned so far: It's nice to be able to get into a place, but it's essential to be able to get out again.

Over at the big black square rectangle of the register, with all the white letters and numbers on it defining every company with space in this building, Judson gazed upward, hoping the guards had lost interest in him (but certainly not looking over there to find out), and found himself marveling at how many different names there are in this world. All individual, most pronounceable. Think of that.

"Help you?"

Judson jumped like a hiccup, and turned to see one of the guards right there next to him, frowning at him, being polite in a very threatening way. "Oh, no!" he blurted. "I'm just . . . waiting for a friend of mine. He didn't come down yet, that's all."

"Where does he work?" the guard asked, pretending to be helpful, and then, more suddenly, more sharply, "Don't look at the board! Where does he work?"

Where does he work? Judson pawed desperately through his short-term memory, in search of just one of those names he'd so recently been reading and marveling on, and every last one of them was gone. His mind was a blank. "Well," he said. "Uh . . ."

"Hey, there you are! Sorry I'm late."

Judson turned his deer-in-the-headlights eyes and there was Andy Kelp, striding with great confidence across the sun-gleaming marble lobby, like the galactic commander in a science-fiction saga. "Oh," Judson said, relieved and bewildered. What words were he supposed to speak? "I," he said, "I forgot where you work. Isn't that stupid?"

"I wish *I* could," Andy said, cheerful as ever. "Let's not go up there, it's too nice a day."

"Oh. Okay."

Andy nodded a greeting at the guard. "How ya doin?"

"Fine," the guard said, but he didn't sound it.

Judson felt the guard's eyes on his back all the way out to Fifth Avenue. Once safely out there among the tourists and the taxis, Andy said, "Let's mosey southward a little." And, as they did so, he said, "Just implanting your facial features on the staff there, eh?"

"I wasn't trying to."

"No? What *were* you trying to do?"

"I felt so bad about John, I thought, why don't I just take a look, see if maybe . . ."

They stopped for a red light among the tourists, many of whom appeared to have been inflated beyond manufacturer's specifications, and Andy said, "My thought exactly. I even went to double-o that golden dome, the least I can do is give a gander to a bank. I get there, I can see you're in need of assistance."

"I was," Judson said humbly.

"See, kid — The light's green."

They crossed, amid all that padding, and Andy said, "See, if you're gonna case a place, it's not a good idea you give them a glossy photograph of yourself. What you do, you come in, you walk over to the elevators,

189

you give that other door the eye, you look at your watch, you shake your head, you walk out. You don't look at guards, you don't stand still, you don't hang around, but when you're outside you've got the situation cold."

"There's no way to get into the vault," Judson said.

"You said that yesterday."

"But now I know it."

"I tell you what," Andy said. "It's a nice day, we're out here anyway, let's go see did John get over it."

24

John wasn't watching football, and May didn't like that at all. Here it was November, the middle of the season, every team still at least theoretically in the running, and John doesn't even sit down to watch Sunday football. Not even the pregame show. It was worrying.

May was in the kitchen, involved in that worrying, when the street doorbell sounded, a noise she was still getting used to, that bell having been on the blink for many years until the landlord abruptly fixed it as a run-up to a rent increase. But now, unasked for and unneeded, here it was working again, and the sound had already trained her enough so that she automatically went to the little round grid in the kitchen wall and said into it, "Hello?"

"It's Andy," said a garbled voice that could have been any Martian.

Andy? Andy doesn't ring doorbells, he

picks locks, you don't know Andy's going to make a visit until he's sitting in the living room.

What was going on here? John doesn't watch football, Andy Kelp doesn't pick locks, the world is coming to an end. "Come on up," she said dubiously, and pushed the button below the grid.

Did he plan to ring the upstairs doorbell, too? Well, we don't have to put up with *that*. So May walked down the corridor from the kitchen to the apartment front door, passing along the way the open door on her right to the room where John sat brooding in the direction of the switched-off television set but not, she knew, actually seeing it.

With the apartment door open, she could hear the asymmetric tramp of feet coming up the stairs; more than one, then. And yes, into view from the staircase came Andy and with him that nice kid Judson who'd attached himself to the group recently.

"Harya," Andy said, approaching. "I brought the kid."

"I see that. Is he the reason you rang the bell?"

Looking a bit sheepish, Andy grinned and said, "Basically, yeah. We don't want to give him too many bad habits all at once."

"Hi, Miss May," Judson said.

"Hi, yourself," May said, and stepped back from the doorway. "Well, come on in. John's in the living room, not watching football."

"Oh," Andy said. "That doesn't sound good."

"That's what I think."

They went in to see John as though entering a sickroom. Brightly, May said, "John, look who's here. It's Andy and Judson."

He sort of looked at them. "Harya," he said, and stopped sort of looking at them.

"Sit down," May said, so Andy and Judson perched uncomfortably on the sofa and she wrung her hands a little, not a normal gesture for her, and said, "Can I get anybody a beer?"

Andy could be seen to be about to say yes, but John, in a voice of doom, said, "No, thanks, May," so Andy closed his mouth again.

"Well," May said, and sat in her own chair, and everybody carefully didn't look at John.

Andy said, "This weather. For November, you know, this weather's pretty good."

"Very sunny out there," Judson added.

"That's nice," May said, and gestured at the window. "In here, you hardly notice."

"Well, it's really sunny," Andy said.

"Good," May said.

And then nobody said anything, for quite some time. Andy and Judson frowned mightily, obviously racking their brains in search of topics of conversation, but nothing. The silence in the room stretched on, and everybody in there except John became increasingly tongue-tied and desperate. John just continued to brood in the direction of the television set. Then:

"The problem is," John said.

Everybody turned to him, very alert. But then he didn't say anything else, just shook his head.

They waited; nothing. Finally May said, "Yes, John? The problem?"

"Well, I'm thinking about it backwards," John said. "That's what's been wrong."

May said, "Backwards? I don't follow."

"When the kid said yesterday, we can't get into the vault —"

"I'm sorry I said that, John," Judson said. "I've been wanting to tell you that, I'm sorry."

"No, you were right," John said. "That's what I've been saying all along, there's no way to get into that vault."

"I'm sorry."

"Fuggedabodit. See, what it is I gotta do, I gotta stop thinking about getting into the vault because I *can't* get into the vault.

That's the backwards part."

Judson said, "It is?"

"The mountain," John explained, "gotta go to whatsisname. Mohammed."

Fearing the worst, May said, "John?"

"You know," John said, and gestured vaguely with both hands. "He won't go to that, so that's gotta go to him. Same with the vault. We can't get in at the chess set, case closed, no discussion, so what we gotta do is get the chess set to come out to us."

"That's brilliant, John," Andy said. "How do we do that?"

"Well," John said, "that's the part I'm working on."

25

Though Fiona and Brian ended their workdays at radically different hours, they began them together, up no later than eight, soon out of the apartment, a stop at Starbucks for coffee and a sweet roll as breakfast on the subway, then the ride downtown together until Fiona got off the train in midtown, Brian continuing on toward his cable company employer's studios down in Tribeca.

This Monday morning was the same, with the usual hurried peck on the lips as Fiona left the train, paused to throw her empty coffee cup into the same trash barrel as always, and walked up the flights of concrete stairs to the street, then down Broadway and over to Fifth, where a poor beggar huddled against the chill air near the entrance to C&I.

Fiona reached into her coat pocket in search of a dollar — she always gave such unfortunates a dollar, not caring how they might spend it — when she realized it wasn't a beggar at all, it was Mr. Dortmunder. Terribly embarrassed, feeling her face flush crimson, hoping he hadn't seen her reach into her pocket or at least hadn't interpreted it for what it was, she forced a large smile onto her face, stopped in front of him and, too brightly, said, "Mr. Dortmunder! Hello again."

"I figured," he said, "we should maybe talk out here, not all the time up in Feinberg. You got a few minutes, we could walk around the block?"

She checked her watch, and she was in fact running a little early today, so she said, "Of course." To make it up to him for mistaking him for a beggar, she said, "I'd be happy to."

"Nice," he said. "So we'll walk."

So they walked, amid the morning scurry of office workers. The Monday crowds on Fifth Avenue were very different from Sunday's; those tourists were still in their hotel rooms, discussing the comparative excitements of a sightseeing bus around Manhattan or a ride on the Staten Island ferry, while the people on the sidewalks this morning were much faster, much leaner, and much more tightly focused on where they were going and why. It was hard for Fiona and Mr. Dortmunder to move among them at the slower pace required for conversation, but they tried, taking the occasional shoulder block along the way.

"What it is," Mr. Dortmunder said, "we got a real problem getting at that thing down in that place, like I told you last time."

"I'm sorry this whole thing got started," she said.

"Well, so am I, but here we are." He shrugged. "The thing is," he said, "your grandfather and the guy working for him, they're pretty set on getting that thing. Or, I mean, *me* getting that thing."

She felt so guilty about this, much worse than mistaking him for a beggar. "Would it help," she said, "if I talked to my grandfather?"

"Defeatist isn't gonna get far with him."

That sounded like her grandfather, all right. Sighing, she said, "I suppose not."

"But there maybe could be another way," he said.

Surprised, ready to be pleased, she said, "Oh, really?"

"Only," he said, "it's gonna mean I'm gonna have to ask you to help out."

She stopped, absorbed a couple rabbit punches from the hurrying throng, and said,

"Oh, *no,* Mr. Dortmunder!"

They'd reached the corner now, and he said, "Come on around here, before they knock you out."

The side street was easier. Walking along it, she said, "You have to understand, Mr. Dortmunder, I'm an attorney. I'm an officer of the court. I can't be involved in crime."

"That's funny," he said. "I've heard of one or two lawyers involved in crime."

"Criminal lawyers, yes."

"That's not what I mean."

A luggage store with an inset entrance wasn't yet open for business. Pulling him into the space, surrounded by luggage behind windows, she said, "Let me explain."

"Sure."

"Feinberg," she said, "is a respectable serious law firm. If they knew I was even *this* much involved in — Mr. Dortmunder, let's be honest here."

"Uh," he said.

"What we're talking about," she said, "is robbery. Burglary. It's a *felony,* Mr. Dortmunder."

"That's what it is, all right."

"You simply can't ask me to be involved in a felony," she said. "I mean, I'm trying to be *good* at what I do."

"I'm not asking," he said, "for you to slip this thing out under your coat or anything. Let me tell you the situation, okay?"

"I'll have to tell my grandfather," she said, "that neither you nor he nor anyone else can expect any help from me of any kind. Not on this matter."

"That's nice," he said. "I'd like to tell him the same thing myself. Will you listen to what I got to say?"

Fiona could be mulish when pushed. Feeling pushed, face closed, she said, "Go right ahead."

"Those specs and pictures you gave me of the thing —"

"*Already* I'm in so deep!"

"Miss Hemlow," he said, "you don't know deep. Here's the thing about those specs. One of the rooks is the wrong weight."

This snagged her attention. "It's what?"

"It weighs three pounds less than the other ones," he said. "We figure, Northwood had a fake made up, sold the real one off for railroad fare."

"My goodness."

"Yeah, I know. Anyway, your company has one of these family members, right?"

"Yes, of course."

"If we could get the news to that one," he said, "that there's a problem with one of the pieces, then maybe there's problems with more than one, maybe somebody in the family was up to some hanky-panky, and maybe he wants to —"

"She."

"Okay. Maybe *she* wants to get the whole chess set investigated by some experts. You know," he said, and his eyes actually gleamed. "Bring it up out of that vault, bring it to the expert's lab or wherever it is, have the thing *there* for a while."

"Oh, my God," she said.

"I can't do it," he pointed out. "You can see that I can't go talk to this person, how do I know any of this stuff? *You* could talk to her."

"Oh, my God," she said, more faintly.

He cocked his head and studied her. "Will you do it? I gotta tell you, it's the only way your grandfather's gonna get the thing."

"I have to," she stammered, "I have to think." And she fled the storefront, leaving him there, looking more than ever like a beggar.

26

When Dortmunder got back to the apartment May was already off to her job, but she'd left a note on a Post-it stuck to the six-pack in the refrigerator, where he'd be sure to see it. "Call Epic on his cell," it read, and gave the number.

"I'd like to call Eppick *in* his cell," he muttered, but transferred the note to the wall beside the phone and dialed.

"Eppick!"

"It's, uh, John. You wanted me to —"

"That's *right*." Eppick sounded in a hurry. "Grab a cab, come —"

Dortmunder waited. "Yeah?"

"— In the lobby."

"What?"

"I'll be there before —"

"Where?"

Silence. Not a hovering silence, or a pregnant silence, more of a bat cave silence; they're all asleep in there. Then a dial tone, so he hung up.

Try again? Why? Dortmunder turned back toward the refrigerator, remembering the six-pack that had been used so effectively as a means of communication, and the phone rang.

Well, there were some things you simply had to go through. He went back and picked up the phone: "Yeah?"

"I'm in this cab, the recep — buildings bounce — soon as you — read me?"

"No."

A little silence, then, "— These cell phones!" It sounded like an expletive might have been deleted.

"I understand," Dortmunder said, "they're the wave of the future."

"Then the future's looking bleak. I want you to —" Dial tone.

"Good-bye," Dortmunder told the dial tone, achieved a can of beer from the six-pack and went to the living room to get the *Daily News* May had been reading earlier this morning. He brought it back to the kitchen table, because he knew damn well Eppick was not a guy to give up, and sat there for a while turning newspaper pages. Since he didn't look at the paper more than a couple times a week, usually when he found one on a subway seat, he could never figure out what all those comic strips were all about. Were those supposed to be punch lines over there on the right?

In the sports section, the standings were about as expected. It occurred to him that sports might be more interesting if the football players wore basketball uniforms and the basketball players wore football uniforms, and the phone rang.

Okay; he went over and answered: "Here."

"*That's* better. John, you gotta grab a cab and come right up to Mr. Hemlow's place."

"The reception's a lot better now."

"I made the cab stop at a pay phone. Come up right away, John, Mr. Hemlow isn't happy."

"Why should Hemlow be happy?"

"No, he isn't happy about *you*. I'll be in the lobby."

Eppick was in a rhinoceros-horn chair in the lobby, and got up from it when Dortmunder was let in by the doorman, who looked as though he wasn't entirely certain this was the right thing to do.

"All right," Eppick said, still impatient. "Let's go."

In the elevator, Dortmunder said, "I seem to be laying out a whole lotta cab money."

"That's because," Eppick said, "you're an

independent contractor."

"Oh," Dortmunder said, and the elevator opened, and a fuming medicine ball awaited them in his wheelchair.

"Gentlemen," Mr. Hemlow spat. Dortmunder hadn't known you could spit a word like "gentlemen," but Mr. Hemlow made it sound easy. "Sit down," he ordered, and the wheelchair spun away toward the view.

Once everybody was in position, Dortmunder and Eppick side by side in the antique chairs, Mr. Hemlow facing them in the middle of the view, Mr. Hemlow, over the tempo-setting twitch of his right knee, lowered a glower at Dortmunder and said, "I understand you spoke to my granddaughter this morning."

"Yeah, I did," Dortmunder said. "Not in the place, on the sidewalk out front."

Eppick glared at Dortmunder's right eye and ear. "You *accosted* her? On the *street?*"

"I didn't accost her. It was a little conversation."

Mr. Hemlow, the lid barely on his rage, said, "You *asked* her to take part in a criminal act."

"I don't see that," Dortmunder said. "Where's the crime? I didn't even ask her to jaywalk."

Eppick said, "Sir, could you back it up a little here? I don't really know what's going on. What did he ask her to do?"

"I just —"

"I'm not asking *you*," Eppick spat. Now everybody was spitting. "I'm asking Mr. Hemlow."

"As I understand it," Mr. Hemlow said, "your associate here has decided it's too much trouble to make his way into that bank vault and retrieve the chess set, so he wants —"

Appalled, Eppick cried, "Your *grand-daughter* to go down there?"

"No, not quite that bad. He wants Fiona to approach Livia Northwood Wheeler and —"

"I'm sorry, sir," Eppick said. "Who?"

"She is the Sgt. Northwood descendant," Mr. Hemlow explained, "who is represented by Fiona's firm in the family lawsuits."

"Oh," Eppick said. "Thank you, sir."

"Fiona's *firm* represents Livia Northwood Wheeler," Mr. Hemlow went on, those little red eyes glowering at Dortmunder. "*Fiona* doesn't represent her, does not have any legitimate reason to speak to the woman, even if she were willing to do what you asked of her."

Eppick said, "Sir, what did . . . John here, ask?"

"Perhaps John himself should tell you," Mr. Hemlow said.

Eppick turned a judgmental gaze on Dortmunder, who shrugged and said, "Sure. We can't get down in there, so I figured, maybe we could get the thing to come out instead. The specs and stuff the granddaughter gave me, which by the way I think was more legally iffy than what I asked her today, those specs showed one piece was too light, and we figure the sergeant switched it for a phony —"

"To give himself a stake," Eppick said, nodding, agreeing with himself. "Very smart."

"Nah, anybody could figure that."

"I meant him."

Mr. Hemlow said, "John here took this information to Fiona and asked her to pass it on to Mrs. Wheeler with a recommendation that she have the entire chess set appraised."

"Which," Dortmunder said, "would bring it up outa that vault."

"Were Fiona to address a client of the firm," Mr. Hemlow said, "without being asked specifically to do so by a partner or an associate, she would be let go at once."

"Fired, you mean," Dortmunder said.

" 'Let go' conveys the same information," Mr. Hemlow said.

Eppick said, "Sir, let me have a word with John, if I may."

"Certainly."

Eppick nodded his thanks, then turned to Dortmunder. "I see what you were trying to do," he said, "and it wasn't bad. I understand that vault is maybe a little tougher than some places you've seen in the past."

"*All* places I've seen in the past."

"Okay. And the idea to get the thing out of the vault to somewhere maybe a little easier to get at, that's good, too."

"Thank you," Dortmunder said, with dignity.

"The problem is, though," Eppick said, "you can't use the granddaughter, not for anything. She started the ball rolling, but now she's out of it. We gotta protect her, we gotta protect her job, we gotta protect her reputation."

"Uh huh."

"She is not," Mr. Hemlow said, "an asset."

Dortmunder frowned, not getting that, but decided to let it slide.

Eppick apparently understood it, though, because he nodded in approval and said,

"Exactly." To Dortmunder he said, "But the idea's a good one. We just gotta find some other way to make some other member of the family want experts to take a look at the chess set."

"Then," Dortmunder said, "Mr. Hemlow, I gotta ask you this. There's one last thing I'd want from your granddaughter, and I think it's okay, but you tell me."

Dubious, head rolling down over the medicine ball more than ever, Mr. Hemlow glowered up through his eyebrows and said, "What would that be?"

"She said, she told me one time, there's seventeen family people in this, everybody suing everybody, all with their own lawyers. Could she get me a list of the seventeen, and which lawyer each one's got?"

Mr. Hemlow thought a minute, but the head was nodding while he did it, not in time with the metronome knee. Then he said, "She could do that."

"Thank you."

"I will arrange for her to compile such a list and give it to me. I will convey it to Johnny here, and he can pass it on to you."

"Great."

"But then," Mr. Hemlow said, "that is the end of it. You will never have contact with my granddaughter ever again."

"Oh, sure," Dortmunder said.

Riding down in the elevator, Dortmunder said, "Whadaya mean, independent contractor?"

"It's one of the job definitions," Eppick told him, "you know, that the government has. Like, if you work for wages, you're a salaried employee, so you can be in a union, but if you're an independent contractor you can't be in a union."

"I'm not in a union," Dortmunder said, and the elevator door opened at the lobby.

Leaving the building, Eppick said, "We're both going downtown. Come on down to the corner, we'll grab a cab. I'll even pay."

Dortmunder said, "But you don't want to give the doorman a dollar to get a cab right here."

"Neither do you," Eppick told him.

So they walked down to the corner and eventually found a cab without help, and as they rode downtown together Dortmunder said, "Tell me more about this independent contractor. Whadaya mean, it's a government definition?"

"It shows where you fit in the workforce," Eppick said. "There's certain things you gotta match up with, and then you're an independent contractor."

"Like what?"

"You don't get a fixed salary every week."

"Okay."

"You don't work in the same office or factory or whatever every day."

"Okay."

"You carry your own tools on the job."

"I do that," Dortmunder said.

"You work without direct supervision."

"You know it."

"There's no withholding tax on what you make."

"Never happened yet."

"The employer or whoever doesn't give you a pension or health care."

"This is my profile to the life," Dortmunder said.

"Then there you are," Eppick said. "And now, go to work on those family members. I think you're onto something there."

"Soon as I get the list," Dortmunder promised.

When May got home that evening, Dortmunder helped by carrying one of the grocery sacks. In the kitchen, he said, "I found out something today."

"Oh?"

Dortmunder smiled. "I am an independent contractor."

She looked at him and put the cereal away. "Oh," she said.

27

Later that same day, Kelp was in his own apartment in the West Thirties, chatting with Anne Marie Carpinaw, the friend he'd made one time on a trip to Washington, DC, and had brought home to protect her from that place. Deciding to raise a certain issue, "You're a woman," Kelp pointed out.

"I believe," Anne Marie said, "that was the first thing you noticed about me."

"It was." Kelp nodded, agreeing with them both. "And as a woman," he said, "I just have this feeling you might maybe have some certain expertise."

"About what?"

"Well, in this case, jewelry."

"Yes, please," she said. "It's never in bad taste, and never out of style."

"Not like that," he said. "A different kind of expertise."

The look she gave him had something caustic in it. "I could show my expertise at sulking, if you like."

"Come on, Anne Marie," Kelp said. "I just wanna pick your brain."

"Well, that's all right, then," she said. "I was wondering when you'd get around to my brain."

"I didn't have that much need for it up till now."

She laughed, but pointed a finger at him. "You're on the lip of the volcano there, pal."

"Then let me ask my question," he said. "It's most likely you don't know the answer, but I definitely don't know the answer, and I gotta start somewhere."

"Go ahead."

They were in their living room, which earlier he had salted with a manila envelope on the coffee table. This he now picked up, and withdrew from it two photos of the red queen from the chess set, plus the sheet giving the queen's dimensions and weight. "What I wanna do," he said, handing her these documents, "is make a fake one of these. It doesn't have to be a hundred percent perfect, because we're gonna paint it with red enamel."

"This is the thing," she said, studying the photos, "that John is working on."

"Well, we both are," Kelp said, "if we get past a couple little problems. And one of them is how to make a copy of that thing there, same size, same shape, pretty much the same weight."

"Well, that's easy," she said. "Particularly if the jewels don't have to match."

"No, they're gonna be painted over. Whadaya mean, it's easy?"

"You came to the right person," she said. "What I will do is turn this over to the Earring Man."

"The who?"

"Women lose earrings," she pointed out. "You know that."

"You find 'em in cabs," Kelp agreed, "you find 'em next to telephones, you find 'em on the floor the morning after the party."

"Exactly," she said. "So there you are, you had a pair of earrings you loved, now you've only got one earring, and one earring isn't going to do anything for anybody except some pathetic guy trying to be hip."

"I've seen those guys, too," Kelp said. "They look like they're off the leash."

"So if you're a woman," Anne Marie went on, "with one earring of a pair you loved, you go to this jeweler that everybody calls Earring Man because he will make you an exact match."

"That's pretty good," Kelp said. "I never knew that."

"I think there's probably an Earring Man, or maybe more than one, in every urban center in the world where women don't have to wear headscarves. The one I know is in DC. I wore earrings a lot more when I was a congressman's daughter than when I'm some heister's moll."

Surprised, Kelp said, "Is that who you are?"

Looking at the photos again, she said, "How much of a hurry are you in for this?"

"Well, since John says we're never gonna get our hands on the real one, I'd say you could take your time."

She nodded, thinking it over. "I still have some unindicted friends down in DC," she said. "I'll make a couple calls and probably fly down tomorrow. He'll most likely want a couple weeks."

"He'll know," Kelp said, "there's a certain amount of secrecy involved here."

"Oh, sure," she said. "Earring Man would never betray a confidence." Grinning at the memory, she said, "The great story about him is the time a woman came in, very sad, with the one earring, and she lost the other in a cab, just like you said. He went to work on it, and a couple days later *another* woman came in with the *other* earring and claimed *she* lost the missing one in a cab.

He never called either of them on it, never found out which one was lying, didn't care."

Kelp said, "Anne Marie, in that case, how come *you* know about it?"

She couldn't believe the question. "Andy," she said, "people *gossip* all the time. That isn't the same as tattling."

Sometimes you know when the explanation you've got is the only explanation you're going to get. "Fine," Kelp said. "Whadaya wanna do about dinner?"

28

It took Fiona two full days, until late afternoon on Wednesday, burrowing into other people's files and records, to compile the list of all the litigating Northwood heirs requested by her grandfather. During this time, her own work suffered, of course, so when she finally had the list printed out and safely inside a manila envelope inside her shoulder bag under her desk, she turned immediately to the concerns and hungers and unfulfilled dreams of *another* enraged family — oil — but had only been at it for twenty minutes when her desk phone rang.

Oh, what now? She didn't have *time* for this, she'd be here till midnight, and what would happen to Brian's dinner, would he prepare some exotic cuisine and then just sit there and watch it congeal, hour after hour? *Why* would people phone her at a time like this?

No choice; she had to answer. "Hemlow,"

she said into the phone, and a clipped British female voice said, "Mr. Tumbril wishes to see you in his office. Now."

Click. Stunned, Fiona put down her phone. Why would a partner in the firm want *her* in his office? And why, of all the partners, Mr. Tumbril? In New York, a city known for fierce litigators the way New Orleans is known for overweight chefs and Los Angeles for fanciful accountants, the name Jay Tumbril was in itself very often enough to make mad dogs settle and homicidal maniacs run screaming from the room.

Well, she'd soon find out what it was about. She made her circuitous way across the Feinberg domain to Mr. Tumbril's corner — of course — office, outside which Mr. Tumbril's British secretary, as lean of head and body as a whippet, accepted her proffered identity, spoke briefly into her phone, and said, "Go in."

Fiona went in, closing the door behind her. She had never been inside Mr. Tumbril's office before, but the office itself wasn't primarily what she immediately saw and reacted to; it was Livia Northwood Wheeler, seated at attention on a pale green sofa along the windowless side wall and gazing at Fiona with an extremely complex expression on her face, appearing to combine apprehension, expectation, doubt, defiance, arrogance, and possibly a few additional herbs for flavor.

"Ms. Hemlow."

Her master's voice. Reluctantly, Fiona turned away from that bouillabaisse of an expression to the much clearer and sterner expression on the face of Jay Tumbril. A tall, large-boned man in his fifties, with a small ferret-like face, he was not quite so fearsome when seated behind his large neat desk, flanked by large clean windows showing views of the jumble of Manhattan, as when he was on his feet, pacing and stalking in front of a jury, but he was still quite fearsome enough. In a smaller voice than any she'd known she possessed, Fiona said, "Yes, sir."

"The last time Mrs. Wheeler visited these offices," Tumbril said, "you approached her as she waited for the elevator. You said I had sent you."

Shocked, Fiona cried, "Oh, no, sir!" Turning in horror toward Mrs. Wheeler, she said, "I didn't say that. I didn't say that at all."

Mrs. Wheeler was no longer looking at her, but at Tumbril instead, and her expression now was a simple combination of surprise and offense. "Jay," she said, "you're misrepresenting me. It was *my* conclusion you'd sent her after me. She denied it at the time."

Tumbril didn't like that. "Why would *I* send her after you?"

"There was a certain amount of rancor in this room at the time of my last visit," she said, apparently unafraid of Tumbril, no matter how much he glared at her. "I thought perhaps you were trying to make peace."

"Why would I do that?" Said with more impatience than curiosity, as though he didn't expect there could be an answer.

Nor was there one. "My mistake," Mrs. Wheeler said.

Accepting victory as his due, Tumbril turned his scowl back on Fiona. "Since I didn't send you to speak to Mrs. Wheeler," he said, "who did?"

"No one, sir."

"It was your own idea."

"Yes, sir."

"Miss Hemlow," Tumbril said, "do you know the firm's policy with regard to young assistants such as yourself making direct contact with clients?"

"Yes, sir," Fiona said, in a voice so small she could barely hear it herself.

"And what is that policy, Miss Hemlow?"

It was one thing to study cross-examination technique in law school, but quite another to undergo it. Fiona said, "Sir, we're not supposed to deal directly with a client unless a partner or associate requests it."

"Jay," Mrs. Wheeler said. "I didn't mean to get this girl in trouble."

"She got herself in trouble, Livia." Tumbril made a little sweeping-away motion toward Fiona, as though she were dust, and said, "She had *no* excuse to speak to you. She never even had work assigned to her to do on your affairs. Why would she speak to you?"

"Well," Mrs. Wheeler said, "she said she admired me."

"Admired you? For what?"

"For the stance I was taking in my suit."

Tumbril sat well back in his large leather chair to gaze with thorough disapproval at Fiona. "You went into the files?"

"Yes, sir."

"Of a case toward which you had absolutely no responsibilities?"

"Yes, sir."

"You searched through matters that were none of your concern," Tumbril summed up, "and then you went to the principal in the matter to toady up to her."

"No, sir, I just —"

"*Yes,* sir! Well, young lady, if you thought you might be advancing yourself with this behind-the-scenes rubbish, you've done quite the reverse. You will go and clear out your desk and wait for security to escort you from the building."

"Jay!"

"I know what I'm doing, Livia. Miss Hemlow, the firm will mail you your final compensation. You will understand we will not be able to give you a reference."

"Yes, sir."

"Good-bye, Miss Hemlow."

Stricken, not yet able to think about what was happening to her, Fiona turned toward the door.

"Young lady," Mrs. Wheeler said, and when Fiona turned her heavy head the older woman had leaned forward to hold out a card. "Phone me," she said.

Hardly knowing she was doing it, Fiona took the card. She couldn't think of a thing to say.

Tumbril could. "You're making a mistake, Livia."

"Not the first one I've made in this office," she told him.

Tumbril threw one last scowl at Fiona. "You may go."

She went.

■ ■ ■ ■

The envelope! If security found that envelope, with all that information on all the Northwood heirs, she'd be worse than fired, she'd be charged with felonies, her reputation would be destroyed forever.

Trying not to look in a desperate hurry, Fiona walked faster than she'd ever walked before through the maze of cubicles to her desk. She pulled the envelope from her shoulder bag, slapped a mailing label on it, wrote her grandfather's name and address on the label, and carried it away, to drop it in an absent person's out basket on her way to the ladies'.

Once in there, she realized she actually did need a stall for a moment, which was just as well because, when she stepped out, security was standing there, frowning at her, a heavyset severe woman in a uniform of brown. She said, "Fiona Hemlow?"

"Yes."

"You're supposed to be at your desk."

"When you're fired," Fiona told her, "it makes you need to go to the ladies' room. I'll just wash my hands."

The security woman followed her back to her cubicle, where her neighbor Imogen widened her eyes but knew enough not to say anything. Fiona took her few personal possessions from her desk, permitted the security woman to search her bag, and then they headed off for the elevators.

Fiona looked at it all, so familiar, so much of her life. All those hunched backs, those computers, telephones, stacks of documents, all of these creatures pulling steadfastly at the oars of this galley while their betters sat out of sight, next to windows.

Fiona smiled. Suddenly a weight had lifted, and she hadn't even known she was carrying it. "You know," she told the security woman, "I'm a very lucky person."

29

Friday afternoon, Anne Marie took a shuttle back up to LaGuardia from DC. Kelp cabbed out there from the city a little ahead of time, so he'd have leisure to find just the right wheels with which to deliver Anne Marie back to their love nest. His first priority, as always, was a car with MD plates, he being firmly of the conviction that doctors have a greater than average experience of the highs and lows of human life, and will therefore whenever possible gravitate toward the high; as in their choice of personal vehicle, for instance.

This trip, however, was more than ordinarily special, as being the return of Anne Marie after three days of travel to and from DC and dealing with the Earring Man while there, all on Kelp's behalf. So, when he began his ramble through long-term parking, keeping an eye out for MD plates and no dust (early in the long term), his other criterion was that he wanted a *woman* doctor's car. In the old days he would have looked for a modest sedan with lower-than-average mileage but more than the usual dents, but times had changed and the old signifiers no longer signified.

Well, something had to signify. Kelp strolled for a while among the wheels on offer, and then he saw a white Lexus RX 400h, the low-fuel-consumption hybrid, and yes, MD plates; unusual on a white car. This doctor drives a hybrid, so this doctor cares about the planet. And the bumper sticker: *The Earth — Our Home — Keep It Tidy.* Uh huh. And when he looked through the driver's window, there was the clincher: *two* bottles of Poland Spring water in the cup holders.

An electronically inclined acquaintance of Kelp's named Wally Knurr had recently sold him, at very little above cost, a carefully restructured universal remote. Originally meant to find its way through the various individual electronic signals of every known TV, VCR, and DVD, the machine now provided the same service for your most recent automobile models, thus bypassing all the physical violence of yesteryear. It took Kelp barely a dozen clicks with the remote to make the Lexus give him the bleep of welcome. He checked inside, to be sure the parking fee ticket was in its place behind the sun visor, saw that it was, locked the Lexus again and went off to find Anne Marie.

Who seemed to be the only one in her group to come down the long ramp from the gates without a briefcase. What she lugged instead was a bulky black leather shoulder bag bouncing on her right hip, which made her look like a particularly fetching stew out of uniform, and from the tail ends of a few conversations he observed as the herd headed this way some of her fellow passengers had dreamed of being in a position to get her even further out of uniform, but forget all that now: her boyfriend's back.

They kissed, to the disgust of the briefcase-toters, and made their way out to long-term, where Anne Marie gazed with pleasure upon the Lexus and said, "For me?"

"I picked it out special."

"You're very thoughtful," Anne Marie told him, as he remoted them into the car.

Once he had the seat adjusted back from somewhere up against the firewall, the Lexus was fine. Kelp happily paid the three-day parking charge and out they went to

Grand Central Parkway, westbound toward the city.

As they drove, he said, "I guess it all went okay, then."

"You owe me four hundred bucks."

"Extra beyond the airfare, you mean. How'd I do that?"

"Mr. Earring Man wanted an advance," she said. "He smelled a felony, and would risk his reputation for no less."

"I can understand that," Kelp said. "You did right to pay him."

"You know, Andy," she said, "I'm not the gang's banker."

"Oh, I know that," Kelp assured her. "Me and John, over the weekend, we'll do a little this and that."

"Good."

"But otherwise, he says no problem, huh?"

"He didn't want to admit how easy it was going to be," she said, "but I could tell."

The 125th Street Bridge was near. "I missed you," he said.

"Good. I missed you, too."

"We'll have a nice dinner out."

She considered that. "We'll have a nice late dinner out," she decided.

30

As far as Dortmunder was concerned, his was a for-profit operation, so he wasn't in love with the idea that, not only was this particular heist impossible, but now they were in the red on the thing to the tune of four hundred bucks. He understood that Anne Marie had done what Anne Marie had to do, but even so.

Over the weekend, to pay this debt, Dortmunder and Kelp made a couple little after-hours visits to some Madison Avenue luxury purveyors so upscale and rarefied the little sign in the door said, *English spoken,* which further necessitated a West Side visit to a fellow named Arnie Albright, known to the authorities as a receiver of stolen goods but to his customers as the guy you went to when you were carrying something you didn't want to carry any more.

Negotiations with Arnie were usually brutish, nasty, and short, the short because

Arnie well knew he had competitors who, while perhaps a little more off the beaten path and certainly noted for bargaining an extremely hard dollar, were also well ahead of Arnie in the acceptable human being category. Arnie knew his customers could only stand to look at him for so long, particularly when, such as now, his recurring wet red rash had returned, to spread over his lumpy face so that he looked as though he'd fallen asleep in a bowl of salsa. When you finally did get the cash, you wanted to go home and wash it.

As for Johnny Eppick and his employer, Mr. Hemlow, Dortmunder assumed the granddaughter was having a little trouble collecting the information he'd requested on all the other heirs, which was also okay, because, once he did get that information, he hadn't the slightest idea what he was going to do with it. So, let sleeping Eppicks lie.

Which he did, until late the following Monday morning, shortly after May had gone off to the Safeway. That's when the phone decided to ring, so Dortmunder put down the *Daily News* — there didn't seem to be anybody he knew in it today — got to his feet, walked to the kitchen, grabbed the receiver, and said, "Yar."

"Mr. Hemlow wants to see us. His place."

Fatalistic, Dortmunder said, "I'm springing for another cab, am I?"

"I don't think you have time to walk," Eppick said, and hung up.

Poker-faced, the doorman said, "The other gentleman is already here."

"Yeah, I see him," Dortmunder said. He was in a bad mood because of having to spend so much of Arnie Albright's money just to get here.

Eppick's manner was not bad-tempered, actually, just guarded. Rising from the rhinoceros-horn chair, he said, "He didn't sound happy."

"Like usual, you mean."

"Maybe worse."

As they rode up in the elevator with its extraneous operator, Eppick said, "We'll just see how it goes."

"That sounds like a plan," Dortmunder agreed.

It was not going to go well. Mr. Hemlow in his wheelchair waited in his usual position on the polished floor of his penthouse, but when they emerged from the elevator he did not spin around, did not zoom over to the view, did not invite them to take a seat. Instead, he stayed where he was, with them on their feet in front of him, and after the elevator had gone away he said, "I wanted to tell you both in person. I don't blame either of you for what happened."

Eppick, sounding alarmed, said, "Something happened?"

"Last Wednesday," Mr. Hemlow said, "my granddaughter was fired. Embarrassed, she didn't tell me, but this morning, in the mail, arrived the list of heirs you asked for."

"You mean John asked for," Eppick said, dodging a bullet.

"Yes, of course."

Mr. Hemlow seemed shrunken this morning, as though some of the stuffing had leaked out of the medicine ball. His eyes and brow were more troubled than hawklike today, and even the red beret perched atop him like a maraschino cherry didn't do much to improve the bad vibe he exuded.

"I phoned her when I received the envelope," he said, "and she explained she'd been fired, had been escorted from the offices by an armed guard, and had just barely time to mail me the envelope before the guard searched her belongings."

"Searched her belongings!" Eppick sounded equal parts astounded and outraged.

Mr. Hemlow's tempo-setting knee kept

double time to the slow sad shake of his head. "That is the corporate form of the farewell interview these days, it appears," he said. "Particularly if the employee has been caught breaking the rules, as Fiona had, and on *my* account. That's what I blame myself for, and no one else."

Dortmunder, who had kind of liked Fiona Hemlow, said, "What kinda rule did she break?"

"She sought out Livia Northwood Wheeler. She had no right to speak to Mrs. Wheeler, no justification for approaching her. A person in Fiona's position — in Fiona's former position — is not to speak until spoken to."

"That's terrible, Mr. Hemlow," Eppick said. He sounded sincerely upset by the news.

"It's my own selfishness caused this to happen," Mr. Hemlow said. "My egotism. Who *cares* about ancient grudges, ancient history? Who can correct a one-hundred-year-old wrong? Nobody. The guilty aren't there any more. The people who *are* there, whatever else they may have done, have never done *me* an injury. And now all I've done is harm my own granddaughter."

"We'll make up for that, Mr. Hemlow," Eppick said, all at once eager. "When we

234

get that —"

"No."

Dortmunder had seen this coming, but apparently Eppick had not. He blinked, and rocked back half a step toward the elevator door. "No? Mr. Hemlow, you don't —"

"I do." For a sagging sack of guts, Mr. Hemlow sounded pretty damn firm. "The chess set can stay where it is," he said. "It's done enough harm in this world, let it rot in that vault."

You bet, Dortmunder thought.

But Eppick was not a man to give up without a fight. "Sir, we've been working on —"

"I know you have, Johnny," Mr. Hemlow said, "and I appreciate it, but the job is over. Send my accountant your final bill, you'll be paid at once."

"Well . . ." Eppick said. "If you're sure."

"I am, Johnny. So thank you, and good-bye."

"Good-bye, sir."

Eppick turned to push the elevator button, but Dortmunder said, "Hey. What about me?"

"Mr. Dortmunder," Mr. Hemlow said, "you have not been in my employ. Johnny has."

"Don't look at me, John," Eppick said,

235

though that's exactly what Dortmunder was doing.

"Why not?"

"Because, John," Eppick said, as though explaining to a bonehead, "you didn't do anything."

Dortmunder couldn't believe it. "I didn't *do* anything? I drove all around New England, sitting on the *floor*. I wracked my brains, trying to figure out the way to get my hands on that chess thing. I done more taxi time than an escort service. I been working my *brain* on this."

"That's between you gentlemen," Mr. Hemlow said. "Good morning." And now he did spin the wheelchair around and sped off, this time through a doorway into a side hall.

Pushing the elevator button at last, Eppick said, "Well, John, I just think you have to count this one up to profit and loss."

Dortmunder didn't say anything. The elevator arrived, they rode down together, and he still didn't say anything. No expression at all appeared on his face.

Out on the sidewalk, Eppick said, "You don't want to make trouble, John. I've still got those pictures."

"I know it," Dortmunder said.

"The least I can do," Eppick said, "I'll

spring for a cab for us, downtown."

"No, thanks," Dortmunder said. He needed to be alone, to think. About revenge. "I'll walk," he said.

31

Like many members of the NYPD, past and present, Johnny Eppick had not lived within the actual five boroughs of New York City for many years; not, in fact, since his second year on the force, when he'd married and left his parents' home in Queens to set up his own new family — two boys and one girl, eventually, now all starting families of their own, none following him into the Job — farther out on Long Island.

Unlike some of his fellows, Eppick had never maintained a little apartment in the city, containing one or a string of surrogate wives, he being of the sort who was content with one family and one home, just so it was completely separate from the Job. The place on East Third Street was new, since his retirement, since he and Rosalie had come to the realization that, while they still loved one another and had no desire for change, it was also true that neither of them could stand his being around the house all the time. He was retired from the Job. Tough; go there anyway. Thus Johnny Eppick For Hire.

He wasn't the first ex-cop to go into private detectiving. The city pension was good, but there isn't a pension anywhere that couldn't use a little supplement, though that wasn't the primary reason so many ex-cops wound up with security companies or armored car outfits or banks. The primary reason was boredom; after the tensions and horrors and pleasures of the Job, it was tough to sit around all day with the remote in one hand and a beer can in the other. Leave that life to the young slobs who hadn't come out of their cocoons yet.

In the earliest days of his retirement years, Eppick had thought about hiring on somewhere, but a life on wages after so many years on the Job had just seemed too much of a comedown. It was time to be his own boss for a while, see how that would play out. So he got his private investigator's license, not hard for an ex-cop, and set up the office down on East Third because it was inexpensive and he didn't feel he was going to have to impress anybody. All he needed was files and a phone. Besides, private eyes were expected to office in grungy neighborhoods.

Once he had his tag and his address, Eppick had caused there to be made letterhead stationery and a business card. He'd spread the word through the cops and the lawyers and the other people he'd met over the years through the Job, and the first fish in the net was Mr. Horace Hemlow.

And what a fish. A keeper, Eppick had thought, rich and honest and dedicated to his obsession. Putting every other potential client on hold, changing his answering machine message to deflect other possible business, he'd devoted himself to Mr. Hemlow, even researching that scuzzy band of crooks to handle the actual dirty work without any possibility of double-cross.

And look what he got for it. Time and expenses. He might as well deliver newspapers, for that kind of money; that would also keep him out of the house.

Okay. After the chess set debacle, Eppick changed his answering machine message once more, made another round of soliciting phone calls, and started to receive smaller but at least not irritating offers of work. Here a jealous wife, there a health freak searching, for genome reasons, for his natural father. It kept him on the move.

■ ■ ■ ■

On a blustery Monday two weeks after the farewell in Mr. Hemlow's apartment, the first Monday in December, Eppick drove to the city, left his Prius in its monthly parking spot in a garage a block from his office, walked the block, took the elevator to his office, entered, and saw in an instant he'd been robbed. Burgled. Cleaned out solid.

Just about everything was gone. Phone, fax, printer, computer, TV, DVD, toaster oven, even the less heavy half of his exercise equipment.

The whole thing had been done with an economy and a professionalism that, even through his outrage, he had to recognize and admire. There was barely a mark on the locks. His three alarm systems, including the one that should have phoned the precinct, had been dismantled or bypassed with casual, almost disdainful, assurance. Everything was gone, and not a footprint was left to mark its passing.

Eppick of course immediately phoned the precinct — on his cell phone, the office phone and answering machine being gone — though he hadn't the slightest expectation anybody would ever track down those

241

crooks. But he needed the report for his insurance, and this haul would certainly lead to a very hefty insurance company check.

And many headaches between now and then, while he replaced everything that had gone away, integrated the new systems, estimated just how much his personal and professional privacy had been violated, and worked out what additional security measures he would have to take to keep the bastards from coming back for a second dip.

The cops who came to make the report were unknown to him, he never having worked in this precinct. They were sympathetic and professional and just a little scornful, exactly as he would be if the roles were reversed. He hated the interview, and ground his teeth in rage once his responders had departed.

Now, the next thing to do was hide this disaster from his two current clients. It would never do for a professional private detective to himself become a crime victim; all credibility would be lost forever. Therefore, after a quick trip farther downtown to an area of electronics stores, he came back with a new telephone–answering machine, which he set up on his ravaged desk and into which, using a much more grating voice than normal, he placed this message:

"Hi. Johnny Eppick here. I came down with something over the weekend I hope isn't flu, so I'm not in the shop today. Leave a message and I hope I'll be here and healthy first thing tomorrow."

The rest of the replacement equipment he'd buy out on the Island, to avoid New York City's sales tax, so he might as well get to it. There was no point hanging around the ransacked office all day.

It was while driving out the LIE, just east of the city line, that the penny finally dropped and one word came into his mind, as though in neon: Dortmunder.

Of course. In the first shock, he hadn't been thinking straight, hadn't connected the dots, but what else could this be? Dortmunder. He had to get even for not scoring anything out of the chess set caper. And, whining all the time about something as minor league as taxi fares, that gave you the measure of the man.

The son of a bitch had waited exactly two weeks, Monday to Monday, just long enough so Eppick wouldn't be able to prove it but he'd have to know it.

And there was more to it than that. All of the other things that were taken were just smoke screen, just icing on the cake. The only theft that really mattered was the computer. That little box where the incriminating pictures of John Dortmunder were stored.

Yes, and when he got back to the office tomorrow and looked in his files — a thing that hadn't occurred to him until just this minute — the copies of those pictures that he'd printed out would also be gone.

I no longer have a handle on John Dortmunder's back, Eppick thought. Dortmunder had needed that handle off of there. Why? Because he's up to something. What is he up to?

Eppick frowned mightily as he drove east toward home.

32

"They're *never* coming back!"

"Nessa," Brady said, over their lunch of nuked frozen fish fingers, nuked frozen french fries, and canned beer, "of course they're coming back. They came all the way up here just to be sure everything was all right."

"Then when they left here," Nessa said, leaning belligerently over her fish fingers in this large elaborate dining room constructed for more diners but less volume, "they must have made sure everything was wrong, because they *aren't coming back!*"

"Come on, Nessa, you don't have to holler, I'm right here in front of you."

"Yet somehow you don't hear me," she said. "Those bozos are not coming back."

Surprised, almost offended on their behalf, he said, "What do you mean, bozos? Those were very serious people."

"Hah."

"They were up here to discuss hiding a very valuable chess set," Brady reminded her. "And *here* was where they meant to hide it. They even pointed out the table in the living room."

"Where they were going to hide it."

"Yes."

"Right out on a table in the living room."

"I told you, Nessa, it was the something letter. You remember Edgar Allan Poe."

"We read *The Raven*," she said, being sulky. "It was very boring."

"Well, he did something else," Brady said, "that said, if you want to hide something, put it right out in plain sight where nobody expects to see it."

"Put it right out in plain sight," Nessa said, "where *I* won't expect to see it, and guess what happens next."

"Well, Edgar Allan Poe is what they were doing," Brady said, "and they're definitely coming back."

"Brady," she said, around a mouthful of fish fingers, as she waved a melodramatic arm toward the far windows, "it's *snowing*."

"I know that."

"Again."

"I know that."

"We're in the mountains in New England in December. Brady, on the TV they're talking about accumulations. You know what accumulations are?"

"Listen, Nessa —"

"You wanna wait here till *spring? Here?*"

The fact was, Brady wouldn't mind if he had to wait here forever. He had this huge house all to himself, he had no responsibilities, he had this really cute girl to go to bed with all the time — though not so much lately, unfortunately — and he had the prospect of this amazingly valuable chess set at the end of the rainbow. So what was the problem?

Well, he'd better not put it that way, because, the truth is, the problem was Nessa. She had some kind of cabin fever or something. She got bored too easily, that's what it came down to. He screwed her as much as he could, or these days as much as she'd put up with, but still she got bored.

He just had to keep his calm, that's all. This was just a phase Nessa was going through, and soon she'd be fine again. Maybe in the spring, when the flowers started to grow, though he sensed it wouldn't be a really smart move to phrase it quite that way.

"Honey," he said, "I heard those guys talk, and I know they meant it, and I know they're coming back, and I know they're serious."

"They're bozos," she said, and filled her mouth with french fries.

He paused, a fish finger in midair. "Why do you keep saying that?"

"They pranced through here," she reminded him, "the four of them, looking all over for just the right place to hide their precious chess set, and they never even saw *us.*"

"Well, neither do those maintenance guys. We're too smart for them, that's all. Just last week the maintenance guys came through and we've been here for *months* now and they *still* don't know we're here."

These were two guys who drove up the first Friday of every month to check the house, flush the toilets, check the smoke alarms, that kind of thing. They were easy to evade, and so Brady and Nessa evaded them.

The very point she now made. "We know they're coming," she said. "They're not searching the place, they're just doing their rounds. Those other bozos suddenly showed up when we didn't know they were coming, they went all through the house with us underfoot —"

"They never went upstairs."

"They went all over downstairs, Brady,

and they never even got a *glimpse* of us, and you say they're *serious?*"

"They'll be back," he insisted.

"Not this winter," she insisted right back. "And I don't want to still be here next spring."

"Where *do* you want to be?"

She looked at him. It was a disquieting look, and it went on quite a long while, during which she consumed most of the rest of the greasy food on her plate. He instinctively felt he shouldn't speak during this examination, shouldn't do anything but let her work out her own thought processes inside her own head. He had no idea why she was so discontented with their paradise — she hadn't been at first — but if he just kept very quiet and very attentive, maybe this whole thing would blow over and they'd get back to the way things used to be. Having fun. Not worrying about anything. Not nagging people all the time.

She licked grease from her fingers. They never could remember napkins, so she rubbed her fingers down the leg of her jeans. She said, "I want to go home."

"What?"

"Not right away," she said.

"Wha, wha, we, you, I —"

"But I want to *see* something first, *be*

somewhere, have things going *on* around me."

"We, we —"

"I think," she said, "I'd like to go south first, maybe down to Florida. Then we can circle back and head for home."

"Nebraska? Nessa? Numbnuts, Nebraska?"

"I miss all the kids," Nessa said.

"No, you don't," Brady told her. "*Those* were the bozos. You don't miss those morons any more than I do."

"I miss *some*thing," she insisted. "But anyway, we've got to leave here. I will not be snowed in on this mountain, so we just have to go, that's all."

Being reasonable, he said, "How? We don't have any money."

"We'll steal things from here," she said. "Things we can sell to pawnshops. Things like mantel clocks and, and toaster ovens. We'll leave here while we can still get out to the main road, and drive south until we get warm, and then maybe in the spring we'll drive by home again and just *look* at it, just see what it looks like after we've been away."

"In the world, you mean."

She looked around the big empty dining room. "This isn't the world, Brady," she said.

In the spring, he thought, I'll come back here, the chess set will be on the table where they said, and *I'll* see it because I know the secret. So for now, let's just keep Nessa happy.

"Okay," he said. "We'll drive south. We'll drive to Florida. We can start tomorrow morning."

"Good." Nessa looked comfortably around at the table. "So at least," she said, "we won't have to wash *these* plates."

It was beside the pool at a motel in Jacksonville, Florida, that they got into conversation with the advance man for an alternative rock band on tour that would be playing in town that weekend. "Come by the room after lunch, I'll give you a couple ducats," he said, and they thanked him, and he grinned and walked off, hairy shoulders, pool water glistening in his beard and ponytail.

A little later Nessa was ready to leave the pool, but Brady was enjoying himself, mostly looking at college girls on spring break, so he said, "I'll just stick around here a little longer." If he wasn't getting as much as he used to from Nessa, at least he could look at these girls, maybe sneak off with one at some point.

But nothing happened, as he'd more or less realized it wouldn't, so an hour later he went back to the room and Nessa wasn't there. Neither was her little suitcase, nor the cash from his wallet.

Brady never saw Nessa again. Without her, he made his circuitous way back home to Numbnuts, was forgiven, got a job in Starbucks, and was a good boy the rest of his life. There came a time when he never even thought about Nessa any more, but still, every once in a while, he did wonder: Whatever happened to that chess set?

■ ■ ■ ■

PART TWO:
PAWN'S REVENGE

■ ■ ■ ■

33

Fiona had a window. She had a window just to the right of her reproduction Empire desk here on the upper floor of Livia Northwood Wheeler's duplex apartment on Fifth Avenue in the Seventies, and she never tired of looking out her window at the sweep of Central Park down below, not even when it was snowing, which it was doing right now. Not a heavy snow like those of January and February, turning the world white and thick and hard to move around in, this was a tentative March snow, the snow of a season that knows its end is near, a mere dusting of white to freshen the mounds of old snow gathered beneath the trees and against the low stone wall that separated the park from Fifth Avenue.

Fiona's job as Livia Northwood Wheeler's personal assistant was interesting in its diversity, but it did leave time for gazing out the window at the park, imagining what the view would be when they came to spring and then to summer. When she wasn't park-gazing, though, there was enough to keep her busy in Mrs. Wheeler's affairs, which were many and varied and mostly uncoordinated.

Mrs. W (as she preferred to be called by the staff) was, for instance, on the boards of many of the city's organizations, as well as a director of a mind-boggling array of corporations. Beyond that, she was a tireless litigant, involved in many more lawsuits than merely those involving her immediate family. Solo, or as a very active member of a class, she was at the moment suing automobile manufacturers, aspirin makers, television networks, department stores, airlines, law firms that had previously represented her, and an array of ex-employees, including two former personal assistants.

While passionately involved in every one of these matters, Mrs. W was not at all coordinated or methodical and never knew exactly where she was in any ongoing concern, whom she owed, who owed her, and where and when the meeting was supposed to take place. She really needed a personal assistant.

And Fiona was perfect for the job. She

was calm, she had no ax to grind, and she had a natural love for detail. Particularly for all the more reprehensible details of Mrs. W's busy life, the double-dealing and chicanery, the stories behind all the lawsuits and all the feuds and all the shifting loyalties among Mrs. W's many rich-lady friends. And, just to make Fiona's life complete, Mrs. W was writing an autobiography!

Talk about history in the raw. Mrs. W had total recall of every slight she'd ever suffered, every snub, every shortchanging, every encounter in which the other party had turned out to be even more grasping, shrewder, and more untrustworthy than she was. She dictated all these steaming memories into a tape recorder in spurts of venom, which Lucy Leebald, Mrs. W's current secretary, had to type out into neat manuscript.

Fiona's role in all this was to read the finished sections of manuscript and establish the chronology of events, since Mrs. W recalled things in no sequence at all and didn't personally care a rap when this or that event had occurred. To put her story in chronological order purely on the basis of internal evidence was, of course, impossible, but it was just exactly the kind of impossibility a history nut goes nuts for.

Fiona, still astonished by the fact three months later, was in heaven. The day she'd been fired by Mr. Tumbril at Feinberg had been a frightening one, somehow liberating but mostly perilous, with no solid future in sight. She'd had to tell Brian, of course (he'd responded with black pudding for dinner), but she told no one else, not even her grandfather, until the following week, when he called her because he'd received that set of names of Northwood heirs she'd mailed on her way out the Feinberg door. Then she'd had to confess, weeping a bit, and he was so repentant, so appalled, so positive it was all his fault, that she was forced to cheer up just so *he* would feel a little better.

He was also responsible for her being here, in this job. It's true Mrs. W had said, at the end of that awful experience, "Call me," but Fiona had had no intention of doing any such thing until Grandfather, hearing her story, insisted she make the call: "Always follow up, Fiona, it's a rule of the world."

So she'd followed up, to find that the invitation to call had been an act of contrition by a woman not at all used to being contrite. She hadn't thought twice about heaving the lackey Fiona Hemlow at the

head of Jay Tumbril, only to discover —
mirabile dictu! — the girl was innocent! And
a victim! Mrs. W's victim as much as Jay
Tumbril's, in fact.

So here she was, and if Mr. Tumbril knew
who answered Mrs. W's office phone these
days, those few times he'd left messages
here, he gave no sign. Nor, of course, did
she.

Tink-tink.

Not the office phone. There were three
phones on Fiona's desk, each with its own
ring — *blip-blip* for the outside line, *bzzzork*
for the in-house line, and *tink-tink* for Mrs.
W's private line from her desk in her own
office across the hall. So: "Good morning,
Mrs. W. It's still snowing."

"Thank you, my dear, I have the Weather
Channel for that. Come in and bring your
pad."

"Yes, ma'am."

Fiona left the office she shared with Lucy
Leebald, crossed the hall with its elevator at
the far end and window at this end with its
identical park view to her own, and into
Mrs. W's office, in which the same windows
somehow offered more light, more air and
more park, and where Mrs. W herself sat at
her more ornate desk and nodded at Fiona
like the queen bee she was. "Good morn-

ing, dear."

"Good morning, Mrs. W."

"Close the door, dear, and sit on the sofa here. You have your pad; good."

The little settee next to Mrs. W's desk was far less comfortable than it looked. Fiona perched on it and looked expectant.

Mrs. W seemed more ruminative than usual this morning. Frowning a little, she watched her hands move small figurines around on her desk as she said, "As I remember, in addition to your law degree, you have a strong interest in the study of history."

"Your memoir is fascinating, Mrs. W."

"Of course it is. But it's a different history I want you to think about now."

"Yes, ma'am?"

"Do you remember a discussion we had — two discussions, I think — about the Chicago chess set?"

Oh, dear. Fiona had been afraid to even mention the chess set, but wanting to help her grandfather in his quest — even if at the moment he believed he'd given it up — she had given it a try. She'd even — when they were looking together at the photos of the pieces on Mrs. W's computer — managed to "discover" the mismatch in weight among the rooks.

But that had been some time ago. She'd given the effort up when she'd seen she was getting nowhere and might even be putting herself at risk. But now Mrs. W herself had raised the issue; for good, or for ill? Heart in her mouth but expression as innocent as ever, Fiona said, "Oh, yes, ma'am. That beautiful chess set."

"You noticed one of the pieces was the wrong weight."

"Oh, I remember that."

"Very observant of you," Mrs. W said, and nodded, agreeing with herself. "That fact kept bothering me, after our discussions, and I soon realized there was far more mystery surrounding that chess set than merely one unexpectedly lighter rook."

Looking alert, interested, Fiona said, "Oh, really?"

"Where is that chess set from?" Mrs. W demanded, glaring severely at Fiona. "Who made it? Where? In what century? It just abruptly appears, with no history, in a sealed glass case in the lobby of my father's company, Gold Castle Realty, when they moved into the Castlewood Building in 1948. Where was it before 1948? Where did my father get it, and when? And now that we know the one piece is lighter than the rest, and is a castle, now we wonder, where did my father get his company name?"

"Gold Castle, you mean."

"Exactly."

Knowing how she could answer every last one of Mrs. W's questions, but how doing so would be absolutely the worst move she could make, Fiona said, "Well, I guess he had to have it somewhere else before he put up the new building."

"But where?" Mrs. W demanded. "And how long had he had it? And who had it before him?" Mrs. W shook her head. "You see, Fiona, the more you study that chess set, the deeper the mystery becomes."

"Yes, ma'am."

"History and mystery," Mrs. W mused. "The words belong together. Fiona, I want you to ferret out the history *and* the mystery of the Chicago chess set."

I am being given, Fiona thought, the one job in all the world at which I have to fail. *I'm* the mystery, Mrs. W, she thought, I'm the mystery and the history, my family and I, and you must never know.

Mrs. W was going on, saying, "I don't mean I want you to devote your life to that, but for at least a little time every day you should work on this problem. What is that chess set, and where did it come from?"

"Yes, ma'am." With the sudden thought

that there might be something useful here, after all, useful to her grandfather and to Mr. Eppick and to Mr. Dortmunder, she said, "Do you think I should go look at the chess set?"

Mrs. W didn't like that idea at all. "What, physically stare at the thing? We know what it looks like, Fiona."

"Yes, of course," Fiona said.

"If it had a label on the bottom reading 'Made In China,' someone would have noticed it before this."

"Yes, ma'am."

"If it ever turns out there *is* a need for a physical examination, I'm sure we could arrange it. But for now, Fiona, the question you are to concern yourself with is provenance. What is that chess set's history? What is its mystery?"

"I'll look into it, Mrs. W," Fiona promised.

34

A blustery Sunday in March, and Dortmunder and Kelp trudged back across the snowy
warehouse roof, following their own reversed footsteps toward the distant fire
escape. They were dressed in black parkas
with the hoods up, black wool trousers,
black leather gloves and black boots, and
the wind snaked through it all anyway. The
plastic backpacks they wore, also black,
were just as empty as when they'd come up
onto this roof, and they were going to stay
that way, at least for today.

It was Kelp who'd lined up the customer
for the video games said to be stacked like
candy bars in the warehouse below, and it
was this customer who'd told them everything they needed to know to effect entry to
the place from above. Everything, that is,
except the existence of the two pit bulls
down there, gleaming like devils in the
safety light.

At first, Kelp had suggested they might be a hologram: "It's a video game place, why not?"

"Go down and pet one," Dortmunder suggested, so that was that. While the pit bulls stared upward, yearning to be best friends but unable to climb the steel rungs mounted on the wall, Dortmunder and Kelp quietly closed the trapdoor they'd opened and turned back, empty-handed. Days like this one could be discouraging.

All at once the opening chords of Beethoven's Ninth burst across the windy air. Dortmunder dropped to the snowy roof, staring around in panic for the orchestra, and then realized Kelp was fumbling in his trouser pocket and murmuring, "Sorry, sorry."

"Sorry?"

"It's my new ringtone," Kelp explained while, without a pause, the invisible orchestra leaped back to the beginning and started all over again.

"Ringtone."

"I usually," Kelp said, finally managing to drag the cell phone out of his pocket, "keep it on vibrate."

"I don't want to know about it," Dortmunder said.

Kelp made the racket go away, put the

machine to his head, and said, "Hello?"

Dortmunder turned away, brushing himself free of dirty snow and reorienting himself vis-à-vis the fire escape, when Kelp said, "Yeah, hold on, wait a minute," then extended the phone toward Dortmunder with a very strange expression on his face: "It's for you."

Dortmunder didn't believe it. "For me? Whadaya mean? People don't go around calling me on *roofs!*"

"He doesn't know where you are," Kelp said. "It's Eppick. Come on, it's for you."

Eppick. Dortmunder hadn't thought of that guy in three months, and had been perfectly prepared to never think of him again, but here was this phone, on this roof, with snowy wind all around, and he was supposed to talk to Johnny Eppick For Hire.

So all right. He took the phone: "Yar?"

"You don't have a cell."

"No thanks to you."

"That's pretty cute," Eppick said. "You weren't at home, you don't have an answering machine either, you might not even have indoor plumbing for all I know. I was gonna leave a message with your friend, call me, but here you are."

"I have indoor plumbing."

"Glad to hear it. Mr. Hemlow is back."

266

"No. I don't want him back."

"But this is good news," Eppick said. "The granddaughter has maybe come through after all. I don't know the details yet. Mr. Hemlow wants to lay it on the two of us."

Dortmunder was about to say no, he hadn't found much profit in his dealings with the firm of Hemlow & Eppick, and besides, Eppick no longer possessed those overly candid photos, but then he thought about the pit bulls to whom he'd so recently been introduced, and his other current prospects, which added up to a round nil, and he thought there might be worse roads to travel than the one that led back to Mr. Hemlow, with whom, at least, with luck, he would not be bit.

But there had to be conditions. "No more taxis."

"I understand, John," Eppick said. "I tell you what. Tell me where you are now, I'll come pick you up."

Dortmunder shook his head. Some days, you just can't win. "I'll take a cab," he said.

Dortmunder stepped into the Riverside Drive lobby as Eppick rose from the rhinoceros-horn chair and dropped somebody's *New York Post* on the seat. The green-uniformed doorman welcomed Dortmunder like an old stranger: "The other gentleman —"

"I remember him."

Eppick stepped forward, serious-faced, arm out as though to shake hands, about which Dortmunder was very ambivalent, but then fortunately he only wanted to grasp Dortmunder's elbow and say, "A word, John, before we go upstairs."

"Sure."

They strolled to a rear corner of the lobby among the oriental rugs on both floor and walls, and Eppick said, "As far as I'm concerned, you know, bygones are bygones."

"That's nice," Dortmunder said.

"Fortunately," Eppick said, "my insurance covered almost everything."

"That's nice."

"And it was a good learning experience, to know where I had to beef up security."

"That's nice."

Eppick peered closely into Dortmunder's face, still holding, though not tightly, Dortmunder's left elbow. "You know what I'm talking about."

"No."

"That's fine, then," Eppick said, and released his elbow to give him a friendly, if perhaps slightly hostile, whack. "Let's go up and have Mr. Hemlow give us the good news."

There was a new extraneous green-uniformed operator hovering over the controls in the elevator. Dortmunder nodded at him. "Harya."

"Sir."

"The other guy go on to pilot's school?"

"I wouldn't know, sir. I'm new here."

"You'll get the hang of it," Dortmunder assured him.

The doorman leaned his head in to tell the newbie, "The penthouse."

"Yes, sir."

So, to the penthouse they went, and there in his wheelchair was Mr. Hemlow, about whom the best you could say was that he probably didn't look any worse. Or not much worse.

"Welcome to you both," Mr. Hemlow said, nodding that head that looked as though it might roll off the medicine ball at any minute. Below, the busy leg tangoed.

"Nice to see you, Mr. Hemlow," Eppick said, and Dortmunder contented himself with a nod, deciding to let Eppick have spoken for both of them.

"Well, come along."

Apparently, everybody was friends again, because the speeding wheelchair led them back to the view and the two chairs side by side. Once they were there, Mr. Hemlow said, "May I offer you two something to drink?"

This was something new, a level of sociability heretofore unknown. Dortmunder might have tried his luck on a bourbon request, but Eppick said, "Oh, we're fine, Mr. Hemlow. So things worked out well for Fiona, did they?"

"Very well indeed." That head might be beaming, in grandfatherly pride. "It seems that Mrs. Livia Northwood Wheeler," he said, "the person Fiona improperly approached, blamed herself for Fiona's being fired, sought her out to be sure she'd be all right, and, in a word, hired her as a personal assistant."

"No kidding!" Eppick loved it.

Mr. Hemlow chuckled, or something. "At an actual increase in pay," he said. "Not much, but some."

"That's great, Mr. Hemlow."

"But that's only the beginning," Mr. Hemlow told him. "Although I'd assured Fiona, and it was the truth, that I had no further interest in the stolen chess set, she now felt she might be in a position to help us all lay our hands on it."

"That would be something," Eppick said.

"Yes, it would. Not wanting to risk her reputation even further, Fiona operated very slowly and carefully, gradually inculcating in Mrs. Wheeler's mind the idea that there just might be something not entirely on the up-and-up about that chess set."

Interested, Eppick said, "How'd she work that, Mr. Hemlow?"

"There was the difference in weight between the rooks," Mr. Hemlow said. "Also, the lack of provenance from before its appearance in Alfred Northwood's possession. Northwood had no family, no money, no discernible background, all matters of supreme significance to a woman like Mrs. Wheeler. Where had this supposedly so valuable object come from?"

Admiring, Eppick said, "Fiona got that point across, did she?"

"She was aided, I have no doubt," Mr. Hemlow said, "by Mrs. Wheeler's natural paranoia. But yes, she did become convinced there was something dubious, shall we say, about that chess set, and now she's given Fiona the task of establishing the set's bona fides."

Eppick gave a single bark of a laugh. "Those bona fides are gonna be tough to come by," he said.

"I don't doubt," Mr. Hemlow said, "that

a diligent researcher could trace the set back to Sgt. Northwood's arrival in this city in 1921 on the train from Chicago. He wouldn't have announced the set's existence at that time, wouldn't have brought it out at all into public view until twenty-seven years later, when he felt secure enough, respectable enough —"

"Rich enough," Eppick suggested.

"That, too." Mr. Hemlow tremored a nod. "*Solid* enough, let us say, that he dared to put the set on display in the lobby of his real estate offices. Announcing without ever quite saying so that *this* elaborate toy of kings was the source of the Northwood fortune."

Eppick said, "What about before . . . when was it? 1921? When he brought the set on the train from Chicago?"

"Yes, 1921." Various parts of Mr. Hemlow, squeezed as they were into the wheelchair, tremored and tangoed and fidgeted and possibly even shrugged. "Before that date," he said, "there is no trace. We three in this room know the actual *owner* a little prior to that time would have been Czar Nicholas II, but even there the property rights are clouded, since apparently Nicholas never actually received the gift. Nor can we ever know the gift-giver's identity or ultimate intention."

"Good for us," Eppick said.

"Possibly." Mr. Hemlow nodded and said, "We can only assume the chess set reached Murmansk sometime in 1917, just as the First World War and the Russian Revolution were both breaking out. The set could move no further, since all the land between Murmansk and St. Petersburg was being fought over, and all trace of it, all paperwork connected to it, even the identity of the sender, all were lost in the double turmoils of war and uprising. By 1918, Nicholas and his entire family had been slaughtered by the Bolsheviks, leaving the question of ownership, if it would ever even arise, further and further in doubt. Surely the Bolsheviks could not be thought to have inherited."

"Not from their own crime," Eppick said.

"Exactly. By 1920, when the American platoon stumbled across the set in a pier-side warehouse in Murmansk, who was the rightful owner? If ever there were such a thing as legitimate spoils of war, that chess set is it. So I suppose it would be permissible to say, if there *are* any potential claimants to ownership of the set, they are the descendants of the ten men in that platoon, including of course myself and my granddaughter."

Dortmunder said, "And the Livia North-wood Whatever. Her."

"Yes, of course," Mr. Hemlow said. "Not all of Mrs. Wheeler's worth is ill-gotten, only ninety percent of it."

Eppick barked that laugh again. "We'll leave them a couple pawns," he said.

"Amusing," Mr. Hemlow said, "but I think not."

Dortmunder said, "How's your grand-daughter gonna try to find out where that thing come from if she already knows where it come from but can't tell anybody?"

"Well, you see," Mr. Hemlow said, perk-ing up as though Dortmunder had just put his finger on a very positive and a very strategic point, "that's the beauty of it, John. Since she knows the answer, she knows what to avoid. She knows to provide Lydia North-wood Wheeler with clues and evidence that lead firmly in some opposite direction."

Dortmunder said, "Which opposite direc-tion?"

"Whichever direction," Mr. Hemlow said, "will lead Mrs. Wheeler to demand the chess set be taken *out* of that vault —"

"Now you're talkin," Dortmunder said.

"— and examined by experts."

Eppick said, "Mr. Hemlow, this is great news."

"Yes, it is." Was that a smile of satisfaction down there in the blubber somewhere? "I wanted you both to know this situation is brewing," he went on, "because I will want you both available when the time comes. But let me remind you of the ground rules."

"Keep away from your granddaughter," Eppick said.

"Exactly so. She survived the previous danger, but I don't want it to happen again."

"Fine by us," Dortmunder said.

"At this point," Mr. Hemlow said, "Fiona is on her own, attempting to steer events. Whatever news may develop, she will communicate it to me, I will communicate it to you, Johnny, and you will communicate it to John."

"Absolutely, sir," Eppick said.

A beady eye from out of the folds focused on Dortmunder. "Is that clear to you as well, John?"

"I don't need to chitchat with grand-daughters," Dortmunder told him. "When that thing comes up outa that vault, just tell me where it is. That's all I need."

"We're all business," Eppick assured Mr. Hemlow, "all the time. Aren't we, John?"

"You bet," Dortmunder said. He was wondering about suggesting he be put on Mr. Hemlow's payroll this time, next to

Eppick, but decided not to waste his breath. He knew what the answer was.

"Well, gentlemen," Mr. Hemlow said, and down inside there he might have been smiling. "It would seem, once again, the game's afoot."

35

Jacques Perly was the only private detective Jay Tumbril knew, or was likely to know. A specialist in the recovery of stolen art, frequently the go-between with the thieves on the one side and the owner/museum/insurer on the other, Perly was a cultured and knowledgeable man, far from the grubby trappings associated with the term "private eye."

Tumbril had known Perly slightly for years, since the Feinberg firm had more than once been peripherally involved in the recovery of valuable art stolen from its clients, and now, although Fiona Hemlow could not fairly be described as either "stolen" or "art," Jacques Perly was the man Jay Tumbril thought to turn to when there were Questions to be Asked.

They met at one that Monday afternoon for lunch at the Tre Mafiosi on Park Avenue, a smooth, hushed culinary temple all in white and green and gold, with, this time of year, pink flowers. Perly had arrived first, as he was supposed to, and he rose with a smile and an outstretched hand when Tony the maître d' escorted Jay to the table. A round, stuffed Cornish game hen of a man, Jacques Perly retained a slight hint of his original Parisian accent. A onetime art student, a failed artist, he viewed the world with a benign pessimism, the mournful good humor of a rich unmarried uncle, who expects nothing and accepts everything.

"Nice to see you, Jacques," Jay said, releasing Perly's hand, as Tony seated him and Angelo distributed menus and Kwa Hong Yo brought rolls, butter, and water. "It's been a while."

"Yes, it has. You've been fine?"

"And you?"

Menus were consulted, food and wine were ordered, and then Jay leaned forward over the display plate, made a steeple of his hands over the plate, and leaned back as Kwa Hong Yo removed the plates. He then leaned forward again, made another steeple, rested chin on steeple like golf ball on tee, and said, "In complete confidence."

"Of course."

"Let's see. How do I begin?"

Perly knew better than to offer advice on

that score, so after a minute Jay said, "A client of ours, a valued client of some years standing, is a very wealthy woman."

"Of course."

"She was introduced, not by me, to a young woman, a young attorney with the firm." Jay picked up a roll and watched himself turn it over and over, as though searching for a secret door. "The young woman had gone outside the normal channels to force a meeting with this client," he told the roll. "That was against the firm's rules." With a quick glance at Perly, he said, "It would be against most firms' rules."

"I can see the security implications," Perly agreed.

Jay dropped the roll onto its bread plate, a little disappointed in it. "Unfortunately," he said, "I was a bit impetuous. In fact, I fired the young woman in the client's presence."

"Who took the young woman's part," Perly suggested.

"Worse," Jay said. "She hired the young woman as her personal assistant."

"Oh, dear."

"Exactly."

Perly considered. "The softer sex," he suggested.

"Possibly," Jay said. "The more willful sex, in any event."

"Speaking of sex," Perly said, now studying his own roll, "is there any chance . . . ?"

"What? No, no! That's not the issue at all!"

Fortunately, the soup arrived at that moment, and when they continued the conversation it was from a slightly different angle. "This young woman," Jay said. "Her manner of forcing herself on the client made me suspicious. What was her motive?"

"To be hired by the client?"

"I don't think so, not at first." Jay shook his head. "I doubt she could have guessed that turn of events in a million years."

"Then what *did* she have in mind?"

"That's the question," Jay said, fixing Perly with a meaningful stare. "That's the question in a nutshell."

"The question that brings us to this lunch."

"Exactly. What is the young woman's ulterior motive? What, if any, risk is there to my client?"

"Yes, of course. And how long ago did this happen?"

"I fired the young woman in December."

"Ah. In time for Christmas."

"That was not ad rem."

"No, of course not." Perly smiled, man to man. "A pleasantry," he said.

"It happened to be when I learned the facts," Jay said, feeling faintly defensive but firmly strangling the feeling in its crib. "As I say, I acted impetuously."

"And what has happened in the three months since?"

"She — the young woman — is ensconced in my client's apartment — not living there, working there, living somewhere else — and every time I phone my client only to hear that young woman's voice and have to leave a confidential message for my client with *her,* it gives me a twinge, a sense of foreboding."

"Yes."

"Finally," Jay explained, "it seemed to me I had to *act* on my instincts, if only to assure myself there was no real . . . problem here."

Perly nodded. Surreptitiously he looked around for the arrival of the entrée while saying, "Just the level of attention and concern I'd expect from you, Jay. But you have no *specific* fears or doubts in connection with this young woman."

"I know nothing about her," Jay complained. "She filled out the usual applications and took the usual tests. I've brought copies of all that for you."

"Good."

"She has a decent education, comes so far as I know from a decent family, has no previous link that I can find with my client at all. But it was *that* client and no other that the young woman went after."

"Wherever there's an action, there is always a motive," Perly said. "What is her motive? That is what you want me to find out."

"Yes."

Perly nodded. "How will I be billing this?"

"To me, at the firm," Jay said. "I'll pass it on to the client's account."

"We are acting on her behalf, after all," Perly agreed. "Even if I don't come up with anything . . . reprehensible."

"Whatever you come up with," Jay told him, "if it at least answers my question about her reasons, I'll be content. And so will the client."

"Naturally."

From within his sleek dark jacket, Perly withdrew a slender black notebook that contained within a strap its own gold pen. Drawing this pen, he said, "I'll need names and addresses and some little details concerning these two ladies."

"Of course."

Seeing Jay hesitate, Perly leaned forward into his arriving main course, smiled, and said, "Confidentiality, Jay. It's considered my greatest virtue."

36

What Brian missed most was the evenings alone. It had been fun, in those days, to come back to the apartment from the cable station before six, futz around with his music, browse in his cookbooks, prepare tonight's dinner in a slow and leisurely fashion, and know that, probably after ten o'clock, he'd get that call: "I'm on my way." He'd turn up the heat under the pots or in the oven, bring out tonight's wine and a couple of glasses and be ready when she walked in the front door.

Being fired from Feinberg had been bad for Fiona but ultimately it had been worse for Brian, because she was over it by now but he was never going to be. He'd never have those evenings to himself, ever again. Or the sense of freedom they had given him, in more ways than one.

As he well knew, it was the irregularity of her days that had made the regularity of his own easier to stand. What had attracted him to both cartooning and cooking in the first place was that both were art, not science. He could cook but he couldn't bake, because baking was chemistry; get one little thing wrong and you've ruined it. The same with cartooning; he couldn't do an exact face or even an exact building, but he could give you the *feel* of it, and that's what made it art.

What he liked about art was that there were no rules. He liked living with no rules. The regularity of his mornings and evenings struck him as too uncomfortably close to living within the rules, so he'd been lifted by Fiona's goofy hours; they'd freed him from the temporal rules by osmosis. But he would of course never tell her that her being fired had taken that pleasure out of his life.

Besides, he was happy for her. She had a better job now, which meant not just more money and better hours but more entertaining things for her to talk about over dinner, Mrs. Wheeler being an endlessly diverting character. He wished sometimes he could figure out a way to turn her into a cartoon and sell it to the station, or maybe some other channel further up the animation food chain. He was creative in some ways, but not in that way, and he regretted it.

Now that they had these longer evenings together, another question was what to do to fill the time between getting home and actually sitting down to dinner, which couldn't possibly happen until two or three hours later. Much of the time was spent with Fiona detailing Mrs. W's latest follies while he worked on dinner, and the rest of the time they'd been filling in with games: Scrabble, backgammon, cribbage.

But the main topic of their evenings was Livia Northwood Wheeler, who was so rich the thought of it made Brian's teeth hurt. She was also apparently as ditzy and over-the-top as any cartoon character you could think of. Brian wanted to meet her. He wanted to laugh, discreetly, at her antics, and he wanted from time to time to find some of her money in his pockets. If he could arrange the meeting, he was sure he could arrange the rest. If only he could arrange the meeting.

Evening after evening, while shifting tiles or moving pegs or arranging tiles into words, he'd drop little hints that he'd like to meet the fabulous Mrs. W. Why not invite her to dinner? "I'm not that bad a cook."

"You're a wonderful cook, as you very well know. 'Quixotic' is a word, isn't it? But we couldn't ask her *here,* Brian."

"Why not? Maybe she'd enjoy slumming."

"Mrs. W? I really doubt that."

If it were summer, or the weather were at least decent, he could suggest a picnic, in Riverside Park, or even on the roof of this building, which had some pretty good views and which some of the tenants did occasionally use for picnics and small parties, though Frisbee had been banned after a couple of unfortunate incidents.

But now, at last, this Monday in March, he had his opportunity, or he thought he did. All day at the station the preparations had been under way, and that's where he got the idea, and could hardly wait to get home, and for Fiona to get home, so he could try it on her. Maybe this time it would happen. But he should be cool about it, not just burst out with the idea, or she'd likely be turned off.

So this evening, though they were both home before six, and moving cribbage pegs inexorably onward by half past, he waited until that game was finished — she won — to even broach the subject. "Guess what's happening this weekend," he said.

She gave him a funny look. Nothing happened on the weekend in March, as all the world knew. Unless St. Patrick's Day came on any day remotely close to the weekend, being any day except Wednesday, as everyone also knew, and as at the moment was not the case. So, "Happening?" she inquired.

"It's the March Madness party at the station," he told her, with a big happy grin.

So there was to be an occurrence on the weekend in March after all, though it didn't actually occur in, or anywhere near, New York City. It was Spring Break, the annual pilgrimage of all America's undergraduate scholars to Florida to take seminars on noncommitment.

Spring Break was a big deal for Brian's station, GRODY, because it homed right in on their target audience. One time, Fiona had asked him, "Who *does* watch that station?" and he'd answered, "The eighteen-to-nineteen-and-a-half-year-old males, an extremely important advertising demographic," and she'd said, "That explains it," whatever that meant.

In any event, GRODY annually marked Spring Break with its March Madness party, at a rented party place down in Soho, limited to station staff and advertisers and local press and cable company minor employees and good friends and whoever else happened to hear about it. All attendees were encouraged to come costumed as one of the cartoon characters from the station, and many did. Brian's Reverend Twisted costume was kept in the back of the closet to be brought out lovingly and hilariously every year, an old if unusual friend. "Oh, I hope it still fits," he always said, which was his March Madness joke.

But now Fiona began to throw cold water on his idea even before she'd heard it, saying, with an exaggerated sigh, "Oh. I suppose we have to go."

"*Have* to go? Come on, Fiona, it's fun, you know it is."

"The first couple of times," she said, "it *was* fun, like visiting a tribe way up the Amazon that had never been marked by civilization."

"Listen —"

"But after a while, Brian," she said, "it becomes just a teeny little bit less fun."

"You never —"

"I'm not saying we won't go," she said. "I'm just saying I'm not as excited about it as I used to be. Brian, March Madness at GRODY does not hold many surprises for me any more."

He knew an opening when he heard one. "Listen," he said, very eager, as though the thought had just this second come to him.

"I know how to put the zing back in the old March Madness."

The look she gave him was labeled *Skepticism.* "How?"

"Invite Mrs. W."

She stared at him as though he'd suddenly grown bat wings on the sides of his head. "Do *what?*"

"Watch *her* watching *them,*" he explained, waving his arms here and there. "You know she's never seen anything like that in her life."

"Yes, I do know that," Fiona said.

"Come on, Fiona," he said. "You know I want to meet her, and there's never a place that's just *right.*"

"And March Madness is just right?"

"It *is.* She'll know ahead of time it's a freak show, you'll explain the whole thing to her, a world she never even suspected existed."

"And wouldn't want to know exists."

"Fiona, invite her." Brian spread his hands above the cribbage board, a supplicant. "That's all I'm asking. Explain what it is, explain how your friend — that's me — wants to meet her, explain it's a goof and we promise to leave the *instant* she's had enough."

"*Any* of it would be more than enough, Brian."

Brian did an elaborate shrug. "If she says no," he said, "then that's that. I won't ever mention it again. But at least *ask* her. Will you do that much?"

"She would think," Fiona said, "I'd lost my mind."

"You'll say it was my idea, your goofy boyfriend's idea. Come on, Fiona. Ask her, will you? Please?"

Fiona sat back, frowning into the middle distance, her fingers tap-tapping on the table beside the cribbage board. Brian waited, afraid to push any more, and at last she gave a kind of resigned sigh and said, "I'll try."

Delighted, he said, "You will? Fiona, you'll really ask her?"

"I said I would," Fiona said, sounding weary.

"Thank you, Fiona," Brian said.

37

On Wednesday afternoon, two days after his lunch with Jay Tumbril, Jacques Perly completed a very encouraging conference with two international art thieves and a sometime producer for the Discovery Channel, then drove back to the city from Fairfield County in bucolic Connecticut. The West Side Highway deposited him onto Fourteenth Street in Manhattan, and a few deft maneuvers later he steered the Lamborghini onto Gansevoort Street, thumbing the beeper on his visor as he did so. The battered old green garage door that obediently lifted in response was in a low squat structure that perfectly suited the neighborhood; an old stone industrial building converted to more upscale uses without losing its original rough appearance.

Perly steered into the building, beeped the door shut, and drove up the curving concrete ramp to where the conversion began.

The high stone exterior walls up here were painted a creamy white, and ceiling spot-lights pinpointed the potted evergreens in front of his office door. This space was large enough for two cars to park, though usually, as now, it contained only Perly's. Leaving the Lamborghini, he crossed to the faux Tudor interior wall and stepped into his reception room, where Della looked up from her typing to say, "Hi, Chief. How'd it go?"

"Well, Della," Perly said, with justifiable pride, "I believe we'll have an amphora on our hands in very short order. *And* thirty minutes of airtime."

"I knew you'd do it, Chief," she said. She'd never tell him, but she loved him madly.

"I thought I might," he admitted. "What's doing here?"

"The crew's reported on that Fiona Hemlow matter," she said. "Jerry sent his stuff over by messenger, Margo e-mailed it in, and Herkimer stopped by with it. Fritz says he'll have pix for you by the end of the day. It's all on your desk."

"Good girl. Man the barricades."

"Always, Chief."

He went into his inner office, a large room with tall windows across the back and a big domed skylight in thick glass, framed in steel. The furniture was clubby and quietly expensive, the wall decorations mostly pictures of recovered art. His desk, large and old and dark wood, had come from one of the daily New York newspapers that had gone under during the final newspaper strike of 1978. He sat at it now and drew to himself the three packets of information delivered by his crew.

Fifteen minutes later, he thumbed the intercom. "Della, get me Jay Tumbril."

"Right, Chief."

It took another six minutes, while he skimmed the reports once more, before he got the buzz, picked up his phone, and said, "Jay."

"I'll put Mr. Tumbril right on," said a girl whose English accent was probably real.

"Fine." Perly had forgotten that Jay Tumbril was one of those people who scored points for himself in some obscure game if he made you get on the line first.

"Jacques."

"Jay."

"That was quick."

"It doesn't take long when there's nothing there."

"Nothing?"

"Well, not much. There's one little — But

we'll get to that. The girl first. Fiona Hemlow."

"Yes."

"She's clean, Jay. A good student, conscientious, as obedient as a nun."

Jay, sounding faintly displeased, said, "Well, that's fine, then."

"Comes from money," Perly went on. "Her grandfather, still alive, was an inventor, a chemist, came up with some patents made him and the rest of the family rich."

"So she's not after Livia's money, is what you're saying."

"*She* isn't, no."

"Yes? I don't follow."

"For the last three years," Perly said, putting a finger on the name on the top sheet of Herkimer's report, "Ms. Hemlow has been shacked up with a character named Brian Clanson."

"He's the one you're dubious about."

"He is." Perly tapped Clanson's name with a fingernail, as behind him his computer dinged that an e-mail was coming in. "I ask myself," he said, "if this character *put up* our little nun to ingratiate herself with Mrs. Wheeler."

"So *he'd* be after her money."

"It's only a possibility," Perly cautioned him. "At this point, I have no reason to believe anything at all. I just look at this character, and I see someone from, to be honest, a white-trash background, a community college education, no contacts of any consequence in the city, and an extremely marginal job as some sort of illustrator for a cable channel aimed at Neanderthals. I can believe Ms. Hemlow hooked up with him because he has that redneck charm and because she's a naïf who thinks well of everybody, but I can also believe Mr. Clanson hooked up with her because she has money, or at least her grandfather does."

"Mmm."

Turning in his swivel chair, Perly saw the e-mail was from Fritz, and opened it. The photographs. "Further than that," he said, "I can believe he came to the conclusion that Mrs. Wheeler was the likeliest prospect among your firm's clients for him to get his hands on."

"So you think he set the girl to go after Mrs. W."

Perly opened the photo marked BC and looked at Brian Clanson, arms folded, leaning against a tree in a park somewhere, big boned but skinny, like a stray dog, with a loose untrustworthy smile. "I'll only say this, Jay," he said, looking Clanson in the eye, "it's out of character for that girl to have imposed herself on Mrs. Wheeler all on her own. There has to have been a reason, and I can't find any other reason in the world except Brian Clanson." And he nodded at the grinning fellow, who showed no repentance.

Jay said, "So you want to look into Clanson a little deeper."

"Let's see if this is the first time," Perly said, "he's tried to work something funny with his betters."

"Go get him," Jay Tumbril said.

38

At the same time that Jacques Perly and Jay Tumbril were discussing the investigation into Fiona Hemlow and Livia Northwood Wheeler, those two ladies, all unknowing of the scrutiny, were discussing the results of Fiona's own investigations. "There's just no record," Fiona was saying, spreading her hands in helplessness as she stood in front of Mrs. W's desk.

Mrs. W had a photo of the chess set displayed on her computer, and she now frowned at it with the same mistrustful expression that Perly, downtown, wore when gazing on the photo of Brian Clanson. "It's vexing," she said. "It's just vexatious."

"Your father, Alfred Northwood," Fiona said, consulting her memo pad, in which she had placed careful and thorough notes of the history just as though she hadn't had it memorized a long time ago, "came to New York from Chicago in 1921. We know that for certain. We know he was in the army in Europe in the First World War and became a sergeant, and went to Chicago after he left the army, though I couldn't find any records of what he was doing there. There's also no record of his having the chess set in the army or in Chicago —"

"Well, certainly not the army," Mrs. W snapped. "Nothing as valuable as *that.*"

"No, ma'am. We know your father's friends and business associates called it the Chicago chess set because he brought it from there, but I can't find any circumstance in which *he* called it the Chicago chess set."

"Or anything else."

"Or anything else," agreed Fiona. "There is no record that he ever said where it came from, or how he happened to own it. I'm sorry, Mrs. W, there's just no history."

"Well, there, you see," Mrs. W said, with an irritated headshake at the picture of the chess set. "Behind every great fortune there is a crime."

Alert, Fiona said, "There is?" because she found that a truly interesting idea.

But now Mrs. W's irritated headshake was directed at Fiona. "Balzac, dear," she said. "*Père Goriot.* And I fear that the crime behind *my* family's fortune may have more than a little to do with that chess set."

"Yes, ma'am."

Again Mrs. W frowned at the picture on the computer screen. "Will the crime be found out? Is there risk in that ugly toy? Is there anything to do other than let sleeping chessmen lie?"

"I don't know, Mrs. W."

"No, you don't. Well, thank you, Fiona. I'll think about this."

"Yes, ma'am." Fiona turned to go, then said, "Mrs. W, there is something else."

"Yes?"

"I wasn't even going to mention it, it's so silly."

"Well, either mention it or don't mention it," Mrs. W told her. "You can't dither forever."

"No, ma'am. It's my boyfriend, Brian."

Mrs. W's eyebrows lowered. "Is something wrong there?"

"Oh, no, nothing like that," Fiona assured her. "It's just — Well, you know, he works for a cable station, and they have a party every year in March, sort of the end of winter and all, and Brian said I should invite you. He's wanted to meet you, and —"

"Been telling tales about me, have you?"

Mrs. W hadn't said that as though she were angry, yet Fiona became very flustered and felt the color rise up into her cheeks.

She couldn't think of a thing to say, but apparently her pink face said it all for her, because Mrs. W nodded and said, "That's all right, dear. I don't mind being an eccentric in other people's stories. I can't imagine what Jay Tumbril says about me, for instance. Tell me about this party."

"It's really very silly," Fiona said. "A lot of the people there dress up in costumes, not everybody. *I* won't."

"Like Halloween," Mrs. W suggested.

"Sort of."

"And when and where is this?"

"Saturday, down in Soho. It starts at eight, but Brian doesn't like to get there until ten."

"Very sensible. Let me think about it."

"Yes, ma'am."

"And," with a sudden snap to her voice, "get me Jay Tumbril on the phone."

"Yes, ma'am."

"I've made up my mind," Mrs. W said. "The time has come to bring in experts, to get to the bottom of this. Fiona, we are going to *look* at that chess set."

39

GRODY was always in the process of expanding, without having either the money or the space to do so. The studio in Tribeca, being the entire third floor of an old industrial building where, in the late nineteenth century, aprons and overalls were manufactured, was always undergoing renovation, the carpenters and electricians with their leather toolbelts like space-age gunbelts and their macho swagger serving as the oil to the water of the staff's resident geeks.

Because the brick exterior walls of the building and the unrepealable law of gravity meant they could never actually add to their territory, the only way to accommodate more offices, more studios and more storage was to keep chopping finer and finer, until the rooms were like closets and the closets had long ago been sacrificed to the need for more space. Hallways had been squeezed to within an inch of the fire code.

And one result of all this adjusting and repacking and clawing for space was that many of the resulting rooms were of unusual shapes, triangles and trapezoids. Long-ago-sacrificed doorways meant many of the routes within the GRODY confines were circuitous indeed. All of which was one reason why the company found it so hard to hire or keep anybody over the age of twenty-five.

Coming to work Thursday morning, after the astonishing news last night that Mrs. W actually would come along to Saturday's March Madness, Brian made his round-about way toward his own office, one of the few octagons in here thus far, in which, no matter which way you faced, the workspace shrank away in front of you. Just after squeezing past two carpenters toting over their shoulders eight-foot lengths of L-shaped metal like bowling alley gutters creased down the middle, only lined along both sides with holes — what was that for? straining beer? — Brian was distracted from his route by a knocking on a window some-where.

Oh; to the left. One of the control rooms was there, with a sealed window to the hall left over from some previous incarnation, and standing in it was Sean Kelly, Brian's shaggy boss, who mouthed things at him through the glass; some sort of question.

But the point of the control room was that it was soundproof, so Brian merely shrugged and pointed helplessly at his ear. Sean nodded, frowned, nodded, and pointed vaguely away with his right hand while doing a finger-up circular motion with his left. Come around and talk to me, in other words.

Sure. Brian nodded, paused to figure out the shortest way from this side of the glass to that side of the glass, and set off, along the way passing an electrician, seated wedged in a corner, still smoking slightly, accepting sustenance in a flask from his fellows.

Brian's route took him past his octagon, which had a doorway but no door because there was nowhere for it to open to. He nodded at it, trekked on, and eventually came to the control room containing both Sean and an expressionless technician seated at the controls, watching a tape of a hilarious animated outer-space drunk scene to be aired at eleven tonight, in competition with the world news. (They expected to win again.)

"Hey, Sean."

"Hey." Sean seemed troubled, in some

vague way. "Man," he said, "you got any problems at home?" Hurriedly, he erased that from the imaginary blackboard between them. "I don't mean none of my *business,* man, you know, I just mean, anything gonna impact us *here."*

Brian could have pointed out that a permanent construction site was all impact, but he cut to the chase: "*What* problem, Sean? I do something wrong?"

"No, man," Sean said. "Nothing *I* know about. It's just, I got this call yesterday, just walking out of the office, this guy, says he's from the enforcement arm of the Better Business Bureau."

"Enforcement arm?"

"That's what he said, man." Sean grinned and scratched his head through his shaggy hair. "Can you see them comin around? 'You gotta give the twenty percent, man, it's right there in your ad.' Might make a nice bit."

"Sean, he wanted to talk to you about *me?* Or just the place?"

"No, man, you, strictly you. Do you borrow from your co-workers —"

"Fat chance."

"Uh huh. Do I know where you cash your checks, have you ever had unexplained absences —"

"Everybody does, Sean."

That quick grin of Sean's came and went. "Sing it, sister. He wants to know, do I think you're having trouble in your home life, interfering with you here, whadoI think your work prospects are —"

"Jesus."

"It was freaky, man." Another grin. "Don't worry, I covered for you."

Suspicion struck Brian. "You goofed on him."

"Naw, man, would I —"

"You would. Wha'd you tell him?"

"I just answered his questions, man, told him you were the number one jock in the shop."

"And? Come on, Sean."

Sean looked slightly sheepish, but still grinned. "Well, I did mention," he said, "those Venusian bordello scenes you do . . ."

"*Lost It in Space.* Yeah?"

"I said, you were so good at it, it's because you think they're real."

"Sean, what did you —"

"No, that's all, man, honest to God. Just sometimes we find you at your desk, you're in this trance state, you're getting laid on Venus. That's *all* I said, man."

"And did he believe you?"

Sean looked amazed at the question.

"Brian? What do *I* know how Earth people think?"

Brian had all that day to figure out what was going on, and yet he didn't.

40

Jay Tumbril had all Thursday night to brood about Livia Northwood Wheeler and the Chicago chess set, which didn't leave much time for sleep, but he couldn't very well do that in the office either, so by eleven Friday morning he was both sleep-deprived and jittering on the edge of panic. He hated to admit there might be a circumstance in which his control of the situation was less than perfect, but there were such circumstances and this was one of them, so it was time to pull the emergency cord.

The point was, if you found yourself in a position so far outside your expertise you hadn't the faintest bloody idea what to do next, then the thing to do next was to call upon someone who *does* have expertise in the area, whatever that area might be. In this case, there was only one expert in the area that Jay knew, so just after eleven he picked up the intercom and said, "Felicity."

"Sir."

"Get me Jacques Perly."

"Sir."

Three minutes later, Felicity was back on the line: "Mr. Perly says he's in his car, northbound on the Franklin Delano Roosevelt Drive, speaking on his hands-free carphone, and wonders if he should ring you back later or will you rough it now."

Jay knew damn well Perly had actually said "the FDR Drive," but Felicity was so proud of her studies to become an American citizen that he merely said, "Thank you, Felicity, I'd rather talk to him now, it's a bit urgent."

"Sir."

Jay broke the connection, and spent the next twenty-five seconds rehearsing how he'd describe the situation. Then the buzz sounded, and he picked up and said, "Jacques."

"I'll put him right on."

"What?"

"Just joking," Perly said.

"I knew that was you, you didn't change your voice or anything. What do you mean, joking?"

"Your secretary said it was urgent."

"Yes, well — Yes, it is. Also, Jacques, extremely confidential."

"We know that."

"Sorry. Didn't mean to insult you. The truth is, I'm a little tense, didn't get much sleep last night . . ."

"You, Jay?"

"It's Livia Northwood Wheeler again!"

"What? The Hemlow girl? Or did Clanson make his move?"

"No, nothing to do with them. This is something completely different."

"Tell me."

Jay forced a deep breath, assembled his thoughts, and said, "Among the items under dispute in the law case involving Mrs. Wheeler and several of her relatives is a chess set, never I believe properly evaluated, but said to be worth in the millions."

"Worth fighting over, in other words."

"Yes. Since the suits began — I'll only say by now they sue and countersue and cross-sue one another to a degree of complexity you could only otherwise find in a map of the New York City subway system — the courts have placed this asset in the care of the law firms involved, four of whom, including us, have offices in this building, so that for the last few years the chess set, called for some reason the Chicago chess set, though I doubt it was made there, has been in the sub-cellar vaults beneath this building."

"And likely to stay there for a while, I should think."

"Except," Jay said, "*now* Mrs. Wheeler wants it brought up and placed somewhere that experts of various stripes may examine it."

"Dangerous."

"Infuriating," Jay corrected him. "As her attorney in this matter, it is up to me to take this request to the court. I unfortunately see no reason why the court would deny it, nor why any of the other litigants would object. I can see that every blessed soul concerned with this matter would like to take a look at that bloody chess set."

"So what's the problem?" Jacques asked.

"Where it is now," Jay told him, "in that vault beneath this building, it is safe as houses."

"But a little too inaccessible," Jacques suggested, "for perusal by experts."

"Exactly. Nor will the bank accept the concept of various people trooping through their vaults. It must come up. But whose task will it be to *keep* the damn thing safe while it's up and about, like the groundhog looking for its shadow?"

"Oh, I see."

"Yes, you do. It is up to *this* firm to find a

site both accessible to the experts and agreeable to, if not the other litigants, at least to their legal representatives."

"And still be safe as houses," Perly suggested.

"If only we could." If Jay had had hair, he'd have torn it. "Not in *these* offices," he said. "We can't keep track of the *copiers* around here. And no other firm has more secure offices. It's not an official investigation, and so we can't ask the police to step in, and in fact for various potential ownership rights and inheritance liabilities, we'd rather *leave* officialdom out of this matter."

"When does she want to make this move?"

"Now! Yesterday!"

"Well, that's not possible. I could make a suggestion, Jay."

"Then why don't you?"

"I'm afraid it — Excuse me, there's a multiple-car collision up ahead, I'll just steer around — Oh, good, the police are on the scene, I'm being waved through — *Oh, my God!* Jay, you never want to see anything like that your whole life long."

"Don't describe it to me."

"I will not."

"You were going to make a suggestion."

"Oh, Lord. Give me a second, Jay."

"Of course."

That must have been horrendous, Jay thought, to rattle Jacques Perly. How much simpler life was when people couldn't tell us what they could see from their cars.

"What I was going to say, Jay —"

"Yes, Jacques."

"— That I was hesitant to make my suggestion because it could seem self-serving."

"*You* want to guard the piece? You're not a sentry, Jacques."

"I wanted to suggest my offices," Jacques said. "Extremely safe, extremely secure, but absolutely accessible. You've been there."

"Well, yes, but — I don't know what to say."

"You would hire private security, of course, 24/7, but the building itself is ideal for you, and I'm sure we could work out a rental acceptable to all concerned. I would have to keep my own business going at the same time, of course."

"Of course. Jacques, the more I think about this —"

"Well, think about one more thing," Jacques told him. "Ah, we're in the snow-belt now."

"Are we?"

"Ask yourself this, Jay. Why now? You said Mrs. Wheeler *now* wanted this, and wanted it at once. Why, Jay? After all these years, why now?"

"I haven't the vaguest idea."

"Could it be, Jay, because of her recent hire?"

"You mean — ?"

"Has Fiona Hemlow put that suggestion into Mrs. Wheeler's head? And did Brian Clanson set the whole thing up? Is Brian Clanson just sitting there, waiting for that chess set to come up out of that vault?"

"Oh, my God."

"I'm already on Clanson, Jay, because of that other thing you asked me to do, though of course he has no idea he's under surveillance. We'll intensify that, study his associates. If your Chicago chess set is in my offices, and Brian Clanson makes a move to snatch it, we'll have him, Jay, in the of   our   ."

"Jacques? You're breaking up."

"We'll   later." And Jacques Perly was gone.

41

Thursday evening was a busy time at the Safeway. The store stayed open late, and people stocked up on their groceries for the weekend. May didn't usually work the evening shift, since the one regularity John really liked in his life was dinner, but sometimes people got sick or fired or mislaid themselves somewhere, and May might be asked to fill in, like tonight. A little after seven now; she could quit at eight, pick out something nice for their evening repast in the deli department that wouldn't take a lot of preparation, and home she'd go. Easy.

The first thing she noticed about the guy was that the only thing he was carrying was a little packet of lightbulbs. He was on her checkout line, the people in front of him and behind him all with carts piled up to their chins, so that at first he just looked like a very easy example of the which-one-doesn't-belong-in-this picture quiz. She stood there, sliding items over the bar code reader, sliding them twice if she didn't hear that *ping* the first time, pushing the items onto the belt to roll on down to tonight's packer, an overweight kid with an overbite whom all the staff here knew only as Pudge, a name he didn't seem to mind, and she kept looking at the guy with the lightbulbs until finally she caught his eye and gestured with her head toward the last checkout line in the row, which was for people with six items or fewer, though the sign actually said *six items or less.* The guy grinned a thank-you and spread his hands a little; he'd rather stay here.

Huh. *Ping. Ping.* Then the lightbulb inside her head went off. He's a cop. He looks like a cop, heavy and self-confident, somebody that nobody would ever call Pudge, and he's doing something a normal person wouldn't do, which is wait in a long line of people buying out the store while he's only got one item. So that would make him not only a cop, but a cop with a particular interest in May, which could not be good news.

Her first thought was that John had been arrested, but her first thought always was that John had been arrested, so her second thought was to reject the first thought. If they'd arrested John, why come *here?* And if they were going to come here, why not just do a real cop thing and jump the line entirely to say what they had to say?

Well, she'd find out soon enough. A few thousand more *pings* and here he was, pushing the little packet of four hundred-watt frosted white bulbs toward her with a ten-dollar bill as he grinned and said, "You know, you really oughta get an answering machine."

He's from Andy, she thought, but she knew he wasn't. She said, "Oh, you must be the man John went to see a couple times."

"Naturally," he said.

Ping. She took the ten and made change as Pudge put the packet of lightbulbs into a plastic bag, and Johnny Eppick For Hire said, "So you be my answering machine. Pass on to John, he should call me. Tell him we got ignition."

I hope John doesn't plan to cheat this man, she thought. I'll have to remind him to be careful. "I'll tell him," she said. "Enjoy your light."

"Better than curse the darkness," he said, and grinned one last time, and carried his lightbulbs into the night.

42

By Friday morning, Dortmunder's irritation had cooled without disappearing. When May had come home last night and told him Eppick had actually braced her right there in the store with his message to call, Dortmunder had at first been outraged. "He talked to you? In the store? He's not supposed to have anything to do with you at all!"

May wasn't as upset as he was, but of course she'd had longer to live with it. She said, "He wasn't bad or anything, John. He just gave me the message for you and bought some lightbulbs."

"Lightbulbs? Listen, he wants to talk to me, he can call *Andy,* like last time."

"Well, he talked to me," she said, "and I thought it was a little weird, but there wasn't anything *wrong* about it."

"You know what it is?" he demanded. "I'll tell you what it is. The message isn't lightbulbs or call me or any of that. The *message* is, 'I can reach out to you. I not only know where you are, I know where your lady friend *works,* I'm on top of you any time I wanna be on top of you,' that's what the message is."

"I think we already knew all that," May said. "Are you going to call him?"

"Some other time. Right now, I'm too irritated."

"Well, go in the living room, and let me get on with dinner," she said, gesturing at tonight's sack of groceries on the kitchen table.

He was hungry. "Okay."

"Have a beer as an appetizer."

"I will," he agreed, and took a can of beer with him to the living room, where he sat and frowned at the switched-off television set while he conducted several imaginary conversations with Johnny Eppick in his head, in which he was much fiercer and made much more telling points than was likely in real life, until May called him to dinner, which was a really good meat loaf, and how she'd whipped that up so fast, with all those ingredients and stuff, straight from working late hours at the Safeway, he had no idea. But it calmed him considerably, and at the end of the meal he said, "I'll call him tomorrow. Not tonight."

"Don't yell at him," she said.

He hesitated, then made the concession. "Okay."

And late this morning, after May'd headed back to the Safeway, he called Eppick's number and got *his* answering machine. "So this is better, is it?" he demanded. "We're in closer communication now, are we? I'm talking to a *machine*." And hung up.

Eppick phoned just after two that afternoon. "I'll give you a place you can walk to," he said. "Meet me at Union Square in half an hour. I'll be on a bench wherever the dealers aren't."

"The dealers won't be wherever *you* are."

"You think I'm that obvious?" Eppick asked him, but he sounded pleased at the idea.

"See you in half an hour," Dortmunder said, and did, walking through the park all bundled up against the raw March air, and Eppick was seated at his ease on a bench amid only civilians, and not many of them at that, because the weather was still a little below par for park bench–sitting. However, Dortmunder joined him and Eppick said, "The granddaughter has come through like a champ."

"You shouldn't talk to May," Dortmunder told him. "It upsets her."

"I'm sorry to hear that," Eppick said, though he didn't sound sorry. "She didn't look upset. Maybe we could get carrier pigeons, you and me."

They'd already veered too far from Dortmunder's practice conversations, so he said, "Tell me about the champ."

"Huh? Oh, the granddaughter." Eppick grinned, pleased at the very thought of the granddaughter. "She's our spy in the enemy camp," he said, "and she's worth her weight in chess sets."

"That's nice."

"They don't know exactly when they're gonna move the set," Eppick said, "because they're still working on the security, but as soon as they know it she knows it, and as soon as she knows it we know it. Or I know it, and you find out when the carrier pigeon gets there."

"Yeah, right."

"But what we do know now," Eppick said, "is the safe place they're gonna move it to. So this is a very nice edge," he pointed out, "because you can case it before the chess set even gets there."

"That's good."

"It's down on Gansevoort Street," Eppick

told him. "It's the office of a private detective down there by the name of Jacques Perly." With an arch look, he said, "*You* wouldn't have any trouble getting into a private detective's office, would you?"

Not rising to the bait, Dortmunder said, "There's gotta be more to it than that. Some office on Gansevoort Street?"

"Well, if there's more to it," Eppick pointed out, "you've got time to find out what it is."

"I'll take a look," Dortmunder said, and glanced around at the snow-flecked park. You could see everybody's breath. "You know, it's kinda cold out here."

"It is," Eppick agreed, "but we've got privacy. But we could leave now."

"Good."

They stood, Eppick not offering to shake hands this time, and Dortmunder said, "Well, anything's gotta be better than that vault."

"Let's hope." Eppick shrugged his coat and scarf up closer to his chin. "You see your friend Kelp a lot, don't you?"

"From time to time."

"I'll leave messages with him."

"That's good," Dortmunder said. "I don't think May would like carrier pigeons."

43

At just about the same time that Dortmunder and Eppick were consulting about the Chicago chess set en plein air, another meeting was coming to order on the exact same topic, but with a very different membership and in a very different setting. The setting, in fact, was the largest conference room in the offices of Feinberg et al, and still it felt crowded. It was a hush-hush top secret meeting attended only by those who absolutely had to be a party to it, and still that meant seventeen people.

Representing both Feinberg and Livia Northwood Wheeler, and therefore more or less conducting the meeting, was Jay Tumbril, accompanied by a stenographer named Stella, who would take notes of the meeting and record it as well, on cassette. Representing the other principal law firms connected with the Northwood matter were nine senior lawyers, the men in navy-blue pinstripe, the women in navy blue pinstripe plus white ruffles. Representing the NYPD, who would monitor the chess set's movements through the city streets, were two senior inspectors from Centre Street, both in uniforms heavy on the brass. Representing Securivan, the company whose armored car would actually transport the set from the sub-basement in this building to the second-floor office of Jacques Perly, were two sternly fit men with identical crew cuts and square jaws, and with brass Marine Corps insignia pins on the lapels of their pastel sport jackets. And finally, representing the intended destination of the set was Jacques Perly, who'd brought along his secretary Della, who would also take notes and make a recording, and who was blinking a lot at the moment, not being used to life outside the office.

Once the necessary introductions had been made and business cards distributed, Jay, at the head of the conference table, stood and looked around at those assembled either at the table or in chairs along the wall, and decided to begin with a quip: "I'm happy that at last, after years of litigation, everyone connected with the matter of the Northwood estate has finally found one area of agreement. Everybody wants a look at that chess set."

Apparently no one else in the room realized that was a quip, so Jay cleared his throat into the silence and said, "We all understand there's a certain degree of peril in this move, particularly if word seeps out that it's about to happen, so I hope everyone here realizes the need for total secrecy on this matter until the move is done."

More silence, which this time Jay took for consent. "When a task is difficult and fraught with peril," he went on, "the wise man turns to the experts. I hope we're all at least that wise, and so I want to turn to the experts in our midst today, from Securivan and from the NYPD. Harry or Larry, would you share your thoughts with us?"

Harry and Larry were the Securivan men. Jay sat down and Larry remained seated as he said, "Keeping a secret that seventeen people in this room already know about, plus the judge and other people at the court, plus one or more people at the bank, plus at least one of the principals in the lawsuit means, not to offend anybody present, but it isn't a secret you're gonna keep secret for very long."

The more senior of the NYPD men present, whose name was Chief Inspector Mologna (pronounced Maloney), now said,

"Speakin for myself, and speakin for the great city of New York, I can tell you right now you already got your secret blowed. This city does not raise up a criminal class that don't have its eyes open and its ears open and its hands open every blessed moment of the night and day. They're out there already and they're waitin for you. You put together a mob scene like we got in this room, of course, you're just engravin an invitation."

"Unfortunately, Chief Inspector," Jay said, "this is the minimum number possible to obtain agreement."

"Oh, I understand," the chief inspector said. "You got your protocols and you got your noses that might get out of joint, so you gotta have this social before you get down to business. But when you *do* get down to business, take it from me, the crooks will be right with you, every step of the way."

Larry of Securivan said, "Harry and I think the chief inspector's right, so, because there are those sharp-eared crooks out there, and, because we don't want to give them too much time to make their own plans, the sooner you make this move the better."

"That's right," the chief inspector said.

"Don't shilly-shally."

Jay said, "No, we certainly don't want to do *that.*"

"Harry and I," Larry said, "think the best time to do this is Sunday night."

"*This* Sunday night?" Jay asked him. "The day after tomorrow?"

"Yes, sir," Larry confirmed. "We'd want to get our armored car into position at the curb downstairs here at oh two hundred hours Monday morning."

His partner Harry spoke up: "This thing weighs, so we're told, a third of a ton. We'll have a crew of four with the armored oar, to bring the object up and place it into the vehicle."

"And we," Chief Inspector Mologna said, "are gonna have patrol cars on that block, and patrol cars up at the next intersection to divert traffic, so you are gonna have *no* vehicles in that area except your van and our patrols."

"This all sounds very good," Jay said.

Jacques Perly said, "When do you think you'd get to my shop?"

Larry considered that. "If we start at oh two hundred hours," he said, "say it takes fifteen minutes to bring the object up and secure it. At that time of night, fifteen or twenty minutes to drive down to your area.

327

You should count on an arrival time of oh two-thirty to oh two-forty hours."

One of the other lawyers present said, "That means the experts could start examining the artifact Monday morning."

"Not quite," Jay said. "We don't want to tell anybody else about the move until after it's made." With a bow toward the chief inspector, he said, "Granted that secrets are difficult or impossible to keep, we'd still like to limit the advance knowledge of the move as much as we can."

Another lawyer said, "But they can start their inspections Tuesday morning, surely."

"I don't see why not."

"Some of our principals," another lawyer said, "and some of our senior partners as well, will certainly want to take this opportunity to see the thing in the flesh, as it were."

"We'll make accommodations for that as we can," Jay assured him. "But we don't want it to become a tourist destination."

That quip got its chuckle, and another lawyer said, "Oh, I think most of us are mature enough to show restraint."

Another lawyer said, "However, speed in assessing the object is also a priority, of course. I understand we're all paying Mr. Perly a per diem for the use of his space, and of course every day the object is out of the vault the risk of theft increases."

Another lawyer said, "What we're talking about here is not one object, but thirty-four. A theft doesn't have to be of the entire piece."

Jay said, "We're arranging for private guards to stay with the object 24/7 while it's at Mr. Perly's. We'll all breathe easier once the set is back in the vault downstairs."

"Amen to that," said another lawyer, and still another lawyer said, "In fact, the per diem is not that much. In this instance, it is truly better to be safe than sorry."

Which caused a general murmur of agreement, followed by Jay saying, "Does that cover it all?"

"I'd like to say one thing," said the chief inspector, and got to his feet. He also picked up his braid-rich hat from the conference table, so he apparently didn't intend to stay much longer. "At oh two hundred hours in the ayem of this comin Monday morning," he informed them all, "I am gonna be asleep in my bed in Bay Shore, Long Island. And I will not be wantin any phone calls." And he put on his hat.

On that note the meeting concluded, having worked out about as satisfactorily as the one just ending in the park downtown.

44

Andy Kelp came home from the department store wearing three suits and two coats. It wasn't really that cold out, but it was still better to wear them than to pay for them.

Anne Marie was at her computer on her desk in the bedroom. She looked at him and said, "Did you put on weight?"

"No," he said. "I put on wool. Let me get these clothes off."

"Okay," she said, and shut her computer down, and the phone rang.

Kelp gave it a look of dislike. "It's gotta be John," he said.

"You do your strip," she told him, "and I'll talk to John."

"Deal."

He got half his new wardrobe off when she said, "It is John, and it sounds like he really does have to talk to you."

"Then I suppose he does. Hello," he told

the phone.

"We've got the place where it's gonna be."

"Where it's gonna be. But it isn't there now."

"No, but it's gonna be there soon, and you and me, we should look it over, look the place over before the thing shows up. A little easier now than later."

This was unfortunately true. Looking at Anne Marie, who had started her own striptease, Kelp said, "So where is this place?"

"Down on Gansevoort Street. An office down there."

"An office? Doesn't sound right."

"I'll give you the details, you know, in other circumstances."

"Okay, but . . ." Kelp looked wistfully toward Anne Marie. "Anne Marie and me, we had plans for this evening, maybe a movie . . . I tell you what."

"Tell me."

"There's a very trendy hotel down there on Gansevoort," Kelp said, "now that the area's gentrified. I could meet you there, in the bar there."

"Fine. When?"

"We should make it pretty late," Kelp said, and looked again at Anne Marie, who was smiling. "I'll meet you in the bar there at midnight," he said, and did, and saw Dortmunder already in position there at the bar.

Kelp had to admit, even seen from behind and across the room, slouched at the bar, John Dortmunder did not go with this setting. Any observant person in the joint would have taken one look at him in this environment and called the cops on general principles.

Fortunately, this hotel did not generally cater to observant persons. It was the kind of place that attracted rail-thin persons of several genders, all of whom sandpapered their cheekbones every evening before leaving their cave. Being unaware of the existence of any other people at all, none of this rather large and very loud mob of trendoids had noticed the creature from another species who had joined their revels. Dortmunder was in perfect concealment with this crowd.

And now there were two aliens at the bar, once Kelp climbed onto the fuschia stool beside him. The bartendress, an action figure in a skintight black dress, dropped a coaster bearing an ad for condoms on the bar in front of Kelp and said, with complete indifference, "Sir?"

Kelp looked at Dortmunder's drink, recognized it, and said, "I'll have what he's having."

"Ew." She rolled her eyes and slanked away.

Kelp observed Dortmunder's glass again, from which in fact Dortmunder was now drinking. "That's bourbon, isn't it?"

"Yeah."

"Two cubes?"

"Yeah." Dortmunder shrugged. "They don't like to leave bourbon all by itself around here," he explained. "They like to muffle it down a little."

Kelp looked up and down the bar and saw that the things in front of the other patrons didn't look so much like drinks as like extraterrestrials. Short extraterrestrials. "Gotcha," he said.

The bartendress might have felt sullied by having to serve a high-test drink, but she did it, and only charged fourteen dollars for the indignity, sliding a five and a one back at him from his original twenty. Kelp sipped his drink, found it to be as requested, and said, "Tell me about this office where they're gonna move the thing."

"It's some hotshot private detective named Perly," Dortmunder said. "What makes it a good place to stash the thing is what we'll find out."

"And the thing's gonna get there soon."

"That's the story."

"Probly in an armored car."

"Probly."

Kelp contemplated the situation, lubricating his brain muscles with a little more bourbon. "Tough to do an armored car on a city street," he said. "Those jobs are more for the countryside."

"Oh, you can do it," Dortmunder said, "but it takes explosives. I'd rather work more quiet than that."

"Oh, you know it." Kelp took a little more of his drink and said, "You look at this place on your way here?"

"No, I figured we oughta get the good news together."

"When do you want to do that?"

"When you finish your drink," Dortmunder said, because, it seemed, he'd finished his.

45

Gansevoort Street is part of the far West Village, an old seafaring section, an elbow of twisted streets and skewed buildings poked into the ribs of the Hudson River. The area is still called the Meatpacking District, though it's been more than half a century since the elevated coal-burning trains from the west came down the left fringe of Manhattan to the slaughterhouses here, towing many cattle cars filled with loud complaint. After the trains were no more, some cows continued to come down by truck, but their heart wasn't in it, and gradually almost an entire industry shriveled away into history.

Commerce hates a vacuum. Into the space abandoned by the doomed cows came small manufacturing and warehousing. Since the area sits next to the actual Greenwich Village, some nightlife grew as well, and when the grungy old nineteenth-century commercial buildings started being converted into pied-à-terres for movie stars, you knew all hope was gone.

Still, the Meatpacking District, even without much by way of the packing of meat, continues to present a varied countenance to the world, part residential, part trendy shops and restaurants, and part storage and light manufacturing. Into this mix Jacques Perly's address blended perfectly, as Dortmunder and Kelp discovered when they strolled down the block.

Perly had done nothing to gussy up the facade. It was a narrow stone building, less than thirty feet across, with a battered metal green garage door to the left and a gray metal unmarked door on the right. Factory-style square-paned metal windows stretched across the second floor, fronted by horizontal bands of narrow black steel that were designed not to look like prison bars, to let in a maximum of light and view, and to slice the fingers off anybody who grabbed them.

Faint light gleamed well back of those upstairs windows. The buildings to both sides were taller, with more seriously lit windows here and there. On the right was a four-story brick tenement that had undergone recent conversion to upscale living, with a very elaborate entrance doorway flanked by carriage lamps. The building on the left, three stories high and also brick, extended down to the corner, with shops on the street floor, plus a small door that would lead up to what looked like modest apartments above.

Dortmunder and Kelp stood surveying this scene a few minutes, being occasionally passed by indifferent pedestrians, they all bundled up and hustling because the wind was pretty brisk over here by the river, and then Kelp said, "You know, I read one time, if you're stuck with a decision you gotta make, there's rules."

"Oh, yeah?"

"Yeah. Depending on circumstances, you pick the most active, the earliest in time, or the one on the left."

"That's what I was thinking, too," Dortmunder said.

"That house on the right there," Kelp said, "that's shielding a very valuable family."

"I know that."

"Whereas, on the left there, the top floor apartment on the right is dark."

"Maybe they're out to that bar we were in," Dortmunder suggested.

"Maybe they'll stay a while," Kelp said, and they crossed the street to find that neither the street door nor the second door behind it offered much resistance.

This was a walk-up, so they walked up, where a narrow hall led them rightward to a door with a brass 3C on it and no light visible through the peephole.

"Could be early to bed, though," Dortmunder said.

"On a Friday night in this neighborhood? I don't think so," Kelp said. "But we'll go in quiet, not to disturb anybody."

"And not to leave any sign we were here."

"Not this time."

Kelp did the honors with the door, and they entered a semi-dark kitchen, illuminated only by distant streetlights from below this level, plus the red-ember glows of all the clocks and other LED lights on all the appliances, giving the room a faint speakeasy air.

"Joe sent me," Kelp whispered.

The kitchen led to a living room of the same size, making the kitchen fairly large and the living room pretty small. And that led to a bedroom which would also have been the same size except that a third of it had been walled off for a bathroom.

The only illumination in the bedroom to boost the streetlights' glow came from the red numerals on the alarm clock. The double bed — happily empty — was on the left, against the bathroom wall. The window to the right looked down at Gansevoort Street, and the one straight ahead beyond the bed, looked down at the roof of Perly's building, which was considerably deeper than wide and featured a large skylight in the rear half.

"I like that skylight," Kelp whispered.

"There's nobody here," Dortmunder said, in a normal voice.

Surprised, Kelp looked around and said, also in a normal voice, "You're right. And I still like that skylight."

Perly's tar-paper flat roof was about six feet below this window. Whatever light they'd seen through his windows had to be toward the front, because nothing at all showed below the skylight glass.

"I like the skylight, too," Dortmunder said, "but there's no point looking in it now."

"No, I know that."

"I wonder," Dortmunder said, "about utility access."

It is not only burglars in New York City who occasionally have trouble getting to the parts of buildings that interest them. In the older and more crowded sections of the city, like the far West Village, the small old structures pressed together in every direction can also make headaches for electric company meter readers, telephone company installers, cable company repairmen, and city inspectors of various stripes. Alleyways, basements, exterior staircases and unmarked doors all have their parts to play in making it possible for these honest working folk to complete their appointed rounds, and just behind them here tiptoe less honest folk, though in their way just as hardworking.

This window out which Dortmunder and Kelp now gazed was a normal double-hung style, with a simple lock on the inside to keep the parts closed. Dortmunder turned this to unlock it, raised the lower sash, felt the cold wind and heard it ruffle papers and cloth here and there behind him, and leaned forward to look out.

Not much snow on the flat roof below, and none on the skylight, which would be warmed from underneath. The roof of Perly's building extended to the left past the end of the building Dortmunder and Kelp were in, and it looked as though there was also space between the far end of the roof and the rear of the building on the next street.

Would anything out there provide utility access of the kind he was looking for? "I can't see," he decided. "Not good enough."

"Let me."

Dortmunder stepped aside so Kelp could take a turn leaning out the window, but then Kelp came back in and said, "I tell you what. I'll go out and see what we got. When I come back, you can help me shimmy up."

"Good."

Kelp, an agile guy, sat on the windowsill, slid his legs over and out, rolled onto his belly and slid backward out the window, holding the sill, coming to a stop with the top of his head just parallel to the bottom of the window opening. "Be right back," he whispered, and headed off to the left.

Dortmunder considered; should he close the window? That was a pretty nippy wind. On the other hand, Kelp wouldn't be gone that long and he wouldn't want to come back to a closed window.

Lights, somewhere behind him. Doorslam.

Nobody cried out, "I'm home!" but nobody had to. Two rooms away, a tenant was shucking out of his or her coat. Two rooms away, a tenant was headed in this direction.

Dortmunder didn't go in for agile, he went in for whatever-works. He managed to go out the window simultaneously headfirst and assfirst, land on several parts that didn't want to be landed on, struggle to his feet, and go loping and limping away as behind him an outraged voice cried, "Hey!", which was followed almost instantly by a window-slam.

Dortmunder did his Quasimodo shuffle two more paces before it occurred to him what would be occurring to the householder at just this instant, which was: That window was locked. Once more he dropped to the roof, with less injury to himself this time, and scrunched against the wall to his left as that window back there yanked loudly upward and the outraged voice repeated, "Hey!"

Silence.

"Who's out there?"

Nobody nobody nobody.

"Is somebody out there?"

Absolutely not.

"I'm calling the cops!"

Fine, good, great; anything, just so you'll get away from that window.

Slam. Suppressing a groan, Dortmunder crawled up the wall until he was vertical and lurched forward, looking out ahead of himself for Kelp.

Who was not there. Was nowhere to be seen. Dortmunder risked stopping for just a second, hand braced against the wall as he scanned the roof, the skylight, the upscale building over to the right with its draped and gated windows, and there was no Kelp. None, not anywhere.

So there was a way off this roof. A way other than back past the person now explaining things to 911. Encouraged by the thought, Dortmunder hobbled on, until the wall to his left came to an end and he could look straight down into inky black.

Now what? No ladders, no staircases, no fire escapes. If there were any way to get down there into that darkness Dortmunder didn't see it. And he was looking, very hard.

The rear of Perly's building was his last hope. He gimped over there, to the low stone wall that separated the roof from empty air, and at first he didn't see anything of use in this direction, either. And then, maybe he did.

There was a larger apartment building across the way, its lighted windows giving some dim illumination to the back of Perly's building, and there, over to the right, some kind of square wrought iron thing like a basket protruded from the wall partway down. He moved over there and saw that it was a kind of tiny iron porch with no roof fronting a second story entrance, with a fire escape leading downward from it.

But how to get to it? The porch or basket

or whatever it was looked very old and rickety, and was at least ten feet below where he stood.

Rungs. Metal rungs, round and rusty, were fixed to the rear wall, marching from here down to the wrought iron. They did not look like things that any sane person would want to find himself on, but this was not a sanity test, this was a question of escape.

Wishing he didn't have to watch what he was doing, Dortmunder sat on the low stone wall, then lay forward to embrace it while dangling his left foot down, feeling around for the top rung. Where the *hell* was it?

Finally he had to shift position so he could turn his head to the left and slither leftward across the stone wall toward the dark drop which, when he could see it, was nowhere near dark enough. In the lightspill from across the way, many items could be seen scrambled together on the concrete paving way down there: metal barrels, old soda bottle cases with soda bottles, lengths of pipe, a couple of sinks, rolls of wire, a broken stroller. Everything but a mattress; no mattresses.

But there was that damn iron rung, not exactly where he'd expected it. He wriggled backward, stabbed for the rung, and got his foot on it at last.

And now what? The first thing he had to do was turn his back on the drop and, while lying crosswise on the stone wall, put as much of his weight as he could on that foot on the rung, prepared at any instant to leap like a cat — an arthritic cat — if the thing gave way.

But it didn't. It held, and now he could ooch himself backward a little bit and put his right foot also on the rung. One deep breath, and he heard that far-off window fly up, and knew the householder was looking for him again. Could he see this far into the darkness, at the shape of a man lying on a stone wall?

Let's not give him enough time to pass that test; Dortmunder clutched the inner edge of the wall with both hands in a death grip, and slid back some more, letting the right foot slide on down past the safety of that rung, paw around, paw some more, and by God, find the next rung!

The transition from the second rung to the third was easier, but then the transition to the fourth was much worse, because that was when his hands had to leave the stone wall and, after several slow days of hanging in midair, at last grasp the top rung tightly enough to leave dents.

Overcome, he remained suspended there a minute or two, breathing like a walrus after a marathon, and then he progressed down, down, down, and there was the porch which was really just an openwork metal floor cantilevered from the building, with a skimpy rail at waist height.

Next to him. The rungs did not descend into the railed metal floor but beside it. So now he was supposed to let go of these beautiful rungs and vault over the goddam rail?

Apparently; the rungs stopped here. Lunge; one hand was on the rail. Lunge; one foot was over the rail but not reaching all the way down to the floor. Lunge; the other hand was on the rail and he tipped forward over it, landing headfirst onto the floor, which shrieked in complaint though it didn't entirely separate from the building.

Up. Holding on to everything he could reach, Dortmunder got to his feet, turned to the wall, and found that the doorway had been bricked up many years ago. This metal structure had not been used for a long time, and it was feeling its age. It seemed to be thinking about leaving the building, what with all this new weight to carry and all.

But here was the fire escape, extending

down at a diagonal across the rear of the building, down one flight to where it stopped at another metal landing, this one with a ladder mounted up against it that could be slid down to descend from there.

Descend? The Perly building was only two stories high. So this space back here went all the way down to basement level.

I'm never gonna see the upper world again, Dortmunder thought. I'm in some kind of horror story, and this is the entrance to Hell.

Well, there was nothing for it; time to descend. Dortmunder started down the fire escape and found it the least horrible part of the experience so far. It was solid iron, securely fastened to the stone of the building, with a good railing and thick gridwork steps.

Too bad it stopped before it got anywhere. Dortmunder reached the lowermost step, which was another platform, though sturdier than the one above, and next to it was the ladder. Studying this, he saw that it operated with a counterweight; if he stood on it, his weight would make it lower. If he got off, the counterweight would lift it back up again. It was clearly an anti-burglar device, operating on the theory that burglars would approach it from below and would be unable to reach up to the bottom rung.

Okay; let's go for a ride on the ladder. Dortmunder stepped onto it, holding tight to the sides, and, after a second's trembling hesitation, it slid smoothly downward with small mouselike chirps and squeaks, descending just like an elevator except, of course, for the elevator cab and the elevator shaft.

The bottom. Dortmunder stepped off onto the cluttered concrete, and the ladder more silently rose away. Only after it departed did he stop to think he'd just now effectively cut off his own retreat. From this point on, there was no way to turn back.

All right, let's deal with what we've got, which is what, exactly? The rear of Perly's building, with more bricked-up windows and a gray metal door, stood before him. The door was rusty, its hinges were rusty, its handle was rusty, and its keyhole was rusty, but the point was, it did have a keyhole. Dortmunder bent to study this keyhole as best he could in the darkness, and it seemed to him Kelp had done a good job in getting through this door without leaving any traces.

And Kelp had to have gone through here. There was no other way. This messy rectangular concrete area back here was one story below street level, enclosed by high walls on all sides. This door was the only way out. Kelp had been ahead of him, and wasn't still in this hole in the ground, so Kelp had to have gone through this door. Could Dortmunder do it just as well, leaving no trace?

Now his competitive juices were stirring, and he forgot all those various aches and pains he'd picked up along the way since toppling out that window. In various interior pockets of his jacket, mostly in the back, were several small tools of his trade, skim-brushed with flat black enamel to keep them from reflecting light. Reaching back there, he brought out a number of these, bent over that lock, and went to work.

Very stiff, the lock was; it reminded him of himself. Except for Kelp, it looked as though nobody'd used this door in quite a while. But at least this stone-and-brick carton he was in was out of the wind, so he could work in relative comfort, without distraction.

And *there.* The door abruptly jolted a quarter-inch toward him, with a popping sound like a cork coming out of a bottle of wine that's turned bad. Dortmunder pulled on it and reluctantly it opened, hinges screaking in protest. As soon as the opening was wide enough, he slid through and pulled the door shut behind himself, creating pitch-blackness.

Now from those useful pockets at the back of his jacket came a tiny flashlight, shorter than a finger. He hadn't wanted it before this, when surrounded by apartment windows, but this kind of interior blackness was perfect for its use. It was sold for the alleged purpose of being attached to a keychain for people wanting to enter and start up their automobiles after dark, but it had other advantages as well, such as giving Dortmunder, when on the job, exactly the amount of light he needed to see that he was in a stone-walled corridor lined with metal storage shelves heaped with the kind of junk people are never going to use again but can't quite bring themselves to get rid of.

Ignoring all that, he stepped down the corridor, and through a doorway on the right he saw a concrete staircase going up. He went up.

The door at the top of these stairs was also gray metal and locked, which seemed excessive, but Dortmunder was on a roll now and went through it with hardly a pause and leaving not a trace of his handiwork. He brushed through the doorway, elbowed the door shut behind himself, and looked around at a place that didn't seem at all converted from its prior industrial uses.

Here was the building's plain metal front door, and over there the garage door, gray rather than green on the inside. A concrete ramp curved upward from the garage door. The space under the ramp and stretching back through the building was taken up with storerooms facing a central corridor and all fronted by barred doors like those on jail cells; unfortunate image.

Dortmunder and his small flashlight took a quick curious look at these rooms and they were full in a way the word "miscellaneous" couldn't quite cover. There was furniture, there was statuary, there were at least two motorcycles, there were office safes piled one atop another, there was what looked like a printing press, there were stacks of computers and other office equipment, and there was a painting of the George Washington Bridge with a truck on fire in the middle of it.

Very strange guy, this Jacques Perly. A private detective. Did people pay him in goods instead of money?

Dortmunder went back to the front of the building and was about to let himself out the street door when he glanced again at that ramp going up. The light source, dim but useful, came from up there.

Would Kelp have checked out the second floor? No. Something told him that Andy Kelp was long gone from this neighborhood. Probably he figured Dortmunder wouldn't be agile enough to get out that window and clear of trouble and so would be somewhere in custody right about now, meaning he'd not be a good person to stand next to for some little while. Dortmunder didn't blame him; if the situation were reversed, he himself would be halfway to Philadelphia.

But what about that ramp? As long as he was here, inside this place, shouldn't he at least take a look-see?

Yes. He walked up the ramp, which curved sharply to the right then straightened along the front wall. This concrete area, just wide enough to K-turn a car in, was flanked on the left by a cream-colored stone wall with a very nice dark wood door. High light fixtures provided the low gleam he'd seen from the street through those industrial windows now high to his right.

Was this nice wooden door locked? Yes. Did it matter? No.

Inside, he found a neat and modest receptionist's office illuminated by a grow light over a side table of small potted plants, all of them legal. He ambled through, and the next door wasn't locked, which made for a change.

This was Jacques Perly's office, very large and very elaborate, spread beneath that skylight. Aware that a private eye might have additional security here and there — even Eppick had had a couple of surprises in his office — Dortmunder tossed the room in slow and careful fashion, using his little flashlight only when he had to, very mindful of that skylight observing him from just above his head.

There were a couple of fruits from this endeavor. On a round oak table in an area away from the main desk, he found notes in a legal pad in crisp tiny handwriting that described the security arrangements to be made to accommodate the coming presence of the Chicago chess set, and those arrangements were elaborate indeed. He also found a copier, switched it on, and copied the pages of notes, putting the copies into a side pocket of his jacket and the legal pad back precisely where he'd picked it up.

There was nothing else much of interest in Perly's office; not to Dortmunder, anyway. He left it and looked at the receptionist's room. Would there be anything of use in here? Very unlikely, but as long as he was passing through he might as well check it out.

It was in the bottom right-hand drawer of the desk that he found it, tucked in the back of the drawer under various cold medicines and lipstick tubes. It was a garage door opener. It was dusty, it was clearly the second opener the company always gives you when the garage door is installed, but it had never been needed and so was long ago forgotten.

If this was the right opener. Dortmunder stepped out to the parking area at the top of the ramp, aimed the opener at the garage door down there, and thumbed it. Immediately the door started to lift, so he thumbed it again and it stopped, with a four-inch-wide gap. A third push of the thumb and back down it went, to close the gap.

Well, this was something. The garage door wasn't quiet, God knew, but it was a possible way in. Dortmunder tucked the opener into the same pocket as the security notes, closed the office door behind himself, and went home.

46

All day Saturday Fiona fretted over tonight's GRODY party. How had she ever let Brian talk her into inviting Mrs. W to March Madness? And what had possessed Mrs. W to say yes?

Was there any way out of this? Could she pretend to be sick? No; Brian would just escort Mrs. W to the party anyway. And if there was one thing in Fiona's fevered imaginings worse than being at GRODY's March Madness party with Mrs. W at her side, it was the thought of Mrs. W at the party *without* Fiona beside her, to explain it, to smooth it as much as possible, to *shield* the woman, if that could be done.

So what could she do to make this not happen? Could she lie to everybody? Lie to Mrs. W that the party had been canceled, lie to Brian that Mrs. W had changed her mind. No; nobody would believe her. Fiona was not at all a good liar — an unfortunate trait in a lawyer — and they'd both see through her at once.

And then, how to explain *why* she'd lied? Well, she couldn't, could she? She could barely explain it to herself, because it wasn't merely the mismatch of GRODY and Mrs. W, it was more than that, it was . . .

Brian.

There wasn't anything *wrong* with Brian, not really. He and Fiona made a very good couple, easygoing, supportive, not demanding. His passion for exotic cookery remained a happy surprise, though somehow not quite as exciting, a teeny bit less of a treat, now that she'd left Feinberg and started a job with normal hours. (She would never mention that to Brian, of course.)

The problem, which she could barely articulate inside her own head because it made her feel guilty, the problem was class. Brian did not come from the same world as Fiona. His people did not live where her people lived, did not school where her people schooled, did not vacation where her people vacationed, did not buy suits — if they bought suits — where her people bought suits. His was a rougher, scruffier, less settled universe of people who hadn't made it, generation after generation, with no prospect for future change. When she was with Brian, Fiona was, in the very slightest way, barely noticeable to the naked eye, slumming.

If she were honest — and she wanted to be — she'd have to admit that her own great-grandfather, Hiram Hemlow, father of her dear grandfather Horace, had come from that same class, the strivers without connections. The stolen chess set might have helped Hiram move up out of the unwashed, but that opportunity was lost.

What had finally made the difference in the Hemlow family was her grandfather Horace, who happened to be an inventive genius. With the prestige and money he made through his inventions he could cut through the nearly invisible barriers of American class, so that the generation after his, the generation of Fiona's father and her aunts and uncles, with money behind them, however fresh, could attend the right schools, move into the right neighborhoods, make the right friends.

The family had moved smoothly into the upper middle class the way it's done in America, not with family, not with history, but with money. And now, a member of barely the third generation at this level, Fiona could look at Brian Clanson and know, with shame and embarrassment but without the slightest question, that he was beneath her.

The knowledge had her tongue-tied, and the further knowledge that she must very soon display Brian to Mrs. W as her chosen escort only made things worse. Mrs. W, as Fiona had every reason to know, was about as class-conscious as anyone she'd ever met. That rambling vitriolic memoir the woman was writing reeked of it. Was Fiona, having acted against her better judgment in a moment of weakness, about to make Mrs. W despise her forever?

Through all of her fretting Brian, of course, remained oblivious, continuing blithely along with his own usual Saturday morning routine, which was to commandeer the big room while he watched the Saturday morning cartoons, an activity he claimed counted as work but which she knew he secretly enjoyed for its own sake, the more childish the better.

Confined to the bedroom with the door closed — it didn't help that much — she paced and worried and searched in vain for a route out of her dilemma, and, finally, a little before eleven, she decided to phone Mrs. W even though she had no idea what she intended to say. But she had to do something, had to start somewhere; perhaps hearing Mrs. W's voice would give her inspiration.

So she sat on the bed, reached for the phone, and it rang. Startled, she picked it up, and heard Mrs. W's voice. "Mrs. W!"

"About this question of costumes," Mrs. W said.

"Mrs. W?"

"I understand, from what you say, many of the partygoers this evening will be in costume."

Oh, she doesn't want to go! Fiona thought, and her heart leaped up: "Oh, *yes,* Mrs. W, all kinds of costumes!"

"That doesn't much help, Fiona, dear: 'all kinds,' you see. What sort of *theme* does one encounter at these events?"

"Theme?" Arrested development, she thought, but didn't say. "I guess," she said, "I suppose, it's popular culture, I guess, cartoon shows and things like that. And vampires, of course."

"Of course," Mrs. W agreed. "Women, I find," she said, "don't improve in vampire costumes."

"The fangs, you mean."

"That would be part of it. I know you won't be in costume, but your friend — Brian — will he?"

"Oh, yes," Fiona said, trying to sound

359

perky rather than resigned. "The same one every year."

"Really? And would it spoil things to tell?"

"Oh, no. It's Reverend Twisted, that's all."

"I'm sorry."

"A cartoon character," Fiona explained. "From cable, you know. A little raunchy."

"His costume is raunchy?"

"No, the cart— What it is, Mrs. W, he's a mock priest, he blesses *all* the bad behavior, he loves the sinner *and* the sin."

"I'm not sure I follow."

Beginning to feel desperate, Fiona said, "The joke is, he's the priest at the orgies, you see."

"And what does he do there?"

"Blesses everybody."

"That's all?"

"Really, yes," Fiona said, realizing she'd never before noticed just how small and toothless a joke the Reverend Twisted actually was.

Mrs. W, calm but dogged, said, "What does he wear in this persona?"

"Well, it's not that — Not that different, really. Just heavy black shoes and a shiny black suit with very wide legs and very wide double-breasted jacket with a bottle of whiskey in the pocket and a kind of white dickey and white makeup on his face and a black hat with a flat brim all the way around."

"I see."

"It's mostly his expression, really," Fiona tried to explain. "You know, it's a leer, he leers for hours, the next day his jaw is very sore."

"For his art," Mrs. W said, with suspect dryness.

"I suppose. He used to carry a Kama Sutra, you know, the way priests carry a Bible? But he lost it a few years ago and never got another."

"We'll just have to imagine it, then," Mrs. W said. "Thank you, my dear, you may have been of help."

"Oh, I hope so," Fiona said, and hung up, and gave herself over to despair. Mrs. W was definitely coming to the party.

47

With a table knife, Dortmunder was trying to find a little more mayo at the bottom of the jar, but mostly finding it on his knuckles, when the phone rang. Licking his fingers, he ambled over to the phone and spoke into it: "Yar."

"I'm thinking," Andy Kelp said, "of giving up my answering machine."

Surprised, Dortmunder said, "You? You live for those gizmos. Call waiting, call forwarding, call lateraling, all those things."

"Maybe not any more. Anne Marie's out today," Kelp explained. "Some old friend of hers from Kansas is showing her New York."

"Right." Dortmunder understood. It's always the out-of-towners who know the real New York. "Statue of Liberty?"

"Empire State Building," Kelp agreed. "Grand Central Station. I think they're even gonna grab a matinee at Radio City Music Hall."

"Anne Marie," Dortmunder said, "has a very good heart."

"First thing attracted me to her. Anyway, I was out myself a little, you know how it is."

"Uh huh."

"I come back just now, there's *three* messages from Eppick. Three, John."

"Maybe he's tensing up," Dortmunder said.

"No maybe about it. Three messages that he wants *me* to ask *you* what's going on. They're not even my messages, John."

"Does he really think," Dortmunder wanted to know, "anybody's gonna tell him what's going on on the *phone?* You're not the only one with those gizmos, you know."

"You tell him that, John, it's you he wants to talk to."

"Maybe later. Listen, satisfy some curiosity."

"Sure."

"How come, when you were in there last night, you didn't go in there?"

"What? In where?"

"Maybe," Dortmunder decided, "we should talk in the open air."

Open air in March should not be approached unwarily. It was in a small triangular park in the West Village called Abingdon Square — sue me — that they huddled together on a bench near the southern apex, where some of the buses only slowed down, but others across Hudson Street stopped for a while, engines growling, to compete with the traffic going past the park south on Hudson then south on Bleecker Street, north on the other part of Hudson and then north on Eighth Avenue, and east on both disconnected parts of Bank Street. There wasn't much wind here, with fairly tall buildings all around except for the children's playground in the triangle just south of this one, so that, if Abingdon Square had been an hourglass, that would be the part with the sand. Not too cold, not too much wind, plenty of ambient noise — some children are louder than buses without even trying — and so a perfect spot for a tête-à-tête.

Having called this conclave, Dortmunder went first: "You were ahead of me, last night, on that roof."

"You went out on that roof?" Kelp was surprised.

"I had to. The householder come home."

"I heard all the fuss," Kelp agreed. "I figured, it was somewhere else in the building and you took off back outa there, or it was the householder and you went through him and then back outa there. I didn't figure you for the roof."

"Neither did I," Dortmunder said. "But there I was. And you were already gone."

"That was the place to be."

"Oh, I know. So I went over and I found those rungs —"

Kelp was astonished, and said so. "John, I'm astonished."

"No choice," Dortmunder said. "Down the rungs, down the fire escape. What got me was how clean you went through that basement door."

"What basement door?"

"Into Perly's building. What other way was there?"

Kelp was now doubly astonished. "You went into Perly's building?"

"What else could I do?"

"Did you never turn around?" Kelp asked him. "Did you never see that humongous apartment house right behind you? You get thirty-seven windows to choose from over there, John."

Dortmunder frowned, thinking back. "I never even looked over there," he admitted.

"And here I thought how terrific you were, you got through that basement door without leaving a mark, got through and out the building and not one single sign of you."

"That's because I wasn't there," Kelp said. "Where I was instead, I went into an apartment where there's nobody home but there's a couple nice de Koonings on the living room wall, so I went uptown to make them on consignment to Stoon, and then I went home. I never figured you to come down that same way. And wasn't that a risk, you go in there before we want to go in there? Did you leave marks, John?"

Insulted, Dortmunder said, "What kind of a question is that? Here I tell you how impressed I am how *you* didn't leave any marks —"

"It was easier for me."

"Granted. But *then,* back last night, you were like my benchmark. So what I left was what you left. Not a trace, Andy, guaranteed."

"Well, that's terrific, you found that way in," Kelp said. "Is that our route on the day?"

"We don't have to do all that," Dortmunder told him. "While I was in there anyway, I looked around, I picked up some stuff."

"Stuff they're gonna miss?"

"Come on, Andy."

"You're right," Kelp said. "I know better than that. Maybe I'm like Eppick, I'm getting a little tense. So what stuff did you come out with?"

"Their extra garage door opener."

Kelp reared back. "Their what?"

"That they don't remember they have," Dortmunder said. "Bottom drawer of the secretary's desk, way in back, under stuff, covered with dust."

"That's pretty good," Kelp admitted.

"Also some other stuff," Dortmunder said. "Perly's an organized guy, he made himself a lot of notes about the exact time the thing's coming down from the bank and all the extra security they're gonna lay on while it's there."

"He didn't."

"He did. Also, he's got a copy machine."

Kelp laughed, in pleasure and amazement. "You got their garage door opener," he said. "You got their security plans."

"Right," Dortmunder said, going for modesty.

Kelp shook his head. "And all I got was a couple de Koonings."

"Well, we took different paths," Dortmunder said, now going for magnanimity.

"We sure did." Seated on the park bench, Kelp watched a bifurcated bus make the long looping U-turn around the triangle, to go from southbound on Hudson to northbound on Eighth. "So what do you think next?" he asked.

"I think," Dortmunder said, "we make a little meet. All of us. At the O.J."

48

"Oh, I hope it still fits."

Brian, gazing down at the Reverend Twisted costume now spread-eagled on the bed like a steamrollered Arthur Dimmesdale, was already leering a bit. How he loved to get into that part!

"Oh, it always fits you and you know it," Fiona said, trying to sound loving rather than irritated, and the phone rang, yet again. "Not again!" she cried.

Brian's leer strengthened. "She's your boss," he said.

This was the last thing Fiona had expected to result from having invited Mrs. W to March Madness. Was this the sixth or seventh call, with hours still ahead before the actual party? Mrs. W had regressed to some antediluvian teenage past, working out her anxieties on the telephone.

Mostly the calls were about costumes, or, that is, the personae inside the costumes.

So far, Fiona had gently but firmly shot down Eleanor Roosevelt, the Gibson Girl, Annie Oakley, and Ella Fitzgerald. (Ella Fitzgerald?)

But the calls hadn't been entirely about the conundrum of Mrs. W's personal disguise for the evening. Should one dine ahead, or would it be a catered affair? Oh, dine ahead, definitely. Then Mrs. W would dine at home and pick up Fiona and Brian later.

Another issue. Would she be the only person of a certain age present at the party? Actually, no. Among the advertisers and other corporate types who might drop in were people of all ages, though the older ones tended to be more often male than female, and mostly interested in a new young companion to chat with.

Well, would there be anyone present whom one (Mrs. W, that is) might know? Not a chance.

Fiona answered the phone in the big room, wondering what the problem would be this time around. "Hello?"

"Do forgive the intrusion, dear —"

"Not at all, Mrs. W. Whatever I can do to help. Do you have another idea for a costume?"

"Well, yes, I do, in fact," Mrs. W said, "but

this time I don't need advice. From what you have said of tonight's festivities, I have now decided on the absolutely perfect masquerade."

"Really?" Tense, worried, wondering if she could talk Mrs. W out of whatever lunge into the past she'd made this time, Fiona said, "Who, Mrs. W?"

"No, my dear, that would be telling. You will be quite impressed when you see me. Now, my car shall pick you up at ten-twenty, is that right?"

"You don't want to tell me." Dread clutched at Fiona's bosom.

"Let it be a surprise, dear."

"I'm sure it will be."

"What I was ringing up about, in fact," Mrs. W went on, "was your friend Brian."

Fiona could see Brian, in fact, in the bedroom, just pulling on the Reverend Twisted trousers, shiny black wool with so much extra material and pleating that he now looked, from the waist down, like a half-blown-up Macy's Thanksgiving Day parade balloon. "Yes, Brian," she said. "What about him?"

"I should have asked this before," Mrs. W said, and she did sound a bit uneasy when she said it. "Will your Brian object to, in effect, escorting two ladies to the event?"

Out of sequence, Brian had put on the flat-brimmed Reverend Twisted hat and was viewing himself in the closet mirror, leering so hard he looked like a Cadillac grille. "He won't mind a bit," Fiona promised Mrs. W. "Trust me."

49

When Dortmunder walked into the O.J. at three minutes past ten that night, Rollo appeared to be deeply involved in taking an inventory, or a census, or something, of the bottles lined up on the backbar, doubling themselves in the mirror that ran along the wall back there. Tongue between teeth and left eye scrinched up like Popeye, he pointed the business end of a pencil at each bottle, sorting like with like and subtracting for mirror image before writing down the results on a piece of stationery from Opryland Hotel. Feeling Rollo shouldn't be disturbed at such a delicate moment, Dortmunder rested a forearm on the bar and watched.

Meanwhile, down at the left end of the bar, the regulars were discussing poker, one of them now saying, "Yeah, but why a flush?"

A second regular cocked his head in

response. "And your question?" he asked.

"Just that," the first one said. "Okay, I mean, a pair, trips, I get that. Even a straight, you can see the concept, your numbers are in a straight line. But why a flush?"

A third regular, who maybe hadn't caught all the nuances of the original question, explained, "That means they're all in the same suit."

The first regular lowered a gaze on him. "And?"

"They just are," the third regular said. "All the same color."

"And?"

A fourth regular, sounding a bit tentative for a regular, said, "Well, if they're red . . ."

"Yeah, fine," the first regular allowed. "That could be. But what about when it's black? What about when it's clubs?"

The second regular, who hadn't been heard from for a while, said, "Well, you wanna talk about that, how come they're called clubs?"

It was the third regular who said, "That's because they look like clubs,"

"No, they don't," the second regular told him. "They look like clovers. Three-leaf clovers."

The fourth regular, still tentative, said,

"So what about spades?"

"They're black," the third regular said.

The fourth regular, suddenly no longer tentative, said, "We know that, dummy, but whado they look like?"

The third regular looked into space. "Dummy?" he asked, as though uncertain of his hearing.

"Well, them," the first regular said. "Them, they look like spades."

"No they don't," the fourth regular said, all tentativeness forgot. "You wanna try to dig a *hole* with one of those things?"

"No," the first regular told him, "I don't wanna dig a hole with one of those things, they're *cards*, you play games with them."

"Dummy?"

"I go back to my original question," the first regular said. "Why a flush?"

"When you lose," the second regular suggested, "your money goes down the toilet."

"What's with this dummy?" the third regular insisted.

"They don't have dummies in poker," the first regular told him. "They have dummies in bridge."

"I can see," the second regular said, "you don't play poker."

"Oh, yeah?" The first regular turned away to call, "Rollo, you got a decka cards?"

Rollo turned half away from his bottle count to say, "No, I'd rather have a license." Then, catching a glimpse of the patient Dortmunder out of the corner of his eye he turned full around and said, "There you are."

"There I am," Dortmunder agreed.

"You got an envelope under your arm."

"That's true."

Having his research materials from Perly's office to bring to the meeting, Dortmunder had commandeered from the trash a manila envelope that had once contained color photos of flat scrubland in Florida that some misguided sales agent had been certain "J. A. Dortmunder or Resident" would eagerly look upon as the site of a "dream vacation or retirement residence." Feeling a little exposed to be walking around with an envelope too big to conceal on his person, he'd written on it *Medical Records,* in the belief that was something nobody would want to look too closely at. "It's just some stuff," he explained to Rollo, "to show the guys."

"Well, you got some guys back there," Rollo told him. "The other bourbon's got your glass."

"Good. I didn't want to disturb you," he

said, gesturing at the bottles along the back-bar.

"You don't disturb me," Rollo said. "It's a place of business."

"Right."

Leaving Rollo and that conversation, Dortmunder walked down to the end of the bar and past the regulars, as the fourth one was saying, "You know what's a very good card game? Frisk."

"Frisk?"

Suddenly tentative again, the fourth regular said, "Isn't that it? Frisk? Like bridge."

Rounding the end of the bar, Dortmunder walked down the hall, past the doors labeled POINTERS and SETTERS with black dog silhouettes, and past the former phone booth, now an unoccupied sentry box containing nothing but notes to and from the lovelorn plus a few frayed wire ends, and into a small square room with a con-crete floor. Beer and liquor cases were stacked against all the walls, floor to ceiling, leaving just space enough for a beat-up old round wooden table with a once-green felt top, this surrounded by half a dozen arm-less wooden chairs. The only light source was a single bare bulb under a round tin reflector hanging from a long black wire over the center of the table.

This was where they would meet, and it turned out, this time Dortmunder was the last to arrive, and as usual, the prize awarded to the last arrival was that he got to sit at the table with his back to the door. Andy Kelp had apparently been the first to show up, since he now sat in the place of utmost security on the opposite side of the table, facing the door. In front of him on the felt stood the bottle of alleged bourbon, plus two short fat glasses, one half full and one containing only ice cubes.

To Kelp's left sat Stan Murch, and to Stan's left Judson Blint, the kid. In front of each of them was a glass of draft beer and between them the saltshaker they shared, it being a tenet of Stan's creed that a little salt sprinkled into a glass of beer would restore a faltering head, a belief the kid had lately signed onto.

Across from those two, more or less taking up that opposite quadrant, was Tiny Bulcher, his fist closed around a glass that looked as though it might have cherry soda in it but which actually contained a mixture of vodka and less expensive Chianti, a drink Tiny claimed was not only robust but also good for the digestion. His digestion, anyway.

It was Tiny who'd been speaking when

Dortmunder entered the room: "If that's his attitude, fine, I put him back in the meat locker."

People tended to look for a distraction when Tiny was telling his stories, so the room significantly brightened when everybody saw Dortmunder walk in. "There you are!" Kelp sang out.

"You got my glass," Dortmunder said, shut the door, and sat with his back to it, putting the envelope on the table in front of him.

"Coming up," Kelp said, and poured into the emptier glass at his disposal, then paused with the bottle hovering. "Good?"

"That's fine," Dortmunder agreed.

As the glass relayed from Kelp to Stan to the kid to Dortmunder, Kelp said, "We just been waiting for you to get here with the stuff."

"You tell them what I got?"

"No," Kelp said. "I thought you'd like that pleasure yourself."

"Thank you, Andy," Dortmunder said, took a sip of his drink, and nodded at the others. "I got it all here," he said, and patted the envelope.

Judson said, "Medical records?"

"That's just the cover story," Dortmunder told him. "Inside, it's a different story."

Kelp said, "He had an interesting night, John did."

"Andy and I," Dortmunder said, "we thought we'd check out the place where the chess set's gonna be when it's outa that damn vault, and the place is a private eye's office down in the West Village."

Judson said, "An office?"

"Well, he's got the whole building."

Stan said, "That's some private eye."

Dortmunder shrugged. "It's only a two-story building. Anyway, what with one thing and another, I'm on this roof I gotta get off, and down into this space behind all these buildings, and *I* thought the only way out was through this Perly's building."

Judson said, "Perly?"

"That's the guy's name. Jacques Perly."

"Very pretty," Tiny said, not as a compliment.

"Anyway," Dortmunder said, "Andy was out ahead of me, turned out he went a different way, through an apartment building I didn't notice."

Stan said, "An apartment building you didn't notice? How do you not notice an apartment building?"

Kelp, to offer some assistance, said, "It was nighttime, Stan, and it was very dark and confusing down in there."

"If you say so," Stan said.

Ignoring that, Dortmunder said, "So I went through Perly's building, without, I might say, leaving one single trace that I went through there. And while I was there, I figured, let's see what it looks like here. So I tossed it, and I found some stuff."

Stan said, "What stuff?"

"Well, their other garage door opener," Dortmunder told him. "I didn't bring that with me, I got it at home."

Stan said, "This is a place with a garage? In Manhattan?"

Kelp said, "You see them sometimes, Stan, with the sign. *No Parking, Active Driveway.*"

"It's an old industrial building," Dortmunder explained. "Converted for Perly."

Abruptly, Judson laughed. "You got their garage door opener! You could go there any time, bing-bing, you're in."

"It's loud," Dortmunder cautioned him. "You go in that way, you're not exactly sneaking up on anybody."

"Still," Judson said. "It's nice."

Kelp said, "John, tell them what else you got."

"Well, Perly is a very organized guy," Dortmunder said, taking from *Medical Records* the sheets of paper covered with copies of Perly's neat small handwriting. "He put down the time the chess set's getting there, who's moving it, the security people they're gonna have then and later, the extra security stuff they're gonna lay on like motion sensors —"

"I hate motion sensors," Tiny said.

"We all do, Tiny," Dortmunder agreed. "Anyway, I made copies, so we can know what he knows."

Tiny said, "How many copies?"

"Just one, Tiny. I didn't wanna hang out there too long."

"Well, I don't wanna hang out *here* too long," Tiny said. "Kid, read it."

So for the next five minutes Judson read Perly's careful notes, while the others listened in a silence that moved steadily toward awe. When he finished, the silence went on for another few seconds, until Kelp said, "They really don't want us in there."

"Not up to them," Tiny said.

"Well, let's do a little recap here," Stan said. "I think I got it, but tell me if I'm right. This guy Perly gets to his office at ten tomorrow night." He looked at Judson. "Right?"

"That's what it says," Judson agreed.

Stan nodded. "He's got stuff to do, get ready for his houseguests. And they're gonna show up at eleven. Am I still right?"

"Absolutely," Judson told him. "These are the security guys and the tech guys with the equipment."

"And with them," Stan said, "they got Tiny's motion sensors."

"I don't like motion sensors," Tiny said.

"We know, Tiny," Stan told him. He looked around. "They also got — what? New phones."

"A cell phone," Kelp said. "And a special landline phone doesn't use Perly's connections."

"They've also got," Dortmunder said, "a metal cabinet with thirty-two lockable drawers for the chess pieces."

"And the complete security thing at the office door like at the airport with the doorway you go through," Stan said. He looked around. "Am I leaving anything out?"

"The moat," Kelp suggested.

Stan frowned at him. "The what?"

"Forget it," Kelp said.

"You can't do a moat in the city," Stan told him.

"I understand that. Just forget it. Go on with the recap. Now they're setting up all this stuff."

"And Perly goes home," Dortmunder said.

"Right," Stan said. "So it's turned over to the security guys now, and when they've got the office the way they like it they call their people at the bank."

"But the people at the bank," Judson said, "they don't move when they get the call. They wait, and they don't move until two o'clock."

"That's right," Dortmunder said. "It's all timed, so they can coordinate with the cops, because they get a cop escort coming down."

"And they figure to get to the office with the armored car," Stan said, "a little after two-thirty in the morning, drive the armored car into the building and up to the second floor and the cops go away. So now it's just the security from the armored car and the security already in the office." He looked around. "And there's some sort of idea that's where we come in."

"That's what we're working on," Dortmunder said.

"The good thing about this," Judson said, and they all looked at him. "Well, kind of good," he said. "We can go in ahead of time. We can go in before they set up."

Stan said, "And then what?"

"I dunno," Judson said. "It's gotta help."

Tiny said, "Dortmunder, does this Pearl

guy live there?"

"No, it's just his office."

"Anybody there right now?"

"No, not until the chess set is gonna get there. Late tomorrow night."

"Then what we do," Tiny said, "we go in there *now*. We look it over, see what we can use. Dortmunder, go get your opener and meet us there."

"I will," Dortmunder said, rising, half-turning so he could at last see the door.

Kelp said, "John, take taxis."

"Oh, I know," Dortmunder said.

50

From the minute she walked in the joint, Mrs. W was the belle of the ball, the queen of the hop, the star of the show. She *was* the top.

Fiona looked on in floods of pleasure and relief, though she'd known it was going to be a triumph from the instant she and Brian had climbed into the limousine and seen what Mrs. W had decided on for her persona this evening. It was perfect, it was inspired, it was *her.* And now the assembled guests of GRODY, in their turn, were being knocked out by it.

The GRODY party, as every year, was taking place in a rented party hall in Soho, a big barnlike space on the third floor of a recent building, accessible only by one special elevator, so that all of security could take place down in the small lobby and be over and forgotten by the time the elevator doors opened onto March Madness.

As usual, the walls of the party space had been decorated this week by GRODY staffers, so that everywhere you turned there were blown-up cartoon drawings, many of them suggestive but none actually filthy. A band consisting mostly of amplifiers scared away the demons down at the far end of the room, pumping out music one certainly hoped would not turn out to be memorable, and a few partygoers danced in a cleared space within its near vicinity, though not exactly with or to it.

Most people, as usual, stood around and shouted at one another, holding drinks in their hands, a surprising number of those drinks being soft, in cans. All of this activity was building toward fever pitch by ten-thirty, when the elevator door opened and Mrs. W stepped out, followed by the completely unnoticeable Fiona and Brian, whose Reverend Twisted was now reduced to nothing but a tall Munchkin.

Yes; that was it. The clunky black lace-up shoes; the black robe; the tall conical black hat; the outsize wart on nose; the green-strawed broom held aloft. It was Margaret Hamilton from *The Wizard of Oz* to the life; to the teeth. "And that goes for your little dog, too!" she cried, exiting the elevator and announcing her presence.

She was an instant hit. Awareness rippled outward through the hall, and people were drawn as by magnets in her direction. People crowded around her, people applauded her, people tried to hold conversations with her, people gave her about thirty drinks. The only sour note in the event, as it were, was the band's attempt to play "Over the Rainbow"; fortunately, most people didn't recognize it.

The first excitement and delight soon passed, and the party returned to approximately where it had been before Mrs. W had made her appearance, only with an extra little frisson created by this new presence in their midst. It isn't every party that has a drop-in from the Wicked Witch of the West, perhaps the most beloved and certainly the best-known villainess in pop culture.

When the first flurry was over and the partygoers had returned to their earlier activities and conversations and the band had gone back to whatever it was they had been assaulting, Mrs. W turned to her companions, thrust her broom at Fiona, said, "Hold this," then turned to Brian and said, "Hold me. I want to dance."

"Yes, ma'am." Wide-eyed, Brian was even forgetting to leer.

Off the two of them went, and Fiona had

to admit that, unlikely couple or not, they did make something of a statement out there on the dance floor, the wicked witch and the wicked priest. Mrs. W danced like someone who'd learned how at parties long ago in eastern Connecticut, and Brian danced like someone who'd learned how at backyard barbeques in southern New Jersey, but somehow the blend worked.

Fiona stood watching, feeling she knew not what, and a guy came by, looked at the broom, and said, "Do you do windows?"

"Ha ha," she said, and went off to find the bar. She knew how she felt; forlorn.

Brian did dance with Fiona a little later, to a somewhat slower number, during which he said, "Mrs. W is really something, isn't she?" He had his leer back by now, which gave the statement a strange coloration.

"I never knew," Fiona said, "she could dance."

"Oh, sure, that's the WASP world she comes from," he said. "They learn all those social things, like they're aristocrats. Remember, they call dances 'formals.' "

"Everybody calls dances 'formals.' "

"Not around here."

"Well, that's true," she admitted.

And something else she had to admit, if

only to herself, was that, while the GRODY party was the same old party it always had been, somehow this year it seemed more benign, more interesting, more fun. It was still the same completely unhomogenized crowd, the callow staff nearly invisible in the sea of outsiders, the twentysomethings dressed as X-Men or Buffy, the thirtysomethings with their more creative versions of roadkill or Messalina, the fortysomethings in their fangs and harlequin masks, the fiftysomethings in their red bow ties and shipboard gowns, the sixtysomethings dressed for some completely different party, but this year it didn't seem fake and strained, it just seemed like people letting their hair down at the end of another damn long winter.

Fiona realized that the only thing that had really changed was her perception. It really still was the same old party, too loud and too late and far too much of a mixed bag, with no coherent reason to exist, but this year that was okay. And it was okay because of Mrs. W.

Fiona watched Mrs. W swirl by, having learned by now how to dance while holding her green broom aloft, and now paired with Brian's shaggy boss, Sean Kelly, who this year had come either as a hobbit or Yoda;

impossible to tell. In any case, he danced like a man in a gorilla suit, but nobody seemed to mind. Mrs. W beamed upon him as they swirled along, and Sean, his grinning face as red as a stoplight, yakked away nonstop.

"Brian," Fiona said, "this is fun."

He leered at her in surprise. "You didn't know?"

Mrs. W didn't want to go home. The party was winding down, the bar closed, the band endlessly packing up like NASA after a moonshot, one a.m. just a memory, and so few people left in the place you could hear each other at a normal tone of voice. But Mrs. W didn't want to go home.

"I have just the place," she said, as they descended in the elevator after she'd called her driver to come pick them up. "I've never been there, but I've read about it. It's supposed to be the most in place ever, in the West Village."

"Oh, Mrs. W," Fiona said. "Are you sure? It's so late."

"New York," Mrs. W reminded her, "is the city that never sleeps."

"And tomorrow," Brian said, still with a residual leer, "is a day off."

"Exactly so."

"But, the . . . the costumes."

"Our hats can stay in the car, Brian's and mine," Mrs. W said, "and so can my wart. We'll keep our coats on."

"Fiona," Brian said, as he held the limo door for the ladies, "let's do it."

"I guess we're going to," she said.

The ride up and over from Soho to the West Village didn't take long, and Mrs. W, more girlish than Fiona had ever seen her, chatted away the whole time. She had apparently been particularly taken by Sean Kelly. "A remarkable comic mind," she pronounced.

"He can be pretty funny," Brian agreed.

And now they were in the West Village, driving slowly down Gansevoort Street while the driver looked for house numbers, and when Fiona looked ahead she saw a group of men coming out of a building up there, and thought, well, we're not the only night owls.

They'd come out of a garage, in fact, those five men, and as they stood on the pavement talking together the green garage door slid downward behind them. They were so animated, even at this hour, all talking at once, pointing this way and that, shrugging their shoulders, shaking their heads, that

Fiona couldn't look away. The limo drove slowly past them, and Fiona watched out the window, and one of them was Mr. Dortmunder.

No. Could it be? She tried to look out the back window, but it was hard to tell at this angle.

Could that really have been Mr. Dortmunder? The five men walked off in the opposite direction, all still gesticulating and talking a blue streak. They were certainly passionate about something or other.

Fiona faced front. There were so many things she didn't understand. Mrs. W had shown an entirely different side of her personality tonight. And now, had that really been John Dortmunder?

"There it is!" Mrs. W sang out.

"Oh, good," Fiona said, and swallowed a yawn.

51

In the careful chronology Perly had written for himself, he would return to his office on Sunday night at ten, to lock away many of his files and personal possessions and wait for the people from Continental Detective Agency to arrive with their equipment at eleven. But the tensions of the week had built up so much that by Sunday he couldn't stand it any more. Sunday evening was traditionally the one night of the week he could set aside for a quiet dinner at home in Westchester with his wife, but tonight he was just too much on edge. He wolfed his dinner, without his usual wine, and shortly before eight he said, "I'm sorry, Marcia, I'm too keyed up to just sit here. I've got to get down to the office."

"There's nothing to do there, Jacques," she pointed out. She was often the sensible one.

"Doesn't matter," he said. "I've got to be there."

And so it was that, an hour ahead of schedule, he and the Lamborghini were headed south on the Hutchinson River Parkway. Just to be in motion was an improvement.

Also, traffic was lighter on the Hutch inbound toward the city on Sunday night, so he made better than usual time. It was only ten minutes to nine when he turned onto Gansevoort Street and thumbed the opener clipped to his visor, and down the block his green garage door rattled upward.

The ceiling lights outside his office at the top of the ramp were kept on all the time, so by their light he drove up the steep ramp as the garage door lowered behind him, and parked in front of his door.

Unlocking that door, he stepped inside, switched on the lights there, and shrugged out of his coat. Fortunately, he didn't hang the coat up in the closet, because at the moment there was a very large and irritable person standing in there, muttering to himself about people who show up an hour early. He draped his coat instead over the chair at Della's desk, and it's also fortunate he didn't happen to look under that desk, or he would surely have noticed a lithe young guy curled around the wastebasket under there.

The door between Della's office and his own was normally kept unlocked, so he just opened it and entered and left it open as he switched on more lights in there. He then went over to sit at his own desk, under which there weren't any people. However, lying on his left side behind the sofa, squeezed between sofa and wall in a place Perly had never intentionally gazed upon, was a carrot-topped guy who looked almost as put out as the big fellow in the other room's closet.

Once at his desk, Perly switched on one more light, the gooseneck lamp there, which gave him concentrated illumination at the desk area but somehow made the rest of the room seem a little darker, though of course not as dark as the night outside his two large well-draped windows facing the rear of the apartment building on the next block. He often closed those maroon drapes at night, and briefly considered doing so again tonight, but then decided the security people would want to know what was out there, so he left the drapes open, which was just as well, because that way he didn't notice the sharp-nosed, keen-eyed guy standing behind the right-side drape of the right-hand window, farthest from his desk. That person had originally taken up a position facing the drape, but at the last instant had turned around, so that now he faced the window, in which he could examine at his leisure the reflection of most of the room, but in which his own dark presence against the dark drape could not be seen from any distance at all.

There had been a third person, another returnee from last night's reconnaissance mission, who had been in this room when the racket of the garage door lifting had alerted everybody to Perly's untimely arrival. This person had been near a closed interior door he'd already established as leading to a bathroom, so he'd popped open the door, popped into the bathroom, popped the door shut, popped it open again while he found the light switch and popped the light on, then popped the door shut again.

It was only when he heard Perly enter the office out there that it occurred to him that (a) Perly might want to utilize this bathroom at some point in the evening, and (b) there was nowhere to hide in the bathroom.

Well, was there? He looked around at a small simple utilitarian bathroom with white-painted walls and white tile floor, white toilet and small white sink and a white-tiled shower the size of the former phone booth back in the O.J.

Could he make use of the shower? Perly wasn't going to take a *shower* here tonight, was he? The shower had a plastic curtain across the opening, but the curtain was a translucent gray; shapes could be seen through it.

He had to do something. He had to get this light turned off, soon, and he had to find some way to disappear. How?

Above the toilet were two shelves, with white hand towels and bath towels. Hurriedly, he grabbed a bath towel, switched off the light, and felt his way into the shower, where he lowered himself until he was seated, knees up to his chin, on the white shower pan in the rear corner away from the drain. As best he could, he covered himself with the bath towel and scrunched up to become as small as possible. White tile, white pan, white towel; with any luck, no foreign shapes would call attention to themselves through the curtain. Sighing, reflecting on how nobody could be trusted, not even people with handwriting as neat as Perly's, he settled down to see what happened next.

Meanwhile, in his office, Perly was opening desk drawers, deciding what he wanted to remove from here and store in the safe in the corner until his visitors should move back out. Absorbed, he didn't hear the small click of the closet door opening in the other room, nor the faint rustle of the lithe young guy unwrapping himself from the wastebasket under Della's desk, nor even the tiny tick of the outer office door opening, but he did hear the quick snip of that door as it closed, and looked up from his desk, frowning.

Had security got here this early? Impossible. He rose, crossed to the doorway between the offices, and looked out at unchanged normality.

It must have been his imagination. Shaking his head, he crossed back to his desk, unaware that the fellow from behind the drape had sped silently across the room to stand behind the door while Perly frowned at his empty outer office, then looped silently around the door and through the doorway as Perly walked back to his desk.

Perly sat; the outer office door tocked shut.

Perly reared back and stared at the doorway. Wasn't that definitely the sound of the door? Was he hearing things?

Something's funny, he thought, and stood again, and this time walked both across his office and across Della's office to open that outer door, lean out, and see nothing out there but his own Lamborghini.

He frowned at the ramp, listening hard, but heard and saw nothing, while the carrot-topped fellow who'd been on the floor behind the sofa squeezed out of there and scampered across both offices to tuck himself into the recently vacated closet.

Perly frowned, still in his doorway, facing his ramp. Nothing. Nobody there. Could temperature changes at night do it?

This time, on returning to his office, Perly resolved to pay no more attention to tiny anonymous noises. They meant nothing. Everything was fine. Nothing could go wrong.

52

"The whole thing's going to hell from the get-go," Tiny said. He didn't sound happy.

"It's goddam Perly's own schedule," Stan complained. "Can't he read his own writing?"

The four had retreated down the ramp to take up a position over by the stairs to the basement. But this wasn't the way things were supposed to be. Relying on Perly's schedule, they'd fitted their own schedule into it like a burglar's hand in a stolen glove. They would get here a little before nine, and they'd have a leisurely time to study the offices for unknown problems — or opportunities, you never knew — and then come down here and continue on down to the basement about a quarter to ten.

Then Perly was supposed to show up, not *now.* Then he would show up, at ten, dammit, and do his packing and his filing until eleven, when Continental Detective Agency people would show up with the security stuff. A little five-handed poker would be played in the basement while Perly and the security guys set things up, and then left, and the office would be in the charge of the two uniformed Continentals, who would call their people at the bank.

Shortly before two in the morning, according to the plan, the game would be ended, and they'd come up from the basement and go on up the ramp to persuade the Continentals to cooperate — Tiny was particularly good at that part. The uniforms would be borrowed from their previous wearers, and whichever of the group they fit best would become the new security detail. When the set showed up, they would accept delivery, then go get the borrowed van they'd stashed around the corner.

Simple. Plain. Nice. No trickery, no complications. But now?

"I think the whole job's in the tank," Tiny said. "And if it is, where we all go is home."

Kelp said, "John's still up there, you know."

Tiny looked around. "Dortmunder? Where is he?"

"He went into the bathroom," Kelp said.

"At a time like this?"

"He went to *hide* in the bathroom."

"You can't hide in bathrooms," Judson said.

Tiny said, "The kid's right."

Kelp, looking for a ray of hope, said, "Does this bathroom have a window?"

Stan, who'd studied all the territory up there as carefully as if he were going to drive around in it, said, "No. One of those exhaust fan things."

"Jump-the-gun Perly," Tiny said, "is gonna take a leak, and guess what. We don't wanna be here when that happens."

Stan said, "What if we just went up and take him prisoner now? There's five of us."

Kelp shook his head. "Perly has to front the operation until the chess set's here."

Tiny said, "So it's time to say good night."

Kelp didn't want to leave with John still stuck up there. "No, wait, Tiny," he said. "Nothing bad's happened yet. We can still hope."

Tiny doubted it. "Hope? Hope what? Hope Perly's blind? Hope he doesn't take leaks? Forget it, Kelp, Dortmunder's history. Where's that door zapper?"

"The garage door opener?" Kelp pointed upward. "John's got it."

"Perfect," Tiny said, then looked around and pointed. "That looks like a door."

"Tiny," Kelp said, "why not wait a little

while, see what happens."

"We don't want to be here," Tiny said, "when Perly makes the phone call. You know the precinct in this neighborhood already has this address on their minds tonight. When Perly calls the precinct, it's already too late to leave here."

"I tell you what," Kelp said. "I'll just go back up there, take a look, see what's going on."

"Couldn't hurt," Stan said. "What the hell, we're here,"

"And if there's a problem," Kelp said, "we can always go out the way John came in last night, the back door out of the basement. Could be some other rich apartments across the way, so it isn't a total loss."

Tiny considered, then shrugged. "Five minutes," he said. "Then I'm outa here, and I won't mind making noise."

"Thanks, Tiny," Kelp said, and turned toward the ramp.

"If you two wind up upstate," Tiny said after him, "I don't visit."

Not feeling that needed an answer, Kelp went on up the ramp. The office door had an automatic lock on it, but he'd already automatically unlocked it once tonight, so he just breezed through it, being very quiet, then tiptoed across the outer office to peek around the corner of the doorway.

There was Perly, seated at his desk, taking folders out of a side drawer. He sorted the folders into two stacks, then reached for more. And just beyond him was the bathroom door.

A distraction might help John, but a distraction would also ruin the heist. Kelp held his position and watched, and Perly stood, picked up one of the stacks of folders, and carried it over to an open safe along the same wall as the bathroom. He stooped to put the folders into the safe, turned around, and went back to the desk.

Twice more Kelp watched Perly sort folders and carry some to the safe. Then he put the rest of the folders back in the drawer, locked the drawer, and stood up to go over to some bookshelves full of tall binders, all neatly marked on their spines with tape. He stood looking at the binders, then turned to look at the bathroom door instead.

Uh oh. Did John make a noise in there?

Perly crossed to the bathroom door and opened it. He switched on the light, stepped in, and closed the door.

Kelp didn't know what to do. Stay here and see if he could help John? Or get fast down the ramp to warn the others?

The toilet flushed.

Kelp frowned at the bathroom door. Water ran in a sink in there. Perly came out, switched off the light, and went back to the bookcase, where he started to sort through the binders as Kelp raced down the ramp and over to the others. In a shrill half-whisper, he said, "Perly went in there!"

"We're gone," Tiny said.

"No, listen," Kelp said. "He went in there, he took a leak, he came out, calm as ever. He never saw John!"

"Impossible," Tiny said.

"But that's what happened, Tiny, I saw it."

Judson said, "Are you sure he's in there?"

"I watched him go in," Kelp said. "And he didn't come back out, or where is he?"

"If he come out," Stan said, "even if Perly didn't see him, we would."

"Tiny," Kelp said, "we can stick around, because somehow John made himself invisible in there."

"Then I will stick around," Tiny said. "I'll want him to tell me how he did it."

53

It was nice the bath towel thing had worked, but other than that, this whole situation sucked. Dortmunder stood in the pitch-black bathroom, hand on the edge of the shower stall so he wouldn't get lost, considered his current position, and decided he didn't like it. He was still stuck in here with a guy outside to whom he would be unable to offer any conceivable explanation as to why this person he'd never seen before was suddenly walking out of his bathroom.

"It must be a space-warp kinda thing. I was just coming out of a bar in Cleveland." No.

Another problem with this place was that Perly himself wanted to make use of it, an experience Dortmunder had found not entirely pleasant. But the capper, and the reason he was standing out here in the dark with the bath towel over his shoulders, turns out, the showerhead had a leak. A slow insidious leak that you don't even notice until all at once the seat of your pants is soaking wet, and you wouldn't mind the opportunity to make use of this bathroom yourself. Which was also impossible.

What could he do to get *out* of here? What about the garage door opener? Would it work at this distance? If he hit the button, would the noise of the door lifting distract Perly and make him run from the room and otherwise behave in a way that would allow Dortmunder to get out of here?

It was worth a try. He took the opener from his pocket, aimed it at the door, and pressed the button.

Nothing. Too far away, or too many walls and doors in between.

What if he were to open the door, just a tiny tiny little bit, maybe while down low on the floor, and stick the opener out at ground level and try it from there?

Anything was better than to stay in here. Dortmunder let go of the shower stall, fumbled around, found the doorknob, and used it for support while he went down on his knees and very slowly, carefully, silently opened the door. He was just about to stick the opener out when he realized he could see Perly's desk out there, and Perly wasn't sitting at it.

So where was he? Was he standing or sitting somewhere that he'd have a fine clear view of an arm sticking out of the bathroom, holding a garage door opener?

The door opened inward. Dortmunder scooted over a bit on his knees until he could open it farther, a little farther, and there was Perly, walking away toward an open shelf-filled closet, his arms full of large binders and his back toward Dortmunder.

Out. Shucking off the bath towel, out he went, on his knees, pulling the door almost closed behind himself. Without a sound, over to the desk he went, down out of Perly's sight, and crouched low to look under the desk.

Over there, beyond the desk and across the polished wood floor, Perly's feet had turned around from that closet and were crossing the room. The feet stopped, then reversed and headed for the closet again, so that his back would be toward both Dortmunder and the doorway out of here.

Dortmunder's run was not graceful, but it got there. Out of Perly's office he galumphed, and paused at the closed outer office door to put the opener away. Then he eased open that door, slid through, admired the Lamborghini parked there for about a fifth of a second, and headed down the ramp.

How to get out of the building. He could just say the hell with it and open the noisy garage door and make a run for it. Or he could hope to get through that other door without attracting Perly's notice upstairs. Or he might go down to the basement and out the back way and see if he could find Kelp's apartment with all the art treasures. Get at least something to show for the night's work.

At the foot of the ramp, he decided the hell with it, let's just get gone, and was reaching in his pocket for the opener when, from his left, Kelp's voice did a loud whisper: "John!"

He turned. All four of his partners in alleged crime were over there, by the stairs that led down to the basement. Kelp gestured to him to come over, so he did and said, "I thought you people were long gone."

"I was," Tiny said. "Perly see you up there?"

"No," Dortmunder said. "But I left a towel on the floor, he might notice that."

Stan said, "Your pants are wet."

"I know," Dortmunder told him. "I'm well aware of that."

Judson said, "So does this mean it's a go again?"

Dortmunder looked around. Perly was upstairs and hadn't been spooked. Nothing else had changed. "Well, how do you like that," he said. "We go back to Plan A."

54

Operation Chess Gambit went off, at least in its earlier parts, without a hitch. The operation, code-named personally by Chief Inspector Francis Xavier Mologna of the NYPD before he'd taken himself off to his home, his wife and his comfortable and capacious bed in Bay Shore, Long Island, began at eleven o'clock, when, just exactly on time, two uniformed and armed operatives of the Continental Detective Agency, plus two of the agency's technical people, rang the street bell at Jacques Perly's office and, having identified themselves through the intercom, were granted admittance. Their unmarked small van drove up the curving ramp, parked next to the Lamborghini, and for the next fifty minutes Perly and the two operatives contented themselves with awkward conversation while the tech people laid out their special gadgets, including sensors on the windows and on the trapdoor to the roof.

When they were finished, the tech people turned their van around with some difficulty, due to the Lamborghini taking up so much of the available space, and at last, after a lot of backing and filling, they drove down the ramp and away. Perly spent another ten minutes giving the operatives last-minute instructions about what was on-limits and what was off-limits in this office — he'd noticed that one of them had already managed to drop a bath towel on the floor — and then he turned the Lamborghini around with not much trouble at all, because he didn't have a second vehicle to contend with and was in any event used to the space, and also drove away, headed for Westchester.

Once Perly was gone, one of the operatives phoned a fellow operative standing by up at the C&I International bank building, to tell him everything was ready for the cargo to be transferred, and then both found themselves comfortable places to sit and curl up with their books. Being a Continental operative could be slow work if you weren't a reader.

Meantime, up in the Bronx, the armored car drove out of the Securivan secure garage facility a few minutes early, at 12:25, and made terrific time coming down to midtown Manhattan, arriving at the C&I International building at 1:10, nearly an hour ahead of schedule. The driver chatted for a while with the four Continental operatives there, all uniformed and armed, who would be doing the heavy lifting, and then somebody said, "Listen, why wait till two o'clock? We're here now, the guys are ready downtown, let's call the cops and tell them we're starting now."

Everybody thought that was a good idea. Get the job done early, get home before sunup. So the NYPD was called, and by the time the Continental operatives, assisted by the guy from the bank, had the chess set mounted on its dolly and brought up out of the vault and across the lobby floor to the entrance there were four patrol cars in position out front.

Sometimes a task has a lot of screwups and irritations in it, but every once in a while you've got a job to do and everything works just fine, not a single problem, and that's how this chess set move went, at least for a while. There was no trouble moving the set, no trouble installing it in the armored car with the four operatives on the bench in there to guard it, and no trouble driving down the mostly deserted streets, accompanied now by only one patrol car.

They arrived at Jacques Perly's building at 1:27 exactly. One of the Continentals in with the chess set radioed the guards upstairs to open the garage door, which they did by pushing the button they'd been shown on the secretary's desk, and down in the basement the five poker players jumped up and said, "What's that? It's the garage door! It isn't even one-thirty!"

They had planned to relieve the guards of their duties and their uniforms at two o'clock, which would have given them a solid half-hour before the chess set would arrive. Fuming, Stan said, "Doesn't *anybody* keep to a goddam schedule?"

"Only us," Dortmunder said. "Come on, let's see what this is."

The five hurried up the stairs just in time to watch the armored car nose into the building and groan tentatively up the ramp, while outside the patrol car went about its business, its nursing detail done. The five stared, all hope gone. This was disaster. They absolutely had to get their hands on that goddam chess set *before* it got into that impossible circle of security inside Perly's office, that was the whole point here.

Over there on the ramp the armored car, angled upward like a turtle crawling over a log, stopped. It moved backward a little, then stopped. It moved forward a little, and very loud scraping sounds were heard. It stopped, moved backward, hitched itself around like a fat man adjusting his shorts, moved forward, and reproduced the scrape sound effect.

"It's too big," Judson said. He sounded stunned.

"These people," Stan said, "can't do anything right."

"Enough is enough," Dortmunder said, stepping forward from the stairwell. "Stan, get the van. Take the kid with you. Tiny, Andy, come on."

Everybody did as they were told, Stan and Judson exiting through the nearby door, Kelp and Tiny following Dortmunder, Kelp saying, "John? What's our plan?"

"We're getting what we came for," Dortmunder said, and yelled at the armored car as it did that scrape thing again, "Hey! Cut it out! Whadaya wanna do, knock down the wall?"

The armored car was completely inside the building now, on the ramp, in a position where it scraped the wall just as much when it went backward as when it went forward. The driver, over on the far side in his closed cab, looked out his right window at Dortmunder and shrugged his arms up in the air: "Whadaya want from *me?*"

Dortmunder went to the rear door of the armored car and banged on the bulletproof window. Cautiously, the door opened an inch, and the Continental in there, his hand on his holstered sidearm, said, "Who are *you?*"

"We work for Perly," Dortmunder told him. "We're the outside security, keep an eye on the place while you people are here, and brother, you *need* us. I got a van here," he went on, as Stan and Judson arrived with it. Turning to Kelp, he said, "Tell him to back it in. As close to the armored car as he can."

Kelp, looking awed, went away to instruct Stan, while Dortmunder said to the Continental, "You're gonna wreck this place. We'll get the chess set out and into the van, then get your truck outa here, then take the set up the ramp with the van. Also, we gotta take pictures of the damage."

"That's Securivan," the Continental told him. "That's not us."

From up above, one of the two Continentals already in position called down, "You need help down there?"

"Stay there," Dortmunder yelled up to him. "You don't wanna compromise the security you got there." Then he had to move briskly out of the way as Stan backed the van into the building and over to the rear of the armored car.

"I guess that's all we can do," the Continental said, and turned to tell his friends in the armored car what was going on. They all climbed out and, with all nine of them lending a hand, it took no time at all to transfer the chess set and its dolly into the van.

Once it was in and the van door shut, Stan drove the van out to the curb with Judson on the seat beside him, Kelp and Tiny sort of vagued themselves out of the scene and down the block, and Dortmunder said to the four Continentals, "You guys want to get in position where you can guide this driver. He's all messed up in here. You two go round front, you get on this side, you get on that side, I'll stand here by the door, be sure there's nobody coming."

Everybody got into position, and Dortmunder stepped back and thumbed the opener in his pocket, then galloped over to shove into the van next to Judson, which then left. The Continentals ran to the closing door, but didn't get there in time. If one of them had been a little spryer he might have been able to roll out under the closing door, but none of them were that spry.

Eventually they got the door open again, with a lot of shouting and recrimination, but the van was nowhere to be seen. Also, nobody had noticed its license number.

55

The longest day of Jacques Perly's life started, appropriately enough, before dawn, with a phone call from the NYPD that woke him from a sound sleep at, according to the green LED readout of his bedside clock, 1:57 a.m., approximately fifty minutes since he'd shut his eyes.

"Jacques? Whuzza?"

"God knows," Jacques muttered, rolling over, lifting onto an elbow, tucking the phone between shoulder and jaw as he switched on the low bedside light and reached for pen and paper, just in case, while saying, "Perly."

"Jacques Perly?"

"That's me."

"This is Detective Krankforth, Midtown South. There has been a robbery at your office, sir."

Jacques was not really yet awake. He said, "A — a burglary?"

"No, sir," Detective Krankforth told him. "There were individuals present on the premises, that upgrades it to a robbery."

"Indi— Oh, my God, the chess set!"

"There are officers at the location," Detective Krankforth told him, "who would like to converse with you as soon as possible."

"I'll be there in an hour," Perly promised, and dropped the phone into its cradle as he scrambled out of bed.

"Jacques? Whuzza?"

"Hell," he told her. "Go back to sleep."

More hell than he'd guessed. He couldn't park in his own building, couldn't even drive down that block. After being impatiently waved off by a traffic cop who didn't want to hear anything he might want to say, he found an all-night garage two blocks away and walked back, shivering in the cold. Three-fifteen in the morning now, nearly the coldest time of the night.

Two television remote trucks were parked outside the yellow crime tape that closed off the block. Whatever had happened here had caused some commotion because people leaned out windows into the cold up and down the block, and other people stood in clumps outside the yellow tape, staring at nothing much.

Perly identified himself to a cop at the tape, who radioed to someone, then nodded and let him in, saying, "See Captain Kransit in the command module."

The command module, in civilian life, was a mobile home, though sporting NYPD blue and white. A uniformed patrolman ushered Perly up the steps and in, where a disgruntled plainclothesman in brown suit and no tie, rawboned, fortyish, craggy-faced, looking exactly like a disgruntled high school science teacher, said, "Mr. Perly? Have a seat."

The front half of the command module contained tables and benches bolted to the floor, with a closed door in a black wall partway back. Perly and Kransit sat facing one another, elbows on table, and Perly said, "The chess set was stolen?"

"We're still trying to work out exactly what happened," Kransit told him. "Somebody's coming down from C&I bank, should have been here by now. You got a valuable chess set delivered to you tonight, is that it?"

"Yes. After I left. The Continental Detective Agency provided uniformed guards, and Securivan made the transfer. NYPD provided escort coming down."

Captain Kransit didn't take notes, but did

consult a yellow legal pad open on the table at his right elbow. "You were not here when this chess set arrived?"

"No, that wasn't necessary. The arrangement is, I'm renting my office to these people while the set is out of its vault for study and evaluation, so once the security people were in place I could go home. That was about twelve-fifteen" — glance at watch — "three hours ago. Can you tell me what happened?"

The microphone/speaker dangling from Kransit's lapel squawked like a chicken, and Kransit told it, "Send him in," then got to his feet. "The bank man's here. Let's go take a look at what we've got."

The command module had been warm, which Perly noticed when he stepped back out to the cobbled street. The man approaching them was black, well over six feet tall, and done up in thick black wool overcoat, plaid scarf and black homburg. He looked like a Negro Theater Ensemble production of *The Third Man.* "Woolley," he announced.

Introductions were made, hands were shaken, and they turned toward Perly's building, where the garage door stood uplifted. "The crime scene is still intact," Kransit said, as they walked. "The vehicle is

423

still inside."

"Well, yes, it would," Perly started, then stopped and started. "It's on the ramp!" And there it was, tilted up, a big, dark, bulky mass of metal, crawling with forensic team members like ants on a rotted eggplant.

Captain Kransit seemed slightly embarrassed on the armored car's behalf. "Yes, sir," he said. "Seems it got stuck in there."

Three or four men in dark blue overalls had been standing near the entrance. Now one of them came over to say, "Captain, we ready to pull this mother out of here?"

"Not just yet," the captain told him. "When forensics is finished."

"It's gonna take some doing," the overalled guy said, not without satisfaction. "Those guys really stepped on their dick in there."

"I'll let you know when," the captain promised, and Perly said, "Captain, what *did* happen? And where are the guards?"

"They were all shaken up by the event," the captain told him. "They've been taken down to Centre Street for a little rest and then a debriefing, but I can tell you both, now that you're here, Mr. Woolley, what occurred here tonight. This armored car arrived at about one-thirty —"

"Well, that's wrong," Perly said. "It was

supposed to appear at two-thirty."

"We'll find out about that," the captain promised him. "But in fact, it did get here at one-thirty, when, too late, they discovered the vehicle was too bulky to make that tight turn up the ramp. Trying to correct, back and fill, you know, they wedged themselves in tighter."

The overalled guy still stood nearby, and now he said, "We might have to take some of that stone wall out."

Perly said, "What? Now you're going to tear my building down?"

"Well, that's a very valuable piece of machinery in there," the overalled guy said.

Perly gave him a dangerous look. "More valuable, do you think," he said, "than my *building?*"

Becoming belatedly cautious, the overalled guy said, "I guess we'll leave that to the insurance companies. I'm out of it." And he walked away to join his pals, dignity intact.

Woolley said, "Captain, so far, we have this vehicle wedged onto this ramp. I take it something happened next."

"Five men appeared, in civilian clothes," the captain told him. "I don't have every detail, but this is based on the preliminary investigations up here, before the witnesses were taken downtown. Five men approached the armored car from over there, said they worked for Mr. Perly."

Woolley said, "They came from *inside* the building?"

"That's right. They were already in place before the armored car arrived. The guards in the car assumed they came from the ground floor offices."

"I don't have ground floor offices," Perly said. "That's all storage."

"The men in the armored car didn't know that," the captain told him. "These men said they were your outside supplemental security, and they had a van with them, and they assisted in transferring the chess set from the armored car to the van, which would be small enough to make the curve up the ramp. Then — the men on the scene have expressed great embarrassment and chagrin over this — the van drove away."

Woolley looked very sad. "I'm afraid, Mr. Perly," he said, "you haven't been very lucky in this affair. No sooner do you take over the responsibility for the chess set than it disappears."

Perly rounded on him. "Responsibility? I never *had* responsibility for that goddam chess set."

"Sir, I am a Christian."

Perly was beside himself. "I don't care if

you're a Girl Scout, my responsibility does not begin until that chess set enters my office. *My office.*" Perly pointed a rage-trembling finger. "That ramp is not my office. Not verifying the size vehicle needed was not my responsibility, and what happens to the chess set before it actually enters my office is also not my responsibility. It was still property entrusted to the *bank* that underwent an armed robbery, not property entrusted to *me.*"

"Er, Mr. Perly," Captain Kransit said, "it wasn't actually an *armed* robbery. None of the thieves showed any weapons. They merely showed up, took the chess set, and went away."

"Which somehow doesn't make things much better," Perly told him. "But the point remains, the bank continues to maintain sole custody of that chess set, as it has for lo these many years, and as it will continue to do until the chess set crosses the threshold into my office."

Woolley shrugged; no skin off his nose. "We'll let the lawyers sort that out," he said.

Envisioning a future full of C&I International bank lawyers, not to mention all the lawyers attached to all those Northwood heirs, Perly turned to glare at that *stupid* Tonka toy stuck in his beautiful building.

It's Clanson, he told himself. Brian Clanson, he set this up somehow. I'm not going to mention his name, not tonight, but I'm going to get the goods on that white-trash son of a bitch if it's the last thing I do.

"All done, Captain," said the head of the forensics team, as at last they all trooped out to the sidewalk, carrying their cases of equipment and samples and supplies.

"Thank you," the captain said, and turned to the blue-overalled crowd. "It's all yours, boys."

"Thanks, Captain!" The boys headed for the armored car. They were all smiling, ear to ear.

Perly closed his eyes.

56

When Fiona got to the office Monday morning, Lucy Leebald, who was already there, typing more of Mrs. W's memoir — Fiona was, in fact, a bit late this morning — said, "Mrs. W says come see her."

"Thanks."

Though she'd had trouble getting out of bed this morning, despite Brian calling to her from the kitchen every three minutes, Fiona did in fact feel better today than yesterday. Saturday night's March Madness party, followed by the pub crawl instigated by Mrs. W, had just about finished her off. She knew she'd drowsed a bit in the limo after the final bar, and Brian had had to hold her arm to steer her from curb to elevator and from elevator to apartment, where she'd slept heavily but not restoratively until almost midday, so that yesterday had become a completely lost and wasted day, but by this morning her recuperation was very nearly complete, so it was with a clear eye and a firm step that she crossed the hall to Mrs. W's office.

Where Mrs. W looked as chipper as the first robin of spring. Fiona had never guessed the woman had such stamina. Closing the door behind her, she said, "Good morning, Mrs. W."

"Good morning, my dear," Mrs. W said, and then, a bit archly, "Where have you been keeping young Brian?"

"Oh, I'm glad you liked him, Mrs. W."

"He's a charming young man. Sit down, dear."

Fiona perched on the uncomfortable settee, notepad in lap, and Mrs. W said, "Apparently, he's quite a talented young man, as well. Some of the decorative work on the walls was his, I understand."

"Yes, ma'am."

"Somehow," Mrs. W said delicately, "that television station — What is it called?"

"GRODY."

"Exactly so. It somehow doesn't seem quite the right place over the long haul," Mrs. W suggested, "for a person of maturity and talent. Wouldn't you say?"

"Brian does enjoy it there," Fiona said, which was as close as she could honestly come to defending his occupation.

"Oh, I'm certain he must. His co-workers are such a jolly lot. Especially that Sean. I quite enjoyed myself with them all."

"Well, your costume was wonderful," Fiona said. "Everyone was just in love with it."

Mrs. W came as close as she could to a simper. "I must admit," she said, "I was pleased at the effect it had. Do you suppose Brian would like to go back to university?"

Surprised, Fiona said, "He has his degree, Mrs. W. In broadcast communications."

"Oh, really?" Mrs. W seemed quite interested. "One obtains a degree in broadcast communications, does one?"

As Fiona looked for a response to that, the phone on Mrs. W's desk tinkled, and she picked it up: "Yes, Lucy? Thank you, dear, I'll speak to him." Smiling at Fiona and holding up one finger to indicate that this wouldn't take long, she pressed the button on the phone and said, "Yes, good morning, Jay. How are you this morning? Really? Why's that? *What?* My God! Jay, how could that — That's horrible, Jay. For all of us, yes. What do the police say? Have they no *idea* — Yes, of course, of course. Well, obviously. Two o'clock. I will be there, Jay."

Mrs. W hung up and turned toward Fiona

431

a thunderstruck face. At this moment, she looked less like the wicked witch of the west and more like Munch's *Scream*. "Unbelievable," she said.

Fiona, bursting with curiosity, said, "What is it, Mrs. W? What's happened?"

"The Chicago chess set has been *stolen*."

"Oh, my God," Fiona said, and inside she was saying, Oh, my God. They did it.

57

Because of its proximity to the Fifty-ninth Street Bridge over to Queens, the easternmost part of East Sixtieth Street is pretty well lined with parking garages, for those members of the bridge and tunnel crowd who prefer to keep their Manhattan driving experience to a minimum; say, seventeen feet. The garages are large, and full, and given to heavy turnover of both customer and employee, so any one of them would make a good place to stash, for just one overnight, an anonymous little van full of chess pieces, if you didn't mind paying the exorbitant fee, just this once.

Dortmunder had not accompanied the van last night — that had been Stan and Judson's duty — but he knew what to look for to find the right garage, and that was Tiny. Yes, there he stood, midblock, looking from a distance like a grand piano about to be hoisted through an upper-floor window.

Approaching, yawning — that had been a late night last night, and this meet was scheduled for 10 a.m. — Dortmunder eventually saw Judson beyond Tiny, and at that moment the kid saw him back and grinned and waved, which caused Tiny to turn around and acknowledge Dortmunder's approach, but did not cause him to grin and wave. He did, however, say, "Kelp's not here yet."

"He's probably waiting for the doctor to get out of the car," Dortmunder said, and to Judson he said, "Stan in there?"

"He should be right out."

"And you got the directions."

Patting his shirt pocket, Judson said, "Andy wrote it all out for me, gave it to me when we met last night."

Tiny said, "What about Kelp calling Eppick to call the guy, make sure the house is open?"

Dortmunder said, "He was gonna do that this morning, before he went for wheels."

"It's a hell of a distance to go," Tiny suggested, "to stash one box."

"Well, its not a stash, Tiny —"

Judson said, "Here comes Andy."

"— it's more of a delivery. The guy that it's his house, he's the customer."

"And we do home deliveries," Tiny commented. "That's real good of us."

Now out of the bowels of the garage came last night's small black van, Stan at the wheel, as simultaneously there came to a halt nearby a bright red Cadillac Colossus with MD plates, an SUV large enough for the rear seat to accommodate a basketball team; or Tiny.

"See you up there," Dortmunder told Judson, waved to Stan at the wheel of the van, and turned to climb into the front passenger seat of the Colossus, as Tiny occupied the rear seat in much the way the Wehrmacht once occupied France.

The van moved off first, Kelp following it down the block to the corner, where the light, for once, was green. The van went straight through the intersection, keeping to the left lane for the bridge approach.

Following, Kelp said, "What's he doing? He's going to Queens."

"Maybe he knows something," Dortmunder said.

"Maybe I do, too," Kelp said, keeping to the right, headed for the northbound entrance to FDR Drive. "We're not going east to Queens, we're going north to New England."

Dortmunder twisted around, to look back past the bulk of Tiny, but the van was already out of sight. "I wonder why he did that," he said.

"We'll ask him up at the compound," Kelp said. "We'll have to wait for them a while, though."

58

Nessa reached behind her to clamp Chick's thrusting hip. "A car!" she cried, her words half muffled by the pillow.

The metronome that was Chick abruptly clenched. "A what?"

"A car! See what it is."

Chick wasted seconds staring around the bedroom, as though expecting to see some car drive through here, but then at last he did hop out of her and out of bed and over to stare out the window. "It *is* a car!" he confirmed. "Two cars!"

Could this be the bozos with the chess set after all? Nessa didn't believe it for a second. "Time to get dressed," she said, feeling grim.

There'd been a few men in Nessa's life since, last November, four months ago, she'd switched from the dreamer Brady to the completely unreliable Hughie the roadie, and if she were the contemplative sort, she would be contemplating right now the fact that her men had not been getting better along the way. Chick, for instance, did not have Brady's deftness with locks, nor Hughie's cleverness and constant cash flow, nor much of anything else to recommend him except a large strong tireless body and an amiable willingness to let Nessa lead him by the nose or some other part, but he was an easy companion in her slow drifting progress toward somewhere or other, so what the hell.

Nessa had not so much hardened in the last four months as jelled toward the person she would eventually be. Leaving Numbnuts with Brady had not been a serious life decision, but just a fun goofy thing to do, on a par with cutting school or piling into a car with a bunch of other kids some summer night to go skinny-dipping out to Lake Gillespie. Leaving Brady for Hughie the roadie had been almost as impulsive and unthinking, but calculation had begun to enter her head: the indolent and unfocused Brady was proving to be useless in her life, but Hughie appeared to be a man with uses. And when he too in very different ways disappointed, there turned out to be somebody else. By now she had become serious enough to understand that she was not yet actually serious, but would be. There was still time to grow up. At the moment, but not forever, she was with Chick, who was gaping out the window, at a loss.

So she pulled on her jeans, crossed to the window next to Chick, said, "Put something *on*," and looked out and down at two simple sedans parked in front of the garage and, did they but know it, parked also in front of Chick's dented gray PT Cruiser, which was at the moment stashed inside that garage. Another complication, maybe.

A total of four people, all bundled up because in Massachusetts it was still definitely winter in late March, had climbed out of the two cars and, as Nessa watched and behind her Chick finally put his clothes on, the four began to pull other things out of the cars to carry with them off to the guesthouse, away to the right. Mops, brooms, squeegees, buckets holding cans and boxes of cleaning supplies.

Servants, these were, two men and two women, come to clean the guesthouse. We're about to have guests.

Won't they come to this house, too? A good thing they started their work over there. Nessa and Chick wouldn't be able to leave this vicinity while their car was bottled up in that garage, but at least they'd have time to erase their presence from this house before any of the cleaners arrived.

There wouldn't be much evidence of their presence to eliminate, in fact, since Nessa and Chick had only slipped past the locked rear gate and into the compound last night. Driving northward, she had told him about the big empty house in the Massachusetts woods, and how Brady had found the way to circumvent the lock, which she could now do as well. She told him about the people who'd showed up at the place to choose somewhere to hide a valuable chess set they planned to bring up, but then how they never did return, with or without anything of value.

"I still think they're bozos," she'd said last night, "but what else've we got to do? We'll stop by there, see if they actually ever did show up with that chess set, sleep in a nice bed, defrost some of the food there, and take off tomorrow."

"Then let's go to Ohio," Chick had said, for no real reason, and she'd said, "Sure. Why not?"

Why not? One place was as good as another, until it would be time to get serious. In the meantime, that chess set might have come in handy, but of course it hadn't been here. If there was one thing Nessa had learned so far in her travels it was this: Bozos are bozos.

59

As Brian saw it, the problem was how to make Mother Mean, the new consort for the Reverend Twisted, recognizably enough the Wicked Witch of the West for the viewer to get it but not so recognizable that all the property rights lawyers of the world would rise up en masse to smite him, and so he was hard at work in his octagonal office at GRODY late this Monday morning, forgetting all about lunch, deeply engrossed in his petty piracy, when someone knocked on the frame of his doorless doorway.

Now what? Looking around with that sudden spasm of guilt known to all pilferers, he saw standing there in his doorway what looked very much like a plainclothes detective, fortyish, a bulky body in a rumpled suit and tie. But he couldn't be, could he? A detective?

"Help you?"

"Brian Clanson?"

"Guilty," Brian said, with a leftover leer.

The man drew a narrow billfold from his inside jacket pocket, flipped it open, and showed Brian an overly designed police badge; too busy. "Detective Penvolk," he said. "I'd like you to come with me, if you would."

More startled than frightened, at least at first, Brian said, "But I'm working here, I . . ."

"It won't take long," Detective Penvolk assured him. "You can just answer a few questions for us."

"What questions?"

"Mr. Clanson," the detective said, with a sudden bit of steel in his voice, "we prefer our interviews in settings other than this."

Well, that made sense. In truth, Brian would have preferred his entire work experience in a setting other than this. However, it didn't seem as though he were going to be given many options at the moment, so Brian obediently rose, saying, "Will this take long?"

"Oh, I don't think so," the detective said. He turned to look both ways along the corridor, then said, "You probably know the shortest way out of here."

"Probably," Brian agreed. "Unless they did some carpentry last night." Nodding to the right, he said, "It should be that way."

The corridors were too narrow to walk two abreast, though people meeting could squeeze past one another. The occasional pregnancy among the staffers was usually blamed on the corridors. Brian therefore led the way, the detective followed him, and Brian said over his shoulder, "Could you tell me what this is all about?"

"Oh, let it wait till we get there," the detective advised.

Brian's boss, Sean Kelly, had his office on the right along here, an elongated rectangle that looked as though it wanted to grow up to be a bowling alley. Sean was at his *Star Trek* replica control panel in there when Brian walked by, and he was deep in conversation with Detective Penvolk's older gloomier brother. Sean rolled his eyes as Brian walked by, though Brian had no idea what he meant by that.

Had something bad happened during March Madness? There hadn't been any overdoses, had there? That was so old century. Still, something was going on, if one detective wants to talk to Brian and another detective wants to talk to Sean.

As they continued down the angling corridor, Brian dropped unconsciously into a prison shuffle, and said over his shoulder,

"The reason I asked, I mean, what this is all about, you know, this kind of thing could make you nervous. I mean, not knowing. What it's all about."

"Oh, don't let it worry you," the detective advised. "If you're innocent, you've got nothing to be afraid of."

Irrepressible at all the wrong times, "Innocent?" Brian asked. "Moi?"

Detective Penvolk chuckled. Faintly.

60

When Kelp steered the Colossus up to the closed gate to Mr. Hemlow's compound in Massachusetts around one-thirty that afternoon, the van was already there, parked in front of the gate. Stan and Judson, with all the time in the world, strolled back and forth on the recently snow-cleared drive, working out the kinks after all those hours in the car.

Looking grim, Kelp said, "I'm not gonna ask him," as he pulled in behind the van.

"I will," Tiny said.

"He'll only tell you," Kelp warned him.

"Then I'll know something," Tiny said.

They all climbed out of the Colossus and said hellos back and forth, and then Tiny said, "Kelp wants to know how you went to Queens and got here first."

"I don't care one way or the other," Kelp said.

"If you're headed north," Stan told them

all, "that's the best way out of midtown. You take the bridge and Northern Boulevard, then the BQE to Grand Central to the Triboro Bridge —"

"And there you are back in Manhattan," Kelp said.

"They call it Triboro because it goes to three boroughs," Stan said. "You take it north to the Bronx, to the Major Deegan, which happens to be the Thruway, which is the widest fastest road in *any* of the boroughs. Meanwhile, when you do it your way, you're in traffic jams on the FDR, traffic jams on the Harlem River Drive *and* traffic jams on the West Side Highway, and you're not even outa Manhattan yet. Also, I suppose you had to fill the tank on that thing six, seven times to get here."

"It is a little thirsty, this beast," Kelp admitted, and spread his hands, forgiving everybody. "But we're all here now, so what difference does it make?"

Judson, admiration in his voice, said, "Stan is one heck of a driver."

"We know," Kelp said.

"Andy," Dortmunder said, before any tension could develop, "you're supposed to buzz them now, aren't you?"

"Right."

Kelp went off to the intercom mounted

447

on the post beside the gate, and Dortmunder said to Stan, "There's a flat clear spot we found the last time in there. That's where we'll switch."

Stan, not sounding thrilled, said, "And I get to drive the monster."

"It's not so bad," Dortmunder told him. "It's kinda like driving a waterbed."

As Kelp got off the intercom, the two halves of the gate swung silently outward. "They say they got lunch ready for us," he said.

"That's a good thing," Tiny said.

They climbed back into the vehicles and drove through, the van moving over to let the Colossus go first. Behind them as they went, the gate closed itself.

Soon Kelp stopped once more, at a spot where, on the left side of the driveway, there was a small clearing. There might have been a little house there at one time, or just a turnaround for cars, or possibly extra parking for parties. Whatever the original idea, the space now was just a small clearing without the usual towering pines, the land at this time of year showing hardy weeds growing up through old snow.

Once again, they all piled out of the cars, but this time Stan and Judson took green plastic tarpaulins from the back of the van and spread them on the weedy patch while the other three dragged the box containing the chess set out far enough to get at the interior box containing the chess pieces. This part of the set was heavy enough all by itself for Tiny, who carried it over to the green tarps, to say, "Huh," before putting it down.

While he was doing that, Dortmunder and Kelp were pulling several cans of spray enamel out of the van and placing them on the periphery of the tarps.

"We'll see you up there," Stan said, when everything was ready.

"Shouldn't take us long," Kelp said. "Save us some lunch."

"Tell Tiny," Stan suggested.

"Don't be too long," Tiny suggested.

Judson gestured at the tarps. "The people up at the house," he said. "What are they supposed to think about all this?"

"They're servants," Tiny told him. "They're supposed to think, what a nice job I got."

"Oh. Okay."

As Stan and Judson got into the front of the Colossus, Tiny resumed his usual occupation of the backseat. Dortmunder and Kelp started rattling spray paint cans, listening to the little balls bounce around inside, and the Colossus disappeared around the next curve into the pines.

Kelp said, "Hold on, I need the red queen."

"Right."

Now they bent to the chess pieces and distributed them into two sections on the tarps, all standing in place, the red-gem pieces over here, the white-gem pieces over there. Kelp took the Earring Man's red queen from his pocket, put the original into his pocket in its place, and now the two of them went to work. Dortmunder sprayed his bunch black, Kelp went for the red. Fortunately, there was very little breeze, so they managed not to spray one another but still could circle the clusters of chessmen and get a pretty good shot at them from all sides.

As they sprayed, Dortmunder said, "We're only switching the one piece. We're leaving a lot of value up here."

"The way I figure," Kelp said, bending to get to the deeper crevices, "the four hundred bucks we paid for the queen was like seed money. We break up the queen and sell the parts and Anne Marie goes back to Earring Man for a few more second-team members, after the chess set heist is yesterday's news. We know the set's gonna stay up here. We just come back from time to time, do another little switcheroo. Money in the bank."

"Kings and queens in the bank," Dortmunder said. "Even better."

The job didn't take long. The box that had held the pieces went back into the van, along with a couple unused cans of paint, and then they got into the van, Kelp driving, to go the rest of the way to the compound.

As they started off, Dortmunder looked back at the two clusters of martial figures spread on the green tarps like a pair of abandoned armies, as though feudalism had just abruptly shut down in this part of the world. He said, "They'll be okay there, right?"

"Sure, why not," Kelp said. "Stay out in the air, dry overnight, tomorrow we'll set them up in that big living room. In the meantime, what could happen?"

61

When Fiona got back from lunch at her favorite bistro down on Seventy-second, it was not quite one-thirty, and Mrs. W was waiting, perhaps patiently, in the office Fiona shared with Lucy Leebald. "You heard me on the phone," she said, "that there is to be a meeting this afternoon about this dreadful event."

"Yes, ma'am."

"I want you with me."

Surprised, Fiona said, "You do?"

"I will want a reliable witness," Mrs. W said. "I may want a lawyer, of which you are still one, and with some familiarity with the case involved. And I may need moral support."

"*You,* Mrs. W?"

"We'll see," said Mrs. W, pulling on her gray suede gloves. "Come along. We'll be back anon, Lucy."

"Yes, ma'am."

The meeting was in a large conference room at Feinberg, her old stamping grounds. It felt very strange to walk through this tasteful gray territory as someone else entirely, no longer a wee beastie, but . . . well. No longer *their* wee beastie, but Mrs. W's wee beastie, a far better job description indeed.

The sleekly dressed secretary who led them through the Feinberg maze was a new one, but that was often the case. They turned at last into a short corridor and there, obviously waiting for them, was Jay Tumbril, as hateful-looking as ever. He gave Fiona a quick dismissive sneer and said to Mrs. W, "You brought her. Good."

"You said you would explain why when we got here," Mrs. W said.

"All in good time," Tumbril said, and gestured to the nearby open door. Inside there, Fiona could see, was the conference room, full of people, none of them looking happy.

But that wasn't the point. She said, "Mrs. W? He *asked* you to bring me?"

"All in good time, as I say," Tumbril answered, and pointed at one of the two low sofas along the corridor. "Wait there, young woman," he said. "Do not try to leave the building."

"Why would I leave the —"

But he had already turned away, ushering Mrs. W in. Without another glance in her direction, he also entered the conference room and shut the door.

This was a dead space in the Feinberg domain, a short corridor with a large conference room on each side, for meetings that wouldn't fit into the smaller rooms such as the one where Fiona had first talked with Mr. Dortmunder. There was no other furniture here than the sofas, each accompanied by a low end table on which reading matter was carelessly stacked, most of it three-year-old *New York* magazines.

Having nothing else to do — leave the building, indeed! — Fiona sat down and tried to find a *New York* too old for her to remember the articles inside.

The meeting went on and on. Fiona read *New York* magazines. She read *TIME* way out of time. She read *Golf Digest.* She even read *Yachting.*

Inside the conference room, the meeting was occasionally stormy. From time to time she could hear voices raised, male and female, though never what they were saying.

Every once in a while, she sensed movement and would look up to see one of her former co-workers staring at her from the end of the corridor. They always fled away like Eloi when she caught their eye, too afraid to be seen with her to allow them to satisfy their curiosity as to why she was here. And to think she used to like some of those people.

The meeting, which had begun at two, didn't end until nearly four, and then seemed to trickle away more than finish. The door opened and people began to come out, but they were all still talking, arguing, gesturing at one another. They paused in the corridor or back in the conference room or the doorway between, to make another point. None of them had grown any happier since the meeting had started. The exodus was like the end of a church service, but hostile.

And then, among the departing parishioners, here came Mrs. W and Jay Tumbril. Fiona stood, the two approached her, and Mrs. W said, "Well, Jay? *Now* will you tell us what it's all about?"

"Ms. Hemlow will, I believe," Tumbril said, and gestured at the closed door to the other conference room. "We'll have some privacy in here."

So the three went in, Tumbril shut the door, and he turned to say, "We might as well sit."

It was a very long conference table. Tumbril sat at its head, with Mrs. W on his left hand and Fiona on his right. Mrs. W said, "Jay, I don't handle suspense particularly well. Say what you have to say."

"Let's give Ms. Hemlow the opportunity." Tumbril turned his spotlight glare on her. "Would you like to tell us about it?"

Bewildered, Fiona said, "About what? I don't know what you mean."

"No?" Another smirk from the senior partner. Sitting back in his chair — they were actually quite comfortable chairs — he said, "Perhaps I should tell you, your coconspirator has already been arrested."

"My what?"

"He's probably already implicating you," Tumbril went on, "putting all the blame on your shoulders to try to make things easier for himself. That's what his sort generally does."

"Jay," Mrs. W said, "you are perplexing the both of us. If you have something to say, man, say it."

"Your sweet little assistant here, Livia," Tumbril told her, "is part of the gang that stole the Chicago chess set."

Fiona felt her face go beet-red, and her heart pounded as though it would explode. How could they have found out? She might have blurted something irretrievably incriminating if Mrs. W hadn't distracted Tumbril from her flaming face by saying, "Jay! Have you lost your mind? This girl couldn't *lift* that thing!"

"She was what I believe the police call the inside man," Tumbril said, "or in this case the inside woman. She's the one passed on to the gang the details of where the set would be kept while out of the vault. That was all they needed."

These few seconds when Tumbril was distracted by having to explain things to Mrs. W were all Fiona needed to get control of herself. She could feel the blood recede from her cheeks as sanity returned to her brain. Whatever had gone wrong, what she had to do now was just keep denying everything, she knew that much. Deny deny deny. But she couldn't help wondering, who had the police caught? Mr. Dortmunder? Somehow, she hoped not.

Mrs. W was saying, "I don't believe that for a second, Jay, and if you weren't blinded by prejudice you wouldn't believe it, either. And how is it you never mentioned this magnificent break in the case during the meeting we all just underwent together?"

"The police don't want it made public," Tumbril told her, "until it's wrapped up. Preferably with a confession. From the fellow they've already got, or possibly from this young lady here."

Now Mrs. W was openly scoffing. "Look at the girl," she said. "She would no more gallivant with a *gang* than you would play basketball."

"Bas— Livia, try not to wander. I told you at the beginning she was up to something. Didn't I? When she flung herself on you in these very offices."

"Flung her —"

"Mr. Tumbril," Fiona said, and, when she had the man's gimlet-eyed attention, "who did they arrest?"

"Ah, yes." The smirk raised itself a notch, and Tumbril leaned forward, the better to observe her reaction. "His name is . . . Brian Clanson. Do you recog—"

"Brian!" This was so astonishing, so absurd, she almost laughed out loud. "Brian? You think —" Then she did laugh, at the thought of Brian organizing a robbery like this. Or organizing anything, for that matter.

But then the laugh cut off in her throat

458

and she too leaned forward. "They *arrested* him?"

"That's what usually happens to thieves. Wouldn't you like to make your plea bargain with the district attorney before he does?"

Brian knows, she thought. I told him about Mr. Dortmunder and the chess set months ago, when I thought it couldn't ever happen. He's certain to remember.

Will he tell the police, to protect himself? But how would that protect him? If he said he didn't do it, but he'd known it was probably going to happen and he hadn't reported it, how would that do anything to save him?

The only thing Brian could possibly do was keep silent and wait for them to realize they'd made a mistake. The only question was, would he understand that was the only thing he could possibly do?

Was there any way she could get to him, talk to him? Would they let him have visitors? But didn't they secretly record jail-house conversations? Wasn't that in the papers all the time, that they weren't supposed to tape private conversations but they did anyway, and then people got convicted of things?

But even if she could see Brian, what could she say to him? And what would Brian say to the police?

Brandishing a self-confidence she didn't at all feel, Fiona said, "Brian didn't have anything to do with stealing that chess set. It is just a stupid mistake, and they'll have to let him go."

"Is that so?" Now Tumbril leaned back, hands folded on his paunch. "And are you claiming the chess set is *not* the reason you approached Mrs. Wheeler?"

Fiona hesitated, and in the hesitation knew that the hesitation itself had given the answer, and so changed her own response even as it was forming. In fact, she was a good lawyer. "No," she said. "I won't deny it. It was because of the chess set."

"Fiona!"

"Tell us more," Tumbril offered, with his little smirk.

"I'll have to tell you the whole story."

"I have all the time in the world," he assured her.

"All right, then," she said. "In 1920 —"

And she went on to tell them the entire history of the chess set and the platoon members' failed efforts to find either it or their missing Sgt. Northwood. She told them of hearing the story from her grandfather, and ended with her coming to work here at Feinberg, where she had learned about the lawsuits with all the Northwoods attached, and with that very same chess set attached.

"And I told my grandfather," she finished, "that at last we knew what had happened to the chess set, so he could at least be content at the end of his life knowing the answer to that awful mystery." Turning to Mrs. W, she said, "And I did want to meet you because of that. Your father stole everything from my great-grandfather, and stole his hope from him, or all of our lives would have been very different."

"Dear God," Mrs. W said, in the faintest voice she'd ever used in her life.

"Tell me about your grandfather," Tumbril suggested, smirking as though he thought he was being sly.

"He's an eighty-year-old millionaire in a wheelchair," she told him, "with a fortune from patents of his inventions in chemistry."

Tumbril blinked, slowly. For the first time, he seemed to have nothing to say.

"And to think," Mrs. W said, "you wanted to accuse this child of *theft.* How long, Jay, do you suppose it would be before that story of hers went public? Our fortune, our *lives,* based on a despicable crime? My *father* stole from his own soldiers!"

"I remember you said, Mrs. W," Fiona

said, "every fortune starts with a great crime."

"Balzac, dear," Mrs. W said. "Always give credit where due."

"Yes, ma'am."

"I do not want to see," Mrs. W told Tumbril, "my name, my family or my face on the cover of *New York*."

"No," Tumbril said. "No, that's true."

"So now, you horse's ass," Mrs. W said, "for once in your life do something sensible. Get on the phone. Get that poor boy out of quod."

62

Johnny Eppick and Mr. Hemlow, having started north in Mr. Hemlow's limousine after lunch, didn't reach the compound until half past four. The trip up, with Mr. Hemlow's wheelchair buckled to the floor so that Mr. Hemlow faced forward toward Eppick on the rear-facing seat behind Pembroke, was not devoid of accomplishment. By the time they arrived, they'd come to a number of satisfactory conclusions.

Mr. Hemlow began, once they were north of the city, by saying, "Johnny, I must tell you, you chose well."

"I'm pleased with John," Eppick agreed. "And his companions, too."

"There are five of them now?"

"That does seem to be what it took." Eppick grinned in an admiring way. "I talked with a couple friends still on the Job, and I must say what they did was as smooth as Mister Softee ice cream. They went up against half a dozen armed professional security men, and pulled the job without a shot being fired, with no violence of any kind, without even a *threat*. Sir, it was a heist even your granddaughter would approve."

"Oh, she'll approve the result, I have no doubt of that." Mr. Hemlow brooded out the window a bit, Eppick watching that profile that itself looked a bit like a Mister Softee ice cream. Then he turned back to Eppick to say, "They will expect to be paid."

"Yes, sir, they will."

"If I intended to sell the set," Mr. Hemlow mused, "it would be a simple matter of giving each a percentage. And you, too, of course."

"Thank you, sir."

"But that would require destroying the set, extracting the individual jewels and melting the gold down into ingots, which would be a far worse crime, in my opinion."

"Absolutely, sir," Eppick said piously.

"So," Mr. Hemlow went on, "since converting the set to cash is out of the question, let us consider what we should offer these fellows as recompense for their good work."

"It will all be coming out of your own pocket, Mr. Hemlow."

"I realize that. On the other hand, my pockets are deep enough to allow me such an indulgence. And when the day is done, I and my descendents will still have the set, with all its value intact."

"That's true, sir."

Mr. Hernlow brooded at the Hutchinson River Parkway a while, and then said, "The question is, what would constitute a proper payment? How much should I offer? What amount would fellows like that think was fair, and what would they think was insulting?"

"That's a very good question, sir," Eppick said. "Give me a minute to think about it."

"Of course."

Now it was Eppick who brooded a while at the Hutch, occasionally nodding or shaking his head as the argument progressed within. Finally he turned back to Mr. Hemlow to say, "If it were me, sir, I would begin by offering them ten thousand dollars apiece. They would not be satisfied with that number."

"I shouldn't think so," Mr. Hemlow said.

"So you would allow them to negotiate with you," Eppick explained, "to argue you up to fifteen or twenty thousand. I'm believing a payout of a hundred thousand dollars would be all right with you."

"Of course. Let me think about this."

"Certainly, sir."

Mr. Hemlow took his turn studying what by now had become Route 684, and did some of his own head-shaking, just visible mixed in there with his normal head-shaking. Then he looked again at Eppick and said, "I think that's too low. I think ten thousand dollars is not a strong enough bargaining first step, but would be seen as an insult. They know as well as we do they did more than ten thousand dollars' worth of work last night."

"That's true."

"I might offer them twenty, however."

"You'll still have the argument, though, sir," Eppick pointed out. "And then you'll wind up at twenty-five or thirty."

"Well, thirty thousand dollars doesn't seem out of the way, considering the job that was done."

"So that would make it a hundred-fifty-thousand-dollar payout for you."

"One hundred eighty thousand," Mr. Hemlow said.

"Sir?"

"You would be getting the same amount, Johnny," Mr. Hemlow said. "In addition to the normal fees I'm paying you."

Astounded, Eppick said, "I would?"

"None of this would have been possible without you, Johnny. You knew how to assemble the team, and you knew how to keep them in good order. You kept them honest."

"In a way," Eppick said.

"Yes, in a way."

Eppick laughed. "Mr. Hemlow," he said, "if I'm getting the same size piece as everybody else, I've been negotiating on the wrong side here."

"It was better that way, Johnny, better for you to think your advice was disinterested. I take it you would be content with thirty thousand dollars."

"Absolutely, sir."

"And the others?"

"I don't see any problem there, sir," Eppick said. "I truly don't."

"Fine."

When they gazed out at the Taconic State Parkway now, both were smiling.

Pembroke buzzed them in at the gate, and they drove the winding road up through the massive pines. Pale late-afternoon light was steadily darkening, the snow around the trees looking gray and tired and old. They drove part of the way up to the house and then Mr. Hemlow barked, "Pembroke! Stop."

467

Pembroke stopped, and Eppick turned to see what Mr. Hemlow was staring at. Out there, in a small clearing beside the road, on green tarpaulins, were two armies of chessmen, one the brightest crimson, the other deepest black.

"Beautiful," Mr. Hemlow breathed. "No one would guess what lies beneath that paint. On, Pembroke."

Pembroke drove on.

63

Mrs. W said, "What's taking so *long?*"

Fiona, seated on the next settee, had wanted to ask the same question, but was still somewhat intimidated by Jay Tumbril, particularly here in his own office, and so had kept silent.

"In my experience," Tumbril answered, "arrest is sudden, but release takes a little longer."

"It's nearly six o'clock," Mrs. W pointed out. "They've had nearly two *hours* to let poor Brian go."

Tumbril started, "Yes, but —" and was interrupted by his phone. "Maybe this is Michael now," he said, reaching for it.

While Fiona, Mrs. W, and Tumbril waited here in Tumbril's office, another Feinberg beastie, not so wee, named Michael, a cadaverous seven-footer in a black suit that made him look like an exclamation point, had been sent to retrieve Brian from the police, after Tumbril had phoned to explain the situation to the assistant district attorney who'd been assigned the case. Now, into the phone, Tumbril said, "Yes, Felicity? Good, put him on. Michael, what's the delay there? *What?* Jacques is absolutely certain of this? Put Roanoke on." That being the name of the assistant DA. Tumbril raised baffled eyebrows at Mrs. W, then said into the phone, "Mr. Roanoke? Jay Tumbril here. Are you certain Jacques Perly's certain? Well, if you don't mind, we'd like to be on our way there as well. Mrs. Livia Northwood Wheeler, with her assistant, and I shall come along personally. We'll get downtown just as rapidly as we can."

Breaking the connection, Tumbril pressed another button on the phone and said, "Felicity, call us a car. Soonest."

Mrs W, increasingly irritated and impatient, said, "Jay? What is this? What's going on? Where's Brian?"

"Jacques Perly," Tumbril said, "the private investigator whose office —"

"Yes, we know who he is. What about him?"

Tumbril spread his hands. "He says he has proof positive Clanson was part of the gang."

Fiona said, "That's ridiculous."

"Jacques is on his way to the DA's office with photographs."

Sounding like Queen Elizabeth the First in a testy mood, Mrs. W said, "I will wish to see these photographs."

"We all will," Tumbril assured her. "That's why I ordered the car."

Perly had arrived ahead of them, an outraged capon, too agitated to sit. He bounced around the small messy office of Assistant DA Noah Roanoke, and began squawking before Mrs. W and Fiona and Tumbril had even finished crossing the threshold: "You were going to let him *go?* You were going to *release* him? After what he did to my building? *And* your chess set!"

"Just a minute, Jacques," Tumbril said, and approached the balding neat metal-bespectacled man behind the room's standard-issue gray metal desk. "Mr. Roanoke?"

Roanoke rose, hand extended. He was as calm as Perly was excited. "Mr. Tumbril," he suggested, as they shook hands.

Tumbril gestured. "Ms. Livia Northwood Wheeler. Her assistant, Fiona Hemlow."

"Please sit," Roanoke offered, and took his own advice.

But nobody else did, because Perly, hav-

471

ing vibrated through the introduction ritual, now said, "I cannot believe this! And you didn't even con*sult* me!"

"If you have evidence, Jacques," Tumbril told him, "I assure you we all want to see it."

"Didn't even consult."

"We're here now, Jacques."

"I've turned the photos over to Noah," Perly said, with a quick brushing-away gesture toward Roanoke.

Who said, "Please, ladies. Those chairs aren't terribly comfortable, but they're better than standing."

Along the wall to the left of the entrance were three gray metal armless chairs with green cushioned seats, the sort of chairs you'd associate with Department of Motor Vehicles waiting rooms rather than doctors' waiting rooms. Since Mrs. W now took the one farthest left, Fiona took the one farthest right, as Roanoke handed a manila folder to Jay, who opened it and said, "Jacques, I'd appreciate it if you'd tell me what I'm looking at here."

"As you know, Jay," Perly said, "we've had our suspicions about young Clanson for some time now, so much so that I began an investigation of the fellow."

Mrs. W almost but didn't quite pop back

up onto her feet. "You did what? To Brian? On whose authority?"

"Jay's," Perly told her. "As your attorney."

"Without telling *me*. And who was supposed to *pay* for this?"

"Mrs. Wheeler," Perly said, "I am sure you will find the result well worth the expense."

"Oh, are you."

"Jacques," Tumbril said, "I'd still like some help here."

"All right," Perly said. "Here's the sequence. On Saturday night, an agent of mine kept tabs on this fellow Clanson, and late that night — just twenty-four hours before the robbery! — photographed him casing my building!"

Tumbril nodded at the folder open in his hands. "Oh, is this him in the backseat?"

"And that is my building, just beyond him. What my man did," Perly said, "when he saw what neighborhood Clanson was headed toward, was to take a faster route, and be in position when the car went by."

"Then this next picture," Tumbril said, "is him and some others getting out of the car. We're farther away here, hard to make it out."

"My man did what he could with a telephoto lens. But I can tell you that's a low-life bar farther down my street. Meeting the rest of the gang there, no doubt."

Mrs. W said, "Jay, let me see those pictures."

As Jay handed her the folder, Fiona slid one chair to the left, so she could look at the photos, too, and Perly said, "Unfortunately, my man couldn't get clear pictures of the others in the car, but he said one was a tough-looking older woman, some sort of harridan, a real Ma Barker type, probably the brains of the gang."

Fiona looked at the photos. In awe, she raised her eyes to look at the stony profile of Mrs. W as that lady said to Perly, with icy calm, "A tough-looking older woman? A harridan? A Ma Barker type?"

"When we get our hands on her," Perly said, "and we will, I can guarantee you she'll have a record as long as your arm."

Now Mrs. W did stand, though not precipitately or with apparent excitement. She stood as a thoughtful judge might stand when about to pronounce a death sentence. "The vehicle Brian is riding in, Mr. Perly," she said, "is mine. *I* am the harridan seated next to him."

Perly blinked at her. "What?"

"The third member of our nefarious gang in my limousine, Mr. Perly," Mrs. W went on, "is Fiona here, my assistant. We had come from a party given by Brian's television station, and we were on our way to a lounge considered at the moment to be the most desirable social venue in the entire city."

Perly's mouth had sagged open during Mrs. W's speech, but nothing had come out of it, so now it closed again. He continued to stare at Mrs. W as though all cerebral function behind those eyes had come to a halt.

Tumbril, clearing his throat, said, "Livia, I don't think Jacques is usually in that neighborhood at night."

"He doesn't seem to be all there by day, either," Mrs. W said, turning her icy gaze on Tumbril. "And if you intend to pay him for this harassment of an innocent boy, Jay, it shall come from *your* pocket, because you are no longer my lawyer."

"Livia, you don't want to —"

"Mr. Roanoke," Mrs. W said, turning toward that interested observer, her manner still steely but less aggressive, "we would like Brian returned to us now."

"Yes, ma'am," Noah Roanoke said.

64

Before dinner, Mr. Hemlow read to them, in the big rustic cathedral-ceilinged living room at the compound, with a staff-laid fire crackling red and orange in the deep stone fireplace, part of a paragraph from Edgar Allan Poe's *The Murders in the Rue Morgue* on the subject of chess: "Yet to calculate is not in itself to analyze. A chess player, for example, does the one without effort at the other. It follows that the game of chess, in its effects upon mental character, is greatly misunderstood. I am not now writing a treatise, but simply prefacing a somewhat peculiar narrative by observations very much at random; I will, therefore, take occasion to assert that the higher powers of the reflective intellect are more decidedly and more usefully tasked by the unostentatious game of draughts than by all the elaborate frivolity of chess. In this latter, where the pieces have different and *bizarre* motions, with various and variable values, what is only complex is mistaken (a not unusual error) for what is profound."

Closing the book, nodding his red-bereted head this way and that, Mr. Hemlow said, "What Poe calls draughts is what we know as the game of checkers."

Kelp said, "I like checkers."

Eppick said, "That's easy. Everybody likes checkers. Shall I put the book back on the shelf, Mr. Hemlow?"

"Thank you."

"My Mom used to read to me," Stan said. "When I was a kid. Mostly biographies of race car drivers."

"It's good when a family shares an interest," Mr. Hemlow said.

No hostess in her right mind would have put together a guest list for dinner like this and hope to make it work, but somehow it wasn't being too bad. Since nobody wanted to do the seven-hour round trip from and to New York in one day, it had been agreed that Mr. Hemlow would open the compound and he himself would spend the night in his ground floor bedroom in the main house with one or two staff members for assistance, while the other six would sleep in the simple but comfortable guesthouse, then head back to the city in the morning. Mr. Hemlow's staff, all local part-timers but loyal over the long term to a generous boss, would make dinner and breakfast, and now, as the group waited for dinner, they were chatting together, not too easily, in the main living room.

Eppick, having returned from putting Poe back in his place, said, "Mr. Hemlow, while we're waiting for dinner here, maybe this is the time to talk a little about recompense."

Nodding, Kelp said, "That sounds good."

"Yes, indeed," Mr. Hemlow said. "Something to whet the appetite, as it were. As you gentlemen know, I do not intend to sell the set but to keep it, right over there." And he gestured to where Kelp had earlier opened out the empty chessboard onto a large side table. "Nor," he added, "is there an accurate figure as to the set's value."

"That's one of the things," Eppick said, "they were gonna be working on in the private eye's office."

Tiny tapped a knuckle on his oak chair arm. "The millions, we know that much," he said. "That's close enough for us."

"Yes, of course." Mr. Hemlow was meeting most of the gang, and especially Tiny, for the first time, and seemed less taken aback than most people when initially rounding a corner to find Tiny Bulcher in their path. It may have been simply that life had already given him so many sharp lefts and rights that he couldn't actually be jolted any more. In any case, he merely gave Tiny's comment a benign response and went on to say, "I think we will all agree that, in this particular instance, the value to be considered is not the worth of the chess set but the worth of the skill and ingenuity and determination demonstrated by yourselves."

Stan said, "A fence would give us ten percent."

"The issue of a fence," Mr. Hemlow said, "does not arise, as this was a commissioned work."

"Unlike most jobs you people pull," Eppick added, "you aren't grabbing something to turn around and sell it. This time, you've been hired to do a little something in your area of expertise. You're like employees here."

Dortmunder said, "So this is the one time I'm not an independent contractor, is that it?"

"In a way," Eppick said. "But of course, without the retirement. Or the health program."

Stan said, "Or the softball team."

"That, too."

Mr. Hemlow said, "The number I was

thinking of, to express my appreciation for a job well done, was twenty thousand dollars a man."

Tiny did that *tock* on the chair arm again. "No, you weren't," he said.

Mr. Hemlow gazed upon Tiny from under his red beret. "I wasn't?"

"A hundred G," Tiny said, "isn't ten per cent of millions."

Eppick said, "It's ten per cent of one million."

"Let's not forget those other millions," Tiny told him.

Mr. Hemlow seemed to chuckle down inside there, unless he was merely having a stroke. Then he said, "I can see why you were chosen to negotiate for the group."

"He chose himself, if you want to know," Dortmunder said.

"Nevertheless," Mr. Hemlow said, "let me see what your friend has to say." To Tiny he said, "How much do *you* think is fair?"

"Not fair," Tiny said. "Right. Fifty G a man."

Even Mr. Hemlow was startled by that one. "A quarter million dollars?"

"Now we're getting there," Tiny said.

"I couldn't possibly," Mr. Hemlow said, "make an outlay that lavish."

"We can still give the thing back," Tiny

said. "Let you try with a more economical bunch. Or just melt it down and sell it off ourselves."

Judson said, "That might be kinda fun, Tiny."

Mr. Hemlow said, "I could go to twenty-five."

"The funny thing about the acoustics in this place," Tiny said, "with the high ceiling and all, sometimes you can't hear a thing."

Dortmunder said, "Mr. Hemlow, I really think you gotta come up a little bit here, just so the guys have a sense of self-esteem outa this."

Mr. Hemlow shuddered all over, even more than usual, while his left leg tapped out a series of SOSes. Then he said, employing the number everybody in the room had known they would end on, "I will give you my absolute top offer, and that is thirty thousand dollars per man. For my *own* self-esteem, I can do no more."

A little silence. Everybody looked at Tiny, who looked around at everybody else and finally said, "You wanna let it go cheap?"

Kelp said, "We're not gonna give it back, Tiny, that's not realistic."

Stan said, "And taking it apart, carrying it around to people like Stoon and Arnie, that's too much like work."

481

Dortmunder said, "You got a deal, Mr. Hemlow."

"Good."

"Dinner," the maid said.

65

Mrs. W insisted on hosting a celebratory dinner, so after Fiona and Brian went back home to the apartment so Brian could shower and change and shake like a leaf and down some medicinal vodka and generally try to get over the horrible experience of having been, for however brief a moment, in the toils of the law, they went back across town in Mrs. W's waiting limo to meet the lady herself at Endi Rhuni, a hot new Thai-Bangladeshi fusion restaurant on East Sixty-third Street, where the vulture wings, when a shipment had come in, were the spécialité de la maison.

Mrs. W was already there, resplendent, as the saying goes, behind a large snowy white round table at a banquette built for six. They joined her, Fiona sliding in to Mrs. W's left, Brian to her right, and Brian began by ordering a little more vodka, just to be certain he was keeping the dosage up to the proper level.

The first business of the occasion was to order a meal. Vulture wings happened to be in residence, so Mrs. W and Brian both ordered some, while Fiona, feeling less adventurous, had the llama steak with yams. Then Mrs. W called for a New Zealand pinot noir she felt good about, the waiter left, and she said, "Brian. Are you quite recovered?"

"Dickens," he said. His voice still shook a bit, but not as much as when he'd first been released to them. "It's Dickens, that's what it is. I never knew what people meant when they said that, when they said Dickensian, you know, that place is Dickensian, or look down there, that's Dickensian. But *now* I do. Boy, believe me, now I do. That was Dickensian."

"It sounds terrible, you poor boy," Mrs. W said.

"I even thought," he said, with a meaningful look at Fiona, "if I knew anything I'd tell, just to get out of there. But then I thought, if I tell, I'm *part* of it, and I'll never get out. So I didn't tell. Not that I knew anything I *could* tell."

"Of course not," Fiona said.

He shook his head. "The place was so awful, I mean just the place. I mean cold, and hard, and *dirty.* But the *people.* Mrs. W, you don't even want to know there *are* people like that."

"No, I'm sure I don't."

"You don't want those people out of there," Brian told her. "You want *me* out of there —"

"Of course."

"But not those people. You don't want those people out of there. Ever. Lock 'em up and throw away the key, there's something *else* I never really understood. You know, I thought, for a while there I thought I was gonna have to spend the *night* there."

"Oh, Brian," Mrs. W said, and squeezed his near forearm in sympathy.

"I thought, how can I do this," Brian went on. "I thought, this is going to destroy me, even if I get out of here someday someday someday, it's going to destroy my talent, how can I ever try to draw something funny ever again or —"

"Oh, Brian," Fiona said, "you'll get over it."

"— put on the Reverend Twisted, knowing *those people* are there. I mean, I'm a different person now, I can't, I can't be like I was —"

"The new Brian may be even better than the old," Mrs. W assured him, and said,

"Oh, your glass is empty," and raised a commanding hand to have his vodka refreshed.

By then the food and wine had started to arrive, so they set to, and the conversation skirted around other topics without ever leaving Brian's life-changing experiences entirely unobserved, and by the end of the meal the tremor in his voice was almost completely gone. They finished with shared desserts — peanut parfait, lychee flan, bees' nest soup — and were happily passing them around when all at once the theme music from *Mighty Mouse* rollicked beneath the table.

"Oh, I forgot!" Brian cried, scrabbling around inside his clothing. "I always turn it off when — I'm just so flustered, I don't know —" He popped the cell phone open and looked in it. "It's the station," he said. "Maybe they want me to take tomorrow off to recover. I better answer it."

The women agreed, and Brian spoke into the phone: "Here I am, out of custody." He grinned. "Hi, Sean, I'm here with Mrs. W and Fiona, we're making the bad memories go away over weird desserts." He nodded at the phone, switched his grin to the women, and said, "Sean says hello."

"And so do we," said Mrs. W.

"What? Sure I can talk." Brian looked

alert, then confused, then terribly hurt. "But *why?* I was *innocent!* Sean, they let me *go.*"

Fiona, startled for him, said, "Brian?"

"But, Sean, it wasn't my *fault.* You've gotta *go?* You lay this on me, and then you've gotta *go?* Sean? Sean?" Staring helplessly at the women, he said, "He went."

"But what was it, dear boy?" Mrs. W wanted to know.

Turning his cell phone off, closing it, moodily returning it to its recess on his person, he said, "They fired me."

"What?"

"I knew it," Fiona said.

Mrs. W reared around to glare at her with a disbelieving, almost angry look. "You knew it? How could you have known it?"

"Just from how Brian looked."

Leaving that side-issue, Mrs. W turned back to say, "Brian, what on earth did they fire you *for?*"

"Cops all over the station, asking questions. Turns out, that private eye'd been doing stuff there, maybe phone taps, nobody knows."

"But what has that to do with *you?*"

"I was what it was all about." Brian gave a hopeless shrug. "At GRODY, they don't wanna be around anything heavy."

"But it wasn't your fault."

"I'd just be a bad reminder."

Fiona said, "Can't your union do anything?"

"They'll try to find me another job."

"Well, this is intolerable," Mrs. W said, and whipped out her own cell phone. "We're not going to take this lying down, Brian. Never take anything lying down."

"No, ma'am."

With the deftness of a master knitter, Mrs. W navigated her cell phone, marching through its address book to the person she wanted, then making the call. Fiona watched and said, "Who are you calling, Mrs. W?"

"Jay. We're not going to put up with this, my dear."

"But, you fired Jay today."

"Oh, nonsense," she said. "I fire him all the time, that doesn't — Jay? Livia. Well, we are also just finishing dinner. Half an hour? Perfect. Call me at home." Slapping the phone shut, she said, "We've finished our desserts. Fiona, dear, we'll have to go on ahead, so I'm afraid I must ask you to put this meal on your credit card and take a taxi home. I'll reimburse you, of course, tomorrow."

"But —"

"Come along, Brian," Mrs. W said, hurrying him ahead of her around the banquette and onto his feet.

Fiona said, "Should I come on to your place, Mrs. W?"

"I do not intend to spend all *night* on this, my dear," Mrs. W told her. "You go on home, and Brian will be along after he's explained the situation to Jay." She started off, then turned back to say, "Dear. Don't overtip."

The reason Fiona overslept is because Brian, having lived a normal regular life far longer than she had, was always the first one out of bed. This morning, without Brian, she slept until nearly nine o'clock, then woke from confused bad dreams with a sudden start.

Without Brian? No, his side of the bed wasn't rumpled. He hadn't . . .

He hadn't come home last night.

First things first. When she came out of the bathroom, she immediately phoned Mrs. W, and recognized Lucy's voice. "Hi, it's Fiona, can I talk to Mrs. W?"

"Oh, you just missed them."

"Just missed? Them?"

"They're on their way to Newark, they're flying to Palm Beach. For about a week, Mrs. W says."

"But who —"

"She says I should find out what she owes you for last night and she'll send you a check."

"But who —"

"She says," Lucy went on, "you had a terrible time of it, and you should take the rest of this week off, and everybody can start all over again next week."

"But who —"

"On salary, she said," Lucy explained.

"*Lucy!* Who did Mrs. W go to Palm Beach with?"

Sounding surprised, Lucy said, "You didn't know? You had to know. She's taking your friend Brian down there to find him a much better job than he had at that cable station. Do you know how much you spent last night?"

"I'll have to, uh, I'll have to figure that out and call you back."

"Fine," Lucy said. "Mrs. W says she'll check in with me when they get to Palm Beach."

"They."

"Enjoy your vacation," Lucy said, and hung up.

So, a little later, did Fiona, though she continued to sit on the sofa in the big room, naked, alone, without breakfast, just looking around at what had suddenly become a very different space.

It must be in their genes, she thought. Her father stole my great-grandfather's future. And now she's stolen my boyfriend.

66

Mr. Hemlow's staff specialized in the kind of breakfast that didn't merely stick to your ribs but weighed them down so much it was a real effort to keep your chin above the level of the table. As a result, it was nearly ten on Tuesday morning before anybody in the compound began to show any vital signs at all, and that was Tiny, whose storage capacity, of course, was larger than everyone else's, so his recovery time tended to be more rapid as well. At last he stood, roamed around the big living room, paused to gaze at the chessboard waiting for its armies, strolled over to the front door and stepped out onto the porch. He left the door open, since the crisp mountain air, while cold, was also a tonic for that logy feeling. A minute later he came back to the doorway to say, "Who moved the Caddy?"

Several mumbles answered him, and then Kelp said, "Nobody, it's over there by the garages."

Standing in the doorway, Tiny looked that way. "The van is over there by the garages. A couple little staff cars are over there by the garages. The Caddy isn't there."

"Impossible," Kelp said. "That's where I left it."

"The Caddy," Tiny told him, "is not something you don't notice."

"I don't get this," Kelp said. Struggling to his feet, he followed Tiny back out into the cold.

Dortmunder roused himself. "I don't like that," he said.

Stan, chin slipping below table level, said, "What don't you like?"

"None of us moved it," Dortmunder said. "That's what I don't like."

Pushing himself two-handed up from the table, he weaved toward the open door. Behind him, Mr. Hemlow said to the hovering servant girl, "Was the upstairs seen to here?"

"No, sir," she said. "Everybody was at the guesthouse and you stayed down here."

"Have somebody look around up there."

"Yes, sir, I'll go."

Dortmunder went out onto the porch. Tiny and Kelp stood where lately the Colossus had stood. They seemed to be discussing the garage, and now Kelp lifted that door, and a car was in there.

Dortmunder went down off the porch and walked over to the garage, and it was a beat-up gray PT Cruiser with New Jersey plates that had been scuffed up with mud to make them hard to read.

Kelp was just closing the driver's door when Dortmunder arrived. "The key's in it," he said, "but nothing personal."

"They were staying here," Dortmunder said, as Judson walked over to join them from the house. "Empty house in the woods, they were smart enough to get in without setting off the alarm."

Tiny said, "Who?"

"We'll never know," Dortmunder said. "The Caddy was in their way, to get at their car. I figure, first they just wanted to move the Caddy over, then they said, what the hell, our car's stolen anyway, let's take the nice one."

Judson said, "How's the chess set?"

Kelp, horror-struck, looked away downhill. "The chess set!"

"Gone," Dortmunder told him.

"I gotta go — I gotta —"

Kelp, with Judson right behind him, climbed into the van. Dortmunder and Tiny turned and made their silent way back to the house, where Dortmunder found a nice old rocking chair not too close to the fire and sat there and waited for events to unfold.

They didn't take long. Kelp and Judson came back with the news that the green tarps were still there. The servant girl came downstairs with a slender pair of cherry-red panties. "They were under a pillow," she said. "What made me look, the bed wasn't made the way we make it."

"How could this have happened?" Mr. Hemlow wanted to know. He'd developed an extra two or three rumba routines this morning.

The answer arrived soon, in the person of Eppick, who came back from inspecting the rear entrance to the compound. "It's been rigged so you can bypass it, if you know how. It doesn't show itself to the eye, but if you know how you can get in. And out."

Mr. Hemlow said, "Johnny, you came up here with John to make sure the place was still secure."

"That was four months ago, Mr. Hemlow. I didn't do any sweep this time. We're all staying here."

Kelp said, "Mr. Hemlow, this is a blow to everybody, but at least you know one thing for sure. The chess set isn't ever going back to the Northwoods."

"Nor is it going," Mr. Hemlow said, "in any fashion at all, to its rightful inheritors."

Tiny, not sympathetic, said, "They can't miss what they didn't have."

"I keep reminding myself," Mr. Hemlow said, "just yesterday, I saw all those pieces, out there, beside the driveway. The lost chess set. I saw it, if only just the once, with these eyes."

"Hold the thought," Tiny suggested. "And before the rest of us get on the road here, let's work out how you're gonna get us our money."

Astonished, Mr. Hemlow said, "Are you serious? The set is *gone.*"

"We delivered it," Tiny said. "We found it and we got it and we delivered it. If this place of yours is a sieve, that's no skin off our nose."

Mr. Hemlow said, "I am not without re-sources."

"That's right, so you can —"

"No, I mean, resources of self-defense." Mr. Hemlow glowered around at all the faces glowering right back at him. "I am not going to pay one hundred and fifty thousand dollars for a chess set I do not have."

Eppick said, "Mr. Hemlow, be fair. They

worked hard. They delivered it to your *door*. And this isn't their fault. You gotta give them *some*thing."

Mr. Hemlow brooded. Never before in the history of the world has a wheelchair-bound sick man surrounded by hostile professional criminals looked less troubled by his situation. The loss of the chess set troubled him. About the attitudes and potential threats of the half-dozen men gathered around him he couldn't have cared less.

But he did finally say, "They deserve something, that's true."

Smiling, Stan said, "I knew you were a decent guy, Mr. Hemlow."

"I do not have the chess set, nor will I ever, but it is true the work was done, and as you point out the Northwoods will never have the set again either. I will pay ten thousand dollars per man."

Stan, no longer smiling, said, "That's a third!"

"Take it or leave it," Mr. Hemlow said. "You'll have a third of the original price. I'll have the chessboard. Fifty thousand dollars is a mighty steep price for a chessboard, gentlemen."

A long slow sigh circled the room. "We'll take it," Dortmunder said.

67

The doctor, when Trooper Hemblatt reached him by phone at his hospital down in New York City, was pretty steamed, and the trooper didn't see as how he could blame the man. "They just came right into the hospital parking lot and waltzed out with my car."

"Yes, sir."

"I had less than seven K on that car."

"Just over seven K now, sir. But at least they didn't bang it up."

"I'll want my garage to do a complete diagnostic on it, as soon as I get it towed down here."

"That's up to you, sir."

"But you got the thieves, did you?"

"We do have two individuals in custody, yes, sir, but we're still sorting that out."

"What do you mean, sorting out?"

"Well, there's little question about the man who was operating the vehicle when it was stopped. Chester Wilcox doesn't deny he took it, sir."

"He was driving it! How could he deny it?"

"Exactly, sir. The one oddity is, he claims he didn't pick it up in New York City, but down in Massachusetts, in some estate down there."

"Massachusetts! I don't even *know* anybody in Massachusetts. He took it from the hospital parking lot, right here on Third Avenue, yesterday morning. You say he was with a woman?"

"*She* claims to be a hitchhiker who boarded the vehicle this morning near New Lebanon, just this side of the New Hampshire state line."

"Is she telling the truth?"

"That's hard to say, sir. Wilcox claims she was with him at the estate, that she was the one, not him, who knew how to find the place, and that it was in fact her idea to take your vehicle, but he doesn't seem to know much about her, other than her first name. He may be telling the truth, but I doubt we'll develop sufficient cause to hold her."

"Just so *he's* put away, and I get my car back. What is he up to, Trooper, claiming he stole my car in some other state and saying some hitchhiker put him up to it? Is he hoping for an insanity defense?"

"I think what Wilcox mostly has is a stupidity defense, sir," Trooper Hemblatt said. "But let me go over the rest of it, if I may."

"There's more?"

"We want to be sure there's nothing missing from the vehicle, sir. Your garage door opener and cell phone and medicated cushion are all there, and the chess pieces are still in the trunk."

"The what?"

"Chess pieces, sir, a full chess set, but without the board. They're pretty heavy, they could be made of cement." This rural part of northern New Hampshire was too remote to know or care about some stolen chess set way down in New York City.

"*I* don't have a chess set." The doctor, on the other hand, was too self-centered to pay much attention to the news.

"It's in the vehicle, sir, in the trunk. Red pieces and black pieces."

"I don't even *play* chess."

"Well, sir, the pieces are there."

"I don't want them. They're not mine, I don't want them."

"I don't think we're gonna get a straight answer from Wilcox, sir. If he says the pieces came from the estate it won't help because he claims he doesn't know where the estate is, and the woman claims never to have been there."

"Trooper, I really don't want that chess set."

Trooper Hemblatt considered. "I tell you what," he said. "If you don't want the set, do you mind if we give it away? There's an old age home in town here, run by the Little Sisters of Eternal Misery. They could probably make a board out of a piece of plywood or something, put some pleasure in the old folks' lives."

"That's very thoughtful of you, Trooper," the doctor said. "You do that."

"I will, sir."

"I'll let you know when I've arranged for the tow."

"Yes, sir. Sorry for all this trouble, sir."

"Oh, well," said the doctor. "All's well that ends well."

ABOUT THE AUTHOR

Donald E. Westlake has written numerous novels over the past thirty-five years under his own name and pseudonyms, including Richard Stark. Many of his books have been made into movies, including *The Hunter,* which became the brilliant film noir *Point Blank,* and the 1999 smash hit *Payback.* He penned the Hollywood scripts for *The Stepfather* and *The Grifters,* which was nominated for an Academy Award for Best Screenplay. The winner of three Edgar awards and a Mystery Writers of America Grand Master, Donald E. Westlake was presented with The Eye, the Private Eye Writers of America's Lifetime Achievement Award, at the Shamus awards. He lives with his wife, Abby Adams, in rural New York State. To learn more, you can visit:
www.donaldwestlake.com